Private Jets

to the awesome staff at V.G.H.
thanks for all your help!
Mark a Ross
Aug 12/2015

A novel by
Mark Ross

This novel is fiction and any situation, organization or character's resemblance to any individuals; living or deceased, fiction or real, is unintentional and purely co-incidental. All rights reserved. No part of this book may be used, reprinted, or reproduced in any manner whatsoever without the express written permission of the author.

Copyright 2012 by Mark Ross

Prologue
Algeria, June 1975

"Here he comes." Mansi spotted the small silhouette camouflaged against the distant gray skies a few seconds before he heard the steady beat of its engine. The plane was two or three kilometers away and approaching from the northeast. It was flying below the clouds and couldn't have been more than five hundred meters high, an easy target.

Gusts blew a light drizzle across the fields. It had rained hard most of the morning, but the steady downpour had relented in the mid afternoon. Uncommon for late June, the drenching spring rains were usually finished for the season by now, but the thick system had moved in yesterday, and the clouds gave way before daybreak. While the lack of light made it look more like a winter's day than the peak of the growing season, the subtropical heat was simmering, steamy, and undeniable. The unexpected moisture might have been a blessing for the farmers, but it certainly wasn't a very good day for flying or waiting for a plane to arrive.

Mansi and his two cousins had been dumbstruck by the Russian's bold offer to deliver the weapons by plane. It was a brazen act, and required a gutsy pilot willing to fly into the center of Algeria loaded with machine guns. It wasn't 1960 anymore.

The country had changed a lot since the revolution had ended in 1962. The eight-year Battle for Algiers had armed most of the men in the country, and carrying weapons had become a way of life. Russian, French, British, American, and Israeli manufacturers had eagerly sold guns to countries all across Africa. President Houari Boumedienne, after seizing power in a bloodless 1965 coup, in order to control the various factions of political and religious interests, had eliminated private ownership of guns. After a few decades of bearing arms and fighting for independence, it was a hard "freedom" for many of the freedom fighters to agree to.

Hashim Nasser, the older of Mansi's two male cousins, agreed with the American way of thinking, although the right to bear arms, was the only thing American he could appreciate.

The largest city in the country, Algiers, was originally known as "Algiers the White" by sailors for the white stucco buildings that could be seen from miles away at sea, but it was the rich farmland that had attracted powerful civilizations to Algeria for thousands of years. It could have been called Algiers the Green. With rainfall annually of over 1,000 millimeters, the northern part of the country had countless bountiful farms and plantations. The fertile land had filled the pockets and fed the armies of its conquerors for centuries.

An hour south the North Tell Atlas Mountains rise in a sudden leap off the lush, fertile plateau that flanks the North African coast from Morocco to Libya. With a peak just over 3,000 meters in height, the mountains even offer skiing at Chsea, which surprises most visitors who expect desert, sand dunes, and camels.

The tiny airstrip close to the mountains that the cousins arranged to meet at was not on any map and not really much more than a dirt road, but the thick orange orchards provided a natural barrier for the short runway and a perfect place to land a small plane unnoticed. Less than a kilometer long, with thick fields on both sides of the road, the little strip had been built during the fifties and was still used for a variety of activities, some legal, some not.

More than ten years after independence, Algeria was still struggling to manage its new democracy, and corruption was rampant. Failed promises, blatant favoritism, and genuine confusion ruled the new nation. The economy was in shambles, devastated by the war, raided and squandered in the name of the public, and justice and employment didn't seem to be high on any political agenda as dozens of varied interests and groups struggled for power and control. Many Algerians felt betrayed by the very men their families had fought and died for. While many of yesterday's *Front de Libération Nationale* war heroes were now leading the new government, many other former comrades and fellow patriots had been branded radicals.

Gendarmerie de la Province d'Algérie, the Algerian National Police forces, had made life in Algeria almost as restrictive as under the French, and an endless proliferation of checkpoints choked the movements of Mansi and his cousins on every highway in the country.

A mixture of different cultures and ethnic backgrounds, all three young men were as Algerian as the fine sand that blew across the endless expanse of the southern half of the country. Hashim was twenty-seven, nine years older than Mansi, but he had been their leader since he was a boy. At ten years old, he had been running messages through the Casbah, past the military checkpoints, and reporting the French positions back to the FLN. His information alone was responsible for the deaths of dozens of soldiers, and, saving the lives of dozens of Algerians.

Mansi Nasser was the youngest of the three, but he wasn't new to violence either. A week after his thirteenth birthday, he had killed someone in a street fight. Since that day over five years ago, he had proven himself in many, many ways. Now, the day he had been promised, his future, was here.

At first, Mansi had been stunned by his older cousin's outrageous and daring plan, but the more Hashim outlined the possibilities, the more Mansi had found the idea impossible to resist. After his father was killed, Mansi and his mother had moved in with his uncle, Kadar Nasser, his wife Asma, Hashim, and Hashim's two sisters, Samia and Fatima. Growing up under the same roof, Mansi had come to idolize Hashim and never questioned any of his decisions. Hashim had planned every detail of every operation that Mansi had ever been a part of. Where, when, what, why and if necessary, who to kill.

Physically, the two men even looked a lot alike, and many people thought they were brothers. Tall for Algerians at almost six feet, their coarse black hair and light coffee-colored skin was just a part of their broken history. Part Berber, part Arabic, too much French, parts unknown, they could trace roots back to the early eighteenth century, just after the pirates had been finally driven out by the French conquest in 1830.

Samzi was twenty-five, seven years older than Mansi, but he looked nothing like his two cousins. By far the shortest of the three at five foot seven, his lighter skin and wild rash of reddish-brown hair was tribute to his father's Spanish roots, but Samzi's loyalty to Hashim was unquestionable. He had spilled blood more than once to prove it.

"It looks like he is alone," Mansi said. He was having a hard time keeping the old binoculars focused on the plane, but he was pretty sure there was only the pilot on board. Drifting right and left at times, sometimes it seemed to be flying sideways. It looked frightening to Mansi. As it lined up for the beginning of the road, it dropped the last fifty feet quickly and then with a few hard bounces, it was down and rolling. The prop kicked up a flurry of leaves, dust, and debris, and the little plane skidded on the muddy surface, but it slowed down quickly and taxied to a stop at the end of the road.

Mansi followed his cousins out of the trees. They approached carefully from the rear of the plane. All three had their weapons out, loaded and ready. The motor died with a cough and a sputter. The propeller spun for a few seconds and then stopped when the engine backfired. The left door popped opened with a groan. Two hands, palms empty, came out first.

The man's accent was heavy, but his French was reasonable. "*Bonjour, mes amis. J'espère que je ne suis pas beaucoup en retard.*"

Mansi looked at his watch. He was almost twenty minutes late.

"*Obtenez notre lentement,*" Hashim waved the nozzle of his machine-gun.

Mansi was surprised when the Russian climbed out. He was short, even shorter than Samzi, about five foot five, heavy, with a sizable gut that was pulling his sticky shirt from his pants. An expensive-looking black leather jacket fit his round body poorly and he grunted as he straightened up. He gasped like he was out of breath and his pallid complexion seemed sad, but a gold tooth glinted in a friendly smile.

"My French is not very good," he said, surprising Mansi when he changed language. "Do you speak English?'

Hashim laughed. "Certainly. Unless you know Arabic?"

"No, just Russian, some French and English."

Mansi looked inside the window on the back of the fuselage. He had never been close to any plane before, and when the rain splattered in a sudden spurt against the thin riveted metal panels, he was surprised at how flimsy it felt. Up front were two worn blue leather seats and what were obviously the controls, but in the small storage area in the rear, he saw the pile of rolled-up gray blankets they were looking for.

"We need to search you," Hashim said, nodding at his younger cousin.

Mansi was thorough, even though an unpleasant smell of nervous sweat was strong on the stocky pilot. Mansi patted him down thoroughly, front and back, and checked the inside of the Russian's calf-high leather boots. No knives.

"All my weapons are in the back of the plane," the man said, grinning easily.

Hashim lowered his machine gun. "Okay. You can put your hands down."

The man dropped his arms and turned around. He stuck his right hand out. "Vladimir Titov. It is good to meet you."

Mansi shook hands first. Titov's hand was firm and surprisingly dry. "Mansi Nasser. It is my pleasure to meet you."

Hashim shook hands without conviction. "How was your flight?"

Vladimir laughed, a deep chuckle that shook his belly. "Rough, banged all over the skies, but this little baby is pretty tough. Ever been up in one of these before?"

Hashim shook his head. "No."

"What kind of plane is it?" Mansi asked.

"A Trainor 252. It's made by the French under license from America," the Russian said hospitably. "Do you know much about small airplanes?"

"No." Mansi couldn't believe it. A Trainor plane, maybe much like the one his father had been killed in. It must be a sign from Allah.

"Trainor doesn't make small ones like this anymore," Vladimir said. "Now they make private jets."

"It doesn't matter," Hashim said, shaking his head to end the questioning. "I hope our requests were not a problem?"

"Not at all." Vladimir shrugged and pointed at the plane. "I have the identification papers and the hardware as promised – a dozen new Russian RPK machine guns."

"You are a man of your word," Hashim said. "That is good. Let us see the papers first."

"I live by my word, as you will see." Vladimir reached into his jacket pocket and pulled out a small brown envelope.

Hashim flipped through the blank pages and a few other documents before handing the package to Mansi. Inside were a passport and a few other pieces of identification. "Do you have a lot of experience with American papers?"

"More than any other country," Vladimir said. "Many people want to get into the United States."

Mansi stared at the passport. They had chosen the name and taken the pictures a few weeks ago, but it was still odd to read. He was no longer Mansi Nasser. He was now Mansi Ruffe.

"Let's see the guns," Hashim said.

Vladimir pushed the door open all the way and folded the pilot's seat forward. He pulled one of the bundles out. It looked heavy. Inside were three shiny new black assault rifles. He handed the cousins one each.

It was heavier than his current Mat 49 submachine gun, and Mansi could feel the quality in the cold, heavy steel, but it wasn't a better choice for him than the French 9mm Parabellum that he had used for the last ten years. The Russian offerings were more military than urban weapons and designed for different battlegrounds and tactics. The RPK boasted selective fire and might be the most mass-produced piece of firepower in the world, but the Mat 49 was still a more desirable weapon for clandestine operations. It was lighter, folded up easily, and was very reliable.

"As a token of my sincerity, these are free," Vladimir said with a smile. "My gifts to you."

Hashim looked amused. He often joked with Mansi about the various meanings people attached to the word *free*. But his words were cautious. "That is most generous of you, my friend, but not often is something given and something not expected in return. How will I repay you?"

"We have common enemies, Hashim. You help us defeat them. You are doing us a favor. No repayment is necessary."

"What enemies do we have in common?"

"The French, the Americans, capitalism," Vladimir said.

Mansi had never met an American, but nobody seemed to like them. "And my papers?"

"No charge. American documents are always free for you. We like to keep their immigration busy." Vladimir laughed. "But if you ever have anything to sell, or any information that you think we might be interested in, I might be a buyer. We have interests in many different areas."

"Who is 'we'?" Hashim reached for one of the boxes of ammunition that Vladimir had pulled out of a separate bag.

"I am a consultant for many different types of Russian imports and exports. Business today is concerned with all kinds of materials and all kinds of information: political, economical, religious, and military. If it's important in one way, chances are it will be important in some other way, too."

"Yes, history teaches us that, my friend." Hashim opened a box of ammunition and dropped a clip of bullets into his hand. "I hope that we can repay the favor. Maybe one day we will be able to return your hospitality."

"We are a patient people, Hashim. Some things take years, we know that. Would you like to place an order now?"

Hashim ordered two hundred machine guns and enough ammunition to win a small war. After the Russian's plane disappeared from sight, Samzi went and retrieved the Renault that been parked behind the trees. No sense revealing anything but what was necessary.

"These were a gift sent by God, my friend," said Hashim, "and his timing, as always, is perfect." He loaded the remaining ammunition and his old gun into the trunk before climbing into the front passenger seat.

"So that's it now, Mansi. Show us what kind of man you are. Bring home a beautiful American boy."

Mansi grinned. He liked the idea of another wife and more children. "Students for school."

"Yes, more students," Hashim said.

They all laughed.

Hashim was serious again. "Never get emotionally involved, Mansi. They will be weapons, instruments of war; children of the jihad, nothing more."

Mansi didn't question. "It is God's will. He gives, he takes away."

"*Tawak Kalto Ul Allah*," Hashim agreed. "Are you ready to go to America?"

Mansi got in the back of the old four-door sedan. "Yes, next week."

Samzi slid the car into gear.

"Your English is better all the time. Soon you two will sound and look like Americans."

"Not a happy thought, cousin," Mansi said. He had doubts about life in America.

Hashim laughed. "And you remember where and what time to meet?" Hashim quizzed him endlessly on the details.

"The baseball fields off Ninth Avenue in Golden Gate Park. The fourth of July at ten a.m."

"And what is your name?"

"Mansi Ruffe."

"You will be the first to go to America."

"It is quite an honor."

Part One

Chapter 1
Ten Years later – 1985

Mansi didn't even pay attention to where they were going. He was thinking about his return to the United States. He had been stunned when Hashim told him he would be returning to try again for a son. Other failures, for a variety of reasons, left their plan far short of their goals, and since Mansi was still quite young at twenty-eight, he could have another family. At first he had been disappointed. He had thought about his return to Algeria for years, but life in America hadn't been all bad, and now he looked forward to a second chance to prove himself.

They slowed as they entered the narrow cobblestone road that led into the oldest part of the city. Built and re-built over the centuries, most of the ten-meter-thick walls of the garrison had long since been torn down, and much of the lower part of the city had been replaced by the wide boulevards and apartment blocks of the French. But the upper half of the old city, the side-by-side white two- and three-story courtyard houses that once served as gracious homes to single families, were now overrun by as many as a dozen families who crowded into the dilapidated buildings that leaned into the narrow, step-lined streets.

Most of the buildings had been built long before steel, and the constant earthquakes that shook when the Arabian tectonic plate ground against the Eurasian tectonic plate, would regularly cause the old buildings to crumble. Considered one of the worst slums in Africa, the Casbah was the face of Algeria itself, a Sunni Muslim community, and any outsiders were immediately apparent. The streets were definitely not on any regular tours, although the few guides who somehow existed in Algeria always made reference to the significant history of the area as they drove by.

Mansi had grown up on the streets of Algiers, and little had changed in the last ten years, the dying buildings a testament to their age as much as the neglect and stagnant poverty that defined the vastly over-crowded hillside. Many of the buildings that fell down were never rebuilt. They were turned into small playgrounds for the hundreds of kids who had nowhere else to play other than the city itself. Located on the hills that rose out of the western end of the city, the Casbah was steps up the hill from the main shopping areas close to the busy downtown that fronted the docks. For all its trouble though, the views were breathtaking. Overlooking the busy docks that lined the crystal blue waters of the Mediterranean Sea, Mansi thought Algiers was as beautiful as any vista in San Francisco. It still felt like home, but after years in the United States, he wondered if even he were safe from the rampant crime that flourished here.

Hashim pointed to a spot on the corner, and the driver tucked the Fiat into the tiny opening behind the large black Citroen. The streets were always crowded in the late afternoon, but nobody paid them any attention. A row of small shops and an open market were busy with shoppers, and the small café at the corner looked busy. Three young men stood beside the door to the café, and they nodded as Mansi and Hashim approached. One of the guards escorted them into the back. It was dark and hard to see, but when the man at the table stood up, Mansi recognized him immediately.

Vladimir Titov stuck out his hand. "It is good to see you, my friends."

Hashim shook hands first. "You remember Mansi?"

"Yes, of course," Vladimir said, "but it's been years since we met." He had put on quite a bit of weight, but his toothy smile was as eager as before.

"Ten years, my friend," Mansi felt like he was starting all over again. "Are you still flying?"

"Yes, but I don't run things quite like the old days," Vladimir grinned.

"Was your plane a Trainor?" Mansi could picture the rainy day years ago when they had first met. He would never forget his surprise.

"Yes, good memory. It's a Trainor 252."

"Yes, I remember," the irony of the small single propeller plane still haunted him. "American design - made in France. I'm surprised you fly such a thing."

Vladimir laughed. "Yes, well they do make good planes. Have you ever been up in a small plane?"

"No."

"Would you like to go up for a flight over the city?"

"Really?"

"You have a few more days before you return." Hashim said

Mansi looked at the Russian. *Was he serious? And in a Trainor plane yet? Why not?* "Okay, my friend. Can we go before Friday?"

Vladimir grinned. "Sure. Either Wednesday or Thursday, weather provided."

The waiter arrived with steaming double cups. The coffee was thick, black, and pungent. Mansi and Hashim added lots of sugar, as they had all their life. Vladimir drank his black.

After the waiter had disappeared, Vladimir reached into his pocket and handed a small brown envelope to Mansi. "As you requested…"

Mansi opened the flap and pulled out a few documents. One was a passport, and he flipped through the pages until he found the photo. It was him, but he was now Mansi Ansour.

"Everything is okay?" Vladimir said anxiously.

"Your documents have always passed immigration with no problem," Hashim said, reaching for Mansi's passport. "What about the rocket launchers?"

"They should arrive in Yemen next week."

"Good. The money is waiting and will be transferred as soon as they are delivered." Hashim handed the passport back to Mansi and stood up. "It's been a pleasure doing business with you."

"And you, too."

Mansi followed his cousin out. "Are you coming to see Jill?"

"Yes, let's go see how your daughter is doing."

A soccer game was underway when they arrived at the madrassa, so they watched from the balcony for a few minutes. Mansi watched with pride as his daughter ran up the outside of the dirt field, deftly dodging two defenders, before her surprisingly hard shot just missed the corner of the goal.

"She is faster than most of those boys," Hashim noted.

Mansi nodded. "I thought you would be amused." He had bought her a soccer ball when she was a baby, and it had always been one of her favorite toys.

"Amused and surprised Mansi. She is most intelligent and already understands quite a bit of French and Arabic. She has quit crying and seems eager to please. Who knows what she will develop into? But this time, you must pray harder for a boy. Allah needs more warriors, not more concubines."

When Jill was born, Mansi had been extremely disappointed and had wanted to kill Linda and the baby. Hashim had remained optimistic and prayed for a boy, but after nine years and only one girl, Mansi felt like he had failed. Many others had already returned with sons, but Hashim had decided that the possibilities of a woman in America were too great to pass up. Time would tell whether Jill could be trained, and, if so, for what purpose, but his daughter had already earned some respect. A few weeks after her arrival at the madrassa, she had beaten up an older boy and given him a nasty black eye. Hashim had roared with laughter when he recounted the story to Mansi, saying it had reinforced his belief that she might be tough enough to be of some use.

She was a beautiful child, with thick, naturally wavy, jet-black hair, startling midnight-black eyes, light-brown cocoa skin, and Linda's soft, delicate features. Even at seven years old, Jill turned heads, and most appraised her a second time. Her mother had always dressed her like the pretty adolescent she was, but she looked more like her father every day. Soon she might pass for a native Algerian.

She was the first girl Hashim had decided to train. While some of the elders had insisted on her wearing a burka, they let her play soccer without the confines of the heavy garments. A few boys had objected to her lack of appropriate attire, but after she punched out the much bigger boy, they had decided to accept her and her strange ways.

"How is my son doing?" For all his disappointments with his daughter, he couldn't have been more proud of his son.

"Very good," said Hashim. "He loves being the spy. Most of the kids tell him everything."

Tariq was almost ten and had been at the madrassa most of his life. He was one of a few Algerians, but no one knew he was related to Hashim or Mansi. Mansi had put him into training at four years old. Alia, Mansi's wife had objected so had divorced her. He had never loved her and never lived with her, but she was a good Muslim girl and she had borne him a fine son. That was all that mattered.

Tariq had loved the conspiracy and initially they made a game of it, but soon he became their inside connection to the problems the young abducted kids were experiencing. Hashim speculated that Tariq could probably run the Madrassa one day; no one would know it better. Mansi couldn't have been more proud of his son. Tall for his age at nine, his hair a mass of black curls, he was a smart kid who already spoke three languages.

But now Mansi needed another son to be a warrior, a son to be a martyr. Who knew what his daughter would be able to deliver. "I pray for many boys, Hashim, and I will not disappoint you this time."

"Good. When do you leave for America, Mr. Mansi Ansour?"

He had wondered about moving back to California, even if it was the southern half this time, but with more than twenty-five million people in the state, it shouldn't matter. That was as many people as all of Algeria.

"In two days. I arrive in Los Angeles on Saturday, June the second."

~~~

Annette yawned and checked the clock as she closed the door behind her. As the owner of the small hair salon for the last three years, she was, as usual, the last one to leave. As she walked the few steps down to the parking lot, the arches of her feet cramped, and for a moment she thought about not going to the party. A long, hot bath sounded better, but she knew Val was looking forward to the evening. Val had turned twenty-one a few months ago and had tried to get Annette out partying almost every weekend since. But she didn't enjoy the nightlife scene, never had, and had felt out of place and old with Val's younger friends.

Approaching thirty and not in any long-term relationship, Annette Madison knew she was the unusual one. Many of the kids she had grown up with were married, many had children, and a few were even divorced. It wasn't for a lack of male attention, however. Five-foot-eight, attractive, athletic and quite fit, blonde and blue-eyed, she could have dated every night, but over the last seven or eight years, she had never seen anyone longer than a few months. Her mother told her she was more mature than most. Annette wasn't sure about that, but the deaths of her father and her fiancé had changed her forever. Now, the blind way most young men lived seemed foolish, and she found herself out of sync with their cars, their sports, and their constant partying.

She dressed simply, in a white cotton sundress with splashes of blue and open sandals. After a quick tuna and egg salad sandwich at the kitchen counter, she drove over to her mother's house to pick up Val. Even though there was almost eight years between them, it was hard to tell. Her younger sister was just as pretty and looked more like her twin than her younger sibling. The tight jeans, red tank top, and black high heels were definitely not intended to hide her figure or her enthusiasm.

On the drive over to the party, Val talked about her new job. "They said if I worked out, there could be a chance to train later as a paralegal."

"What exactly does a paralegal do?"

"It's an assistant, sort of. Prepare documents, do research. Help the attorneys get ready for trials."

"Will you know how to sue somebody?"

"I guess, but that could take a few years." Val laughed. "First I have to do a lot of filing."

George Baylor's house was only a few blocks away, and when they parked, they could hear the music blaring.

Val grinned. "Wow, sounds like a big party."

As they entered the single-story rancher, people waved and shouted hello. Annette stopped and talked to a few friends as she made her way through the crowded living room, but the music was loud and it was hard to hear, so they headed for the back yard. George, as usual, was tending the bar. He waved at them to come over.

"Hi, George."

"Hi, Nettie. Hi, Val. Boy, you girls look great!" George had gained quite a bit of weight in his twenties and lost most of his hair, but his friendly smile was as honest and innocent as his easy personality. He looked ten years older than Annette, but they had known each other since sixth grade.

She leaned over the bar and gave him a kiss on the cheek. "You say the nicest things, George. And you? Another great party?"

"Ah, that is yet to be seen." George was well known for his summer-time bashes. He pointed to the well-stocked bar. "What will it be?"

"How about a margarita?" Annette said. She noticed an interesting-looking man standing at the end of the wooden bar. He smiled at her. She wondered if she had met him before, but immediately thought that he was too handsome to forget.

"Specialty of the house, but of course you know that." George started pouring mix into the blender. He nodded towards the mystery man. "Have you met Mansi?"

Annette was trying to figure out if he was European, or maybe from South America. She smiled and introduced herself. "Hi, I'm Annette. Everyone calls me Nettie. This is my sister Val." As he slid a step closer, she could see he was much better looking than she had thought at first. His white teeth were almost dazzling, his ruddy olive complexion full of character, and his deep black eyes a stark contrast to his warm and sincere voice.

"It's nice to meet you," he said. "This is a good party."

"It's nice to meet you, too." Annette was surprised that he didn't have much of an accent. "George has the best parties. Is this your first?"

George put his arm around his guest and said, "Mansi was just transferred here from Paris. It's all new to him."

Annette loved everything French. "Paris? Really? Are you French?"

"No, I am Algerian, but some of my ancestors are from France."

"Algeria? Our dad went there."

"He did?" Mansi's smile disappeared into an odd, questioning look. "When was that?"

"After the war. He was in the Navy." Every time a National Geographic special was on TV, her father had talked about the Roman ruins outside Algiers at a place called Tipasa. It had fascinated him, and he had always hoped to go back someday. "The fleet stopped there a few times."

"Oh." Mansi looked confused. "After which war?"

"Which war? World War Two." She couldn't think of another war. "I guess it was the early fifties, because he got out in 1955."

"Yes, that makes sense. The Allies made Algiers their North African headquarters." He smiled again, and his eyes seemed to pour into hers. "U.S. ships were there for many years."

"Which war did you think I meant?"

"Algeria had a war of independence from '54 to '62. I grew up during it."

"You grew up . . ." She hesitated as she realized what he had said. ". . . during a war?"

"Yes. Not an education for a child." Mansi's smile disappeared again. "But it is much safer these days, and besides, we're all moving over here."

She laughed. "Yes, it's hard to beat southern California. It's pretty nice here."

"Yes, beautiful. Actually, it's like parts of Africa. Both are north of the Tropic of Cancer, and parts of Algeria actually have similar weather much of the year."

"I've never met anyone from Africa." As soon as she said it, she thought it sounded dumb.

Mansi took her left hand and kissed it. *"L'Afrique n'avait jamais vu une telle beauté comme le vôtre."*

Annette giggled. "What does that mean?"

"Africa has never seen such beauty as yours."

Annette was not sure if he was serious or kidding and was almost stuck for words before she thought of a reply. "That sounds like Paris talking, not Africa."

They all laughed, and George said, "Smooth, Mansi. Really smooth. Can I use that line sometime?"

"American girls have a confidence that is not present in most women from other countries," Mansi said. "It is a very attractive quality. American women are easy to admire, especially beautiful blondes."

Annette felt hot and wondered if she was blushing. She teased him back. "That's closer to the truth. It's really the blonde hair, isn't it?"

He nodded. "There are not many blonde women in any of Africa, and I think you both look like movie stars."

Loud blasts froze their kidding as fireworks started exploding high over the rooftops. Everyone headed for the street, where the pyrotechnic display was visible on the far side of the park. One after another, the sizzling rockets shot into the night, their bright splashes of color irresistible and mesmerizing. Annette and Mansi watched the show together and talked about a lot of different things. She found him intelligent and funny, and his soft manner was quite endearing, a wonderful change from the over-confident boys who prowled the bars of Southern California. She wondered if he felt any attraction to her, but she didn't have to wait long to find out.

As they were leaving, he stopped her at the front door. "It was a very good party. I will remember it for a long time, my first fourth of July."

"Your first party at George's, too." She was glad she had come. Mansi was very charming and had a different perspective than anyone she had ever met.

"I was wondering if I might call you?" he said. "Maybe we could go out for a drink. I'll try not to embarrass myself again with any more overused pickup lines." His eyes flickered with hope.

"You didn't embarrass yourself at all. It was nice to talk about something other than baseball and the weather. I'll give you my number if you promise to tell me more about Europe." She slipped a business card out of her purse. "Call me at work; it's a private line. If I'm busy and can't pick up, there's an answering machine. Leave a message, and I'll call you back."

Mansi put the card in his pocket, then leaned closer and kissed her gently on the cheek. "I look forward to seeing your pretty smile again."

Annette could smell his musky scent and realized she found him fascinating. "What did you study in Paris? Good behavior?"

"No, that was my mother's doing. She was very proper about manners, but that's a long story for another time."

She could hardly wait.

~~~

The familiar double knock on the door announced her sister's arrival. When Annette turned around to open the door, Val was already inside.

"It's me," Val said.

Annette hugged her sister. "He just called."

"Who? That French guy?"

"He's not French. He's Algerian."

Val turned the TV on and flopped on the tan leather couch. "Are you going out with him?"

"Yeah, but I'm not sure what to think. I've never dated anyone like him before."

Val laughed. "Go out with him, Nettie. He's been to all the places you want to go, and he seems real classy."

"Yes, and very confident. It seemed to me he knows exactly what he wants out of life." Annette had peppered him with questions at the party.

"As long as he's not all work and no play."

Annette dwelled on the words for a second, but Mansi had been serious and funny. "He makes me laugh."

Val laughed. "Well, then, that settles it. That's Mom's main criteria."

"Humor is good, but he has a confidence that one can only earn. I bet his mother is proud of him. He speaks four languages and works all over the world."

"What would our mother think of him?"

That had crossed her mind more than once. "You didn't tell her about him, did you?"

"No, not yet."

"Should I even care what Mom would think?" Annette pictured her mother first, then Mansi. "But he's very charming, and that smile . . . What's not to like?"

~~~

Mansi felt good about his prospects. Annette's tone had told him she had been waiting for his call. He couldn't believe how much she looked like his first wife and wondered if that was good or bad. Certainly he liked blondes.

He hid the flowers behind his back and knocked firmly on her apartment door. There was no sound. He waited what seemed like thirty seconds and raised his hand to knock again, but then he heard footsteps. The doorknob turned.

She looked happy to see him. "Hi, Mansi."

"Hi, Annette." He pulled the flowers out from behind his back. "Beautiful flowers for a beautiful lady." He meant it; she looked stunning. Her blonde hair cascaded down her shoulders, and her dark blue silk blouse and tight white skirt hugged all her curves.

Her blue eyes danced as they surveyed the colorful bouquet, and her sexy smile answered any doubts he had.

"Mansi, you shouldn't have. But they're beautiful, thank you." She took the flowers and kissed him on the cheek. "That was very sweet of you."

He could smell her sweet perfume. The soft touch of her lips was almost too much to resist. "I'm glad you like them."

"They're gorgeous. Let me put them in water. Please, come in."

He closed the door and glanced around while she searched for a vase. "Your apartment is nice, very cozy," he said. It was tastefully decorated in a beachy look, with rattan furniture, hardwood floors, lots of plants, and bamboo window shades. Family pictures lined the small hallway, including several featuring someone in a small plane. Another picture showed Annette with her arms around a young man. They both looked to be teenagers, maybe an old boyfriend.

"Thanks," she called out from the kitchen. "It's small, but I did the best I could."

"I think it's beautiful. I should have you decorate my place." He wondered if she always kept her place so clean. Linda had been really messy, and it had made him crazy.

"Why? Is it a typical guy's place? Posters of girls and cars?"

Mansi chuckled at the repulsive thought. "No, nothing like that. Just quite bare. I haven't done anything yet. I only moved in a month ago. You could have a blank canvas."

"Well, it's something we can talk about." Annette set the flowers on her small dining table. "The flowers are beautiful. Thank you again. Ready?"

The restaurant was not too busy, so Mansi asked for a corner booth. He was always more comfortable when no one was listening too close. The waiters made a few extra passes to gawk at Annette, but then left them alone. George had told him Annette liked Italian restaurants and suggested he try at Il Fornaio in Irvine.

She relaxed into the soft armchair that the waiter had pulled out, "Have you been here before?"

Little lies never worked. "No, George recommended it," he confessed.

"Ah, well, George certainly knows food."

"George is a fountain of information and help. I don't know what I would do without him." Mansi had asked him for a number of things when he was moving in.

"You don't seem like the weak and defenseless type," she joked.

"Yes, well new country and all," She was flirty, that was good.

"How is it that you speak English so well?"

He had been asked that before but knew it would seem unusual, "School, University, Business, English is the language of the world."

"Well you speak it better than many Californians."

"I don't know about that, but they probably speak Spanish much better."

"Do you have any brothers or sisters?" she asked.

He was glad she changed the subject, "One brother." Hashim was his brother in many ways and had been part of his life forever, "he is married, has two daughters, and lives just outside of Algiers."

"How old are the girls?"

"Sixteen and eighteen. Maja and Kashia." Women liked a man with family ties, and he did think of Hashim's daughters as his nieces.

"Pretty names. They sound cute."

"They are, but they were disappointed that they never had a boy."

"Two girls and a boy . . . That sounds like the perfect family. Where do your parents live?"

The game was on. "My father was killed in 1962 during one of the last battles in the war with the French. He was a freedom fighter and died a hero."

Annette's expression immediately changed to one of sincere concern. Sympathy was a powerful emotion.

"Mansi, I'm so sorry," she said. "But you must be very proud of him." She reached for his hand and caressed it gently, but let go before he could respond. "Is your mother still alive?"

"Yes. She almost didn't make it, either, when our house was burnt to the ground in the middle of the night. My mother was lucky to get us out alive."

"That's so sad. Not a much of a childhood for you and your brother."

"I don't even remember my father, but his death was not in vain. Algeria finally drove the French out." He was proud of his father's heroic sacrifice, even if most of the story wasn't quite true.

"That must have been really tough on your mother."

"Yes, I'm sure it was." She was clearly touched by his confession. "I don't usually tell people this, not for a while at least . . ." Annette dabbed at tears that quickly formed in her eyes. "But my father died ten years ago."

He wanted to smile. He could and would use that to his advantage. "I'm so sorry to hear that. That's terrible." He hesitated and asked in his best sympathetic voice, "Can I ask . . . how did your father die?"

"Nothing as gallant as your father. It was a car accident. It wasn't his fault; he was hit by a drunk driver."

Mansi reached for her hand and held it firmly. "That's a tragedy. Such a waste of life. But dead is dead, and losing one's family is the ultimate loss." Her hand didn't flinch under his. "It must have been very hard for your mother, too."

"Yes." Annette withdrew her hand from his, but not without a warm squeeze. "She had to go back to work. Dad was still years away from retirement."

"Yes, mothers have to carry on afterwards. My father gave his life for his country; my mother gave hers so her children could have a chance. I owe her everything." He phrased his words carefully. He did respect his mother, but not in a way an American would understand.

"It seems to me you have made a lot of your life so far," Annette said. "Your mother must be very proud of you."

"She is, but she worries about me. She thinks America is a land of sin. She says she prays for me every day." Dealing with his religion was always a good way to test the waters.

"Land of sin? Why does she say that?"

"My mother is a strict Muslim, and the American way of life is contrary to the traditions she knows."

"What do you think? Is American the land of sin?"

"America is the land of plenty, the land of temptation, and temptation can lead to greed. Where there is greed, there is sin. I think one must choose carefully."

"Your mom might be right." Annette changed the subject. "What did your father do for a living?"

"He built fishing boats."

"Really? My father built things, too. Planes."

Planes? "That sounds more interesting than boats." Mansi was intrigued.

"To me, it's interesting that they both were builders."

"What kind of planes did your father build?"

"Private planes, at a company called Trainor Jets in Long Beach."

Mansi stiffened. "That sounds very interesting," he said reflexively. *Trainor? Like Vladimir's plane? Like the one his father* …"do they build small propeller planes, too?"

"They used to, why?"

Mansi knew he shouldn't say anything, but his answer was harmless, "I got a ride in a Trainor 252 a few months ago. It was my first time up in a small plane and it was pretty incredible."

"That's a really old model I think, where was this?"

"Algeria." Mansi could still picture the flight over Algiers. Looking down over the Casbah and the Bay of Algiers had been incredible. The green-blue sea was dazzling in the summer heat, and the city of white looked clean and pure from a distance.

Annette smiled. "So you want to be a pilot now?"

Mansi grinned. "No."

"My father worked there for twenty years, did all kinds of jobs, but when he died, he was manager of wing construction for the Freedom One executive jet."

"Do you fly?" Mansi thought it was quite the coincidence that her father had worked at the manufacturing plant and wondered what Hashim would think.

"No, Dad used to take me up with him and tried to get me interested, but it was never for me." Annette sipped from her wine. "Tell me about being an oil consultant."

He wished she hadn't changed the subject. "I help oil companies decide when and where to invest, help them analyze what projects are viable. I've worked for UniOil for seven years now. Los Angeles is a promotion and should keep me here for a long time. Who knows, maybe I'll decide to stay." His degree was in civil engineering, but he had specialized in soils and minored in geology.

"Well, you wouldn't be the first person to do that. California is full of people who came to visit and stayed."

Mansi filled their glasses with the last of the red wine. He had chosen a bottle of Robert Mondavi, a delicious cabernet sauvignon from the Napa Valley in Northern California that he thought could hold its own against most French wines. Drinking was a sin, but it was part of life in America, almost unavoidable in business and he had come to enjoy a glass or two. Hopefully Allah would understand it was part of his cover, part of his duty to blend in as much as possible.

"I know why they stay," he said. "The beauty in California is amazing!"

Annette laughed. "Do all Algerians lay it on so thick?"

"It's the French in me. I can't help it." He could see she enjoyed the flirting, so he raised his glass, intertwined his arm with hers, and all of a sudden they were face to face. Her delicious perfume was very inviting. "Here's to a lovely lady and a lovely night."

"You flatter me, but it is a lovely night," she clinked glasses, then slid out of the embrace. "Tell me about Paris."

"What do you want to know? It's a beautiful city, and there is much to see."

"It has so much history, so much culture. It's one of the greatest cities in the world."

He wondered if it would be hard to get her to go on a trip with him. "Los Angeles is a world-class city, too."

"Not like Paris. L.A. is so new, so flashy. L.A. isn't style, it's money. Paris has been there for hundreds of years."

"You sound like you really like Paris. You should go sometime."

"I've been saying I'm going for years. I'll get there someday."

They talked about dozens of different subjects, and when the night was over, he could sense that she really liked him. Her eyes sparkled with delight when she laughed and she listened with rapt attention to every word he said. At her door, he wondered what would be appropriate, but she answered his unspoken question when she turned to him and pulled him close. She teased him with the tip of her tongue, and when he responded, her lips melted into his. Soft, warm, and so sweet, the kiss was deep and passionate. She wrapped her arms around his neck, and he could feel the heat of her firm body. When he tried to pull her closer, however, she pulled away.

"I had a nice time, Mansi. I really did. Call me again."

"I will, Annette."

She blew him a kiss and disappeared inside her apartment. Mansi almost skipped as he headed down the hallway. Annette might just be the perfect mother for his next family.

Chapter 2

It had been a long time since Annette had felt this good about a man; and she debated if telling her mother anything at this early stage was a good idea. Who knew what would happen? But she couldn't stop thinking about Mansi and figured her sister was bound to say something anyway. She went over the next night and was glad to find her mother all alone.

"Was he fun?" her mother asked.

Marie Madison seemed to have aged twenty years since the death of her husband over ten years ago, but she was still an attractive woman. At five foot five, she played tennis regularly with Annette, and her blue eyes still sparkled on occasion. She had gone back to work at a doctor's office and was now the office manager, a job she loved and hated equally. Annette had tried unsuccessfully to get her mother to consider dating too, but Marie turned down eager patients every week.

"Fun?" Annette said. "Well, he's not a practical joker, but he likes to laugh, and he's easy to talk to." Annette had found Mansi's humor to be either light and flirtatious, or serious and intellectual, and she had found herself laughing at both.

"You know my motto. Men must be able to make you laugh and smile."

She wondered if her mother would ever find someone who would make her smile again, Marie hadn't dated at all since her husband's death, "He did, Mom, but in different ways. I think he is very interesting. He's traveled a lot and knows far more about the world than I do. He says it's because he's involved in an international business."

"Doesn't sound like your regular guy?"

"No, that he's not," She could feel her mother's disapproval already, "maybe that's why I find him attractive."

"Where do his parents live?" One question after another, at least her mom was predictable.

"His mother lives in Algiers, but his father died years ago in the Algerian civil war."

"Did you tell him about your father?"

"Yes."

Her mother raised her eyebrows in surprise. "So you both have that in common. Did you tell him about Paul?"

"No, not yet." *She had felt so comfortable with Mansi, she had almost told him, but one tragedy at a time.*

"What about children? Does he want children?" Marie asked.

"Mom, it's a little bit early to talk about that. It was our first date."

"I don't know . . . You talked about death."

"Yeah, well, I didn't plan that, but after he told me about his father, it seemed like the right time." She felt like she was defending herself.

"How old is he?"

"Twenty-nine."

"Has he ever been married before?"

"He didn't say, and I didn't ask that, either." She thought a gentleman would have said something, but she would fit it into the conversation next time.

"Maybe he's just a playboy." Her mom's thought had already crossed her mind. Mansi was good looking, very charming and he caught a few eyes himself.

"Maybe, but when he was with me, it was like I was the only thing that mattered." It seemed as if his eyes had never left hers at dinner, and he looked at her with an intensity and focus that was most flattering. "He didn't even bat an eye when another girl walked by."

"That's because you're so pretty."

"Seriously, Mom, he doesn't stare at my breasts. He looks me in the eye. He seems very sincere." His deep black eyes pulled at her like magnets.

"Are you going to see him again?"

"I hope so."

"You didn't invite him to the presentation at Trainor Jets, did you?"

It had crossed her mind. "No."

"What about his religion?"

Annette had wondered if that would bother her mother. "What about it?"

"What religion is he?"

"He's a Muslim."

"Do you know how they treat their women?" Marie warned. "It's not like in the U.S."

"He's been a perfect gentleman," Annette insisted. Not only was he polite, he was courteous and extremely gracious, and she wondered if he could win her mother over. "Maybe I'll bring him by someday. You'll see."

~~~

Lying in bed that night, thinking about Mansi a lot, Annette couldn't help comparing him to Paul, but there was little to compare. Paul was a small town boy who liked baseball and who had wanted to own his own construction business someday, but at nineteen, he had died just a hired hand with a dream. Mansi had traveled all over the world, spoke four languages and could talk world politics as easily as the World Cup. He called it football and confused her at first, but he surprised her by naming a few of the stars in the NFL too. Why did she find such two different men attractive? She even wondered who she would choose if she had the choice.

Not a day went by that she didn't think about her father and her fiancé and most nights ended with the sad memories of the day more than ten years ago that had taken the two men she loved away from her on the same day. Her father, Harold Madison, had been a flight instructor at Trainor Jets for seventeen years. He was still working part-time, and her fiancé, Paul Corbet, was one of his eager students. Ironically, her father had always said his chances were mathematically greater of being killed on the road than in the sky. Tragically, he had been right.

On their way home from the Long Beach Airport after an afternoon flying lesson, Harold and his fledgling top gun had been T-boned by an intoxicated driver at four o'clock in the afternoon. The drunk's pickup truck was traveling extremely fast and pushed

Harold's Mustang a hundred yards down North Lakewood Boulevard before crashing into the curb and bursting into fire. The autopsy showed all three men in the two vehicles had died instantly.

When the two policemen had shown up at their front door, Annette's mother had collapsed. The accident had stunned the community and made national news, but while the story was off the front page the next day, the emptiness and pain had only begun for Annette.

It had been a tragedy for Paul's parents and his two sisters, horrific for her mother Marie, and devastating for her eleven-year-old sister Val. Certainly, it was a nightmare for everyone whose lives were touched, but Annette had lost twice – both the men in her life. The two men she loved. The horror of a future without them in it had seemed unlivable, undesirable; unreal. The guilt and agony had just seemed to get worse with every day that passed without her father and Paul. At first she found herself praying to a God she hadn't really believed in, praying for some kind of answer, trying to understand how any God could take life and destroy families and futures so indiscriminately, the last few years she just tried not to ask herself too many questions she couldn't answer. What sense did it all make?

Mansi comments about his father had her wondering which of life's struggles really mattered. His father had died a hero and he was obviously proud of that. Did that make his death okay? Images of her father's funeral came rushing back and she felt the hot tears slip silently down her cheek.

Mack Trainor, the owner of Trainor Jets, provided the perfect place for the service. The main hangar at the Long Beach plant was the ideal spot to remember Harold Madison and over three hundred mourners had been easily accommodated in the massive building. The various aircraft that her father had worked on over the years were lined up on the tarmac outside, and one of the flight school's Trainor 252s was parked in the back of the cavernous room.

The ceremony was more tribute than religion. Forty-nine-year-old Harold Madison hadn't attended church regularly since his teens, but the priest had known him since the eighth grade. Eulogies by friends and co-workers were funny, personal, genuine, and ringing with the sadness of life's empty promise, but none were more heartfelt than the words of Mack Trainor.

Founder and major stockholder of Trainor Jets, Inc., Mack Trainor was one of the hundreds from work who had attended the service, but Mack and Harold's relationship had been more than just the boss and employee. Harold had worked for Mack for over twenty years and had been the first instructor Mack had hired in the company-sponsored flight school. Harold had even taught Mack's son Art how to fly when he was a teenager. Annette had never realized how good her father's relationship had been with Mack Trainor until after her father's death, when Mack's kindness and generosity had been so graciously extended.

In the time that Harold worked at Trainor Jets, they had grown the flight school to five part-time instructors and graduated hundreds of students. Many had gone on to become commercial-airline-rated transport pilots, and a quite a few were pilots in all four branches of the military.

The loss had opened Annette's eyes to the reality that the world didn't stop for anyone. Her life was shattered, but like the difference that one or two cars made to the traffic, one or two lives just didn't seem to matter. The world went on without hesitation, judgment, or remorse, but life would never be the same for the lives forever shattered. How many other people around the world had died that day? Thousands, maybe tens of thousands, died every day from one cause or another. It was part of the pulse of life.

Her father's ashes – what remained – were spread over the Pacific Ocean off Long Beach on July 24, 1975. Both Annette and Val joined their mother for the flight, which was also courtesy of Trainor Jets. One of Harold's fellow instructors served as the pilot.

Paul's funeral service was a much smaller affair, held at the Calvary church on Fairview Avenue in Costa Mesa. Paul hadn't attended for years, but his parents did, especially his mother, and she had chosen her place of worship for his goodbye. Annette wondered what he would think about all this.

She knew Paul had many questions about the ways of Christianity and Catholicism, but it hadn't been a regular part of his life. Wherever the souls of two men were now, Annette could find no valid message in the emotional devastation left behind. When Mack Trainor's plane had crashed two weeks later, she found herself at another funeral. It was hard to believe. What kind of God would induce such suffering? Part of her had wished she had been buried too.

~~~

Standing on the platform overlooking the tarmac at the Long Beach Airport, Art couldn't hear his own words. He paused in his speech and waited for the crowd to settle down. It had been almost ten years since his father's death and five since he'd been officially elected President of Trainor Jets. He knew he was young for the position at forty-one, even if his disappearing hair made most think he was older, but it was passion and vision that had propelled him to the top as much as his stock options.

He could feel the dampness under his arms. Five thousand invitations had gone out, and it looked like most had shown up. It was the biggest audience he had ever addressed but he thought he was doing okay. The crowd had even laughed at his first few jokes.

His father had made introducing a new aircraft a major event in Long Beach since the 1930s. Even when Trainor had been building small troop carriers for the Army, they had celebrated the new models and designs. His father had taught him to never forget that all the employees, shareholders, suppliers, creditors, media, and politicians were just as important to their success as the customers. It had taken him about thirty minutes to thank everyone, from the union to his wife, but that wasn't what they had all come for.

"Trainor, Trainor, Trainor . . ." the crowd chanted.

Art grinned and raised his hands again. This time the crowd settled down. "As many of you know, the Freedom One and the Freedom Two continue to serve our clients in perfect comfort and will continue to do so for many years to come. But new technologies and competitors have raised the high bar. The Freedom Three might be based on the Freedom Two, but it is bigger and better and state of the *art* in every way." He emphasized his name and paused for its effect while some laughed. "The Freedom Three is fifteen feet longer, it's faster, it's safer, and it will carry Trainor Jets into the next century and beyond."

It had been over twenty years since Bill Lear had introduced the world to business jets. The Learjet 23, the world's first private jet, had been developed from the bones of a failed Swiss fighter jet, the FFA P-16. While the Learjet had been revolutionary at the time and had offered a huge step in executive travel, its size and limited range had only spawned the need for larger jets with greater range and capabilities. In 1966, Gulfstream, a leader in corporate transport since the late fifties, introduced the G-II. Completely revamped from their successful G-I turboprop, the twin 2100 hp Rolls Royce Dart engines had been replaced with the much more powerful Rolls Royce Spey turbojets. The first large-cabin corporate jet had been born.

The wide-body G series and the new G-III quickly became the leaders in the industry. With world-wide reach and unparalleled comfort, the name Gulfstream epitomized the word *luxury*. Now, Trainor Jets was playing catch-up. The Freedom Three had been planned long before Art took the helm and while it was a huge improvement over the Freedom Two, it was already old technology. Customer surveys had been positive, but the early sales numbers were weak.

Art had agonized over every word of his speech. There were only a few major players manufacturing business jets in the world, and each and every new aircraft offered by his competitors had been instrumental in the development of the Freedom Three. Most attending today's unveiling didn't care about the history and evolution of the private jet, so he tried to keep his explanations as simple as possible.

He smiled at the enthusiastic crowd and went on. "Technical specifications might bore many of you, but you will notice one major difference: the size of the plane and the cabin. Passenger comfort has been dramatically improved. The Freedom Three has a cabin height of six feet three inches, and is almost eight feet wide inside, so moving about is no longer a problem. Depending on the customer's requirements, the airframe can now include a full-size conference table or even a bed big enough to fit a basketball star."

On either side of the stage, huge white tarps covered what were obviously a row of airplanes. It was a tradition. Ten planes were available for inspection by anyone who wished to see the inside.

"Ladies and gentlemen, I give you . . . the Freedom Three." Art turned and waved his arms. The tarps slid off the jets and the audience gasped in approval. With six windows down each side, the new models seemed to dwarf the Freedom One and even the Freedom Twos that were parked on the other side of the tarmac. At almost seventy-five feet in length and with an empty weight of almost 30,000 pounds, the new jet's payload and range were more than twice its predecessor. With a crew of three and designed to carry up to sixteen passengers over 4,000 miles, the Freedom Three could fly nonstop from New York to London. The words *Trainor Jets* were splashed along the pearl-white fuselages in a racy black font that looked very chic and oozed sex appeal.

Attendants were waiting at the stanchions beside the steps to the planes. The crowd got out of their seats and quickly formed queues for the chance to inspect one of the jets. This had always been popular with the crowd. Most would never see the inside of one any other way.

Art was glad to be off the stage. As good a speaker as everyone said he was getting to be, he enjoyed meeting people much more one-on-one. He walked over to the front of one of the lines. As he shook hands and answered questions with the curious and enthusiastic, he spotted three women moving through the stanchions: the Madison family. Art hadn't seen them since his father's funeral ten years ago. *Wow, have the girls grown up.* The mother smiled when she saw him, and he winked. In a few minutes, they were at the front of the line.

"Mrs. Madison, Annette, Val, hi." Art gave Marie a quick embrace before offering his hand to the girls. "It's nice to see you."

Marie beamed. "It's nice to see you, too, Art. It's been a long time. I wasn't sure you would even remember."

"Forget?" Art said. "We go back a long time and have a history, as they say. How are you?"

Art would never forget the two funerals ten years ago. The Madison funeral had been Mack's last public appearance before his plane had crashed two weeks later. Harold's death, and then his fathers, thinking about the pain of the senseless deaths could still bring a lump to his throat.

Marie turned to smile at her daughters. "We're all very well. Thank you for asking. How are you? It's your company now, isn't it?"

Only mothers could be so innocently direct. He grinned. "It's certainly not my company, it's the stockholders'. But things are looking pretty good. I hope I didn't bore you with my long speech."

"Not at all," Annette said. "It's very exciting. This plane is amazing. It's so much bigger."

"Wait till you see the inside." The model behind him was a custom order for a Hollywood actor, but for privacy reasons, he would never mention that. "How about a personal tour?" He took Marie's hand and helped her up the steps.

"We would never see these incredible planes any other way," Marie said as she peered into the cabin tentatively before stepping inside. "It is beautiful, really beautiful."

"Thanks, Mrs. Madison." Art caught the attendant's eye and had him hold back the next group in order to give the three women a little privacy. Art had selected the different interior configurations for the display. A few of the aircraft were outfitted with the maximum number of seats and designed more for small groups. This particular aircraft had been designed for only a select few.

Up front, the cockpit boasted the latest in avionics from Honeywell, including the new autopilot hardware and LCD displays. A small jump seat folded into the door frame for the optional flight attendant. Brazilian mahogany wood adorned the small galley and bar at the top of the steps, and an assortment of liquors and wines was visible through the glass doors. A sophisticated audio and video entertainment system was stored in the bottom of the cabinet, but speakers, TV screens, and remote controls were located throughout the cabin.

Inside the main cabin, four Italian leather captain's chairs occupied the front section. All could slide and swivel and would recline into beds if necessary. The rear section of the spacious cabin boasted two large couches that lined the walls and a small conference table that would fold down and connect to the couches to form a king-sized bed. Three different shades of brown accented the tan leather, and with the soft, indirect lighting, it looked more like a cozy living room than an airplane. A lavatory finished in rich brown marble and gold fixtures was hidden discreetly behind the beautiful imported wood of the rear bulkhead.

"It's incredible, and so much bigger," Marie said. "You can stand up."

"Yes, all but the really tall guys," Art said. He was just under six feet, and he had a few inches to spare.

"They just keep getting better and better," Marie said as she tried one of the couches. "What are you going to do next? Go to the moon?"

Art laughed. "No, my dream is next-generation planes that will change the way we fly forever. In twenty years, I believe there will be planes with no pilots." His vision shocked some. Some thought he was nuts.

"No pilots?" Marie said dubiously.

"Yup."

Annette looked confused. "Really? How do they fly?"

"Computers, Annette. Computers."

~~~

It was almost a week before Mansi called Annette, but he could tell she had been waiting, and they talked for over an hour on the phone. He tried to end the conversation with another dinner invitation, but Annette surprised him by suggesting they go to Disneyland. He readily agreed and pretended he had never been. On the drive over, he asked a few questions that he knew the answers to, but she was happy to play tour guide. When they got there, they just walked around for a while. After seeing most of the park and a few of the tamer rides, he stopped her at the indoor roller coaster, Space Mountain.

Annette didn't take much convincing, but she screamed as they rushed through the dark and down the steep inclines. Mansi wrapped one arm around her and enjoyed the feeling as her warm body was pushed backwards into his embrace as the coaster threw itself around the tight track. When the ride was over, he took her hand to help her out, but she stumbled and almost fell.

"I'm sorry," she said. "I'm a little dizzy, I guess."

Mansi held her tighter. "Are you sure that you are okay?"

"I'm fine. I just caught my foot." She grinned. "Did you like the ride?"

"Yes." He had been here a few times with Jill, and it was their favorite ride. "It was very exciting."

Annette pushed her hair back. "I can't believe you've never been on a rollercoaster before."

"It's not an Algerian thing, but I loved it. Thanks for suggesting we come here."

"It's always a lot of fun here. You can come here and forget all your troubles. This is the happiest place on earth." Annette pointed to the words on the huge marquee sign over the entrance to the park.

He laughed. "Troubles? What troubles? Today we are at the happiest place on earth. What could be better than that?"

They stayed until late, long after the impressive fireworks were over, the warm summer California night perfect for walking and talking. As they pulled up in front of her apartment, she stopped him when he started to park the car. "I have to work early tomorrow, so I'm going to run off, but I had fun tonight." She opened her door a little, then leaned over and kissed him. "My mother told me men should be fun. Today was fun."

"It was. A classic American day – going to Disneyland. I will remember that for a long time. Can I call you again?"

Annette smiled seductively as she backed out of the car. "You better."

He watched her cute derriere sashay up the walk. Things couldn't be going better.

~~~

Mansi called a few days later, and they talked on the phone for a long time again. She seemed to be interested in everything he said. When he asked her if she would like to go dancing Friday night, she quickly agreed.

When he picked her up, he was almost speechless. He knew she was beautiful, but he didn't expect her to look so sexy. A silky sleeveless black top barely covered her more than ample breasts, and a tight red leather skirt looked like it was painted on. She wore the black high heels he had heard the guys at the office call CFM shoes. He wondered if he could be so lucky.

The club, a trendy spot called Angels, was loud, so they had to lean in close and talk directly into each other's ears. She didn't seem to mind. Soon, he had her laughing as he mixed up his languages as much as the truth, but he could see she was falling for him. On the slow songs, she seemed to drape herself around him. When he declined a third drink, saying he had to drive, he could see she was impressed. They ordered water before heading back to the dance floor, and when he kissed her tenderly during a slow song, it felt like her body was glued to his. She must have felt how much she affected him.

At her apartment door, they kissed passionately for a few minutes before she pushed the door wide open. "Would you like to come in?"

"It's late . . ."

"It's the weekend." She pulled him by the arm. "You can stay up a little later."

He followed her in and sat down on the couch as she turned on a stereo and a few lights. He glanced at the bedroom on his left. The door was half-closed, but he could see the bed was made. She returned with two glasses of water, but she put them on the table, sat down, and cuddled up. Mansi felt her tongue run along his neck as she left little kisses on her way to his mouth.

She purred in his ear. "Are you ready for this?"

"Ready for what?" Was she thinking what he was thinking?

"A physical relationship?"

"No." He had thought about bringing protection. "Where's the nearest drugstore?"

She laughed. "That's not what I meant, silly, but that is part of it. I meant, are you ready for a girlfriend? I'm not seeing anyone but you."

"I am not seeing anyone else, and you are the only woman I want to see."

"That's nice." She looked him in the eye. "I'm not on the pill."

"That's okay." He had condoms at home but hadn't figured he would need them yet. "We should use some kind of protection, anyway."

"I'll use the pill if we're going steady," she said, "but I'm not now." She sat up, and a funny look crossed her face. "Is this all okay with your religion?"

"Islam teaches many things, Annette, but as you see, I tend to live a conservative Western lifestyle. I care about you a lot, and I think about you all the time. I'm not sure if I know what true love is, or what our future will be, but physical intimacy is part of a loving and healthy relationship between a man and a woman."

"That's sweet." She wrapped her arms around him and pushed him back on the couch.

~~~

The salon was busy and noisy. Debbie Stromberg was her last customer of the day and an old friend. Annette had to tell her about Mansi. She and Debbie had met in the eleventh grade at Costa Mesa High when they shared a desk and giggles in their chemistry class. They had remained good friends ever since. Debbie was a pretty redhead with beautiful green eyes, but her pale complexion was ill-suited for the sunny skies of Orange County. Annette could see the red sunburn lines on her shoulders.

"Massi who?" Debbie said.

"Mansi. M-A-N-S-I. Mansi Ansour. His ancestors were French."

"Does he speak French?"

"French, English, Arabic, Spanish, and something called Berber."

"Wow, this gets better all the time. Does he have family here?" Debbie watched her fine hair slide down the front of the yellow plastic gown that she had wrapped around her.

"No, they're all in Algeria."

"What religion is he?"

"He's a Muslim." Annette looked for her friend's reaction in the mirror.

Debbie looked up and met Annette's stare. "Muslim men have some pretty archaic thoughts about their women. Have you talked about that?"

"Yes, we've talked about religion. He is not a fanatic and is more Western than anything."

"Well, Islam has its own rules, and their women don't have the rights we have here."

"It's just not that important to me," she countered. "He brought it up, but he says he doesn't care what religion I am."

"Well, he sounds very modern and open-minded. Is he good-looking?"

"Yes."

"And . . ."

"And what?" Annette tried not to smile. It wasn't just that she was having sex again; it was how good their lovemaking had been. Mansi was the most attentive and generous lover she had ever been with, and his soft but strong hands made her crazy.

Chapter 3

Mansi waited until after they had made love to tell her. Annette lay cuddled beside him with her hand gently caressing his chest. She would be disappointed, but that was part of his plan. A little test of faith he liked to think. They had been together almost every night in the last two weeks, and London would be welcome. He would be able to visit the mosque on a daily basis for a change.

"I'm sorry," he said. "I know you were looking forward to Catalina."

"It's okay." Her smile was gone. "Don't the English have Labor Day, too?"

"No, they don't celebrate the same holidays as the U.S. I'm sorry, Annette, but if I had more notice sometime, would you want to go with me?"

"What do you mean?"

"I mean, if I get enough notice about a trip to Europe, maybe you would like to come?"

"Really?" Her voice suggested she would say yes.

"Yes. Not this time, and who knows, it might be a while before my next trip. But I wouldn't have to work every minute, and I would love to show you the city. I know it quite well." He already had another trip scheduled.

"That sounds like a nice idea, it really does, but I would have to have enough time to reschedule my appointments. A few weeks' notice, at least."

He was gone for a week and returned eager to keep things moving. The ocean was one of Annette's favorite places, and she would find it romantic, so he drove down to Huntington Beach and they walked out to the end of the pier. Fishermen lined the sides, but nobody seemed to be catching anything. He hoped his luck was better. "How would you like to go to London next month?"

Annette turned. Her eyes had already said yes. "London? Why? Do you have to go?"

He nodded. "Meetings with Shell just got confirmed yesterday. What do you think? I know it's not Paris." A trip to Paris was also in the works, but one at a time.

"London sounds fantastic. When are you going?"

"The first week of October. I leave on Saturday the fifth and return the following Friday. If you come, we could stay a few days longer, maybe through the weekend?

"That sounds wonderful. Are you sure I wouldn't be a problem?"

He wanted to laugh. "Absolutely not, Annette. I'll have to work most of the days, but I will have some free time, and all of my evenings are mine."

"How much is the airfare?"

"I'm inviting you. You don't have to pay."

"That's far too generous. I can't accept that."

"The tickets will be free, from my frequent flyer plan. I have lots of miles saved, and I will never use them all."

"I'm used to paying my own way."

"I can understand that, but I have enough miles for a dozen trips to Europe, and if I don't use them, they'll expire."

"Are you sure?"

"Yes. In fact, maybe Val wants to go, too? That way, the two of you can sightsee together while I'm at work."

"Val?"

"Sure, why not? I have plenty of miles for another ticket. Do you think she would like to go?"

"I don't know, but why her?"

"That way, you won't be alone all day when I am at work. What do you think? We would have to book the tickets soon." He didn't really care much either way, but such a seemingly unselfish gesture might help his cause.

"I don't know if Val would want to be a third wheel," Annette replied. "And I'd want to pay my share of all the other expenses."

"My hotel rooms are paid by the company, but whatever you're comfortable with. I just thought you'd like to see London."

"I've always wanted to go."

"Well then, come. October is off-season, but that's good. It's far less crowded at that time of the year."

"Val would want her own room."

"Of course. What about you? Do you need your own room, too?"

"I don't think so." Her kisses answered his question.

"Then it's yes? I should book the tickets?" Wine and dine them, and most women couldn't resist. A splash caught their attention, and they turned to see a fisherman reeling in a fish. Mansi thought it was a good sign. When Annette turned back and smiled her wonderful smile, he knew something was biting.

"Give me a few days," she said. "I'll see if I can reschedule my clients, and I'll talk to Val tomorrow night."

~~~

Annette called Val before work the next morning. Her sister was stunned, but she was game for most things and agreed almost immediately. Her mother was not so keen and wanted to meet Mansi before her two daughters went halfway around the world with him. Annette called Mansi a few hours later and accepted. They made a date to meet on Wednesday night to plan the trip, and she went over early to tell her mom a little bit more about her new guy.

"You'll like him," Val assured her. "He's nothing like any guy she's dated before." Val seemed to have found new qualities in Mansi.

Annette thought for sure her mother would warm up, too, but she couldn't have been more wrong. Why, she didn't know, but it was obvious the moment he arrived. Her mother stood back beside the kitchen, her arms folded. Mansi was on time, looked very handsome, and was dressed conservatively, as usual, in a nice tan sports shirt and dark blue pressed slacks. He even brought gifts, a tin of English shortbread cookies and a package of Earl Grey Tea.

"Mom, this is Mansi Ansour," Annette said, taking the gifts and setting them on the coffee table.

Mansi's smile was as brilliant as ever. "It's nice to meet you, Mrs. Madison."

"It's nice to meet you, Mansi," Marie said politely, but didn't return his smile.

Annette turned to her sister. "And you know Val."

Val grinned. "Hi, Mansi. This is a very generous offer. I told Annette yes, but if it doesn't work out, I understand."

"Work out? There is nothing to work out. The reservations are all set."

Annette kissed Mansi on the cheek and steered him towards the sofa. "Can I get you anything?"

"No, thanks." Mansi set his maps down on the coffee table.

Marie pulled out a chair in the dining room. "You've been to London before, Mansi?" she asked.

"Yes, many times, Mrs. Madison. I used to live in Paris, and it was a short trip from there. Have you ever been?"

"No, of course not."

"It is quite a city, a lot of history. Maybe you should come, too? I have more than enough miles for another free ticket."

Marie was stunned by the offer. "Me? I couldn't possibly do that."

Annette wasn't sure she wanted her mother there. "Really, Mansi?"

"Sure, why not? Wouldn't that be nice? Mother and daughters on vacation together."

Marie turned him down again. "Don't think any more of it. I'm not going anywhere."

Mansi unfolded one of the maps. "I've brought some maps. Maybe this will help. This is a map of the London Underground, the subway system. It is the best way to get around the city, especially if the weather is bad."

~~~

The sun was just starting to crest the mountains behind Los Angeles the next morning when Mansi stopped his car. Other than the older model Ford parked a few car lengths ahead, the graveyard was empty. The early morning sky was a hazy pink, and it looked like it was going to be a nice day after the clouds burned off.

A door opened on the Ford, and Samzi got out. "It is good to see you," he said.

"It is good to see you, too, Samzi." Mansi embraced his cousin warmly; it had been almost four months since they had last seen each other in Algiers in May. "Not quite as scenic as our first meeting in San Francisco ten years ago."

"Yes, I find myself more cautious as time goes on. But this city of the dead seemed appropriate, wouldn't you say?" Samzi gestured around to the tombstones and crosses.

"Yes, I suppose." Mansi looked at the thousands of graves that extended as far as he could see. "If we could kill this many people, that would be good."

Samzi laughed. "This many dead? With your daughter? That is unlikely. Maybe one important but stupid individual, but not this many."

"How is Jill doing? It seems it will be such a long time before we know what she will be capable of."

"Hashim's plans have always been long-term," Samzi assured him. "Do not worry."

"Ten years for a daughter, not a fair return. I should have had a half-dozen sons in all those years." His daughter's future was yet to be determined, but he knew Hashim wouldn't hesitate to kill her if she didn't work out or something went wrong.

"What about this new woman?"

Mansi couldn't stop thinking about Annette. "Yes, I believe she will be willing."

"She is falling in love with you?"

"Yes, I think so. She is much like Linda – blonde, pretty, trusting. I am taking her to London next week."

~~~

Mansi spent Sunday helping the girls get oriented with the tube. One of the first places they visited was Trafalgar Square. Built in the early 1800s, it was one of the more popular tourist attractions in London. Surrounded by magnificent buildings on all sides, the tall obelisk, elegant fountains, and four massive bronze lions were a favorite spot for both locals and visitors. Today was no exception. Hundreds of people walked around posing for pictures while others lolled about eating lunch and enjoying the nice day. For October, twelve degrees was balmy by English standards. Traffic poured through the intersection in a confused but orderly way, and double-decker buses slowed down in front of the monument as their guides spouted off the history of the area and pointed out the various buildings that formed the perimeter.

They stopped in the middle of the plaza beside Nelson's column, and Mansi scattered the pigeons with a wave of his arm, sending the hundreds of birds flapping into the sky. "What do you think, Annette?"

"It's incredible, so different from the States." She spun around in a slow circle to take it all in.

Val pointed to the large statue. "Who is this supposed to be?"

Mansi was amused at their ignorance. "It is Lord Horatio Nelson. Trafalgar Square was named after a famous naval battle he fought in 1805."

"I take it he won."

Mansi chuckled. "Yes, and changed history. Napoleon had promised an invasion of England for years, but Nelson employed new naval tactics, defeated a much larger force, and won decisively. Unfortunately, he was himself killed in action."

"That's a shame," Annette said.

"He died a hero, saved his country and changed the course of history. I don't know if he would have wanted it any other way." For Mansi, there was no higher honor.

~~~

Mansi left early on Monday morning for the mosque. He told Annette he would be going directly to his first meeting from there. There were dozens of mosques in London, but he chose a different one every time. No sense setting any pattern that could be identified. The London Central Mosque had been completed in 1978 and was one of the largest in the city. It was easy to get to, in between two tube stops and only minutes from the hotel. The main hall could hold almost 2,000 worshippers and was usually filled to overflowing. Today was no exception.

As Mansi entered, he spotted Hashim on the far side of the massive room.

Hashim met him outside after the prayers, the Salah, were finished. "So, all goes as planned?"

Mansi smiled as they walked slowly down the busy street. It was still very early, and the sun was just starting to rise, but the service workers of London were already scurrying to their jobs. "All goes very well, Hashim. I am sure she is falling in love with me."

"Good. I hope wedding bells are soon to be in your future."

"As do I."

Hashim looked around to make sure no one was too close. He spoke quietly. "The ship will be taken today."

"The *Achille Lauro*?"

"Yes."

"Is our money in place?"

"Yes, spread across various tourist, travel and cruise ship companies." Hashim's quick chuckle made it sound like they were enjoying a good joke. "It doesn't take much to send the fear of God into Western investors."

~~~

Annette was a little disappointed that Mansi had to work so much, but she was definitely glad her sister had come. Mansi had left before dawn every morning, and she would have been lonely by herself. Val had been perfect company, and they had explored the city from one end of the London Underground to the other. The cool, damp London climate lived up to its billing, but the sisters hardly noticed as they layered up with a few key English wool purchases.

On the last night, Mansi took them to the London Theatre. Their seats were about ten rows back, just off the aisle, perfect. The play, *Amadeus*, left both girls breathless. All Mansi had told them was that it was the story of Mozart and his music. Annette had never seen anything like it before, and, despite the sad ending, she was delighted with the passionate performance. It was a wonderful way to end their trip.

The next morning, as they were packing their bags, Annette stopped Mansi as he pulled his suits out of the closet. "I had a wonderful time," she said. "Thank you so much for inviting us."

He smiled. "Thank you for coming."

"It's too bad you had to work so much."

"Business travel can be very boring, lots of meetings and too many business dinners. It was great to have you two around. Guess what? I might have another trip coming up."

"Back to London?"

"No, but I might have a trip to Paris in a few months."

"Paris? Really?" She wanted to go. Could she get away again?

"Yes, but I won't know for another few weeks. We are trying to set up a meeting for the week before Christmas. It could be fun; the French decorate for the holidays with a passion."

~~~

Annette woke up at noon the day after they arrived back in California. She didn't feel like getting up, so she lay in bed and thought about how happy she felt. Images of London danced through her mind, and she could almost hear the final magnificent crescendos of the play. But it wasn't just that. It was Mansi. He had worked a lot, but otherwise he had been the perfect tour guide in every way. He had helped them plan each day and had even met them for lunch in a couple of different English pubs. Nights they were all together, and while he had held her hand and kissed her a little in public, he never once embarrassed Val or made her feel uncomfortable. Annette hadn't been sure how romantic the trip might be, but he amazed her with his physical stamina. He left early in the morning for work and had much longer days than the girls, but he always had lots of energy for making love. At the end of the day, in the middle of the night and in the early, early morning, he had been more than eager.

She tried to remember how passionate Paul had been, and a vague memory of their first time made her giggle. Their parents had left them alone for the first time one summer when they were sixteen, and they couldn't stop themselves. They had both been virgins, and while Paul had been fun in bed, it had taken a few months before she finally relaxed enough to have an orgasm. The very few boys she had slept with since his death were always in a rush.

Mansi was never in a rush, yet he was far more aggressive and had taken her to a level of sexual intimacy she had never known existed. He would massage her, kiss her, touch her, play with her, and delight her as he made love to her entire body. He could make her tremble with desire and cry for more, and the intensity and number of her orgasms made her weak. Was that part of love? Was she finally letting go of Paul? Was she finally allowing herself to trust a man again?

The phone startled her from her daydream. "Hello."

"Good afternoon." It was her mother. "How are you feeling?"

"I'm okay, just getting up now. Is Val up?" She wondered how much her sister had told her mother about their trip.

"She just woke up a little while ago. She must have slept for fifteen hours. How about you?"

"I woke up around three, then fell back to sleep about six. I was going to come over." Annette knew she didn't need to ask.

"Of course. Val's told me about some of your trip. You better tell me your side of it."

Annette was over to her mother's house in minutes and could smell the tea brewing when she walked in. Instantly, she wanted to go back to England again.

Her mother looked happy. "Hi, dear. Val was just telling me about the theatre."

Val came down the hall, her hair a mess. "Hi."

"Hi," Annette said as she hugged her mother. "It was wonderful, Mom. The play is a big hit. I read all about it in *The London Times* on the plane on the way back. The story is true and tragic, but it was an incredible performance."

"It sounds like it."

Val's gift, a ceramic replica of the Tower Bridge, was on the kitchen table. Annette offered her mother the small, heavy, wrapped gift she had in her hands. "Here, Mom. I got you something."

Marie delicately untied the pretty green ribbon and opened the little cardboard box. Inside were a set of teacups with saucers, all with pictures of London landmarks. "They are beautiful, Annette. Thank you." She kissed her daughter on the cheek, then looked at the different photos etched on the delicate china. "Perfect. The tea is almost ready."

"Did Val tell you about the changing of the guards at Buckingham Palace?"

"Not yet, but she did tell me you are going to Paris."

Annette blushed. "Maybe."

"Aren't you overdoing it?" Marie's look made no mistake about her feelings.

"I don't know. Maybe. I know he's different from any guy I've ever dated before. I know I really like him."

"Don't you think things are moving a little fast?"

"What do you mean?"

"You hardly date for years, and then all of a sudden you're sleeping with this guy and willing to just drop everything and go anywhere with him."

"All of a sudden?" Annette hated defending herself. "I've known him for four months now, and we've spent a lot of time together. We have a great time together. Isn't that what's important? I've dated enough guys to know what I like."

Her mother rolled her eyes before answering. "You haven't dated anyone for more than a few weeks since Paul died. Now, in a few months, you're getting serious with this guy."

"Maybe I'm finally ready, or maybe I was just waiting for someone different. He is a true gentleman. He's funny, educated, good-looking, and he treats me like a princess. What's not to like?" She wanted to add how good he was in bed.

"What about his religious beliefs? Have you talked about that anymore?"

"Yes, we did, a few times. He does believe religion and faith are important. God is watching, is what he says. He believes that if he lives a good life, a life of purpose, that God will be watching, and he will be rewarded."

"What does that mean?" Her mother sounded angry.

"It sounds like a good moderate approach that would work in most religions, don't you think?" Annette definitely thought so. "But I don't give religion that much importance anymore. As long as he isn't a fanatic, or doesn't try to force his beliefs on me, should it matter?"

"I'd be a fool to tell you that religion or race should matter, but sometimes it still does. Some countries have very different laws and customs, and I don't want you to be taken advantage of."

"Nobody's taking advantage of me." Annette wished her mother would not be so negative. She was happier than she had been in years.

~~~

Paris was everything she had hoped it would be. Famous landmarks were on every corner, and Mansi had been right: holiday festivities and decorations lavishly adorned the shops and streets. When they arrived, the weather was warm for December, almost ten degrees, so they walked the streets while Mansi played tour guide. The trip up the Eiffel Tower was amazing, and the view incredible. Notre Dame, the Arc de Triomphe, the Place de la Concorde . . . It was just as grand as she had hoped. Mansi had to work more than he had thought, but Annette spent the extra hours wandering down the endless halls of the Louvre. She was fascinated by the Egyptian artifacts and vowed to get to Africa one day.

Their last day was beautiful, with not a cloud in the sky. As pretty as it was, however, the wind had turned cold. After a breakfast at a little café on the north side of the Seine River, they had to return to the hotel for an extra layer to ward off the biting breeze. They decided to take a bus tour, which was a great way to see the city, although most of what the tour guide rattled on about was lost to their ears. The bus was less than half full, and they snuggled in the back, as interested in each other as they were in the history that slid past their window. Annette knew she would remember this trip forever and hoped they would come back again.

The Regina Hotel was as beautiful as it was close, and she had been delighted when she opened the heavy curtains and discovered they had a view of the north side of the Louvre and the Eiffel Tower. Luxurious in a style she had never seen before, the high, coved ceiling, ornate woodwork, and antique furnishings made her feel like she had stepped back in time. The grand entrance and reception area dazzled her, and while the four-star hotel had been built over a hundred years ago and might not have been the best in Paris, for her it was perfect and exactly what she had dreamed about.

After a lovely dinner in the hotel restaurant, Mansi suggested they go for their last evening walk. They had retired early a few nights in a row, content after walking all day, to crawl into bed and warm each other up. Tonight, however, the city smelled fresh and alive.

"It's just like in the movies, but much more crowded," Annette said with a shiver. It was colder than it had been all week, but the streets were still thick with couples and friends, young and old. Chic boutiques, intent on seducing the weak, offered nothing but the best. She loved it.

Mansi stopped and fastened the top button on her coat. "Saturday night walking the Avenue des Champs-Élysées, that's a big thing in Paris for tourists and for locals."

"It is beautiful, really beautiful." Annette loved the look of the city at night. The shimmering lights gave the noisy and constant traffic that flowed up the magnificent boulevard a surreal look.

"Not much has changed here for centuries. Paris has always has been a beautiful city. You know, Algiers is very similar."

"Really? I hadn't gotten that impression from you. I thought it was half destroyed by war?"

"Yes, well, some of it was, but one good thing the French did in Algeria was construct great buildings. Their architecture is stamped all over the city. Well, over the European quarter, anyway."

"That sounds pretty nice."

"If it were peaceful, it would be. The city is built on a hill overlooking the Bay of Algiers and the Mediterranean Sea. Everyone, from the Romans, to the Arabs, to the Spanish, left their ideas of grandeur on the city before the French took over in the early nineteenth century. Even pirates lived there for a long time. It definitely has a lot of history."

"Maybe we should go there sometime."

"You wouldn't want to go at this time," Mansi said. "It is still unsafe, especially for Americans."

"You said that before. Is it really that bad?" She wished she had brought a warmer coat.

Mansi wrapped his arm around her and pulled her close. "Yes, the new President is just as corrupt as the old one. People are starving, crime is very high."

"Americans don't seem too well liked anywhere over there these days."

Mansi had told her some of the history of Algeria, but she understood little of the struggle that still tore at the country decades after the French had been forced out.

"Did you see the movie?" he asked.

"What movie?"

"*The Battle for Algiers*. It was done quite a while ago, but most of it was filmed on location. It was quite realistic in some ways. The French were bastards."

"Maybe I'll try and rent it."

"You should cherish your life in America. Much of the world is not so fortunate."

Annette had suffered, but knew it wasn't the same. "My father used to tell us that, too."

"My father died for our freedom, but the people are not free yet. The country is still run by liars and thieves. Maybe someday Algeria will be a good place to visit, but not now."

"You must be very proud of your father. He paid the ultimate sacrifice for your freedom."

"I am very proud of him. His life was of purpose. After almost a hundred and fifty years, Algeria is free of the French, free to make our own history, free to make our own mistakes." Mansi led her through the throngs of people towards the corner where the Arc de Triomphe was magnificently lit up. "Look – isn't it beautiful?"

Annette couldn't have agreed more. Paris was everything she had expected and more. She didn't even notice the man taking a picture of her from a car as it sped by.

~~~

Mansi fondled the photo. It was a fantastic picture. Annette looked beautiful. She was looking almost straight at the camera, with a big, happy smile. They were bundled up, and Mansi stood right beside her, but his face was slightly blocked and he was unrecognizable. Perfect. He dropped it back onto the table.

"My first trip to Paris in ten years, and I see you two love birds," Hashim said with a laugh.

The large café was still quiet and just the way they liked it. It was only seven a.m., and their flight didn't leave until the afternoon. Annette was still asleep. "What do you think?"

"She is beautiful, Mansi, truly beautiful. Your children will be beautiful."

Mansi felt blessed. He enjoyed her charms completely, and he was sure she was falling in love with him. "Do you think she likes me?"

Hashim looked surprised by the question and grinned foolishly in return. "Likes you? The way she looks at you . . . she loves you, cousin. At least, last night she did."

"I am glad you agree. I thought so." Mansi hadn't gotten more than four or five hours of sleep the last few nights and was actually looking forward to the long plane flight home. "I'll ask her soon."

"Good. I'm sorry I'm late, but here's what you were waiting for." Hashim reached inside his heavy brown car coat. It reached halfway to his knees, and Mansi wondered what else he had in there. He pulled out a thick coffee-table book and handed it to Mansi. It was titled *Dream Machines* and featured a picture of the new Land Rover on the cover, one of Mansi's personal dream automobiles. A rich, deep blue beauty, it was parked overlooking a huge cliff. "I thought you would like the book, too."

"And you were right." Mansi flipped the thick glossy pages open to where the brown envelope was taped inside. The middle of the book had been cut out to accommodate the courier package. He lifted the package out and looked inside at the stack of U.S. one-hundred-dollar bills and a few pieces of paper. He left the cash and pulled out the papers. His name was listed as an authorized signature for a corporation from the Bahamas, and the account showed a balance of almost $150,000 dollars.

"Allah is good," Mansi said. "Thank you."

"There is nine thousand five hundred in cash, just under the limit." Hashim gave him back the picture of Annette. "Time to move forward?"

"Yes, very soon. I think she is ready."

~~~

They got back home a week before Christmas. As much as Annette wanted a few days to get over the jet lag, some of her clients had left messages, so she dragged herself in to work the next day. She scheduled her friend last.

"So?" Debbie asked as soon as she sat down in the chair. "How was Paris?"

Annette had told the story a few times already, but it still felt good. "Pretty darn wonderful. We had a great time."

"How was the weather?" Debbie teased. "Cold enough to cool you two lovers down?"

Annette blushed. It had been a very romantic trip; much more so than with Val. Mansi had wined her and dined her in some fabulous restaurants and lavish nightclubs. "It was a little colder than London, but I bought a few nice things."

"So, how's everything with this guy? Still hot and heavy?"

Annette couldn't have hidden the truth if she had wanted to. "Things are great. I've seen and done more in six months with Mansi than I have in years."

"Sounds serious, Nettie. Are you ready?"

Annette combed through Debbie's hair, then looked at her own reflection in the mirror. "I don't know how serious he is. He's very affectionate and very romantic, but he's never said he loves me."

Debbie laughed. "Most guys won't say that even when they do. Do you love him?"

She was struggling with that very question.

Chapter 4

"That's where my father used to work," Annette said, pointing. A pretty Asian reporter was standing in front of a row of Trainor private jets.

Mansi turned up the volume on the TV. "I remember you telling me. What's going on?"

"I don't know."

The reporter had walked over to a platform where a news conference looked ready to start and turned to face the camera. A huge Trainor Jets logo covered the backdrop behind the podium. "This is Tanu Tissii, reporting live from the Trainor Jets manufacturing plant in Long Beach, California. Sales of the company's Freedom Three model were a disappointment, victim of a soft global economy. Unless they can find a way to increase their market share, the company's future is far from certain. Trainor Jets could be sold, maybe even gone after being an institution at Dougherty Field for over forty years, and with it, thousands of jobs and millions of dollars."

"Wow, I bet my mother doesn't know this."

A picture of a well-dressed older man in a jacket and tie flashed onto a corner of the screen. The reporter went on, "Meetings this week with billionaire Jack Pelton have started wild take-over rumors, as Pelton Enterprises already owns ten percent of the Trainor stock. CEO Art Trainor and Jack Pelton will be making a joint announcement in the next few minutes."

"We were just there a few months ago," Annette said. "I've been in one of those planes."

Mansi looked surprised. "You flew in one of those?"

"No, I went in one that was parked on the ground. They always have a big deal when they introduce a plane, and they invite a lot of people. After the speech, you can go inside one."

"That must have been interesting."

Art had seemed so positive when they had met. "Yes, but I didn't realize the company was in trouble. He never indicated they had financial problems."

The TV zoomed in as Art Trainor walked out onto the stage.

Art stepped up to the microphone, and the TV cameras zoomed in on his face. "Ladies and gentlemen, thank you so much for coming. Today is another milestone day for Trainor Jets, and we think you will like what you hear. As you all know, Trainor Jets has suffered with the rest of the industry as general aviation sales continue to slump, but in the problem lies the answer. If the demand for our planes has decreased, we need to find or create new opportunities that will increase the market for our jets." Art paused for a moment, then continued with his newfound comparison, "Much like William Boeing in the 1920s, when he helped create an airmail service and then an airline that needed his planes, Pelton Industries and Trainor Jets have put together a solution that will keep the plant in Long Beach manufacturing hundreds of jets well into the next century."

Cheers from the crowd erupted as the TV camera zoomed back to include the other man, well dressed, wearing a dark power suit and a cool smile, his trademark.

Art held up a few sheets of paper. "Pelton Industries is going to purchase all of Trainor Jets' real estate holdings in Long Beach California, buildings and land, for eight hundred million dollars. Trainor Jets will then lease back every square foot and have the option, and the first right of refusal to purchase all our property back in ten years. Our unions have agreed to wage rollbacks in exchange for profit-sharing in the future, a future that now looks exceptionally bright as Pelton Industries and Trainor Jets have formed a new company called Fly America."

Art turned as a banner behind the stage automatically rolled down, displaying the words *FLY AMERICA* stenciled across a Trainor jet photographed at cruising altitude. "Ladies and gentleman, Mr. Jack Pelton."

The applause was not anywhere near as loud as it had been for Art. Jack waved and took the mike. "Fly America is going to offer fractional ownership of planes, much in the same way time-share condos work. This concept is not new and is supported by extensive market research. Most private aircraft owners actually only fly a few hundred hours a year, leaving the planes on the ground most of the time and available for use. This will bring the cost of private air travel down, and the demand is sure to soar. Our projections are that this business will grow by at least ten percent a year for the next twenty years. Fly America will buy every Freedom Three jet that Trainor Jets can build and more."

The crowd burst into applause.

"Good news, I guess," Annette said.

~~~

Mansi was sure Annette loved him. Everything pointed to it. After six months, they stayed at each other's place most nights. It was almost like being married already. He waited until they were finished with dinner and the restaurant was half-empty, and then he went for it. He fumbled in his pocket for the small box as he reached over and took her left hand. "I know we have very different backgrounds, Annette, but since I met you, my life has been nothing short of wonderful." He pulled out the beautiful diamond ring. "Will you marry me?"

Annette looked shocked. "Marry you? Are you serious?" She watched as Mansi slipped the ring on her finger. It was a large round stone, with a row of diamonds on either side.

"Of course I'm serious. I love you, and I want you to be my wife."

"Mansi, there are so many things I don't know about you," she stammered, "so many things that you don't know about me . . ."

Mansi kissed her and pulled her close. "Don't know? What do you want to know? I'm almost thirty years old; I have never been married, but have always wanted to. I love you and want to marry you. What else do you need to know?"

"I can't say that I haven't thought about it. I think I love you, too. What about your religion?"

Mansi had anticipated the question. "What do you mean?"

"Do I have to convert? I'm not sure about all that."

He had never liked the idea of a nonbeliever as the mother of any of his children, but it just didn't matter. "No, you don't have to change anything. I will always have my faith; you can have yours. That is not important to me. I love you. That's what's important."

"I know you still go to the mosques in Los Angeles. What about our children? Will they need to be raised as Muslims?"

"We can introduce religion to the children later in life." The thought made him think of Jill, and he wondered how she was doing. "They can make their own choices."

"What if they don't follow any religion?"

"Does this mean yes?" He had her.

"Will we still live in Costa Mesa?"

"We will live wherever you want. That makes no difference to me."

"There is something else I never told you," Annette said slowly.

"What? What could possibly make a difference? I love you."

"I never told you that I was . . ." tears ran down her cheeks. "I was engaged once before."

"You were?" Why hadn't she told him this before?

"Yes, but . . . he died." She choked on the words.

Mansi didn't know what to say at first, but hoped it wouldn't stop her from marrying him. "That's awful. How did he die?"

She reached for her napkin and dabbed at her wet eyes. "His name was Paul. He died in the same car crash as my father."

What? Why didn't she mention that before? "That is so awful, Annette. I'm so sorry. You must have been devastated."

"I was. I didn't date anyone for years."

"It's not something one ever gets over. But it doesn't change how I feel about you." Her past pain didn't matter much, as long as there was no other man still out there.

"Thank you." She smiled. "I love you, Mansi. I just don't know if I could take it if anything ever happened to you."

"Life can't promise that an accident won't take either of our lives tomorrow Annette, but life must go on." Linda crossed his mind, and he wondered how his first wife had taken the loss of her daughter. "You are a beautiful woman with your whole life ahead of you."

"I know, but I thought you should know."

"Thank you for telling me, but it doesn't change the way I feel. I love you and want you to marry me."

"Are you sure?"

"Yes, Annette. I am positive." Hashim would be furious if she backed out now.

She didn't say anything for a moment, but then her smile returned. "Yes, Mansi, yes. I do love you, and I will marry you!"

"This is fantastic. I will make you very happy!" He pulled his chair closer, and they kissed passionately for several minutes.

Annette pulled away. "So, kids? You still want children?"

"Absolutely. I've always wanted to have a family, and you're the incredible woman I want to do that with. I know you will make a great mother."

"You're very sweet, Mansi. It sounds wonderful. What kind of ceremony would we have?"

"Algerian traditions are much different from American. What if we just had a simple civil wedding, a non-religious ceremony?" He had been through this before.

"That sounds like a good idea. What about your family? Will they come?"

"My brother, maybe. My mother will be very unhappy that I am not marrying an Algerian girl, but that doesn't matter."

"You are making this too easy. When do you think we should get married?"

"How about this spring? Say, March?"

~~~

She made sure Val was out before she went over to see her mother. Thoughts of her engagement to Paul ran through her mind, and she hoped her mother would react better this time, but her mother's prior comments about Mansi didn't give her much comfort. She had thought about just eloping and running away to Las Vegas.

"Has something happened?" Marie said.

Annette nodded. "Yes, something good." She had resisted answering any questions over the phone.

"Why do you look so worried?"

"Because I don't know how you are going to take the news."

"What news?" Marie set her coffee cup down on the kitchen table.

"Mansi proposed last night, and I said yes."

Marie looked shocked. "You're going to get married?"

"Yes, Mother. In March."

"Isn't that a little soon?"

"I don't know. That gives us three months. How long should we wait? We love each other, and it's not like we're kids." Annette had hardly slept last night, but the more she thought about it, the better she felt.

"You've only know him for six months."

"So? You told me you married Dad after only four months."

"That was different."

"Why?"

"I was pregnant." Marie's face froze. "You're not pregnant, are you?"

"No, Mother. I've been taking the pill since just after I met Mansi."

"Well, thank God for that."

"Why? It was okay for you."

"Things were different then. We didn't have the pill. You were an accident." Marie immediately fashioned an apologetic smile. "A much-welcomed accident."

"Thanks." Annette knew she wasn't planned, but it hurt anyway, and she felt the tears start. "I thought you would be happy for me."

Marie put her arms around her daughter and hugged her. "I'm sorry. It just seems sudden after all these years, and I don't want you to get hurt."

"You, better than most, know there are no guarantees in life. Mansi loves me, and I love him. Isn't that what's important?"

"Yes, dear, it is." Marie softened. "I never told you how mad my mother was at me for getting pregnant. She didn't think your dad would ever amount to anything. I'm sorry for reacting so negatively, but there is something about Mansi that I can't put my finger on. I'm probably just being an overprotective mother."

"I'm happy, Mom, really happy, and I think Mansi will make a great husband and father."

"I'm sure you're right, but don't follow my footsteps. Wait a while before you have kids. Enjoy being married before you complicate your life with children."

"I will, Mom." Her mother had been critical of Paul and didn't think he was going to amount to anything, either. She had warned Annette about getting pregnant then, too.

~~~

Mansi watched the KLM 747 climb out over the Pacific Ocean. He liked meeting at the beach. The rhythmic pounding of the surf was soothing, and the intermittent roar of the jets taking off from LAX could baffle any listening device.

"Congratulations," Samzi said. "You work quickly. That is good."

Mansi shrugged. "I'm not twenty anymore, and time is moving quickly. At this age, Americans have a different perspective on marriage, and a short courtship is quite normal."

"When is the happy day?"

"March fifteenth. Will you come?"

"You want me to be best man?"

"Sure, why not? Nobody will check your I.D."

"Okay. Any other babes there?" Samzi sneered.

"Her sister looks just like her. The two of them together?" Mansi had thought about it a few times when Val had fallen asleep on the couch while they were all watching TV. "It's a fantasy of mine."

Samzi laughed. "You sound like an American, never satisfied. Just get somebody pregnant, okay?"

"I will do my best. You can be sure I will be working for Allah every night." They both laughed as another jumbo jet roared overhead. "Do you have the pills yet?"

"They will be ready next week."

"Maybe our family will arrive sooner than she thinks." Mansi thought of Jill. "How's my daughter doing?"

"She continues to do exceptionally well." Samzi smiled at a pretty woman that jogged by. She never paid him any attention. "She could turn out to be an asset yet."

Mansi had not seen her for almost eight months. "Does she show any particular skills?"

"She is very bright, and she's stronger and tougher than most of the boys. A tomboy, I think the Americans would call her."

Mansi still had many doubts. "I will consider Jill a test run until I get a boy, but it will be interesting to see what happens with her."

"We will do our best. She is definitely a special case. When will you get back?" Mansi stopped as a couple of young girls with a small white dog walked by. "It will be some time, maybe a few months after the wedding."

Samzi got up and patted his younger cousin on the shoulder. "I wonder if your daughter will still love you then?"

~~~

The wedding was a small affair on a yacht in the Newport Beach harbor. Annette had arranged a short cruise around the bay with the captain of the charter boat a few weeks earlier, and Mansi had loved it. He had been amazed by the luxury homes that crowded the narrow peninsula and the shoreline, especially when the captain told him most were second homes. Upon inspection, that was somewhat obvious by the number of houses that were shuttered and the yachts that lay still in the slips in front.

The weather was perfect, as usual, seventy-five degrees Fahrenheit, blue skies and only a few puffy clouds that provided the occasional bit of shade. Annette had frolicked on the local beaches in the surf since a young girl, and she loved the smell of the ocean. Something about the salt, the wind, and the crashing waves brought back memories of the happy days of her youth, and she saw it as a good omen. This was meant to be.

As Mansi had suggested, the late afternoon ceremony would be simple and non-religious. To Annette's initial delight, an old family friend of Mansi's from Algiers was in town and had been glad to act as best man, but gentlemen he wasn't. She struggled politely with his name, Imazari Tanndoor, but his obvious leer and a few rude remarks to Val were totally inappropriate. In the end, she wished he had never come. Mansi seemed to enjoy his company and laughed hard at a few jokes, but whether they were in Arabic, Berber, French, or Spanish, she had no idea what her husband-to-be saw in his unpleasant friend. She was glad when he left shortly after the vows had been exchanged. They partied until almost 10:00 before leaving Val and a few friends to clean up. After a short but extremely passionate night in the Four Seasons Hotel, they flew out of the Orange County airport directly to Maui.

Annette had been to Hawaii once before, to Waikiki with a girlfriend, and she loved the hot, steamy climate, but she had never seen accommodations like this before. Their small but romantic thatched hut was hidden deep in the stand of trees. Very private, with a secluded balcony and an awesome ocean view. They never left the room for the first two days.

"Honey, shouldn't we get out for a while?" she said finally as they lay in bed one afternoon. "Maybe go out for dinner?" She was starved.

Mansi rolled over. "Yes, you are right. Enough making love. Time for real food. We have probably eaten everything good on the room service menu, anyway."

"That's what making babies would be like. You have to have sex all the time, day and night." Annette wondered why she had said that.

"Really? That doesn't sound too bad. Sex morning, noon, and night." Mansi reached for her breasts. "Try to have as much chance as possible for those two little cells to find each other. I think I'm going to like making babies."

"I know we have talked about having children, but I'd ideally like to have kids in a few years."

"That's what I was thinking, too. But you sure make it sound like fun trying to have a baby." Mansi rolled closer and trailed his tongue along her torso. "Do you think a person could have too much sex?"

Annette returned back to Southern California a very happily married woman. Mansi moved into her apartment, and it felt like they were still on their honeymoon. They made love every night, sometimes more often. Annette figured it must be the Frenchman in him.

~~~

A few months after the honeymoon, Mansi came home with a surprise. He had to go Algeria on a business trip at the end of June. Annette was disappointed. It would be the first time they had been apart since they were married.

"What about George's party?" she complained. "It's the anniversary of when we met – one year."

"Annette, what do you want me to do? Tell my boss I can't go?"

"I'm sorry, but the honeymoon is hardly over."

"I have a major opportunity coming up, and in the business world, timing is everything. I have to go."

Annette knew she was being selfish. He had told her before they were married that he would continue to travel. "I thought you said Algeria was not that safe these days."

"In some places, yes, but not so much for me. It is Westerners who are at risk."

"Yes, well, you look like a Westerner." She didn't want to sound too much the part of the worried little woman, but he could be very hard to reach when he was away on business.

"I suppose you're right." Mansi laughed. "That's funny."

He dressed like an American, lived an American's lifestyle, and had married an American. Annette couldn't understand why he thought it was funny.

~~~

The tired old terminal at the Algiers airport built during World War II had never been designed for international flights, and when three large passenger jets landed around the same time, the immigration line-up was long and slow. Mansi stood in the thick queue for a few minutes, then went over and spoke to one of the guards. The man directed him over to the empty crew-only booth. The inspector smiled when Mansi started speaking in Arabic, and he was through in minutes.

Hashim was waiting outside. "Welcome home. It is good to see you."

"It is even better to see you, Hashim. It is always so good to come home. Are you still coming to America next month?"

"Yes, as planned, but surely life must be tolerable? You have a new wife, another beautiful blonde. Did you get the pills?" He snickered.

"Yes."

"Good. Hopefully she can get pregnant quickly."

"I am trying. I am trying very hard." Mansi laughed. "How is Jill doing?"

"She does better every week. She doesn't cry anymore, and her French is coming along quite well." Hashim opened the back door of the Renault and let Mansi in first. The driver nodded a silent greeting as they pulled into the steady stream of traffic.

It had been almost six months since he had seen his daughter, and while Samzi had relayed encouraging progress reports, Mansi had been anxious to see for himself how she was doing. "Is it worth continuing with her?"

"You know better than I Mansi; that many Americans talk about the day a woman becomes president. Margaret Thatcher's election in England has made anything possible for women in Western society. That is their foolish decision, but I think that could help us. In another ten years, this girl could have her choice of jobs, and she can go places a man cannot."

Mansi was aware of the determination of American females. Both his wives were far more independent than any Muslim woman he had ever known. "I will follow your wishes, Hashim, but understand that my priority is to have a son. Now that I am married again, I cannot promise how often I can get back to see the girl."

"I understand a boy is the priority, but you need to have your daughter accept you back into her life. We have convinced her that it was her own fault, that she was a very bad girl and her mother didn't want her, but that you still love her. She will be happy to see you. The time is right."

"Yours is a grand plan, and many seeds must be planted in order to harvest even one crop."

"That is so true, so true, but it's also true that sometimes struggles against the greatest of odds produce the greatest of successes." Hashim tapped his driver on the shoulder and pointed to the left. "If Allah is willing, even a woman may carry out an important mission."

It took less than fifteen minutes to reach the small complex on the outside of the city. The cluster of buildings appeared quite run down, but two rows of barbed wire running along the high wall suggested there was something of value inside. Mansi knew the security precautions were as much for keeping people in as it was for keeping them out. Hashim knocked three times, paused, and then added three more. After a few moments, the door opened.

The guard apologized as he let them in. "Please excuse my delay. Please, enter."

Hashim barked, "Go get the American girl." The young man hurried off.

Mansi walked over to the window on the far side of the room. Outside, seated in a half-circle surrounding an older instructor, a group of young boys were reciting the Koran. He studied their faces and tried to guess where they were from. A few were blonde and appeared to be of some kind of Nordic descent, several were Asian, two were black. He couldn't tell where most of the others were from, but Hashim had told him they now had children with passports from over twenty different countries.

The guard returned in less than a minute, towing Jill by the arm. She looked more like a boy than a girl. Her hair had been cut extremely short, and she was dressed in drab green dungarees.

When she recognized her father, her expression immediately changed, and she started to cry. "Daddy, Daddy, Daddy!"

The guard let her go, and she ran straight into Mansi's arms. He picked her up and held her tightly. "How's my baby girl? You've grown so much." He couldn't believe how tall she was. She must have grown three or four inches since he had last seen her.

Jill sobbed as tears rolled down her cheeks. "Daddy, I missed you so much."

Mansi held her close. "It's okay, Jill. Daddy is here now, and everything is going to be okay."

It only took a few minutes for Jill to stop crying, and she smiled when Mansi asked about school. "I am reading the Koran, Daddy. My teacher says I am doing very well. Do you want me to read for you?"

"Yes, that would be wonderful. Can you read it in French?"

Jill beamed. *"Oui, mon pappa."*

"You have learned well. I am sure when your mother hears this she will be very pleased."

Jill's expression changed instantly. "I am doing the best I can. Tell Mommy that I will do better. She will see that I love her." She started to cry.

"Don't cry," Mansi snapped. "Your mother hates a weak girl. If you cry, she will never come and see you."

Jill stopped instantly. "I'm sorry, Daddy. I'm sorry. Please don't tell Mommy."

"You have to change, Jill. You have to become a soldier of God, and you must serve your God to deserve your family."

"Yes, Father, I will, you shall see. I will become the best, better than the boys."

"I hope so. I really hope so." Mansi doubted she would ever amount to much, but after almost ten years in America, she was all he had so far.

~~~

A few days before Mansi was due back, Annette realized her period was late. She should have been menstruating by now, and as she counted off the weeks on the calendar on the wall, she realized it was almost six weeks since her last cycle. She wondered what could have happened; she had been diligent about taking her pills. Still, part of her hoped it was true. For all their plans of waiting, the thought of being a mother sounded wonderful. She picked up the phone to call her doctor. She made the appointment late in the day, figuring she wouldn't want to go back to work if she found out she was pregnant.

The receptionist told her to have a seat, but it didn't take long before she was whisked down the corridor and into an examination room. She waited patiently for the tests to be run, but by the time Dr. Lee came back, his smile only confirmed what she already knew.

"Congratulations, Mrs. Ansour. You are going to have a baby."

She grinned. "I thought so. I feel different. It's hard to pinpoint, but I knew something was happening."

"You'll feel more changes every day. Is this a planned baby?"

His direct question made her feel guilty. "Yes and no. My husband and I both want children, but we hadn't talked about it happening so soon." She laughed nervously. "We've only been married a few months, and as you know, I've been taking the pill."

"Yes, that is a surprise," the doctor agreed, but he smiled as if it didn't matter. "But it's not like you're nineteen, either. You're almost thirty years old, and that's a good age to start a family."

"Yes, I suppose. It's just that I was still enjoying being a newlywed. This changes everything."

"Life comes without warning sometimes. I hope this can be a wonderful new addition to your life."

"I hope my husband thinks so, too." Annette was pretty sure Mansi was going to be happy.

"I'm sure he will love the child, too. Babies can bring such joy to life. You will see. I have six children, and they surprise me every day."

Annette thought six might be a bit too much. "When am I due?"

"The middle of February." The doctor grinned as if that was the most wonderful time of the year. "An early spring baby."

The doctor was right; life had a way of just happening. Mansi had said repeatedly that he wanted children.

Annette went straight over to her mother's house, but Marie's car wasn't there, only Val's blue VW bug. Annette felt like running up the walk, but she wondered how much exercise she should do now.

Inside, Val was watching TV.

Annette blurted it out. "I'm pregnant. I'm due in February. I can't believe it. I've been taking the pill."

"Pregnant? Really? Wow!" Val looked unsure. "Is this good news or bad news?"

"Good news, I think. You know I've always wanted children. It's just a little sudden."

"Have you told Mansi?"

"Not yet. I think I'll wait till he gets back; it's only a few more days. I'll surprise him." Annette patted her belly. "I sure hope he's ready for kids, because it's a little late now."

"He loves you, and he's no kid, either. I bet he'll be really happy."

"I hope so. I hope he's ready to be a father."

The noise of a car stopping made both girls look to the front door.

"Must be Mom," Annette guessed.

"Hi," Marie said as she entered. She looked back and forth. "What's going on?"

"You're going to be a grandmother!" Annette blurted it out.

"You're pregnant?" Marie obviously wasn't as thrilled.

"Unless you have any other kids I don't know about."

Marie didn't look overjoyed, but she managed a quick smile. "When is the baby due?"

"February thirteenth."

"Does Mansi know?"

"Not yet. He'll be back on Thursday. I'll tell him then."

Annette didn't say anything to anyone at work for the next few days; she wanted to tell Mansi first. She drove up to LAX daydreaming, feeling like she was in a movie. Just married, husband returning from a business trip, and as she got out of the car, she wondered how the story would end. "Hi, baby. Did you have a good trip?"

"It was fine, but I missed you." He set down his bags, wrapped his arms around Annette, and kissed her.

She wanted to tell him right there, but decided to wait until they got in the car. She was pretty sure she was going to start crying. She asked him about his trip, but hardly heard his answer and stopped him as he reached for the keys. "Wait. There's something I want to tell you." She searched his eyes for any sign that this was a bad time.

"What is it?" Mansi looked concerned. "Is everything okay?"

"Yes, I think so. I hope you do, too. I'm pregnant!"

His jaw dropped. "This is wonderful news, Annette, wonderful news."

"It's so sudden. I know we had talked about children, but maybe this is too soon?"

"I think it's fantastic." Mansi started kissing her. "This is great! I'm going to be a daddy."

"I love you, Mansi. I really love you."

The drive home was full of happy chatter. They wondered whether it would be a boy or a girl, and they laughed over different names. Mansi shocked her when he speculated about twin boys, and by the time they had driven the thirty-five miles back to Costa Mesa, they had talked about everything from diapers to university.

~~~

At first, Annette's condo had been fine. The bedroom was quite big and it had lots of closets, so Mansi had moved some of his stuff in and stored the rest. Annette's apartment might have room for a crib in the corner of the bedroom, but not much else.

Mansi brought it up after dinner a few nights later. "Why don't we buy a house?" The apartment already felt too small, now that he had made up his mind.

Annette turned from putting away the dishes. "I don't have much money saved, and if I'm not working, can we afford it?"

"I have saved a lot of money," Mansi said. "How much do I need for a down-payment?" He didn't like that he had to be friendly to all the people in the condo building, that they would come to know him. A home offered far more privacy and ambiguity.

"I'm not sure. It depends on the cost of the house."

"I have well over a hundred thousand dollars in the bank. How much is a house?"

Annette was stunned; they had never discussed money before. "Really? Wow! I think a nice three-bedroom house costs around two hundred thousand. Honey, that's a lot of money."

"I told you the oil business paid quite well, and I have lived on my expense account for years. This is what I've saved all my money for. Why don't you start looking? Maybe we can move in before the baby is born."

Annette couldn't have been more delighted and knew exactly who to call. Her friend Debbie had gotten her real estate license last year. They spent the next month looking at neighborhoods from Huntington Beach to Irvine, but she liked the older homes and bigger yards in Costa Mesa.

Mansi had only seen a few houses on Annette's short list and hadn't really liked anything so far, so she hoped he would like the one today. Debbie was parked out front waiting for them when they arrived. The single-story house was cute. It was a soft medium brown with white trim, had a nicely landscaped front yard, and a well-cared-for look. Annette let Mansi look around for a few minutes. She had already seen it.

"Well, what do you think?" she asked.

Mansi stopped in the generous kitchen. "I like it. It seems quite spacious."

"Look at the back yard." Annette knew that was important to him. She opened the sliding door.

Mansi walked outside and looked around. "I like it, Annette, but it is your decision. If you want it, let's buy it."

"Really?"

"Sure, if you want, I like it." Mansi took another look at the back yard. It was quite private, with bushes that formed a solid fence on all sides.

"Are you sure? We can look at more."

"No, I like this one. It has enough room, and it's big enough if we have a few children." He grinned. "The home is for the woman, for the family. For me, it's fine. You decide."

Annette smiled at her husband; he was so easy to get along with.

~~~

Samzi was waiting when Mansi drove up. The graveyard was quiet, as usual. "This is great news, Mansi. Finally, another child. When is it due?"

Mansi laughed. "February, Friday the thirteenth." The date was ironical.

"So, for you, my friend, the future now has a date."

"It seems like a long time, but it will come soon enough."

"Making history takes time, Mansi. There is no easy way, no shortcuts. Don't worry, my friend, you have done well. You will have two swords, two chances to become immortal."

Samzi pointed at an inscription on a large, expensive headstone. The dead man had lived over eighty-four years. "Imagine, my friend. This man lived so long, long enough for two lives. So shall you."

"I think maybe I have lived three lives already."

"Three wives, three families." Samzi's laugh was not very sympathetic.

"How is Jill doing?"

"Good, very good. She is far ahead of the other new students. You won't fool her with Arabic anymore, and she beat up another boy."

"She did?" Mansi grinned. Even Tariq hadn't been forced to prove himself as much as Jill had. "Anybody seriously hurt?"

"No, a bloody nose, not broken. A crying kid, that's all."

"Doesn't sound like much to worry about." Both kids would have had two week's confinement, but at least she was coming out relatively unscathed. Many of the kids took a few beatings trying to figure out where they fit in. He wondered if Hashim was thinking about allowing any more girls into the Madrassa, "No, Tariq broke it up. He's quite the little peacekeeper, that one."

"Politician." Mansi could picture his ten-year-old son acting as a referee. "Just like his grandfather."

"Yes, well, he's quite the asset. There's not much that goes on in there that we don't know about." Samzi stopped at another grave. The small inscription was sad. The young girl had lived to be only six.

"And the mental training with Jill?" Mansi asked, sitting down on the stone wall that ran between two levels of the cemetery. Low, thin clouds hid the early morning sun, and the horizon turned intense orange. It looked like a massive fire was just over the horizon, and the edge was going to burst into flames any second. "How goes that?"

"Very well. She never talks about her mother anymore and hasn't for quite a while, but she does talk about making you proud. It would be good if you could get back to see her a little more regularly."

<center>~~~</center>

On Friday, February 13, 1987, Annette gave birth to a healthy baby boy. She had started having pains just after dinner, and after her water broke, they rushed to Hoag Hospital. Dr. Lee arrived soon after, and just before midnight she became a mother. Mansi, Marie, and Val were there to share her joy.

The doctor held her newborn son up for her to see. "It's a boy!"

Annette was exhausted but elated as she took her son in her arms for the first time. She knew Mansi would be delighted, and he was.

"He's beautiful, a beautiful boy. My prayers have been answered." Mansi reached for the tiny bundle.

"Be careful," Annette said. She could see the love in her husband's eyes.

Mansi cradled the sleeping infant and grinned.

Val asked, "Have you named him yet?"

Annette smiled. "We are going to call him Derek."

"I knew a Derek when I was growing up," Marie said. "Everyone called him Derry."

Annette mused, "Kind of like my name, I guess."

Val asked, "Why Derek? Where does that come from? It doesn't sound French."

Annette had asked the same thing when Mansi had first suggested the name.

"No, it's not," Mansi explained. "Derek means someone of strength. In ancient times, it meant a ruler of people."

Marie, surprisingly, helped erase any doubts Annette harbored. "I like it. It's not too common, yet not something that will trip him up a lot later in life."

Annette knew her mother must have been relieved when Mansi had suggested the non-Arabic name. "I had suggested Darcy if it had been a girl."

"Derek Ansour, not your average name," Marie said.

~~~

Annette came home a few days later with their new baby. Mansi couldn't have been a prouder or more distracted father. He opened her door, took Derek out of her arms, and left her sitting in the car as he rushed inside, cradling the baby. Annette watched him run off in disbelief. She got out slowly, and as she stood up, he came running out, without the baby, apologized, and helped her up the short walk to the house. It was a sign of things to come.

Annette didn't think about work for the first few weeks, but when she brought up the idea of going back to work, Mansi exploded. She had never seen him mad before and she was shocked. He was dead set against her returning to work.

"The most important years are the first years. Can't you go back to work after Derek is in school?"

Annette was floored by his negative demeanor. "What about my business? It's taken me ten years to build up a good business."

"I do not believe in mothers working. Women should be with their children. There are a lot of experts who think a mother staying home at least until grade school is a good idea."

"Yes, I know, and part of me likes that idea, but if I don't go back to work now, I'll have to start all over again, build up a new client base."

"Why can't you wait until Derek is in school? Then he won't need you anymore."

Annette was stung by his words. "He will still need me, just not all the time."

"Maybe we should try to have another baby. They say two children are better adjusted than single children."

"Maybe we should talk about how many children you really want on your little soccer team." She felt herself soften.

"Just one more, a year or two behind Derek. Wouldn't that be perfect?"

Annette looked down at their son sleeping quietly in her lap. She could see the blanket moving slowly with his heartbeat. "What do you think, Derry?" She whispered. "Do you want a little sister? How about a brother?"

She agreed not to go back to work for a few years. They would try to have another baby in a few months and see what happened.

Chapter 5
7 Years Later - May 1994

Annette never did go back to work. Mansi started to travel more; Europe, North Africa, the Middle East. Sometimes he would be gone for a few weeks at a time. For Annette, the romance and vacations in Europe had been replaced by diapers and afternoons at the local Wal-Mart.

While Mansi continued to insist he would love another child, the passion was quickly disappearing. At first she thought it was just business, but he seemed more distant each time he returned from a trip. When she tried to talk to him about it, he would usually shrug it off without really answering, but a few times he lost his temper and it really scared her.

Mansi made a huge deal out of Derek's seventh birthday, calling him a man, and then one month later, he had forgotten about their wedding anniversary. He apologized and bought her some flowers but a few weeks later they had another fight. Neither one had apologized; and they both went to sleep mad again. Then, without discussing it with him, Annette had registered for the real estate course. When he saw the books on the desk, he accused her of going behind his back and said he couldn't trust her anymore. When she protested he said he didn't care anymore. Now, he said, he didn't care if she worked or not. Derek would be in school next year and would not need her. He even suggested that he could raise the boy if she wanted to work all the time.

She prayed he would change his mind and not come to the roll-out at Trainor Jets, but on Wednesday morning he pretended like nothing had happened and made plans to meet her in the parking lot at the golf course on Lakeview Blvd. It was less than a mile from the gates to the plant. Mansi would leave his car there and pick it up afterwards.

Derek's kindergarten was finished at noon, so Annette had decided to take him to his first unveiling. He was really excited. Planes were his favorite toys and he would point every time he saw one.

"I remember when Trainor rolled out their first jet, and we all came to watch," Marie said. "Your father was so happy. You remember, Nettie?"

"Sure, I remember. It was the first time we got to go inside." Annette had only been seven years old herself at the time, but she would never forget sitting in the pilot's seat. It had been the company's first jet, and although Annette had been too young to understand, it was the first new model released under the revised corporate name change. No longer Trainor Planes, the company name had been officially changed in 1964 to Trainor Jets. The Freedom One was rolled out on July 9, 1965, and the sleek six-passenger twin-engine jet had been an instant success. The business aircraft industry had still been in its infancy, but demand had poured in from around the globe as executives lined up to embrace the benefits and speed afforded by the flexibility of owning their own personal plane.

Her dad had taken a few photos of her in the Freedom One, a cute shot in the pilot's seat gripping the steering controls, and another standing in the aisle in the main cabin. At just over four feet, Annette had run up and down the aisle while her mother and father had to crouch. They had joked about the plane being built for midgets.

"Your father thought the company was going to take off again," Marie said with a smile.

"Very funny." Annette slowed down for the twisty off-ramp. "What's going on with the company financially now?"

"I guess they worked out something. All I know is Jack Alston said they never did get bought out, and apparently things have turned around. He said that they have a lot of orders for their new plane." Marie looked across the airfield. The Trainor sign could be seen high atop a huge building at the far corner of the field.

Annette turned into the parking lot. Sure enough, Mansi's Buick was parked down at the end by the driving range. She pulled up and stopped. "Look, Derek, it's your Daddy."

Derek was glued to the window, watching the small planes that were coming in for landing at the runways across the road, but he immediately bounced over to the other side of the back seat. "Daddy!"

Mansi jumped in. "Hi, Derek. How's my boy? Hi, Nettie. Hi, Marie."

"We're going to see the planes," Derek said. He held up a tiny model airplane Mansi had bought him and swooped it through the air.

"You don't have to do this, Mansi. It's probably not going to be too exciting."

He shrugged. "I would like to see this. An insider's view of the private aircraft industry. I'm sure it will be very interesting."

"We're hardly insiders," Marie said.

The long stream of cars was directed around to the side of the hangar to a roped-off area on the grass at the end of the runway. They parked in the shade behind the hangar and joined the crowd headed for the tarmac, where huge tarps covered a row of planes. Dozens of older-model jets lined the apron. Annette was surprised at how big the new planes were. They seemed much larger than the previous models. A stage in the center was covered with pictures of all the planes the company had made over the years, from the early mail transports to the boxy cargo C-211's they had produced for the army for twenty years. Two huge video displays on the sides of the platform showed a changing array of pictures of prior models landing and taking off, and the words *Freedom Four* flashed across the screens intermittently in anticipation of what was to come.

When the two men walked out onto the stage, the crowd burst into applause and people started chanting, "Trainor, Trainor, Trainor . . ."

"That's Art Trainor on the left, the bald guy," Annette said, pointing him out to Mansi.

"That's the guy you know?" Mansi said. "The big cheese?"

"Yes, I told you, my father taught him how to fly."

Art stepped forward and took the microphone. "Welcome, ladies and gentlemen, honored guests, dedicated employees, trusting investors, and valued suppliers. Thank you so much for joining us today." Art paused as the crowd cheered.

When the applause settled down, he continued, "Today is another big day at Trainor Jets, and another day made possible by the cooperation and hard work of our employees. It was also made possible by the financial support of Pelton Industries and by the resounding success of Fly America. But, as I have always said, it's the future that counts, and that future has never looked brighter for Trainor Jets."

People cheered enthusiastically, but the clamor didn't last long. They wanted to hear what Art had to say.

"Today we are proud to bring you the fantastic new Freedom Four. As you might be able to tell, the Freedom Four is far bigger than its predecessor, and while it is built on the same basic airframe as the Freedom Three, make no mistake. This is a new generation of aircraft."

As customary, ten planes were hidden under the huge tarps, while the company's previous three models were parked in neat rows for the obvious and inevitable comparison. Still dazzling to most, the narrow body fuselage of the Freedom One and the wider Freedom Two jets routinely ferried business executives all over the country, but the prior generation of airframes seemed tiny and outdated in comparison to the huge cabins of the Freedom Three and the Freedom Four.

"It is far bigger and superior to anything we have ever built." Partial pictures of the new interior cabin flashed across the huge video screens behind the stage. "And new composite materials have saved hundreds of pounds off the airframe while increasing payloads by thousands of pounds. The Freedom Four's much larger wingspan and high-performance, fuel-efficient Rolls Royce engines can carry a dozen passengers from Los Angeles to London nonstop, literally putting the world within easy reach of its seven-thousand-mile range."

Annette looked down at Derek. He must have had no idea what Art was saying, yet he seemed totally mesmerized. She thought her dad would have liked the idea of another pilot in the family.

Art went on, "But the Freedom Four is only the first of two models planned for this airframe. NASA, the FAA, and private industry have come together in a project called AGATE, which stands for Advanced General Aviation Experiments. One of their goals is to increase the use of hundreds, maybe thousands of smaller airports around the country. A new program, the Small Air Transportation System, or SATS, will open up significant new demand for air services in the short term, as well as provide the basic infrastructure for the next generation of computerization."

Art took a drink of water and continued, "Digital mapping of the entire commercial airspace will be able to locate any plane, anywhere in the United States to within one meter – at forty thousand feet, or at a gate at O'Hare. We will know where every plane in the sky is . . . exactly. Pilots will never be off course, air to air collisions would be impossible, it could eliminate many kinds of accidents."

The tour afterwards was as popular as ever, and Annette was glad when Art never noticed them in the line and then disappeared. Mansi hadn't quite grasped Marie's story about the personal tour they had taken years ago, and seemed more awestruck by the luxury than anything else. The Freedom Four was much longer inside and seemed even more decadent than the Freedom Three. Twelve captain's chairs, tastefully decorated in gray leather, were spread spaciously around the cabin. Two small tables formed intimate seating areas. One was set with an exquisite dining arrangement for four. Crystal glasses, white linen napkins, sterling silverware, and classic Royal Doulton china offered service fit for a king. A bottle of Dom Perignon in a heavy stainless steel bucket said it all. The other polished mahogany table was all business, and two state-of-the-art Dell laptop computers were open and running. Pictures of the Freedom Four were visible on the bright, colorful LCD screens.

Mansi sat in one of the sumptuous chairs and slid the seat back into a reclining position. "It's hard to believe people can really afford something like this for their personal use," he said.

At home that night, both Mansi and Derek couldn't stop talking about the planes. Derek didn't care about the technologies, but UAV's had been introduced during Operation Desert storm in Iraq in 1990 and the pilotless drones had been in the news frequently. The technology fascinated many aviation buffs.

Art had hushed the crowd with his revelation of Operation Anvil, a now declassified secret bombing technique that had pilots baling out of bomb laden planes that were then flown by other pilots via remote camera into buildings and targets in Nazi Germany.

"Remote control planes in World War II; that was amazing." Mansi had been amused.

Annette was surprised by her husband's enthusiasm for the planes and future of flying, for her the plant was still oddly familiar and she had just enjoyed the delight on Derek's face when she had sat him in the pilot's seat. She had taken a picture much like the one of her father had taken of her thirty years ago.

~~~

Annette had a doctor's appointment a few days later, but she felt tired and didn't feel like going out. It was her annual check-up, but other than the last few days, or some argument with Mansi, she felt absolutely fine and knew she was really fit. She had gotten back into running a few years ago, and her weekly tennis matches had her in better shape than ever. Even Mansi had noticed. The weather hadn't helped her mood today. It was raining. It never rained in Orange County, but it drizzled all day, enough to get damp and cold. Enough to make the roads slippery, which was unusual for Southern California.

"Are you sure?" She said in disbelief. "Pregnant?" *Not now.* Even with the strain in their marriage, she had never returned to the pill, but the news stunned her, they didn't even make love that often anymore.

"Yes, there is no mistake, Mrs. Ansour." Dr. Lee smiled and set down the report. "Maybe eight weeks."

"Shit." That meant a Christmas baby. "Sorry, I didn't mean it that way, but after all this time, I'm surprised."

"Children pick their own time. My six are twelve years apart." He had told her that a few times over the years.

"Yes, well, this will be eight years. When am I due?"

"December twentieth."

~~~

Mansi's work phone rang. It was Annette. "Mansi, something important has happened," she said.

"What is it? You know I am busy." He couldn't help but think ahead a few months when he wouldn't have to worry about her problems anymore. It was the same reaction he had experienced at the end of his marriage to Linda, and while it was obvious to most that they weren't getting along too well lately, no one would have guessed how much he hated her. He was off to Saudi Arabia in two days.

"Mansi! What kind of a hello is that?"

"I'm sorry, Annette, but I am busy." She didn't call him at work often.

"Well, stop being busy for a second and sit down. You'll need to save your energy." Annette paused. "You're going to be a father again."

His breath caught. "Are you pregnant?"

"Unless you have another wife." Her attempt at humor surprised him, but she answered before he could reply. "Yes, that means I'm pregnant."

"We're going to have a baby?" He wondered what Hashim would want to do now. They had given up on more children with Annette a long time ago. "That's good news. Babies are always good news. Do you want to try those tests this time?'

"Which tests?"

"The ones for determining the sex of the baby."

"I hadn't thought about it."

"Let's do it. Then we will know and can start planning."

"Planning what?"

What would they do if it were another boy? Certainly it would complicate the plans they had for Derek.

Annette wasn't sure she wanted to know the sex of their unborn child, but Mansi talked her into it. She said she was just delighted to be pregnant again, and he pretended he was, too. But when the amniocentesis tests indicated it was a girl, he was immensely relieved and started making his final plans for Derek's trip.

~~~

It was late and getting dark when he spotted Samzi, sitting on the sand not more than a few yards from the water. His cousin waved him over. "So, nothing changes," Samzi said. "We proceed as planned."

Mansi sat down and stared out at the ocean. The sun was just disappearing over the horizon in a large fireball. It was a beautiful sight and a good omen. "Yes, we don't need another girl."

"Yes, it is probably better this way." Samzi looked up as a JAL 747 crawled into the sky above them.

"It does provide a perfect reason for Annette not to go," Mansi mused. He had thought of the ruse and was sure it would go better than the first time with Jill. His daughter had started crying for her mommy on the plane to Europe, and he had put half of a sleeping pill in her food. It had caused a few questions at immigration when he couldn't keep her awake. If Derek was excited to see his grandmother, however, he should be easy to travel with. Annette would be almost five months pregnant by the end of June and in no condition to travel halfway around the world.

"You can always come back for the girl later," Samzi said.

He hadn't thought about that and grinned. "Double whammy, they would call it, but why not." That was a great idea.

~~~

Annette sorted through the mail eagerly. She was looking for confirmation of her real estate exam date. One letter, handwritten, was different than the rest. Its stamp and odd postmarks told part of the story. It was from Algeria, from Mansi's brother. His mother had gall bladder cancer and was dying; they thought she had a few months, at best. They wanted him to come home, and his mother's last wish was to see her grandson.

Mansi put down the letter. "I have to go, Annette."

"Do we all have to go?"

"No, but she wants me to bring Derek."

"What does that mean?"

"You can stay and study for your real estate test. I will take Derek."

"Maybe I should go, too?" Annette didn't feel comfortable with the idea, but it made some sense. "It's probably the right thing to do."

"I have to go, but I understand if you don't want to. She was never gracious enough to want to meet you, or to come and visit us. Besides, traveling pregnant could be full of problems."

That had already crossed Annette's mind. "Are you sure?"

"Yes, I think it would be the best overall compromise."

"I do need to study for those tests."

Derek had snuck out of his room and was watching quietly from the hallway.

"It's okay, son," Mansi said. "You can come out."

Derek looked at Annette as if for approval, but walked over to his father.

Mansi picked his son up. "Would you like to go and see your grandmother?"

Derek nodded slowly. "Okay."

Annette remembered what Mansi had told her about Algeria. "Mansi, you never took me there because you said it was too dangerous. Now you want to take our seven-year-old son? Are you sure about this?"

"We will stay away from all the trouble. My brother will pick us up at the airport. I have to go, Annette. She is dying."

"But, Derry?"

"His grandmother wants to see him before she dies."

"Doesn't sound like I have much choice."

~~~

Located in the center of the sprawling airport, on the western side of the busy loop, the Tom Bradley International Terminal at Los Angeles Airport was chaotic as ever. Thousands of passengers and well-wishers crowded the massive building, and most of the airline counters had thick queues. Mansi had taken more baggage than Annette thought was necessary, so they had arrived early to check in and stand in the security line. It had taken over an hour, and at a full three months now, that was a long time for Annette to stand on the hard tile floors. Annette was secretly glad she wasn't making the long trip, even if she was still worried and would miss her son terribly. But seeing him leave was harder than she thought.

At Gate 41B, all the passengers had boarded and the agent had just announced the imminent departure of the flight. The massive black nose of the British Airways 747 filled the large glass windows, and she could see the pilots in their seats making final preparations.

"Annette, we have to go," Mansi said.

"You have fun, Derry, and I'll see you soon. Mommy loves you." She kissed her son as Mansi pulled Derek out of her arms and set him down on the floor.

The ticket agent came over. "Sir, please. You have to board the plane right now."

"You have a good time, Derry," Annette said. "Mommy loves you and is going to miss you." Annette gave her son one last kiss on the cheek and then kissed her husband. "You be careful, Mansi. Come home safe."

"That has always been my intention." Mansi picked up his carry-on, and father and son headed through the door and down the ramp.

Derek turned back and waved. "Bye, Mommy."

"Bye, Derry. I'll see you soon." Annette had never been apart from her son for more than few hours since he was born, and while Mansi had reassured her a dozen times that everything would be all right, something inside her felt cold and empty. These would be the longest two weeks of her life.

~~~

Hashim met Mansi at the Algiers airport and was delighted when he saw the boy. "He is perfect. Well done." Derek was sleepy and didn't say a word. He wore typical American clothes: Jeans, white t-shirt, runners, and a blue jacket. Those would be gone in hours.

"Home at last," Mansi said in Arabic. "And I've brought my prize."

"So I see, so I see," Hashim said. "Hopefully he is as gifted as his sister."

The trip from the airport into the center of Algiers was less than twenty kilometers, but the roads were congested and deteriorated quickly when they got off the highway. Hashim's driver drove like only a local could; weaving in and out the traffic, making sudden turns and ignoring all the speed limits. His familiarity with the narrow, irregular streets ensured that they weren't followed. They parked on a quiet corner in the Casbah. Not considered safe for Westerners, the Old Quarter was not somewhere anyone went uninvited or alone, but when the aging Fiat pulled over and stopped, the few old men who shuffled by never even glanced at the car. Hashim waited until the men were gone.

With the coast clear, he got out and motioned for Mansi and Derek to follow. He knocked at the door of the second building, and a small peephole slid open. The door opened, and they slipped inside.

A young man was waiting. Mansi felt really proud. He had two sons. They were now together, and the oldest one would train the other to be the warrior he could never be.

Tariq laughed when he saw Derek and said in Arabic, "That is my brother? He looks a little soft to be a Nasser, Father."

Tariq had stopped growing a few years ago, but he had made up for size with attitude. At eighteen, he was a key piece of the continuing success of their special school. A student in most ways, he was still one of them, but he had also become the de-facto leader to the other teachers and students. He was a walking embodiment of exactly the kind of blind faith that was required by everyone involved in the training program. There could be no exceptions.

"You are blessed, Father," his eldest son said. "He is truly a beautiful child. He will open many doors."

"Yes, I think you are right," Mansi said. "Let us begin his training right away. His journey will be a long one." Mansi had waited for this moment for almost twenty years. A true warrior.

Tariq dug inside his pocket and pulled out a small camera. "Let me take his picture. I can have his Algerian passport tomorrow. I take it there was no problem bringing the child from America?"

Mansi shrugged. "His mother thinks he is on holiday, visiting his sick grandmother."

They all laughed as Mansi pulled Derek over to one side.

He spoke English to his son. "Stand here and look at that man. He is going to take your picture."

Derek rubbed his eyes. He would never know what was happening. He would never know what plans they had for him. He would never even know that Tariq was his half-brother.

When he dropped his small hands, Tariq snapped a few shots. "That's good. Are we ready to begin?"

"We are going to drop him off right now," Mansi said. "They are waiting for us."

"Wait until you see the girl," said Hashim. "She is doing very well, very well indeed."

Mansi wondered if she was ready. "How is her French?"

"Her French is better than the French. I tell you, the girl is tougher, faster, and more determined to succeed than most of the boys."

They had been traveling for over twenty hours, and as soon as they started driving again, Derek fell asleep. When they stopped ten minutes later, Mansi picked him up and carried him inside. The old man inside pointed to an open door down the dark hallway. Mansi laid his sleeping son down on the dirty mattress and covered him with the one thin blanket. He closed the door quietly, slid the deadbolt shut, and left without a word. Thoughts of what was to come ran through his mind. Ten years of training, ten years of mind control, ten years of discipline. Only then would Derek be ready for the third phase of his life, like Jill was now. The old man led the way, and he followed eagerly. They turned a corner and went up the stairs. At the end of the hall, he knocked on the door.

A voice inside, muffled but distinctly female, was quick to answer. "Who is it?"

"It is your father."

He could hear her rustling inside, and in a moment the door burst open. She had grown since he last saw her, and the baggy fatigues did little to compliment her blossoming teenage figure, but nothing could hide her pleasure. "Daddy!" She wrapped her arms around him.

There had been a time when he didn't think this day would come, but his daughter had surprised everyone. "Hi, Jill, it is wonderful to see you." They sat down together on the bed in her small room. A small reading lamp was the only light, and a Koran was lying open on the tiny table.

"Nobody told me you were coming," she said.

He did not get back to see her regularly, and it had been months since his last visit, but she never said a word anymore. They rarely told her when he was coming, and if they did, often he would not show up, disappointing her, but ensuring she would be grateful when he did visit.

"Your teachers say you are doing well."

She had become the best student in the class and excelled in a number of areas, including math, sciences, and languages.

"And I am studying those tests you gave me."

"Good." They had brainwashed her and played mind games with her since the beginning, but now was the most important part, her commitment. Certainly she was tough, but could she pull the trigger? He told her to pack a few clothes; they would be going away for a few days.

"How long will we be going? Can I ask where we are going?"

"A father and daughter trip, a few days, just the two of us. We'll take our guns, maybe do some shooting."

"I've gotten much better since I saw you last." She beamed.

"I bet you have."

They drove south of the city into the mountains. A few hours out, Mansi slowed down as they approached the small village and turned up the narrow, bumpy road. He stopped as three armed men appeared out of the shadows. They recognized him almost immediately and laughed when they saw the girl, then stepped back and waved the car through. Mansi made a sharp turn down a hill, where lights were visible a few miles away at the bottom of the small valley. Jill had been thoroughly disciplined and didn't ask any more questions about their final destination.

As they rolled down the hill, he told her what the purpose of their trip was. "Everyone does it. You know that. Half of your school has already been here."

"I know, Father, but I'm scared."

"And you should be. If you weren't, you wouldn't be worthy. But the scared student can become the fearless warrior. Being afraid can make one much more careful, and that will be very important later."

"I know, but I don't want to know anything about him. It is a man, isn't it?"

He had made sure it wasn't. "No, Jill, it is not a man."

Jill looked like she wanted to cry, and she bit her lip when she replied. "What is she guilty of?"

"She is an American spy. She has been convicted of espionage." The woman was just a lost and foolish tourist. The endless deserts of Algeria were irresistible and lethal in many ways, and people vanished all the time.

Jill set the trigger selector on her AK-47 for a three-round burst, but she chambered a full clip. When she was done, Mansi walked her down to one of the wood huts with candles flickering inside. It took a few seconds before their eyes adjusted and they could make out the woman, tied to the wall, her mouth covered by tape. They could see the fear seared on the woman's face.

"Would you like me to wait outside?" Mansi tested his daughter every step of the way.

"No, Father, I can do it." Jill pulled the safety off her gun and raised it to her hip.

Mansi knew she couldn't miss at this close range, but that wasn't the point. It didn't take long for a bullet to travel ten feet. When Jill pulled the trigger, the woman's face froze in horror for a second or two, and then her head fell forward and bounced once on her chest. The ropes held her slack body from falling as the blood started to ooze steadily out of the three holes that formed a neat triangle pattern on her chest.

Mansi didn't say a word, but he was not surprised. Jill had become quite a marksman and handled a weapon far better than anyone would have imagined. He might have to go back for that unborn daughter of his someday after all.

Jill stared at the body for a few seconds and then smiled at her father. "It was much easier than I thought."

"Killing is easy, Jill." Mansi looked at the woman's dead body. "Living takes courage; dying takes faith."

"Yes, Daddy."

He waited until they were in the car and on the way back to tell her the news. "Remember when I told you that someday you might move back to the United States? Well, that time is now."

"Really? Back to America?"

"Yes. Back to live with your mother like we planned."

Jill's smile disappeared. "I hope it won't be for too long."

Mansi laughed. "No, a year or so, then college. How are you doing in school?"

"I am studying hard. I will make you proud, you will see. I can speak four languages. I am a brown belt and the best forward on the team."

"That's very good. Write your mother. Tell her that you are coming back, because I have decided you should be educated in the United States."

"I don't know what to say to her. I hardly remember her."

"Just be pleasant, tell her you are looking forward to moving back. She'll be thrilled."

"Are you going to live in California, too?" Jill said.

"Yes, but I doubt your mother will take me back." He laughed and got up to go. "Write your letter to your mother immediately. We will move back in two months."

The two weeks had dragged by for Annette, and she spent most of it studying, but she had missed her son terribly and had counted the days until they returned. She checked the flight number on the calendar one last time. The big red words *UNITED # 1023, 8:15 PM* were circled. As she opened the front door to leave, the phone rang. She hesitated before picking it up. She didn't have the time to get into any long conversations. "Hello?"

"Annette, it's Mansi."

"Mansi? Are you here already?" Had she made a mistake on his arrival time?

"No, but I thought I would let you know that we are all right."

"What's the matter?" Annette could sense something in his voice. "Has something happened to Derry?"

"No, Derek is fine, but . . . we're not coming back. I've decided to stay here."

She froze. "Stay there? For how long?"

"Forever," he said coldly. "I have decided I don't want to live in the United States anymore. I want to raise Derek in Algeria."

"Are you crazy?" she blurted. Her heart began to race. "You can't do that. He's my son, too. What about us?" Tears started to slide down Annette's cheeks, and she felt like she was choking.

"I am getting a divorce. My mind is made up."

Annette couldn't believe it. This couldn't be happening. "He's my son, too. You can't just take him away from me. I'm his mother! Divorce? This is crazy!"

"I do not want my son brought up in America. His family is here."

"His family is there? We are your family. What about me?" She heard herself start to scream.

"Our differences are greater than I thought. I do not love you anymore. I don't care about the baby."

She took a deep breath, struggling to calm herself. "Mansi, you can't take Derry from me. I'll take you to court." He couldn't take her son away that easily, could he?

Mansi laughed. "American courts . . . Sue me, I don't care. They have no jurisdiction in Algeria."

"I'll go to the U.S. Embassy. Derry is an American citizen; they'll force you to give him back." She would have the law all over him.

"He now has dual citizenship, and he has decided he wants to stay in Algeria. Forget you ever had a son."

The line went dead, and she screamed at it, "You bastard. You can't do this! Mansi, Mansi, Mansi!" The phone slipped from her hand, and she exploded into tears.

Chapter 6

It took Annette a few minutes to stop crying and settle herself down. What should she do first? What could she do? Her mother was the only one she had to call, but she hesitated before dialing. What would her mother say about Mansi now? She could feel a vein throbbing in her neck, and she realized her heart was racing. Realizing that she might pass out, she went into the living room and sat down. Her hands trembled as she raised the phone to her ear and dialed.

"Hello."

"Mom, something terrible has happened. Mansi just called me from Algeria. He said he's never coming back, and he's keeping Derek." She started sobbing again.

"Never coming back? Why would he do that? What happened?"

"He said he doesn't love me anymore. He said he didn't want Derek to be raised in the United States. Mom, what can I do? I can't lose my son!"

"What? He can't do that. He's your son, too." Her mother's tone was full of fury.

"He said I should forget I ever had a son." She choked on the word *forget*.

"Annette, stop crying. I can hardly understand you."

She tried again. "Mansi said he is staying in Algeria and keeping Derek. He said they are never coming back."

"But . . . Derek is an American citizen. Mansi can't just take him. That's kidnapping." Marie sounded confident.

"That's what I said. He said Derry now has dual citizenship." She had heard the term before, but wasn't sure how it would affect her. "What does that mean?"

"I don't know. I think you need to call the police, or maybe the U.S. Embassy."

"Yes, I'll call somebody. Please come over. I need you."

"I'll be there as quick as I can."

Annette didn't know who to call next, so she just dialed 911. It was answered on the first ring. "Hello, this is Corporal Jensen of the Costa Mesa Police Department." The voice was male, young, and official. "What is the nature of your emergency?"

"My son has been kidnapped."

"When and where did this happen, ma'am?"

"I just learned about it a few minutes ago. His father took him on vacation to Algeria two weeks ago – that's where he's from. Now he says he's not coming back; that he's going to keep our son there." She started crying again. "I don't know . . ."

The officer cut her off. "Ma'am; that is not the type of emergency I can help you with. This sounds like a case of child abduction. You need to call our regular business number. Let me give that to you."

"I'm sorry. Just a moment, let me get a pen." She wrote the number on the back of the phone book, thanked the officer, and hung up. Tears flooded down her face as she dialed again. She pictured the Costa Mesa Police Station on Fair Drive across from the parking lot of the Orange County Fair Grounds. She had just been there to get fingerprints for her real estate license application. Would the local police really be able to help her in Africa? She wondered if she should call the Orange County sheriff.

The on-duty female officer at the station was very gracious and filled out a lengthy missing persons report, but advised her that she needed to contact the State Department, as it was an international affair. An official complaint was good, and the police would broadcast Mansi's and Derek's names and descriptions out to dozens of cooperating law enforcement agencies around the world. The officer wouldn't promise too much more than that, but suggested a police investigator might call her back later and asked if she could bring a picture into the station. Annette managed to thank her and hung up. On one hand, she realized they couldn't just rush off to Algeria, but on the other, she had hoped someone could do something right now.

She broke down the moment her mother and sister walked in and could hardly talk without sobbing. Eventually, she managed to stammer out what she knew.

"But why would Mansi do this?" Marie questioned again.

Annette shook her head helplessly. "I don't know. All he said was that he didn't love me anymore and he wanted Derek to be raised in Algeria. That was it."

"Was there any sign he was thinking of leaving you before this?"

"Signs, no, but the letter from his brother was very unusual. I don't think he had ever received a letter from Algeria before. Maybe that was part of the plan to give him reason to take Derry."

"That bastard."

It was almost 3:00 a.m. when her mother made her go lie down. Getting her son back was going to be very difficult; another call to the Orange County sheriff's office had made that very clear. They referred her to some of the same agencies she had been given by the police. She tossed and turned and cried so much her stomach hurt.

The pain of losing her father and Paul came flooding back, and she wondered how her mother had ever coped. Losing her son would be the ultimate loss. She just couldn't let it happen. Ten years ago, it had seemed like her world had been stolen from her, but losing her son felt far worse already. She prayed to a God she didn't even think she believed in anymore. She prayed that she could fall asleep and that this was a nightmare, and when she woke up everything would be all right. She slept poorly, not for long, and she thought of her baby. The stress on her certainly wouldn't be good for her baby.

At 6:00 a.m., she called the American Center for Missing Children in Washington, D.C. They were very knowledgeable and answered most of her questions, but the answers weren't very encouraging. She was shocked to learn that there were thousands of similar kidnappings every year. The worst part was that Algeria was not a participant to the Hague Convention on the Civil Aspects of International Child Abduction, and that meant that no formal relationship existed to resolve cases like hers. The counselor suggested she try an attorney who specialized in such work.

She hung up and sobbed hopelessly for a few minutes. Marie tried to soothe her, and between sobs she managed to stammer out the helpless situation that had been explained by the woman in Washington. "Mom, she was really nice, but I could hear the resignation in her voice when I told her it was Algeria. She said it was going to be really tough and told me I would need an international attorney."

"Can't they help at all?"

"Not really. If Derry was in the United States, yes, but not in Algeria. She said that the government will officially request his return, but she didn't sound very optimistic."

"Where do you find an international attorney?" Marie asked.

"She gave me the name of two attorneys in Los Angeles and the name of a contact at the State Department." Annette checked the clock; it was far too early to call anyone on the West Coast.

"I'm sure one of the attorneys at my office will know someone," Val said. "I'll call as soon as the office opens."

"If you need any help with money," said her mother, "I can help. Lawyers can be very expensive."

She hadn't even thought about money. "Thanks. I have about fifteen thousand dollars saved. I guess I'll have to go back to work sooner than I thought."

"It's not any of my business, dear . . ." Marie hesitated. "But did Mansi have a separate bank account?"

"Yes, we both did. But he also put money in a joint account, enough to pay the bills. There's not much there, though. Why?"

"What about the house? Is it in both your names?"

"Yes."

"You need to get any money that is in that joint account out right away. What about his car?"

"I'm assuming you are going to get a divorce, too," Val said, "and get the house into your name. This probably qualifies as abandonment."

Her head hurt. Just before 9:00, she reached someone at the State Department. When she started crying on the phone and couldn't talk, her mother took over and made an appointment for later that morning. Marie also phoned in and took the day off to drive her up to Los Angeles.

"I look awful," Annette said as she stared at herself in the small mirror. "Maybe that's good. Maybe they'll feel sorry for me."

Her mother hadn't slept much more than she had. "I have a lot more sleeping pills," she said.

"I shouldn't take them. I'm pregnant."

"You'll need to get some sleep somehow."

The office was stuffy and formal, but it didn't take long before they were called in for their appointment, and it didn't take long before Annette started crying again.

The special agent, Diane Elter, was probably in her late forties. Gray hair was visible in her medium-brown curls, and her black suit would have been stiff were it not for her soft green eyes that seemed to match her silky blouse and handsome shoes.

She was sympathetic but frank. "This is not going to be easy, Mrs. Ansour. The Hague Convention is the only international law on child abduction, and Algeria is not a member country. We will, of course, officially demand that the Algerian government return the child, but that's all we can do officially."

"But my son is an American citizen, and he has been kidnapped!" Annette pleaded. "That must be against the law."

"By American law, yes. But by Islamic law, at age seven, a boy becomes the responsibility of the father. In Algeria, that makes your husband the legal custodian there."

"But how can they do that without talking to me? I'm the boy's mother!"

"Women have very little voice in Algeria. The husband can divorce the wife for no reason and take the children. Why do you think your husband did this? Were you not getting along?"

"I told you what he said his reasons were. Our relationship had lost a lot of its fire, but there were no indications of anything like this."

Mrs. Elter wasn't very optimistic, and it showed in her weak smile and her official reply. "I will file a complaint with the Algerian embassy in Washington, request that your husband return the child, and we will contact his employer, UniOil. But that's all we can do."

"How long will that take?"

"We'll contact them immediately. Their response I cannot guarantee. Corporations usually respond quickly, especially foreign companies like UniOil, because they want to stay in good favor with us. As far as the government; as I said, Algeria is most uncooperative. Sometimes we don't hear anything for months."

"You're not very encouraging," Marie said. "I expected more from my government." She was just as disappointed as Annette.

"I'm trying to be straight with you, Mrs. Madison. Our success in these countries has been very poor, and I don't want to give you any false hope."

"Is there anything you can suggest I should do?"

"We will try all official channels, but yes, you should consult an international attorney who has experience in Algeria. Private investigators have found a few children, and there are a few support groups that might be able to help you."

Annette thought Diane Elter sounded like everyone else. "What if I go to Algeria myself?"

"I would strongly advise against that. The country is considered very unsafe for Americans." Diane pulled out a copy of the U.S. Department of State travel advisories. "Here. You can read about it in here."

When she got home, Annette called an attorney Val's firm had referred her to. He sounded supportive, and she felt a sense of urgency in his voice. He made time for her the next day. Marie made her some food, but she didn't feel hungry and didn't eat more than a few bites. She kept telling herself to stay positive, that at least Derry was okay. He was not dead, and she had hope. Someday she would see her son again. Someday soon.

Her mother gave her a sleeping pill, but she wouldn't take it. She lay still, trying to will herself to sleep, and she did, but not for more than a few minutes at a time. Her dreams were ragged and confusing, and when she woke up at four o'clock, she went to Derek's room to look for him, hoping against all reason that he somehow would be there sleeping quietly. The house was silent, but the full moon was in the western sky and lit up Derek's room in an eerie gray. His bed was undisturbed. She bent down and fondled the empty spot where he would normally curl up and picked up his pillow. She could smell the shampoo she used on his hair. As she lay down and hugged his pillow, the tears started to roll down her cheek. When would this nightmare end?

Bratton, Dickens, and Silverberg were on the twenty-first floor of the steel downtown high-rise. The high-speed elevator opened directly into the waiting area of the law offices. Annette had been to Val's office a few times, but it was nothing like this. Contemporary yet elegant, the polished granite floors opened onto an impressive waiting room and a view west all the way to the ocean. A dozen or so brown leather chairs were set casually in front of the floor-to-ceiling windows, where a few other clients were quietly waiting.

The attractive young woman at the reception desk smiled brightly. "Hi, may I help you?"

"Yes, my name is Ansour." Annette knew she must look a wreck. She couldn't have slept for more than a few hours in the last two days. "I have an appointment with Richard Bratton."

"Yes, he is expecting you. Please have a seat. I'll tell him you're here."

In a few minutes, a woman came out. "Hi, I'm Brenda, Mr. Bratton's assistant. Please come this way." Brenda was a pretty woman with a dark complexion that suggested a mixed heritage. She appeared to be in her late fifties. She led the way down the hall to an open door. Standing to one side, she motioned for Annette and Marie to enter.

Inside, Richard stood up and came around his desk to greet them. He was older than she had expected, but his cheerful smile and firm handshake seemed sincere and confident. Tall and lanky, he was impeccable in a dark blue suit and deep red silk tie, and looked every bit the successful attorney she hoped he was.

"Mrs. Ansour, it is nice to meet you."

"It's nice to meet you, too. Thanks for seeing us on such short notice. This is my mother, Marie Madison."

"Nice to meet you, Mrs. Madison." Richard indicated the four wingback chairs set off to one side. "Please, sit down."

"Thank you." Annette sat down quickly. She almost felt she owed him an apology. "I must have sounded hysterical on the phone."

Richard smiled. "Not at all. Frightened and worried, yes, but it's only to be expected."

"How do we get started?"

"We already have."

That sounds positive for a change.

Richard stood up and retrieved a letter from his desk. He handed it to Annette. "I have written an attorney in Algiers, one who specializes in these things."

"How long will it take to get an answer?" She scrolled through the wordy request.

"We should hear back within a month if they're willing to take the case."

"A month?" She heard the panic rise in her voice.

"Things move a lot slower in Algeria, but don't worry," he assured her. "I will follow up with a call in a week."

"You said 'if' they were willing to take the case. I thought I was hiring you."

"You are, but we will need to work with someone over there. There is no way we can do anything without them. We would get stonewalled at every turn. It's not a country where we can easily send in private investigators. Better to work with the locals. They'll have a much better chance of finding your son."

Annette remembered what her mother had said about expensive lawyers. "Do I have to pay them, too?"

"We will pay them, with your approval, from funds you give us. But yes, they have to be paid. There is no other way."

Annette turned to look at her mother.

Marie shrugged her shoulders. "I told you I would help you."

"Is money going to be a problem?" Richard asked.

Annette shook her head. "No, not in the amounts we talked about on the phone."

"Good. Are you ready to move forward? Time is always a major factor in tracking someone, and so far the trail is only a few days old."

Annette opened her purse. "Yes, I have no choice. As fast as you can. How much money do you need now?"

"Five thousand dollars." Richard caught Annette's gaze and appraised her one more time. "It could go up from there."

"He's my son. Money is only money. I'll sell my house if I have to." She would spend everything she had to get Derek back. It had occurred to the women that Mansi might have been up to other sinister activities, as well. "Can you check on the house, too?"

"Check what?"

Annette wasn't sure. "I don't know. That he hasn't sold it or mortgaged it?"

"Who is on the title to your home?"

"My husband and I. Can I get him taken off the title?"

"Not easily, and it will take time," Richard said.

"Can you help me with that?"

"I can't personally, but a few of our attorneys specialize in real estate and divorce if necessary. I'll have Brenda make an appointment for you with Donna Appleton. I think you'll like her, and she has a lot of experience." He paused. "Is there anything else that I need to know?"

Annette sighed wearily. "I'm pregnant with Mansi's baby."

~~~

It was ninety degrees in the windless July afternoon and a great day for flying. High layers of thin cirrus clouds took a little of the sting out of the midsummer heat, but the tarmac was ten degrees warmer and sticky, so Art had the new Freedom Four executive business jet prepared and waiting inside the air-conditioned hangar.

Delivery of a new plane to its owners was a joyous affair, and Art was always delighted to meet with clients, but Senator Norman Kingston was much more than a very special customer.

Art gave the interior one last appraisal, but it was perfect. With dark polished wood and rich Italian leathers, it was tastefully done and luxurious in every detail. Smoked acrylic glass partitions midway down the fifty-five-foot cabin separated the front section with its groupings of seats from the back, where an off-white circular couch with throw pillows faced the rear of the plane. Two more tan leather captain's chairs in the rear completed a casual living room effect.

The sound of heavy car doors and footsteps announced Norman's arrival. Satisfied that everything was in order, Art stuck his head out the door. Two security men ran up the stairs to the jet while two others formed a small perimeter around the Lincoln parked at the bottom of the steps.

"Mr. Trainor? I'm Don Bingham. Is everything ready to go?" The man's grip was firm but brief. The other man didn't even glance at Art as he entered the cabin and started an inspection.

"Yes, sir." Art said. "The crew got here a little while ago." He had joked with the two easygoing pilots, one man and one woman. Both had over twenty years at United Airlines.

"Good. Give us a few minutes, would you?"

Art had seen many of the new security measures before, but Don and his partner had some sleek new hardware, and they were obviously well-trained professionals. Using two different types of meters, they swept the sumptuous interior in a precise manner – every piece of furniture, all the hidden pockets and storage spots, every door and cupboard. It didn't take long before they had cleared the plane and nodded their approval. Don stuck his head in the cockpit and checked with the flight crew. "Everything good up here?"

"We're good to go here," said the female pilot as she leaned back and smiled. "Everything looks fine. She's a beauty."

"Great," said Don. "I'll get the Senator." He waved at the men guarding the Lincoln Town Car. One opened the rear door, and two men got out.

Art had seen Norman at the Freedom Four's introduction ceremony earlier in the year, but he hadn't seen the other man for years. He hustled down the stairs to greet them. "Senator Kingston. It's great to see you."

"It's great to see you, too, Art, and please, it's always Norman to you." Norman's handshake was as strong and confident as ever. Two years into his first term, he brimmed with enthusiasm as he introduced his companion. "Art, I believe you know Colonel, Les is catching a ride back to Washington with me."

"Nice to see you again, Mr. Trainor."

"Colonel Wilby, it's been a long time. Nice to see you, too, and congratulations on the promotions. Please, call me Art."

Norman pointed up the stairs. "Do you have a few minutes? There's something we would like to talk to you about."

"Of course. After you." Art followed them up and into the plane. He was surprised when Don Bingham ordered the pilots to do another inspection of the exterior, but as the cabin door closed behind them, it quickly made sense.

"My men just swept the plane," Norman said. "No one is listening, are they?"

"No, not on our end. Your plane does have the technology to monitor on-board conversations, but the equipment is currently turned off."

"Good, because for now, this is just between us, okay?" Norman's tone demanded a firm understanding.

Art nodded. "Yes, sir." He hoped he hadn't done anything to offend his friend. "Is everything okay?"

Norman laughed. "Just fine, Art. Les is now in charge of some of those special projects at the Pentagon. I thought you two might have something to talk about."

Art thought that sounded like good news for Trainor Jets.

"As you probably know," Wilby said, "UAVs were a huge part of our success in operation Desert Storm and Desert Shield. The success of the Predator in Iraq, Bosnia, and Afghanistan has changed a lot of minds. I think your concept of pilotless planes of all types has a lot of merit. What the Air Force thinks is up to them, but they are much more open-minded these days."

"So you really think we won't need pilots someday?" Norman said.

"Yes, sir," Art wanted to kiss his friend for his continued support. "Computers could fly the planes today, but significant assets and infrastructure on the ground will need to be designed and installed before anything commercial can happen."

"That will be quite a task, to equip five thousand airports," Wilby said. "But it's impressive thinking, it really is, and I do think the military should seriously consider funding a joint research project with Trainor Jets. If, as you say, one of the main barriers to pilotless, computer-flown, civilian commercial aviation is new air traffic control systems, that barrier doesn't exist for the military and combat applications."

"No, sir." Art had suggested it in a dozen interviews. "The military could have remote-control centers hundreds or even thousands of miles away. Just like your other UAVs do now."

"Yes. It's a very attractive option. God knows saving all those pilots alone would make it all worthwhile." Wilby was pleased.

Norman smiled and added, "Probably get us a few votes, too."

"Yes, sir," Wilby agreed. "And rightfully so."

They talked for a few more minutes about training pilots who would never be killed and the millions of dollars that would save the American taxpayers, before Don Bingham knocked at the cabin door and suggested it was time to depart. Art couldn't have been more delighted when they exchanged business cards and the colonel promised to have Trainor Jets come to the Pentagon one day soon, so they could discuss their needs on an official basis.

~~~

"That meeting is tomorrow." Annette had mixed feelings about going to the women's support group, but everyone, from her lawyer to her mother, insisted she should attend. "I guess I'd better see what they're all about."

"I'll go with you."

"Thanks, Mom, but you can't go everywhere with me."

She took Harbor Avenue to the San Diego Freeway and turned north, glad she wasn't going south for a change. The off-ramp for South Coast Plaza was backed up for a mile. *Could be a big sale*, she thought, but the massive shopping center, the largest and most successful mall in the country, pulled in thousands of visitors, tourists, and shoppers every day. At close to three million square feet, the seemingly endless selection of stores had been a key benefactor and contributor to the incessant growth that had fed Orange County for the last four decades.

The traffic was reasonably thin for a Tuesday evening, although with a half-dozen lanes in both directions, it was really only quiet on Christmas Day mornings. The 405 north-to-south freeway carried thousands of residents, commuters, and tourists, infinitely and randomly mixed with some of the heaviest truck traffic in the world as business of every kind shipped in and out of the busy Southern California ports. The highway ran from the Canadian border to San Diego, and Tijuana, Mexico, was built at the gates to the bottom of the state and less than a hundred miles from downtown Los Angeles. Close to twenty million humans inhabited the lower few hundred miles of coastline in the southwest corner of the huge state, and it seemed like everyone owned a car. Tijuana had become a local economic powerhouse and a model for Mexico itself, but its recent success was only increasing the enormous burden on the overflowing freeway systems of its American neighbor.

Annette would reminisce with her mother about when the 405 freeway had been built in the mid-sixties, when bulldozers had cut a swath through the east side of Costa Mesa, buying up houses and knocking them down to make room for the massive highway. When she had learned to drive ten years later, part of the test had included a few miles on the freeway, and she could still remember how little traffic there had been back then. As she passed the off-ramp to the 605, she was glad she didn't have to take it. She could get to L.A. that way, too, but she hated that road. The freeway was one of the worst, day or night, seven days a week, and the constant and heavy tractor-trailer traffic on the busy Long Beach Harbor Freeway was very intimidating in a small car.

The monthly meeting of the Southern California chapter of the American Center for Missing Children was in a large conference room at the back of the Hilton hotel in downtown Los Angeles. She was glad for the underground parking lot; the core of the city was not the nicest place, especially in the evening as the local residents drifted out into the streets. When she got to the meeting room, she was impressed. She hadn't been quite sure what to expect, but had definitely anticipated something smaller. Hundreds of women were waiting for the meeting to get underway.

Nancy Dario was the chapter president and introduced herself at the door. She was younger and shorter than Annette had pictured from her voice, and more fashionable. She was extremely friendly and her severe gray business suit didn't match the fire in her dark eyes. Annette figured she was Italian, just like her beautiful black pumps.

Nancy seemed to know everyone by name. She pointed out a few other mothers who had children in Algeria and suggested Annette talk to them. "I'm glad you came to us, Annette. I hope we can help you."

"You have been so kind already," Annette replied. "Thank you for taking so much time on the phone yesterday." They had talked for half an hour. Annette had broken down twice telling her story.

"We want to do anything we can to help you. How are you doing? Are you sleeping?"

She hadn't slept more than a few hours at a time and was grateful for her mother's supply of sleeping pills. She was using only half a pill at a time, but it had helped a little the last few days.

"It's been the longest week of my life," she said. It felt like a month. "And it seems so hopeless already."

"Now, don't say that. I told you, one mother from Algeria is getting her daughter back in a few weeks. Your case is still so new, maybe the police will find something." Nancy put her arm around Annette. She had been mothering lost parents for years. "Do you have someone to talk to?"

Annette nodded. "Yes, my mother, and my sister a bit."

"No, I mean professionally?"

"No." *A shrink?*

Nancy pulled a business card out of her wallet. "Here, let me give you a referral. We have professional grief counselors on staff with a lot of experience with parents who have gone through what you now face. They could be a big help. Would you call them?"

Annette nodded slowly as she read name on the card: *Anita Sanchez*. "Thank you for your concern," she said. Annette had never discussed her problems with anyone other than her mother. "Do you really think it will help?"

"Yes, and whether you know it or not, you are in a state of shock right now. Please just talk things through with her. You'll see. She will be a lot of help."

"Okay. It can't hurt." It would surely be painful to dump all her guilt on someone she hardly knew, but her mother and Val hated Mansi so completely now, and the guilt was spinning her life in a painful spiral she would have never thought possible. "Where is her office?"

"Call her, and you can talk on the phone or arrange to meet. It's up to you. I think you will like her. She's really nice. About your age, too."

Annette slipped the card into her purse. "Is she expensive?"

"She's free. She's a professional psychologist who donates her time. Most of the women here donate their time."

Annette was more impressed by the minute. She sighed. "I'm so glad I came tonight. Driving up, I wasn't sure if this was the right place for me. But you seem so well organized. Have you managed to get quite a few children back?"

"Yes, dozens over the years, and we've managed to establish contact in hundreds more. Look, here comes Linda Smythe right now. She's the woman getting her daughter back from Algeria." Nancy turned to the attractive blonde who walked up. "Linda, it's so good to see you. Let me introduce Annette Ansour."

Linda was about the same age as Annette. "Hi, Annette. It's nice to meet you."

"I understand that you're getting your child back soon. That is great news. I'm so happy for you." She felt a little encouraged already – a child abducted to the same country years ago.

Linda lit up like a candle. "Thank you. I had almost given up, but then a few weeks ago I got a letter from my daughter. She said her father decided she should be educated in the United States, and he's allowing her to move back."

"That's wonderful," Annette said. "How long has your daughter been gone?"

Linda looked pleased. "Ten years."

"Oh, God!"

Chapter 7

"How is Derek doing?" Mansi asked.

Mansi stood a few feet back of the railing. He didn't want his son to see him yet. Derek was seated on the dirt floor in the middle of a class of about twenty boys ranged from seven to seventeen. They were all dressed in loose khaki combat fatigues and leaned forward to listen to Tariq, who stood at the front, reading from the Koran.

"He cried for the first few days, but some discipline has stopped all that," Hashim whispered.

"He looks thin. Has he being eating?" Mansi prayed to Allah everyday that nothing would derail his son's progress now that he was finally here.

"Not at first, but once again, a little persuasion has made all the difference. He cleans his bowl now."

"Can he understand anything in Arabic yet?"

"Not much." Hashim pointed at Tariq, who had come around and stopped behind Derek. "Listen."

The two men stepped into the shadows at the end of the balcony where they were closer and could hear better. The students knew they were sometimes observed from the dark covered porch, but they were forbidden to look. Even if they did, the third-story room was impossible to see into.

Tariq was speaking in Arabic. "Derek has much to learn. You are his friends, his family, his teachers. Teach him language, teach him strength. He may look like a girl . . ." The students snickered but stopped quickly at Tariq's sharp look.

"His name is from the name Theodoric. It means strength. In ancient times, it meant ruler of the people, one capable of huge feats. Someday, Allah willing, Derek will bring a great victory for the jihad."

Tariq switched to English. His accent was clipped, almost British as he addressed Derek. "English is one of four languages you need to know here. All these students will help you learn the others. Remember, your goals here are the same, but your happiness here depends on your cooperation. Do you understand?"

Derek's eyes welled up, and he burst into tears. When the kids started laughing, it only made him cry harder. But when his older brother swatted him with the back of his hand, he stopped almost immediately.

"I don't think Derek is as strong as Jill was, but he will learn," Hashim said. "Are you ready to return to America?"

Hashim's words stung, and for once Mansi hoped his cousin was wrong. "Yes. Once again, I am a new man."

"Mansi Yaccine. I like the sound of it. Very continental."

"Thirty-eight is not too old for Allah." Mansi thought about finding another American wife. Hashim had made him an offer he couldn't refuse: one million U.S. dollars, half paid before he left, and the other half paid with compounded interest when he returned. He would be a very rich man.

"Do not worry about expenses. We have lots of money. Buy her heart if you have to." Hashim snickered. "Get me one more generation of soldier. The others have not done so well, and many children have been lost."

~~~

Annette left early Wednesday morning for her appointment with Donna Appleton. She had some papers to sign to start the abandonment process, and she was surprised when she was led into Richard's office instead of Donna's. He was on the phone and motioned for her to sit down in one of the chairs in front of his desk.

"Thank you. Can you send them over? Yes, right now." He hung up and smiled. "Hi, Annette. This is good timing. Some photos are coming across on the fax machine right now."

"Photos of what?"

Richard was excited. "Your husband. I think we found your husband. Brenda will bring the pictures in as soon as they come in.

Our man on the other side seems quite sure that they have found Mansi."

She didn't care about Mansi anymore. "Did they find Derek?"

"I don't think so. Just your husband."

There was a knock, and Brenda entered. She hurried over to Richard's desk and handed him the photos. He looked at them quickly, then set the two pictures down on his desk so Annette could see.

"Yes, that's him!" She was elated. "Where were these taken?" The pictures were a little blurry, but it was definitely Mansi. She felt hopeful for the first time in days.

"In Algiers, outside a café."

Annette stared at the photos. There were three other men in the pictures, as well, but no sign of her son. "Can we follow him to find Derek?"

"They have tried to follow him, but he always shakes the tail. One night, a truck cut our man off and almost forced him off a bridge. Our investigator was sure it was intentional."

"Can we have him arrested?"

"We can try, but your prospects are very poor. The courts there will most likely favor the father. Honestly, Annette, even if we find Derek, I don't know what you can do about it."

"Maybe if I go there and talk to Mansi face to face, I can convince him to at least let me see Derek."

Richard frowned. "You know I can't advise you to go over there. It's much too dangerous. Besides, you're pregnant. Let us handle it. If we follow him long enough, eventually he will lead us to the child. Then maybe we can arrange something."

"Eventually? I can't afford to hire you forever. I'm only five months along and can still travel. I can do this if I go now." She was just starting to feel the baby inside her, but Derek had not been a problem pregnancy, and she was sure she could make the trip if they left soon.

"Annette, Algeria is not like going to Mexico or London. Algeria has an entirely different culture, a culture not friendly for women. And the hospitals are not like ours. You can't go over there; it just wouldn't be safe."

Annette listened patiently while Richard went on about doing things slowly, but her mind was already made up. "This firm that you've hired over there, can't they provide some security?"

"Yes, but what will going there accomplish at this point? If our investigators find Derek, then maybe you can go and try to reason with your husband."

"You have already told me how limited my options are. Well, my time is limited, too." It was now or never. "I figure if I'm there and can talk face to face with Mansi, maybe he'll at least let me see Derek or allow me to stay in touch somehow."

"You know that is not very likely." Richard stood up, came around, and sat on the front edge of his desk.

It was the only chance she had. "Not likely, but not impossible," she countered. "I have to go and try. It's been over a month now. I feel like if I don't try, I'll never see my son again."

"If it was some other country, I would say okay, but not there. The State Department has had a travel warning there for years. It is considered very dangerous. Westerners get killed all the time."

"You said we could hire someone to protect us," Annette said. She wondered if Richard was just being a little too cautious. Algeria was not even in the Middle East; it was in Africa. Maybe Mansi had purposely overstated the danger. Maybe he had never wanted her to go for other reasons.

"Yes, but that still won't guarantee your safety," Richard said. "They use bombs, guns, they don't care. You would be in serious danger."

"I have to try." She realized she had to. It just couldn't be that bad. "Wouldn't you if it was your son?"

"I have a son and daughter, and that very thought has occurred to me many times over the years while I have tried to help other parents, but I still can't advise you to go. Think it over. Having you in trouble over there, too, sure wouldn't help you get Derek back."

"I know, but I'll be really careful. I won't go wandering around by myself. I'll only go with the security. But I have to try."

Annette talked it through for a few days with her mother and sister, and while they were all worried about the danger, they were outraged at Mansi's betrayal and felt compelled to do something. Annette felt extremely guilty. In hindsight, it now seemed as if the signs had been there, and she cursed herself for letting Mansi and Derek go alone.

Marie volunteered to go with her. The trip was set up quickly; they would go in a week. Everyone hoped Mansi would still be there when they arrived. The night before they left, her mother came over for a last-minute change. Annette had already dyed her own hair dark brown.

"Over here, Mom," Annette said, patting the chair by the sink.

Her mother pulled the cape tight around her neck and stared at her long, thick blonde hair in the mirror. "I can't believe I'm doing this."

"Why? What's the big deal? You've been hiding that gray for years. We can dye it back when we get home."

"Yes, but I've always been a blonde."

"And you can be one again, but the less we stand out, the better." Annette started at top and brushed in the brown dye. "I packed dark colors and a few shawls. After we get there and see what the women are wearing, we can find a few things to help us fit in."

~~~

The Air France 737 banked left over the rich blue Mediterranean Sea as it began its long, gradual descent to the Algiers airport. With just over an hour on the ground in New York, their connection on American Airlines through JFK had gone quickly, but the three-hour layover in Paris had seemed like six. They had arrived at Charles De Gaulle Airport at 7:00 in the morning, after eleven hours of flying and a nine-hour time change that turned their over-tired body clocks upside down.

Neither Annette nor her mother had slept more than a few hours on the overnight flight. After stumbling their way through customs and immigration, they were left to navigate the maze of the French airport on their own. Annette had to ask directions three times before they found their way to terminal 2B and gate 24. When she had come to Paris with Mansi, he had handled everything, from their flights to their meals, and she hadn't paid much attention. On her own now, she felt poorly prepared. She hoped their contact in Algiers spoke good English.

The Algiers flight was short, less than two hours, and Annette felt her anger boil when she realized that her husband had lied about that, too. Apparently, it was far easier to get there from Europe than Mansi had told her. He had said it was hard to get flights, but their plane was half-empty, and booking had not been any problem.

She could see the city of Algiers in the distance. It looked bigger than she had thought it would as it stretched out across the mouth of an enormous, perfectly carved half-moon bay. The mountains in the southern sky surprised her. She had expected desert, but lush green farmlands dotted the landscape. As they turned and lined up for landing, they were suddenly right over top of the city. She loved the history of London and Paris, but no matter how beautiful and old Algiers was, Richard's warnings and her own fears cast a darkening shadow over the sun-drenched North African city.

The terminal was small and had seen better times. Signs in Arabic and French meant nothing, so they just followed the stream of passengers downstairs to the immigration lines. The queue moved slowly, and she heard someone say three international flights had arrived at almost the same time. The continuous slow-motion shuffle of the seemingly infinite lines took another forty-five minutes, but soon they were being questioned by an immigration officer who looked at the two women suspiciously and did not seem to believe their story about a vacation. He called a superior, but after their travel visas and passports had been checked and rechecked by a few different men, they were suddenly free to go.

Outside the customs office, near the entrance to the arrivals hall, a small mustached man held up a placard with the name *ANSOUR* printed clearly in big black letters. Annette caught the man's attention.

As he headed in her direction, a much larger man fell in behind him. He looked more European to her than anything. A dark sports jacket covered a black turtleneck and black pants. Although he was young and reasonably good-looking, the long, thin scar on the side of his neck gave him a sinister look. Annette hoped he was on their side.

"I am expecting Mrs. Annette Ansour," said the smaller man, surprising her with his good English.

"Yes, I am Annette Ansour." Annette offered her hand. "This is my mother, Marie Madison."

"I am Muti Hayan. It is my pleasure to meet you." He shook their hands and pointed to the other man, who had stopped a few steps behind him. "This man is my security guard. Please come with me. I have a car waiting."

Without offering to help with their bags, the men turned to go. Things were obviously different here. Annette and Marie followed the men outside to the curb, where an older, dusty black Mercedes was waiting. Its engine was running, and the driver looked back impatiently when they walked up. The bodyguard opened the trunk and then stood off to the side. Annette threw their bags in the trunk and followed her mother into the back seat. Muti climbed in last and closed the door. The bodyguard sat up front. Even with the windows open, it was hot.

After they pulled away, Muti got right to the point. "Thank you for coming so quickly. We checked on Wednesday, and your husband was at the café again, so it appears we may be lucky and catch him."

"When will that be?"

"Tomorrow, if you want."

"Why not today?" Annette looked at her mother. They were exhausted from the long journey and had been traveling for almost twenty hours. The drive from the airport wound its way west along the beach. It reminded her of Mexico. Things looked either half-finished or very rundown. It looked like a poor country.

"Today is Friday, which is the weekend here. The café will be closed. Tomorrow, Saturday, will be better."

"And until then?"

"You can go to the hotel. Maybe you need some sleep?"

"Yes, that's probably a good idea. What about later? Are we close to anything? Can we walk around?" Annette didn't feel like shopping, but figured walking would give her a much better feel for the city.

As the driver turned off the highway and down a smaller street into what looked like a busy downtown, soldiers with guns looked up as they sped by. Muti nodded at the armed men. "No, that is not a good idea. Stay in the hotel, don't try to go out. It is not safe, especially at night, and especially not for foreigners."

Annette had hoped that things wouldn't be as bad as Richard had warned, but it looked like they were. "Okay," she said. "We'll just wait for you and enjoy the room service."

Security guards stood at the gated entrance to the El Aurassi Hotel and checked everyone's papers thoroughly before letting the car in. Annette wasn't sure whose side they were on, but as relieved as she was to be inside the large compound, she immediately felt trapped. She had a sinking feeling that the enemy was literally waiting at the gates.

The hotel was much more modern than she had expected, and its square, grand, contemporary architecture surprised her. It had been obvious as they drove up that it would have good views from its prominent perch overlooking the heart of the city, but the panorama from their room on the eighth floor was magnificent. The sun behind the hotel in the western sky sparkled across the water in the huge harbor, and the ships glinted like diamonds in the high afternoon sun. Annette wondered again why Mansi had spoken so poorly of his country.

The room was large, with two single beds, and decorated in an odd mix of styles, but it was comfortable. The modern bone-white chest of drawers and new Panasonic TV looked out of place with the antique chairs and desk, but the two beds weren't overly soft, and that was the most important thing at the moment.

They ate in one of the three restaurants and then slept for six hours. Annette woke up around two o'clock in the morning, her mother was up and reading quietly. They both fell asleep again around four o'clock, only to be woken a few hours later by a wailing of voices and sounds. Annette went out to the balcony and listened to strange sounds that lasted only a few minutes – music mixed with words. She couldn't understand anything, but knew from Mansi that it was the Muslim call to morning prayers.

They both fell asleep again and didn't get up until the maids knocked on the door just before noon. Annette didn't feel very rested, but she didn't care about sleep. Maybe she would see her son tonight, and that was all that mattered.

They went downstairs and found a few shops open, where they bought a few things to help cover up. Annette wondered if it even mattered. Even with dark hair, their pale complexions and Western clothes labeled them anything but locals.

Muti was on time and waiting just before four o'clock. This time, the bodyguard from the day before was joined by another man, just as big. Both wore similar dark clothes and neither one smiled when the women got in the car. She tried to keep her sense of direction as they wound through the short, hilly streets, but after a few minutes, she was all turned around and had completely lost her bearings. Dozens of steep, narrow walkways disappeared between the decaying buildings, and the rough roads twisted around the buildings in a medieval way, obviously never designed for automobiles.

A few of the streets had markets, and small crowds of people moved about, sampling and selecting fresh fruits and vegetables. Almost all the women were wearing a hijab of one form or another which hid their hair completely. Many even wore burkas and veils. Annette tucked at her hair, hoping it was all inside the colorful scarf she had bought. Islam was to be respected here.

The roads got narrower, with many wide enough for only one car. Finally, they stopped in front of a row of old, dilapidated commercial buildings. Most were closed or not in business. An old man who sat near the corner nodded towards the narrow walkway that ran down between two of the vacant buildings.

Muti smiled his understanding. "Your husband is here. Let us go quickly."

The bodyguard scanned the street, but there were only a few men scurrying off home. He got out first and Annette could see a machine gun under his loose jacket. She didn't know whether to feel comforted or worried. The men boxed the two women in between them as they entered the dark alley.

Annette blinked as her eyes adjusted to the low light. Then she realized that Mansi and four men were walking straight toward them. All wore white robes, but he was easy to recognize.

Mansi stopped dead in his tracks. He looked stunned, and his hateful glare jumped back and forth between the two women before boring into Annette.

"Annette . . . what are you doing here?"

"I've come for Derek."

"That is not possible. Derek does not want to see you."

"Mansi, he's my son, too. I want to see him. Please, for God's sake."

Mansi tried to walk around her, but Annette put her hand out and blocked him. "Mansi, I've come thousands of miles. Please, I'm begging you, at least let me see him."

Mansi pushed her hand away but stopped. They were less than a foot apart. He smiled as if it was business. "It's too late. He is in school here, and he loves it."

"Can't you at least let me see him?" Annette had thought of a lot of things on the plane, and while most of her questions might never be answered, she knew she would do anything to get her son back. "Let me ask him if he wants to stay here or come home."

Mansi shook his head. "No, Annette, that is not going to happen. He is being well fed and well cared-for. He likes it here. That is all you need to know."

Marie put her arm around her daughter. "Mansi, this is inhumane. She is his mother."

"Inhumane? I called you and told you he was okay. Not calling would have been inhumane. You might never have known what happened to him. Some fathers don't call. Consider yourself lucky."

"What about mothers?" Annette cried. "What about my rights?"

Mansi chuckled. "In this country, the mother has no rights. Excuse me. I have to go."

Mansi's companions formed a circle around him, and they pushed by Annette and into the street. A red Peugeot had pulled up to the curb, and Mansi reached for the door handle.

Muti had been silent during the exchange, but he raised his hand and called out to Mansi's retreating back, "I have notified the authorities. They will seek to have custody of the child returned to the mother."

Mansi stopped and turned around. He glared at Muti for a few seconds before replying. Annette recognized the furious anger from some of their arguments the last few years. He sounded and looked capable of anything.

"I don't know who you are, but I know your face now, and I won't forget it." Mansi's threat was heavy with hatred. "Don't even think about threatening me."

Annette couldn't fathom the depth of the venom in her husband's voice. What had happened to the kind man she knew? "Mansi, what does Derek want? Can't you at least ask him if he would like to see his mother?"

"I think you should forget that you ever had a son. For you, your son is dead."

~~~

Mansi had been shocked by Annette's appearance, but it didn't change anything. He would have to be more careful, but he would be back in the U.S. soon enough. They wouldn't be looking for him there, at least not under his new alias. Plans for Jill stayed exactly the same. He had never even mentioned Annette or Derek to his daughter. Their paths had never, and would never, cross.

The graveyard was stunning when Mansi stopped there. The sun was just starting to rise between the uneven rows of headstones, and many of the old graves looked pink in the early light. Situated high on a hill overlooking the Mediterranean Sea, the graveyard had been there for centuries and was the resting place for many of Algeria's heroes.

Mansi thought it was an incredible place to be buried and a sacred place to talk. Here, amongst the ghosts of the past, God was listening.

"You remember coming here before?" he asked Jill.

"Yes, a few times, but it was a long time ago." She leaned against the car, stretching her legs and arching her back.

"Five years ago, when we went on one of our field trips."

"And when I first came to Algeria."

"Yes, that's right. Now, once again, when you leave." Mansi never got sentimental anymore. He had visited the grave and read the inscription so many times that it just fueled his commitment and his anger.

They walked over to a small stone cross with a few words on it.

<blockquote>
Yassi Nasser
Born May 15, 1933
Died Aug 5, 1961
His blood, spilled by the hands
of the murdering capitalists,
helps carry us to our freedom,
and for that sacrifice,
we are forever grateful.
</blockquote>

"He would be very proud of you, Jill, very proud. You will have opportunities he never could have dreamed of. You will have a chance for a much bigger victory."

Jill ran her hand over the words in the stone. "I hope I can be as brave as he was."

"You have already proven your courage. Now is the time to prove your cunning. It is not the brawn of mankind that changes the world, it is the brain. Study hard, get a good education, and your time will come. Enjoy America for a few years."

"Ours is such a distant target, Father, so far in the future. Sometimes it seems impossible."

"History is never made quickly. One's goals must be far-reaching to be able to make a great statement. Loftier ambitions usually require more commitment, more time. Be patient, my girl. Be patient."

"Will I see you in the States?"

"Yes. Not often, but we will stay in touch."

~~~

Muti had made an appointment the next day at the United States Embassy. Annette was glad to see the U.S. Marines stationed outside when they arrived and felt safer the moment she entered the gate. The three-story white stone building was old, beautiful, and impressive, but inside, it was all business.

In minutes, they were shown into a magnificent office twice the size of her living room, where they were greeted by Don Larton, a special assistant to the ambassador. Don appeared to be in his early fifties, and she hoped he was every bit the hardworking civil servant he looked to be. He wore a dark suit, white shirt, blue tie, and glasses that hung around his neck like evidence of his dedication. He motioned to the seating area in front of the fireplace and the green leather chairs. "Please, sit down," he said.

Annette sat in the chair closest to him. "Thank you, Mr. Larton. I appreciate you seeing us like this."

He smiled. "Please, call me Don. I understand how difficult this must be, and I wish I could be of more help."

"Can't you just take a few Marines and go get him?"

Don didn't return her jesting smile. "That's only in the movies. We have no jurisdiction here, and your case is very complicated. I made a few inquiries after your call. Your son is now a citizen of Algeria. There is nothing we can do."

"I'm the mother. Don't I get any say?"

Don shook his head slowly. "Not in Algeria."

Annette couldn't believe how backwards things seemed to be. "What about Derek's rights? Maybe his father has kidnapped him against his will?"

"Islamic law gives custody to the fathers at age seven."

"Can't we at least force him to produce Derek? Then we can ask Derek what he wants, where and with whom he wants to live."

"Mothers have no rights of custody here, so we can't force them to do anything. You can ask for anything you want, but they don't even have to respond."

Don sounded apologetic, but his tone was quite final. It was obvious the government's position here was the same as back in the States.

After leaving the embassy, Muti took them to the local police station to file desertion and abandonment charges. She never understood a word of what was said until Muti explained it later, but she did understand the scornful looks both she and her mother received from the Algerian police officers. The police only agreed to look into the matter. Muti wasn't certain that anything would happen but wanted Annette's complaint to be on record. It felt hopeless. They waited the last few days, hoping Mansi might be spotted again, or maybe even Derek, but Muti had no more news. They hired one of the security guards from the hotel to go for a walk with them, but after hiking the hills and avoiding the hostile glances, they decided that wasn't too smart an idea. Twice they had been confronted by small pockets of adolescent youths, pickpockets and thieves, the guard said. Many were Derek's age, and the sad reality of what kind of education her son might receive there was almost too much to think about.

On their last night, Muti took them to his brother's house for dinner. Up in the hills in Boozrea, the gated compound sat high above the city, and the night lights stretched farther than she would have thought. Muti's brother Amin was a businessman who owned cafés and apartments. Pictures of Amin with a group of youths were very ominous. They all had rifles or machine guns. Muti explained that his brother was a friend of President Liamine Zeroual, and they had been comrades in arms during the revolution. Muti told Annette on the way home that he had been too young, but his brother had been a key figure and heavily involved. Amin didn't speak much English, but his feelings for the radicals who continued to try to turn Algeria into an Islamic state were clear. As much as he was a devout Sunni Muslim, he didn't agree in any way with the fundamentalists – terrorists, he called them – who had been causing so many problems for the citizens of Algeria the last few years.

The next morning, Muti drove them to the airport, full of apologies. They would find Mansi again, he said, but this time they would tail him until they found the boy, too. Annette felt a tremendous sense of loss the moment the plane took off. She had failed, utterly and completely. The short flight to Paris seemed twice as long as it had on the way out, and she cried most of the way.

A reasonable layover in Paris had them on the way to New York within a few hours. Things both Mansi and her mother had said gnawed at her conscience. Remembering the deaths of her father and Paul was not something she liked to do, but Derek was alive, and who knows what might happen in the future. The two deaths had been a far greater loss than her current fate.

Had she ever really appreciated what her mother had gone through?

"How did you find the strength to get up every morning?" she asked her mother. "I don't know if I'll ever sleep again."

Marie adjusted her pillow as she turned in her seat to face Annette. "You were my only reason to live. You and Val. The first few days afterwards, I wanted to be dead, too, but every time I felt like I just couldn't go on, I would think about you two and how much you needed me. If it hadn't been for you two, I might have killed myself. I would lie awake for hours watching you girls sleep, but deep inside of me I knew I had to go on. I knew there were better days ahead."

Annette thought of her unborn child. While the fact that Mansi was the father was not something she liked to think about, there was another life that depended on her already and she was happy for that.

Marie rubbed her daughter's hands as if they were cold. "I had no idea what the future would hold, but you two needed me, and that gave me strength. If I had been all alone, I don't know if I would have made it. That might sound cowardly, but every time I felt sorry for myself, sorry that I had lost my man, my future, and my reason for living, I would think of you two."

Annette had never heard such a confession from her mother before. "You thought of suicide?"

"Only briefly, the first few days when I thought about how much I was going to miss your father. I loved him a lot and thought I had lost my reason to live, but I was wrong. You were my reason to live."

Annette looked down at her abdomen. She wasn't showing too much yet.

Her mother saw her look and reached over and patted her tummy. "You have a baby on the way. You have another reason to live. Life is never just about you. It's about the others in your life. As you know all too well, there are no guarantees. No road map to happiness. Life is about hope. Life is about caring for others, and in a few months you will have someone who needs you, someone who doesn't know what you have been through. You have to be strong. Hopefully, someday, somehow, Derek will return to your life. He is alive, and for that, there is always hope."

Her mother was right. Derek was still alive, and someday, somehow, Annette would get him back in her life. She prayed to her god, her merciful god of all gods, that until such a day, he would at least be healthy and happy.

~~~

Annette sat down in the second row. She had been home for a week, and despite what her mother said, she had been depressed most of the time. As she watched the eager women fill the large room, thoughts and images of Algiers made her think about how many thousands of parents across the world might be in a nightmare just like hers. Thousands and thousands of mothers, and a few fathers, whose children were kidnapped internationally and domestically . . . everybody had their own horror story.

Nancy Dario opened the meeting by thanking their new financial sponsors and reviewing what it meant for the group's efforts. A ten-million-dollar endowment was going to cover a lot of cases where funds were an issue, and Annette was surprised to hear where payoffs had worked. In a few cases, they had simply paid the offending parent money to give the child back. Sad news included seven new cases in California alone, and in one tragic kidnapping, the death of the child in an apparent murder-suicide at the hands of his own father. Annette had made her mother's words her mantra. *At least my son is alive.*

Nancy had other good news. Two mothers were set to be reunited with their children in the next few weeks. In both cases, the association had been instrumental in helping achieve the safe return of the kidnapped infants.

After a brief question-and-answer session, Nancy moved on. "Okay, enough of that for now. Let's get to the real reason we are here tonight."

Many of the women had tears running down their faces, applauding as the mother and daughter walked on stage. It was something they all dreamed about. Nancy held up a hand to hush the crowd and introduced the two women. "It is my great pleasure to introduce you to Linda Smythe and her daughter, Jill Ruffe."

The room exploded in cheers. Annette could see how delighted Linda looked as she wrapped her arms around her daughter's shoulders in a big hug, but the girl didn't respond and stood perfectly still, her hands at her side. Annette wondered why the teenager wasn't happier.

Nancy smiled as the applause died. "Linda has recently moved here from the Bay area, but she has been a member of our organization up there for ten years, and she never lost faith."

The women cheered furiously again, and Annette realized tears were pouring down her face. She wondered if it would be ten years before she saw her son again. She tried to imagine what he would look like at seventeen. How tall would he be? Would he still have that great smile? Would he be happier to see her than this girl was?

Nancy beamed. "Jill's return is a great example of why we must never give up. Children come back to us for a variety of reasons. We never know which strategy or tactic is going to work. In Jill's case, her father agreed she should get a good education. Thank God for our great schools and universities." As the women laughed and cheered again, Nancy offered the microphone to Linda. "How about a few words from the happy mother?"

Linda looked nervous, but her words were sweet. "I pray for all of you that someday this might be your daughter. Have faith. Your child could come home next."

The women started to clap but quickly hushed as Linda spoke again. "Today, I'm so happy to introduce you to my daughter, Jill Ruffe."

The teenager looked around the room, but never seemed to focus on anyone and never even attempted a smile. Annette thought she looked really tired and wondered how recently Jill had returned. The long flight could knock anybody out.

Linda went on. "There were days I thought this would never happen. Those were the days that you helped me. I wondered if any of us would ever get our children back, but now I know for a fact there's hope for the rest of you. Now's the time for us to get another child back."

When the meeting was over, Annette introduced herself, not sure if Linda would remember. "Hi, I'm Annette Madison. We met last month."

"Sure, I remember you. This is my daughter, Jill Ruffe."

"Hi, Jill. It's a pleasure to meet you. Are you glad to be back in the United States?"

Jill didn't answer for a moment, but after a slight nudge from her mother, she managed a polite response. "Algeria wasn't that bad, but I think I will like living in America."

"Is it okay to ask about Algeria?" Annette asked, looking at Linda. She felt foolish but couldn't stop herself.

Linda turned to her daughter. "This is the woman I told you about. Her son is in Algiers. Can she ask you a few questions?"

Jill blinked. "Okay."

"I was just there last week," Annette said. "It was a little scary." Annette thought she was being kind. She'd had a few scary nightmares about the city, Mansi, and Derek.

"You went to Algiers?" Linda answered, surprised. "Did you find your son?"

"No." Annette felt her emotions reach for her throat. "I'll tell you about that some other time."

"Okay."

Annette turned back to Jill. "Did you live with your father there?"

"Yes, and my aunt and uncle and their four kids."

"Did you see other American kids over there?"

"No, there were very few Westerners, maybe some adult Americans in business, but I never saw any kids."

"Did you ever hear of a blonde boy named Derek? His dad took him there about a month ago."

"No, I didn't meet any other Americans," Jill warned, serious about something for the first time. "It is very dangerous for Americans. They could easily get killed in the street."

Annette didn't want to pursue that line of thought.

"Mother, I have to go to the bathroom," Jill said, ending the conversation.

"Sure, it's over there." Linda pointed to the back of the hall. "I'll wait here."

Jill didn't say anything else and left. Linda watched her go and then turned back to Annette. "She says she hardly remembers me, so we're getting to know each other all over again."

"Yes, I'm sure. Ten years is a long time, but you must be so happy."

"I am. I really am. She's not as happy and bubbly as I thought she would be at seventeen, but she sure likes flying."

"Flying?"

"Yes." Linda looked proud. "She is going to start taking flying lessons."

"Really?"

"My second husband, Hank, has his private pilot's license. He took her up a few days ago to cheer her up, and now she wants to learn how to fly."

"Well, that's terrific. My father flew small planes, too. Trainors."

"Hank says that's what she'll probably learn to fly on, too."

A few other women came over to talk to Linda, so Annette congratulated her one more time and left. It had been a wonderfully happy night on one hand, but the reality that it could be ten years before she saw Derek again was almost too much to accept.

Pulling out of the underground parking lot, she turned left on Wilshire Blvd. As she picked up speed, the light turned yellow, and she had to stop at La Cienega. She didn't go up to Los Angeles often and was amazed by how busy it was at 9:30 at night. As the steady stream of cars passed in front of her, the driver of a light-colored sedan looked in her direction. He didn't see her as he accelerated through the intersection, but Annette's mouth dropped open. In a moment he was gone, hidden by the heavy traffic in both directions, but she knew who she had seen.

"Mansi! That was Mansi!" she screamed, then watched helplessly as the car disappeared.

She thought about trying to chase him and then wondered if she had made a mistake. Mansi, here? Now? In L.A.? The light changed green, and she realized it was probably already too late, but she turned left and headed south. She didn't see the car again, but stayed on La Cienega until it went under the 405 freeway before she gave up. Her imagination played games with her all the way home. Her mother and Val didn't know what to think.

She called Diane Elter the next morning. "I swear it was him. He didn't look right at me, but I had a good, long look at him. It was definitely him."

"Let me run his name and see if anything comes up."

She called back a few hours later. "Annette, I had the State Department run his name, but they show no signs of entry into the country. It must have been someone who looked a lot like him."

"Maybe he came in under another name."

"Why would he do that?"

"To avoid me."

"Yes, well, I guess that's possible, not probable. Not many fake passports get by immigration these days."

"Can't you run his fingerprints or see if he has two passports?"

"Unless he has a criminal record, we have no way of matching records," Diane added. "And at this point, it is still on the government's wish list to have a national fingerprint database."

"So there's nothing you can do?"

"If you see him again or can get a license plate number, I'll do everything I can. But otherwise, nothing has changed officially with Algeria, and it doesn't look like anything will change anytime soon. There is nothing else I can do. I'm sorry."

"No, I'm sorry to have bothered you," Annette said. "Thanks for calling me back." When she put the phone down, she couldn't hold back any longer. As the tears splashed on the back of her hand, she started sobbing.

Marie never went back to work. She retired and moved into Annette's spare bedroom. Val moved into Derek's room. They cried together, they laughed together, and they decided that men were a curse. Val swore she was never getting married. As much as they hated Mansi, however, they all loved Derek and longed for the day when they would get him back in their lives.

On Thursday, December 9, 1994, Annette gave birth to a healthy baby girl. The baby didn't reduce the pain of the loss of Derek, but as the pregnancy had come to term, she had seen the opportunity of another child as more of a blessing than ever before. Having a girl now seemed much more desirable. Enough men for now. First her father and her fiancé, now her husband and her son. She lost them in twos. She changed her name back to her maiden name, so her daughter was born Darcy Marie Madison. Derek would always be Ansour, and she hoped he would understand, but she wondered what she would tell her daughter about her dysfunctional family years from now.

Chapter 8
Ten years later - December 2004

Mansi had only been to Toronto a few times over the years and never during the winter, but he had made his reservations, left sunny Southern California, and headed to chilly Canada without a word. It was much colder than he had thought it would be, and the snow was almost a foot deep.

Customs was, as usual, no problem, and he was standing at the Enterprise rental counter in less than thirty minutes. An all-wheel-drive Ford 500, as his cousin had dictated, was waiting for him. Good thing he had a reservation, the agent said. It was the last four-wheel-drive they had. He was glad he had bought a ski jacket too.

The big car would be comfortable for the long trip. He had only driven in the snow a few times in his life, but figured if the conditions were bad, he would drive slower. It was four days back to L.A. and he certainly wouldn't be speeding.

The directions were easy to follow, and they met at the park at 6:00 am. It was noisy but deserted under the superstructure of the freeway. Traffic on the Don Valley Parkway above was building on its way to capacity as a continuous stream of commuters rushed overhead. Down below, though, amongst the trees, they were all alone. Mansi parked beside the small white Toyota Corolla his cousin was leaning up against. Samzi wore a huge black ski parka, but his hands were bare and he was rubbing them together.

The snow crunched under Mansi's feet as he got out. "Good morning, Samzi. This is quite the spot, alone, yet in the middle of everything."

"Yes, and perfect for our needs. Is everything okay?" Samzi's breath was visible in the cold air.

Mansi turned to the brown rental car. "As specified."

"Good." Samzi turned at the sound of an approaching car. It was a white Chevy van, and as it pulled up, Mansi recognized the driver. Hashim hadn't said anything about anyone else.

Vladimir Titov got out. "It is good to see you, comrades."

"And you, too, my friend," said Mansi.

Vladimir smelled like stale liquor to Mansi. They embraced and exchanged greetings, a bear hug more than anything. Mansi hadn't seen the Russian for a long time and was surprised that the man was still doing business. It had been thirty years since they had first met.

"And Samzi?" Vladimir said. "This is the last place I thought I would meet you."

Samzi's outstretched hand pulled Vladimir in for another hug.

"Not quite the beautiful weather we have in Algeria, but something you are probably familiar with, comrade," Samzi said with a laugh.

Vladimir grinned. "Yes, a nice day for July in Moscow."

Mansi thought Vladimir looked happy, almost jovial.

Samzi seemed to agree. "You look well, my friend."

"Every day there is still color in a man's face is a victory." Vladimir looked comfortable and almost stylish in a heavy, bomber-style jacket with a big white fur collar. The matching leather boots looked warm, but his trendy torn jeans seemed out of place, as if taken from someone else's closet.

"Victory is what we need, my friend, another major victory," said Samzi. "As you know, our brothers have been very successful recently, but the infidels are making things harder all the time."

"Yes, that's true. Getting goods into America has gotten much tougher these days."

"Getting people in is much more difficult, too. It is necessary to have assets already in the country, home grown, as they say. Your offer couldn't come at a better time." Samzi was pleased.

"As they say, timing is everything. The weapons were only recently acquired, but they are available immediately."

Mansi had to ask, "What kind of weapons are we talking about?"

Vladimir glanced at Samzi, who nodded his approval. "Suitcase nukes," he said. "Seems Russia won't be needing them anymore."

"Suitcase nukes?" Mansi didn't think he had heard right. "What is that?"

"Small atomic bombs. Two kilotons. Small enough to fit in a large suitcase."

Mother of God! "I guess I heard about those things years ago." He remembered vague stories but had never known if they were true or not.

"Russia would deny it officially, but they do exist, and they are portable. Easy to transport too." Vladimir's sneer revealed his gold tooth. "But the best part, this one is already in America."

"And we can pick it up tomorrow?" Samzi confirmed.

Mansi had wondered what his role was going to be.

"As soon as the money is transferred," Vladimir said, "I will give you the key to the storage locker that it is stored in. The locker is outside of Chicago, in a suburb just off the freeway. Easy to get in and easy to get out." He pulled out a sheet of paper and handed it to Samzi. A bank account number was the only thing on the otherwise blank page.

~~~

"What are you watching now?" Val said.

It was New Year's Eve, almost midnight back east. Annette had been invited to a few parties, she had decided, as usual, to stay home. A single mother for the last ten years, she hadn't been out past midnight for a long time. She had been flipping through the other channels while Val was in the bathroom and had come across an old movie she had always wanted to see. "It's *The Battle of Algiers*. Mansi told me about it years ago. I had forgotten all about it."

Val watched for a moment. A brutal street fight had ensued between soldiers and a mob. "It looks like a revolution."

"It was – the Algerian Revolution in the late fifties and early sixties. Those army guys are the French, pretty ruthless." This was what Mansi had seen and experienced. *What kind of a man does that breed?* She wondered. "Mansi grew up during this war. He said he saw dead people in the streets all the time. I never doubted him for a moment, and I can't feel any sympathy for him now, but God, what an awful childhood."

Val didn't say anything as they watched the French colonel set up the trap for the freedom fighters in the back of the building. When gunfire broke out, Annette picked up the remote and changed the channel. The party at Times Square in New York City was in full swing.

Annette hadn't been following the movie that well and figured she could rent it later. She did wish Val would get out more. "You're probably missing a good party at George's."

Val shrugged. "New Year's Eve is overrated. Most of the guys just get drunk." She was on her third glass of white wine.

"You might meet someone."

"I thought you liked me," her sister said with a laugh. The wine was starting to kick in.

"Just because I met Mansi at a party at George's, you don't have to be afraid of every man you meet."

"I'm not. I just haven't met anyone interesting lately. What about you? Meet any single good-looking men looking for a nice big home in Newport Beach?"

"Are you kidding? And what, they want me? A forty-seven-year-old divorcee with a nine-year-old daughter and an ax to grind? I've given up on knights in shining armor on big white horses." Annette doubted she would ever marry again.

"Well, then, don't bug me about my dating. After everything you've been through, I'm thinking about turning gay."

"Sometimes I almost feel gay, it's been so long since I've been with a man." Annette laughed as she thought about her small collection of toys. "Thank God for batteries."

Val pointed at the TV. "Look. Here it goes."

It was only nine o'clock on the West Coast as the ball started its slow slide down to New Year's Eve on the East Coast. Fireworks started exploding high above the towering buildings, and a roar erupted from the happy crowd as they all started cheering, dancing, clapping, and singing. The familiar sounds of "Auld Lang Syne" brought smiles to both sisters as they joined in on the chorus, then the ball hit the bottom. It was officially 2005. Annette couldn't help but remember the fireworks nineteen years ago when she had met Mansi. Was it really that long ago?

~~~

A few days later, Annette was just getting ready to leave for work when a moving truck pulled up next door. She had shown the house herself a few times and knew it had been sold by someone from the Century 21 office. She had wondered when the new owners would be moving in.

As the men opened up the long trailer and set the ramp in place, a dark blue Chevy Suburban pulled up into the driveway. A man got out of the driver's side. He was tall and wide, not overweight, but barrel-chested. With his sandy blonde hair and a stocky build, he looked like he could be a truck driver.

Annette figured he was probably in his late forties, maybe early fifties. She watched as he walked around the front of the truck to the passenger door. It opened just as he reached for the handle, and a young girl got out. The girl was dressed in a cute orange dress and looked to be eight or nine years old. She ran excitedly up to the front door. The man walked across the lawn and pulled out the *For Sale* sign. As he did, he looked up and caught Annette watching him. He smiled a big friendly grin and waved. Caught staring, Annette felt awkward, but forced a smile and waved back.

A few days later, Annette had a busy day on her mind and wasn't paying much attention as she backed out of her driveway. She looked in her rearview mirror just in time to slam on the brakes. A police car was parked on the street, and she had almost hit it. A police officer got out.

She rolled down her window as the officer came over to her car. "Sorry about that. I was in a hurry and wasn't looking. Are you okay?"

"No harm done." The cap came off, and she recognized the officer. It was her new neighbor. He flashed a big grin at her. "Heck of a way to meet my neighbor, though."

"Then I owe you another apology. I haven't even come over to introduce myself. I'm Annette Madison. Welcome to the neighborhood."

"Not to worry. We've been busy getting settled. My name is Cliff Billings." He stuck his hand out.

She reached out her window. "Hi."

"It's nice to meet you, Annette. I see you've got a little girl, too. Looks like she's a few years older than mine."

"Darcy is ten. How old is your daughter?"

"Lisa is almost nine."

"She looks darling."

"Thanks. She's a great kid. Maybe we can get the two of them together?"

"That would be nice," Annette said, surprising herself. "Listen, I'm barbequing tomorrow night. Would you and your family like to come over?"

Cliff chuckled. "A barbeque? In January? Only in California. That sounds nice. It's just me and Lisa, though."

"I live with my mother and sister as well. Can you handle just women?" *A single father next door?* Marie and Val would be surprised, too.

He grinned. "Not a problem."

"Okay. Say, about six?"

Was it his uniform? He did have a warm and easy smile. She wondered what her mother would say.

It turned out be a perfect night. The wind had died down, and it was quite warm. Annette had a fresh salad with avocado, grilled steaks, corn on the cob, and her specialty, barbequed cabbage. Cliff complimented her on all of it.

"Are you from the area?" Her mother asked.

"No, Montana," he said. "I just moved down here." Cliff sat down in one of the lawn chairs and stretched his legs. "New job. I'm a deputy sheriff here in Orange County."

Marie smiled. "Well, that's nice, having a policeman on the block. I feel safer already."

Cliff laughed. "I checked all the statistics. It seems Costa Mesa is a pretty safe place to live already."

"It is, and a friendly place, too," Annette said. "If you ever need anything, let me know. I've lived in Costa Mesa all my life."

"That's nice of you to offer. I'm sure I'll be pestering you soon enough, but it's not all new to me. I went to Long Beach State in the late seventies."

"Oh, you must have been down this way before, then."

"Sure, and in Newport Beach in the summer."

Annette thought they could have probably crossed paths. She had hung out down at the beach for quite a few years.

"What about babysitters?" Cliff said. "Know any of those?"

"My sister and mother are my two babysitters," Annette said, looking at the two young girls playing with Darcy's dolls, oblivious to the adults' gazes. "It sure looks like they get along great."

"Yeah, they do, don't they? Maybe we can work something out."

"Your daughter is darling," Val said. "I look after Darcy all the time. Feel free to bring her over anytime."

"That would be great," Cliff said. "I might just take you up on that sometime."

"Who looks after her when you're at work now?" Annette said.

"I take her to a daycare, over on Harbor."

All the women didn't say anything for a few seconds, until Marie asked the question that was on all their minds. "Are you raising your daughter on your own?"

Cliff nodded. "Yes, I am." He looked away for a moment, and his voice cracked. "My wife was killed by a drunk driver eight years ago, a few months after Lisa was born. Joanne, my wife, had gone back to work part-time, and I was home babysitting. I still blame myself sometimes."

Marie's jaw dropped. "I'm so sorry. How awful for you. That's terrible."

"It was, but life goes on, doesn't it? I was a mess for a few weeks, but I had an infant daughter. I had to get it together quick."

"Annette lost her father to a drunken driver and has had to raise Darcy by herself, too," Marie said.

Annette shot her mother a look. "Mom . . ." She had not wanted to get this personal with a man she hardly knew. "Surely that could have waited?"

"I'm sorry to hear that," Cliff said. "I know how devastating and sudden that is."

Her mom had laid most of her cards on the table already, so Annette filled in the blanks. "My father, her husband, died twenty years ago, and I still think about him every day. But you're right, life goes on, and kids grow up fast."

"Where is Darcy's father?"

Fair enough, Annette thought. She looked at her mother for support. Marie just shrugged her shoulders. Annette took a deep breath and tried to keep it short. "Well, that's another ugly story. The father abducted our other child, a boy, when he was seven and took him to Algeria. That was over ten years ago. Darcy was born after he kidnapped Derek and left. I've been trying to get my son back ever since."

It was Cliff's turn to be dumbstruck. "You have a son who was kidnapped by his own father?"

"Yes, and taken to a country that won't help me get him back."

"Can't the State Department help?"

"No. They've tried the official line, but the Algerians just don't respond. Any other suggestions?"

He shook his head. "Unfortunately, international child law is not my area of expertise. Do you have any contact with your son?"

Annette often said that she would be happy if she knew where he was and that he was okay. The civil unrest might just swallow him up, an innocent bystander, or he might become a misguided revolutionary. Her mind had dreamt up many ugly possibilities. "No, and he's almost seventeen now."

"I've heard many of those children try to come back later, on their own, when they're old enough," Cliff said.

"Yes, I've heard that, too. I just hope he stays alive. That country is really dangerous; he could get killed before he has a chance to grow up."

"I know little about Algeria, but it is on the government's warning list. Maybe you need to hire somebody and go get him out yourself?"

Marie laughed. "That sure sounds like a Montana trooper. Are you going to get the cavalry?"

Cliff grinned sheepishly. "I'm sorry. That was a stupid thing to say."

"Actually, I've been there," Annette said, knowing the whole story would come out now. "It makes the Wild West look tame."

Cliff's eyes widened. "You went to Algeria looking for your son?"

She nodded. "We even found my ex-husband, but that was the last I ever saw of him."

"That's pretty amazing. Who is we?"

Annette looked at her mother. "Mom went with me."

"Just the two of you? How did that go?"

Annette sighed. "That's a long story." She was surprised how much she liked looking at Cliff. His smile was genuine and inviting, and she loved his happy and compassionate eyes. Physically, he couldn't have been more different from Mansi. Taller and husky, his sandy blonde hair and fair complexion were far from Mansi's dark complexion and black eyes. But she liked was the way he seemed to listen to her and look at her with every bit of his attention.

~~~

Hashim's request was a surprise. Mansi wondered if it had anything to do with Jill's promotion. She was getting more valuable by the day. He had pretty much forgotten about his first wife after Jill had left home and joined the Air Force, but Linda had been going through Jill's old room a few months ago and found a few of Mansi's letters to his daughter from years ago. While the letters were innocent enough to the casual observer, they did contain coded instructions on how and when to meet.

Jill had been mad about the privacy invasion and worried when her mother revealed that she had kept a file on Mansi since the day her daughter was taken away. Police reports, letters from the FBI, pictures, newspaper clippings, everything.

Hashim decided it was time to eliminate the liability.

Jill gave her father a complete layout of the house and helped him decide when would be the best time. Her stepfather, Hank, was going to be out of town for the weekend at a golf tournament in Palm Springs, and her mother would be home all alone. Linda was now a home care nurse and had a small supply of drugs on hand. They would make it look like a drug-related killing.

He parked several blocks away and entered the park from the other side. It turned out to be the perfect night, as the temperatures had dropped and a low fog crept in from the coast and cut visibility to a few hundred yards. At 3:00 a.m., it was cold and the streets were deserted. There were no alarms to worry about, and the house was set back from the street on a large lot that backed to the park. Approaching the house from the east side, he found the window in the attached garage completely hidden by the tall hedges, just like Jill had said. It was perfect. The master bedroom was on the other end of the house, and any small noise was very unlikely to be heard. In a few minutes, he had covered the window with duct tape, and one quick blow with his rubber hammer cracked the thin window into large pieces that hung in the air. He pulled the sticky chunks of glass away and climbed into the garage. No sounds, no lights, and the kitchen door unlocked as it apparently always was.

His soft-soled shoes were silent on the floor tiles of the kitchen but with the concrete slab of the single-story house and the carpeted hallway, he didn't have to worry. The master bedroom was at the far end of the house and the door to Linda's bedroom was open. She was sleeping on her back and never had a chance. The nine-millimeter Beretta was fitted with a brand-new Abraxas Titanium silencer, and it merely coughed politely as he fired three times at close range. Her body jumped at each shot, but the bullets were well placed and she died without even a whimper.

He found the filing cabinet in her office and removed the entire file before sliding the door to the cabinet closed. In the corner of the room, a small black bag contained her medical supplies. He spilled most of the over-the-counter medications on the floor before taking what he wanted. In the bathroom he left a few things to throw the cops. A used syringe, a cigarette butt he had picked up at random, and the left-handed glove from a set he had bought used at a Goodwill store.

He left through the back door and walked quietly across the park. Glancing around, he saw no one and no lights on in any of the houses. The gun he would throw into the ocean, but he had filed the serial numbers off just in case. Jill would keep him updated, but he was confident that the police would find no leads and the case would soon be forgotten.

~~~

Cliff ran the name through the computer a few days later. He almost didn't want to know, but he had been a cop too long not to respect his hunches. *Sure enough. What a freaking small world!* Marie Madison and her two daughters were even mentioned by first names in the official report. Memories of that day thirty years ago still haunted him. He hadn't even been a cop then, but it was his first fatal vehicle accident. He had been working as a security guard on the gate for a few weeks and was relieving a few different guys who were on summer vacation. He had been the first one on the scene and poorly prepared for a double fatality. Harold Madison's Ford Fairmont was virtually unrecognizable. Dragged down the street for a few hundred feet before it hit the curb and exploded, it had been the most gruesome tragedy Cliff had ever been first responder on.

The two men, no more than names twenty years ago, Harold Madison and Paul Sonnen, naturally had lives with women in them, and those women lived next door.

Of all the women in Southern California, it was absolutely amazing. He hadn't even thought about the accident for years. He had to tell Annette, but wasn't quite sure how. Running her name through the computer was against a few rules, but hopefully that wouldn't bother her too much, because he found so much about her that he really liked. Telling her that and the truth could be tricky.

~~~

Mansi heard the sound of someone running up the stairs, the old wood groaning under the pounding footsteps. It had to be Derek, excited his father was here, and a man soon, but still a teenager at heart. It would be many years before Derek would be of value, but Mansi couldn't help but be proud. His son would never know that he was following in his half-sister's footsteps, but both were well on their way to great things.

Just like Jill, they had convinced him that his mother didn't love him and had never wanted him. Now, ten years after he had left his tiny car bed in California, he despised Annette and could curse her in a multi-language parody that had everyone howling as he mixed metaphors and adjectives in a spew of anger not present in many seventeen-year-old boys.

"Father . . . you weren't expected," Derek said, panting from the rush up the three flights of stairs.

"Get your things," Mansi replied. "We are going on a trip."

Mansi told him the purpose of their trip on the drive out to the mountains. Derek never said a word. All the students had to pass the test. There were no options.

Mansi stopped at the bottom of the narrow valley, close to a few caves that opened into the side of the rocky cliff. "Are you ready?"

Derek looked around. It was dark and hard to see. "Yes, Father. I have been waiting for this moment."

Mansi got out and turned on a small flashlight. He pointed it at the side of the hill and found the entrance to the cave. Inside, it was surprisingly large, and a tunnel disappeared into the dark, but they didn't have to go very far. On one side of the room, two men were tied together. Mouths duct-taped, standing back to back, hands and legs bound, they were fastened to the wall by a couple of solid hooks. They looked terrified.

"There has been a change in the test, Derek. Chances are, if you ever have to kill, it will be at extremely close range. I know you always thought you would use your rifle and kill at a distance, but that will be easy compared to this. Here, use this gun." Mansi offered Derek a handgun, its barrel polished smooth by years of use.

Derek raised the gun.

"You only have one bullet, so you will have to kill one man with a knife." Mansi slid a small dagger out of his robe.

Derek lowered the gun and reached for the knife. He tucked it into the waistband of his dungarees.

Mansi watched carefully. His son's immediate behavior and decision-making was almost as important as the outcome.

Derek walked over to the man on the right, who was taller, maybe forty, with dark brown hair. His eyes begged for mercy. Derek lifted the gun to the man's forehead. His hand and the gun were visibly shaking, but after only the slightest hesitation, he pulled the trigger. The bullet made a tiny hole just above the man's nose before exploding out of the back of the man's skull and into the second man's head. Blood and brain tissue splattered all over the dirt wall as the life poured out of the two men. The first man died instantly, and his body sagged against his friend, who was still alive but missing half of his face. The bullet had exited through his left cheek. When he tried to scream, he choked on the blood, and nothing came out but a sick gurgling sound.

Mansi watched the man struggle for a second, then hissed at his son. "That didn't work, did it? Now you're going to have to finish him off with the knife."

Derek grimaced as he drove the knife into the man's chest. When he pulled it out, blood gushed out of the wound. As it poured down the man's torso, the body went limp. Derek gagged and dropped the knife. His hands went to his face, but it was too late, and he threw up all over the bloody victims.

Mansi laughed and picked up the knife. As Derek staggered backwards, Mansi ripped the blade across the man's throat, severing the head from the body. It landed with an awful thud, and then all was quiet. "Have a little compassion. Kill them quickly."

Derek wiped his hands on his pants. He stared at the bloody scene quietly before replying. "Next time, give me two bullets. This is a little messy for me."

It was a two-hour drive back into Algiers, and Mansi quizzed his son on dozens of subjects, but Derek had been a top student and not only answered his questions, but challenged Mansi. His final performance in the caves had been a little soft, but the two men had died.

Some students couldn't pull the trigger, but the ones who did were in all the way. "Are you ready to go to America?"

"Like we talked about? To go to university?" Derek had been slumped against the car door. He sat up.

"There is no changing your mind. Money is not like sand in the desert."

"I want to do this, Father. All my life I have been trained to become your sword."

"That might not be necessary, but our goals and our loyalties must be the same."

"Of course." His answer was a whisper.

"It might be years before you ever live a pure life again." His cousin had used these same words three decades ago and Mansi still hadn't returned.

"I know, but I'll study hard, and that will keep me busy. I'll make you proud."

Two generations of Nasser men had studied abroad and received a university degree. Derek, whatever his outcome might be, still represented another generation who would now have a first-class education and a chance to help Algeria find true independence.

"Make your grandfather proud," Mansi said. "He's the one responsible for your education. Maybe someday you can return his favor." Fiction together with the truth had become the reality for Derek.

"I look forward to that day, Father," Derek said, sounding proud of the future achievement already.

Mansi thought about the day ten years ago when he had taken Derek. He had been so happy just to go on vacation with his poppa, but Derek changed quickly, and soon Mansi was addressed as *Father*. Now, his son was well-educated in many different ways, and looked and sounded like the American that he was.

"You'll travel alone," Mansi explained. He had already looked at the details. "It's your first time on a plane, and a big trip and all that, so you will be a little nervous, anyway. They'll understand. You'll fly to Paris, then direct to Los Angeles.

"How soon will this happen?"

"Soon, in the next month or so. We need to get you into school before the semester starts."

"Do you know what my mission will be?"

Mansi shook his head. "No, no one does, Derek. Time will tell. For now, you get a good education and have some fun. When the right time and right opportunity comes along, Allah will tell us."

~~~

It was busy as always, and Art had to pass through three different checkpoints on the way to the high-level office on the inner courtyard. The endless hallways that efficiently tied the five sections of the building together were confusing to infrequent visitors. He had been in the Pentagon so many times in the last ten years that he could give directions, but today was different. He was meeting his old friend, General Les Wilby, to discuss the final review of a military version of his proposed pilotless aircraft control system. Today was the day of truth.

He was called in almost immediately. Leslie, the general's longtime aide, escorted him into the spacious office. "General Wilby, Mr. Trainor."

"Thank you, Leslie. Please close the door behind you."

They shook hands, and the general pointed to the two easy chairs in front of the desk. Pictures of pilots lined the walls of the office. Art knew from past visits that many of those men had been killed in flying accidents, military, combat, and civilian. Pilots had been expendable for far too long. On the table were two copies of an official report.

Wilby was smiling. "Read the summary on page eleven."

The cover was simple and self-explanatory:

Proposed Implementation of the
Trainor Jet Autopilot System in Combat

Art picked up the thick report; it had to be three hundred pages. He found the Executive section and started reading.

With a success rate close to 100%, indications are the software could be implemented to eliminate all military pilots, combat and support. Advances in the Automatic Air Collision Avoidance System (ACAS), coupled with improvements in satellite-based Global Positioning Systems, have provided an integrated software platform that has eliminated the need for onboard pilots.

Future air wars could be fought from safe distances, deep inside underground based control units, and no pilot's life would ever be at risk. Development of Unmanned Aerial Vehicles (UAV) during the eighties and nineties was instrumental in the overwhelming success in the Gulf and Iraq Wars and the continuing war on terrorism. These improvements have paved the way for the next generation of fighter jets and air superiority. This long-awaited technology is now ready to fulfill its greatest potential.

When he turned the page, Wilby chuckled. "Do you need to read more? They love it. They want it. Congratulations."

Art reached for the officer's outstretched hand. This was fantastic news. "I can't thank you enough, Les. You have been a great supporter, and I know this wouldn't have happened without your help."

"Your extraordinary program has been a great help to me, too, Art. There are a lot of people here who believe in this technology and the lives it will save, and that includes your old friend."

"How is Senator Kingston?" Art asked.

"He's real good, and he said to say hello. He's going to give this his full support."

"That's fantastic." Washington might have something to say about that, but having his friend backing him wouldn't hurt. "You have been an incredible help. I hope you get another star."

Wilby laughed. "Yeah, well, don't get too excited yet. This is far from a done deal, and it'll take time. The President is going to want to see some serious problem-free airtime in your birds before he starts laying off pilots."

Art couldn't wait to call Bill Simpson and share the good news. "Yes, sir, and we understand. Our first plane is still three or four years away, but once we're certified, we will build as many as we can. We'll get those pilotless planes up flying cargo, and we'll rack up thousands of hours in no time."

"You do that, and your friend might get re-elected," Wilby said.

"And a fourth star for the general?" Art had extended an open offer to the general should he ever retire from the U.S. Air Force. Certainly Les Wilby was worth far more than what the military was paying him. In his early fifties, he was highly regarded for his leadership in Iraq and considered a very attractive candidate for many reasons and many positions. Senator Norman Kingston was General Les Wilby's biggest fan, a known mentor and ardent supporter of a grassroots campaign to get the general to run for elected office in the next election.

"I just want to save lives, Art," Wilby said, smiling. "We're going to nickname the program 'NO LOSS.'"

Chapter 9

It took a few weeks before Cliff asked Annette out. They had talked briefly a few times as they were coming and going, and she wondered if she had read him wrong. When he finally called, however, he apologized, saying he had been studying for an exam. He suggested dinner, and when she agreed, he asked her to pick the restaurant. The waiter recognized her at the little Italian restaurant and found them an empty booth by the window. It was cozy and private.

She had told Cliff it was California casual, and his checked brown sports jacket, T-shirt, and jeans looked perfect. Annette had pinned her hair up and slipped on a yellow halter top, blue jeans, and a white sweater. Small heels spiced it up just enough.

They talked about everything, but mostly about family. Annette couldn't believe how easy it was to open up to him. He shared her pain in many ways, and she wondered if she had reached the moment when she could trust a man again.

Cliff told her all about his wife's death, his challenges with caring for the baby, and his decision to move. She struggled to fight back tears at his pain, laughed when he made fun of his country ways, and was impressed with his compassion for her open wound.

"There's nothing else you can do?" he asked.

Annette shrugged. "If you can think of something else, I'm willing to give it a try." She didn't let herself get too optimistic about Derek's return anymore.

"If anything ever happened to Lisa, I don't know if I could handle it as well as you have." He touched her hand. His caress was warm and surprisingly soft. "Your nightmare still goes on, but ours is behind us."

Annette didn't move her hand. "You didn't see me the first few years after he left. I was a mess. I had no job, almost lost my house. Thank God for my mother and for Val. I would never have made it without their support."

"I know what you mean." Cliff gave her hand a reassuring squeeze and then released it. "I ended up moving in with my folks. My father had just retired, and they took over. I don't know how I would have done it without them, either. Thank God for family."

"Why did you move down here now? Wouldn't having your family close by have been a good environment for Lisa?"

"Absolutely, but my problem was twofold. My folks moved in with me for a few years, but I ended up abusing them by working far too hard to avoid dealing with the pain, and they ended up raising Lisa. I knew it was tough on them and not really fair. For me, the distances are so great up there, that ten- or twelve-hour days are normal, and it was wearing me out."

"And that's better down here?"

"Yes, here there is overtime, but it's not a daily occurrence, and there is no travel time. Besides, I went to college here and had always wanted to return." He paused. "Listen, Annette, there's something I need to tell you. It's kind of odd, but I feel I should mention it."

She could see the worry crease his face. "Nothing bad, I hope?"

"No, not anymore. Just an odd connection in life, but it is something I feel like I need to disclose."

"Sounds official."

He nodded. "Sort of. I worked part-time at Trainor Jets as a security guard while I was going to college down here."

"Really? What a small world." She felt relieved that was all it was. Then something occurred to her. "Did you know my father?"

"No . . . but I was on duty the night he was killed. I didn't see the accident happen, but I was on the scene before the police or the ambulance."

"Are you serious?"

"Yes. I'm sorry. I didn't know if or how to tell you. It was a long time ago, but I just felt I had to tell you."

She was stunned but instantly felt sorry for Cliff. The pictures of the crash scene had been horrible. It would have been very difficult for anyone. "That's an incredible coincidence. It must have been awful."

"I didn't bring it up to talk about it or upset you in any way. I didn't remember the name until after dinner last week, and I double-checked. I wanted to ask you out the day after your barbeque, but I didn't know what to say. All I can say is, I'm sorry for your loss."

"Thanks for telling me." She wondered if this was some kind of ironic twist of fate that had brought Cliff into her life. Either way, it didn't matter. She liked Cliff and felt she could trust him more all the time. Perhaps his being a policeman helped her perception of him, but he seemed so genuine, so caring, and she saw how loving he was with his daughter. "But after years on the force, I'm sure that wasn't your only fatality."

"No."

"It was a long time ago. Let's forget it, okay?"

He grinned and gave her hand another caress. "Thanks for being so understanding."

She liked his hand touching hers, and she fondled it back. "Tell me about the fishing."

Cliff looked confused. "What fishing?"

"The fishing back in Montana, silly. I was trying to change the subject."

His worry turned to joy. "Well, you should have seen the one that got away."

Annette laughed. If they continued to see each other, there would be plenty of time to talk about the serious stuff again.

~~~

"It was in the paper," Annette told her mother as Marie settled into her favorite chair. "The show is on at seven."

The new Freedom Five and its autopilot system had been all over the news when Trainor Jets had first announced their totally automated, computer-operated airplane a few months ago. Dozens of critics had debated scores of reasons why the planes still needed pilots and why the concept just wouldn't work, but the entire world had anxiously waited for the unveiling Art Trainor had promised. Annette could hear Darcy and Lisa laughing. They were playing with dolls and not paying any attention to their parents.

"The stock has been doing really well for years now," Marie said, "Even when all those tech stocks crashed."

Annette turned on the TV and clicked through the channels. She stopped when she saw someone giving a speech in front of a row of corporate jets. "It's Art Trainor. Wow, he's getting old."

"We're all getting older, dear," her mother said, pulling her chair up a little closer.

Art was standing on a small platform, with a few rows of the company's different jets lined up behind him. A wireless microphone was discreetly clipped to his lapel. The words *Trainor Jets* were embroidered into the left front pocket of the white cotton coat. He looked happy.

"The past ten years have been nothing short of amazing times at Trainor Jets," he began. "We have sold more Freedom Fours than we ever thought possible, almost twice as many. Our fractional aircraft ownership company, Fly America, has flourished, and profits have never been greater. But now is not the time to be complacent. The events of 9/11 changed air travel forever, and Trainor Jets wants to make sure that never happens again." He turned and pointed to the airplanes.

"Today, as we speak, computer technologies now perform many different tasks automatically, and some aircraft can actually take off, fly thousands of miles, and land without a pilot ever touching the controls. What we propose is to take the concept one step further and eliminate the need for pilots all together."

A quiet chatter broke out. Art raised his hands, and the crowd, eager to hear more, fell deadly silent. He continued, "We are offering a true autopilot system, from engines on to power shutdown. The statistics are clear; more airplane accidents are caused by pilot error than by equipment failure; and with computers doing virtually everything else, it makes no sense to keep a man in the middle. Aviation has had many incredible milestones in its first century, but I think the best is yet to come. Trainor Jets wants to fly where nobody has ever flown before."

"He's had that dream for a long time," Annette said.

"Shhhh." Marie frowned and turned the volume up a few notches on the remote.

Art went on, "Our current Freedom Four will provide the basic airframe for the new Freedom Five, but interior space and range will increase with the removal of pilot controls and equipment. Now, the two seats in the nose of the airplane will have the best views in all of aviation."

A view of the inside of a jet flashed across the screen. In the cockpit were two beautiful black leather recliners.

Art's face appeared superimposed over a corner of the giant screen, and he grinned. "This plane represents a true frontier, one that will change air travel forever. But, like the Wright Brothers, we have many critics, and the road to success will not be without many challenges." He uttered the word *challenges* proudly. "The massive computer network required by the federal government to build a digital highway in the sky is being constructed as we speak and will provide the perfect framework for our software to guide planes through any sky and any weather. A NASA-sponsored program, the Advanced General Aviation Transport Experiments, AGATE, has digitally mapped the entire sky above the United States. Through the magic of computers, we can now control an airplane anywhere in the sky." Art stopped and took a drink of water.

To Annette, it still sounded incredible.

"The Freedom Five project has an ambitious schedule, with our first prototype scheduled for rollout in 2010, and then, depending on testing and deployment of the new federal computer and radar systems; delivery by the year 2012. All those details are included with the press release." Art waved a small booklet, and dozens of hands shot up.

The TV view switched back to an on-scene news reporter. "Okay, there you have it. Trainor Jets have just announced plans for a new seventeen-seat private business jet that has no pilots – I repeat, no pilots."

"Thanks, Bob," said the anchorwoman. The camera view switched back to the attractive Asian woman at the news station. She swiveled to face her co-host. "John, do you think the American public is actually going to get in one of those things?"

"Originally, the FAA said certification would be next to impossible," John said, "and some swore it would never happen in their lifetime; but things have changed. Perhaps the military's success with all their new drones has opened the way."

"That's a good point, and probably true," Tanu replied. "But drones over Iraq is a long way from laptops over America."

John laughed. "Yes, well, Art Trainor obviously thinks people will get on his planes, and they have approval to start building."

The anchorwoman looked down at her notes. "The fantastic success in the Gulf War with UAVs, Unmanned Aerial Vehicles, has spawned many discussions on drones and pilotless aircraft. Obviously the military believes in it. Is this just a natural progression of that technology?"

"After the success in Desert Storm, the Marines formed the 1st Unmanned Aerial Vehicle (UAV) Company on January 15, 1996. Their UAV weapons have given the U.S. air reconnaissance and strike capabilities like never before, with no risk to pilots. Maybe the technology is ready for paying passengers. As you know, I was a war correspondent in Baghdad in 2003 when the key targets were destroyed in those dazzling displays of total surprise and pinpoint bombing. And the Afghan war relies on Predators more than conventional planes for combat and surveillance. Seems to me this technology has already earned a few stripes. What about you, Tanu? Aren't you a private pilot? Would you go up in a plane without pilots?"

Tanu smiled and turned back to the shot of the Trainor jets lined up neatly on the runway. "I am a pilot, John. In fact, I learned to fly as part of the Trainor company's flight program at the Long Beach Airport, and my dad retired after thirty-five years at the company. I'm definitely biased, but yes, once they're thoroughly tested, I probably would get in one."

" CAAV, some have penned the new plane." John said. "Commercial Automatic Aviation Vehicle."

Tanu laughed, "Yes, I heard that. I also heard PAAV, which stands for Personal Automatic Aviation Vehicle."

John nodded his agreement. "Well, whatever they call it, if Trainor Jets has anything to say about it, we all have one of these in our garage soon."

Art's dream is coming true, Annette thought.

"I wonder if your father taught her how to fly, too?" Marie said.

"She's too young," Annette said.

"I suppose. I wonder if I would get on one of those planes?"

"It would still be built by Trainor, Mom." Annette didn't know if she would have the courage to get in one, but figured she could never afford it, anyway.

"That's true," Marie said, "But no pilots?"
"I can't wait for the next roll-out."

~~~

His cousins were together near the back. They nodded when Mansi slipped in. The room was getting too small. Mansi found an opening beside a few of the students. Tariq was in the left front corner, as was his custom, and Derek was standing only a few places ahead of Mansi. It might be the last time they shared prayers together.

It had been unusually cool for Algiers, dropping to a low of six degrees Celsius. Mansi felt stiff in his lower back as he bent forward, repeating the words of the Salat for the untold thousandth time. He spoke in Arabic, but he was thinking in English about other things.

> *"Bismil laahir rahmaanir raheem.*
> *Al hamdu lillahi rabbil `aalameen.*
> *Ar rahmaanir raheem.*
> *Maaliki yawmid deen.*
> *Eyyaaka na`budu, wa eyyaaka nasta`een*
> *Eh'denas siraatal mustaqeem."*

> "In the name of GOD, Most Gracious, Most Merciful
> Praise be to GOD, Lord of the universe
> Most Gracious, Most Merciful
> Master of the Day of Judgment
> You alone we worship; You alone we ask for help.
> Guide us in the right path."

Mansi had calculated that if one was truly faithful – which he had certainly not been – and performed prayers as required by the Koran five times a day for seventy-five years, one would have performed the holy ritual over 136,000 times. He never felt too blasphemous about missing a few prayers, but today his thoughts were elsewhere, and he couldn't help but reflect on the life he had forged.

His family, four children borne over two decades to four wives; were on the verge of great things. Jill kept getting one promotion after another. Derek would be returning to America and entering university; and Dawn would be kidnapped next month to begin her training. A cycle, the Americans called it. Finally, after a lifetime of preparation, his offspring would start to bear gifts.

What would his father think? Yassi's goal had been simpler. He had wanted a place to educate and train leaders for Algeria – leaders not only on the battlefield, but in the intellectual arenas, too. The education and living in London had taught his father how so many struggles were won by brains, not brawn. Thus he had organized a Madrassa, a small Islamic school, the curriculum very demanding mentally, physically, emotionally, and religiously.

Funded in part by interested benefactors and by the fees they charged, in 1963, with the city in chaos, the small, quiet school had flourished. They had even turned away children every month, many kids whose parents were dead or afraid for their life in the streets of Algiers. The eight-year war of independence had left many homeless, many dead, and a good education was almost impossible. Damaged schools, frightened parents, and terrified teachers left many parents little choice, and Yassi's school offered a safe haven as much as the promise of a superior education.

The new Algerian government did not bother them. Yassi was a hero of the revolution, and one of the more educated Arabs in Algiers, respected both in the business community and on the political battlefield, long before he had found the row of buildings forty years ago. Shelled mercilessly by the freedom fighters before the French had abandoned the outpost, the group of structures that surrounded the courtyard was perfect. Part garrison, part stockyard, the looters had gotten the best of it before Yassi had quietly purchased the derelict property and the land for a few blocks around it.

It still looked deserted from the street, and while the three-story buildings needed more than a few repairs, inside, they were much more functional and quite spacious. Joined by wide hallways to the buildings on either side, the back of the main building opened onto a fairly large courtyard that was completely enclosed. The continuous row of two and three-story buildings eliminated any prying eyes.

The madrassa had opened modestly, with only a few students, and the cousins were three of the nine boys. Hashim and Samzi had been teenagers, but Mansi had started with two other boys who were also seven. Yassi insisted they learn English; it was the language of business, and the language of their enemies. Two instructors, both also schooled in England, and veterans of the war, had worked hard to fill the curious minds as the young men to be morphed into *mujadhin* of the future. Within a few years, the heavy discipline, single-minded focus, and unrelenting training turned the innocent young boys into the sneakiest of little warriors. At ten, Mansi, like many of the others, could easily handle an AK-47, pick a pocket, ask for lunch in French or English, and recite most of the Koran. He was a child to the French soldiers, but a soldier to the jihad.

Things had changed a lot since Yassi's death. Algerians had been outraged that Yassi Nasser, one of their fine young politicians, had been murdered, and donations to their cause poured in, along with many new fresh perspectives. Too many young Algerian men had been lost in the struggle for freedom and justice.

It was Hashim's idea. "Why let our own blood die in battle?" he had said. "Why not enlist the lives of others on our behalf?" They had no spies like the CIA, but understood the pain it took to raise their own sons and turn them into soldiers. Why not raise and train others to do their bidding? Why not employ others who could fit in much better in times of trouble, men who were already part of the landscape, with one foot in the country already?

How to get good young candidates was a problem. They tried kidnapping, but that took a lot of effort, and out of the three boys they managed to get into Algiers, only one was left. One had escaped, and one had been beaten to death by a classmate.

Hashim's idea made so much sense, and they all loved the irony of it. While the chosen few were off obtaining a magnificent education at Western universities abroad, why not have bastard children with infidel women and bring the children back for training as soldiers? A new way to recruit soldiers. A better way to fulfill the jihad.

Hashim found himself agreeing once more with the Americans. Mansi thought it was ironic, but the United States had been sending their young off to die in wars for decades. What was a few more? Children raised to die in battle – a renewable resource, Hashim had called it.

They assembled a list of countries and had no shortage of students who wished to go abroad for a good education and a chance to serve God. The young men were hand-picked for their devotion and understood the commitment it would take. They would marry, raise the children in a loving family home in the child's native country until age seven, then they would kidnap their own kids and bring them back to Algeria for the next ten years of their lives.

The father's right to custody would guarantee that they would become dual citizens and the mother would never see her child again. Soon, the child would forget he ever had a mother. At seven, they would be the perfect age for indoctrination, their minds ripe for knowledge and the truth. Prayers five times a day, the Koran the only book allowed.

Derek never knew he had siblings. Tariq had watched out for him, like he had Jill, especially the first few years, until his young half-brother understood what it took to survive. But both siblings had learned to defend themselves, both verbally and physically. New recruits could get pretty despondent over the loss of their lives, their friends, and their parents, but bad behavior was quickly silenced.

Mansi had given the lives of his three generations of American children to God the day they were born, and while their deaths would hopefully be a moment to celebrate, he had bonded with them in a fusion of necessity and blood that made him proud. They were his seeds, and someday their deeds would bring him tremendous glory.

Tariq was different. He loved his first born, his Algerian Muslim son, with all his heart, and he knew Tariq loved him and understood he was totally different from Mansi's other offspring, and meant for a much different purpose. He was not meant to die young, but rather destined to have Algerian sons to further the family bloodline.

Mansi loved him as much as a father as a friend, as comrades in arms, men of a common purpose. Tariq had not only done a great job training Derek, he was turning out fifteen or twenty well-disciplined young soldiers every year. Tariq had been managing the Madrassa since 1998, and the school was flourishing. Like Mansi and Hashim before him, Tariq had lived in the labyrinth of the dying old buildings most of his life, first as a student, then as an instructor. Now he was in control of the entire complex and over fifty devoted employees. Extremely disciplined, he demanded perfection from his staff, but his modest, hard-working style quickly earned him the respect, trust, and ultimate commitment of everyone involved. A graduate of the program himself, he understood what was required of both the instructors and the students to survive.

Hashim was delighted with the school's progress. The nineteen potential graduates this year were the second most ever. There were now twelve different instructors, all university-educated and all very committed to the cause. Tariq and two of the men were involved in mind control and military training, and led the study of the Koran.

The other nine men and one woman taught typical but accelerated English, French, Arabic, math, history, and geography classes. All were carefully selected and trained to provide an extra layer of care for the children, and absolute silence was part of their lucrative and rigid employment contract.

Tariq had known nothing his entire life but training and plotting and planning, and that would go on for years. Would Derek be the success Jill was? She was doing fantastic and was being sent to a fighter school at the Top Gun Navy base in San Diego next month. Her incredible success and regular promotions over the years continued to astound everyone, and they had decided to see how far the Air Force would promote her.

At the end of prayers, Mansi met Tariq in his office. A map of the world on the wall sported dozens of little pins posted around the globe. Their warriors were now in twenty-seven different nations.

"So Father, a special one finds his wings. If he is anything like his sister, he could develop into big things, too."

"You have a done a remarkable job, as always, Tariq." When the kids left, they were so thoroughly trained, their loyalty was unquestioned. "Thank you."

Tariq nodded his thanks. "Thank you for your continued support. We now have one hundred and seven warriors in place. One day, Islam will control this world."

"I think it already does."

The world had been running scared for years since 9/11, and they had pushed the world economy into a massive slump that had cost Western nations and businesses trillions of dollars worldwide. Continuing struggles in the Middle East and across other developing Islamic nations fueled more press than any Cold War ever had, and from Russia to America, the world was terrified of the Islamic freedom fighter.

"I will be back soon with my next and last girl," Mansi said. "I hope she is half of our Jill." Hashim liked to kid him about his initial disappointment almost thirty years ago.

"Three generations of soldiers," Tariq mused. "That is a lot of lives."

Mansi laughed. "Lives, or lies? A lot of both, I guess."

Tariq nodded, but he didn't laugh. "You never lied to me, Father. We have lived a life of purpose."

"Not a family life, but war changes all that."

"You had a good family. I am proud to be your son." Tariq loved all the rumors about his globe-trotting father and his trail of ex-wives. Mansi had quite a reputation.

"You are meant to be my future, Tariq. That was clear from the beginning. I do wish you would marry, and marry soon. You are almost thirty, and I am still without a grandson."

"Yes, well, you know I have a new girl. Maybe she can give me a boy." Tariq heard a few noises down the hall and got up to go. "I'll see you when you two get back."

Mansi laughed. "I hope it's the two of us."

"You've never let us down yet, Father."

~~~

Annette hadn't dated for over five years after Mansi had left, and then she'd had a succession of first dates. Nothing serious had developed though, and she had seriously wondered if she could ever love a man again. All the men in her life were gone, and she didn't know if she ever wanted to go through that kind of pain again. When her father and Paul had died, one counselor had suggested to her that, man or woman, the pain of the loss could be the same. After Derek had been taken, she realized that losing a child was the ultimate agony, but as much as she despised what Mansi had done, she longed for the companionship of a man.

Cliff was so different from Paul and Mansi, and she couldn't get him out of her mind. Physically, he was bigger, but emotionally he seemed a bigger man, too. Maybe it was the tragedy that he had experienced, maybe it was just maturity, but he was so easy to talk to, and after he confided in her about her father's accident, she knew she could trust him. Her mother probably loved Cliff in some way, too. She called him the proverbial "salt-of-the-earth type of guy" with no hidden agenda.

It took three months of dating before they slept together. It had been on her mind long before that, but kids and life gave them little opportunity. One Saturday, it just happened. They had gone to a movie and had been surprised at the lineup as they drove into the parking lot. When they found out that the new hit show was almost sold out and there were no seats together, they decided to go back to Cliff's house and watch a movie instead. They opened a bottle of wine and surfed through the channels, but there wasn't anything that looked too interesting. She laughed when he suggested dancing and thought he was kidding, but then he turned the lights down low, put on a Frank Sinatra record, and reached for her hand.

He bowed. "Could I have the pleasure of this dance?"

Cliff turned out to be a much better dancer than she would have thought, and in a few songs, she found herself melting in his arms. They danced on and off for a few hours before she realized she wanted it to happen tonight. After a few more slow songs, she suggested maybe they would be more comfortable in the bedroom. They had joked with each other about how little sex that they'd had in the last ten years. Somehow that absence made it a little easier, knowing it would be starting over for both of them. Cliff was slow and tender, and she came more times than she could count. She wondered how she had lived without sex all this time. They cuddled afterwards and spooned like only two lovers could, but then she felt her throat tighten, and she started to cry.

"What's wrong?" Cliff asked, kissing the back of her head.

"Nothing with you," she whispered. "It's me . . . I hope I'm not bad luck for you. I haven't had very good luck with men in my life so far."

"Then I get to be the knight in shining armor."

"You already are."

"It's you I want to save; it's you I want to love."

Annette blinked at the word *love*. "What are you saying?"

"I love you, Annette. I have for a while now."

"Really?" She choked. "Really?"

"Yes, I do. I love you so much. You are the best thing that has happened to me in a long, long time." Cliff pulled the hair away from her back and kissed her softly on the neck. It felt divine.

"Cliff Billings, I never thought it would happen again, but I think I love you, too."

"You do?" He tried to sit up, but she pulled him back down into the bundle of sheets.

"I do. I wasn't sure if I could ever love a man again, but I do. I love you." She turned to meet his kiss. What had she been waiting for?

"I'm glad to hear you can love again."

"That's because you are so wonderful." She felt the hot tears run down her face and onto his as she kissed him, but she didn't care. They were the first tears of joy she had shed in a long, long time. "I am very happy you came into my life."

"I feel the same way about you, Annette. I really do."

~~~

A few weeks later, Marie received an invitation to the special presentation at Trainor Jets in Long Beach. The invitation was to Mrs. Madison and her family, but Annette figured Art wouldn't mind if she brought her new boyfriend and his daughter. Trainor Jets was presenting mockups of its latest model, the Freedom Five, the revolutionary new plane Art had dreamed about for decades and they had seen on TV earlier. The jet was apparently still years away from FAA certification, but preliminary models were set up for inspection.

Annette couldn't believe the number of media people who were there. Dozens of cameras filmed the new airplanes inside and out. They were state of the art in almost every way, and the high-tech presentation was impressive. Three computer simulations displayed on the dozen large monitors spread behind the stage were looped with panoramic footage of various Trainor aircraft superimposed over shots of the world's most glamorous cities, including Sydney, New York, Paris, and London. The computer image of the couple sitting leisurely in the nose of the new jet as it landed was mind-boggling.

Cliff was as excited as Derek and Mansi had been years ago, and after Art's speech, they lined up to see the inside. Annette wasn't surprised to see Art Trainor greeting visitors. She thought he must be near retirement age, but he seemed much younger as he worked the crowd with his normal enthusiasm.

"It's the Madisons!" Art exclaimed. "How splendid to see you." His smile was wide and warm as ever.

"Mr. Trainor, you did it," Marie said.

"Not yet, dear, not yet, but soon. And remember, it's Art."

"Art, this is Cliff Billings," Annette said, introducing her fiancé.

Art pumped Cliff's hand. "Cliff, it's nice to meet you."

"Thanks, Mr. Trainor, but we've actually met before. I used to work for you as a security guard, many, many years ago. You introduced yourself one time."

Art searched Cliff's face but shook his head. "I'm sorry, but I just can't place you."

"It was only part-time, and it was a long, long time ago, but I was impressed you had made the effort to say hello."

"I try to say to hi to everyone at the plant, but over the years, there have been thousands of employees. Where do you work now, Cliff?"

"I'm a deputy sheriff in Orange County."

"I feel safer, even though you're outside your jurisdiction," Art joked. "Come, let me tell you about this new plane. Care to sit down and test the chairs?"

The cockpit was now a room built for two. Marie sat down in the right black leather chair. She leaned back. "It's really soft."

Cliff took the left-hand seat. He was grinning like a kid. "Wow! There are no controls!"

No wheel, no stick, no throttles, no rudder pedals, no banks of switches and lights, just a bank of four nineteen-inch LCD video panels. The cockpit was paneled in the same ebony wood that accented much of the main cabin, and it looked more like an investment banker's desk than the business end of a jet. Four cup holders looked large enough for grande lattes.

"Controls? Sure there are." Art leaned forward and tapped one of the recessed buttons that were just below the counter that ran under the screens. A door in the center of the lower console slid open. A black wireless keyboard, with a built-in mouse, sat in the middle of drawer. "Here you go."

"Wow," Cliff repeated.

"That's how you control the plane?" Marie shook her head in disbelief. "Harold would never have believed it."

"He probably wouldn't like me anymore," Art joked. "One day, they're not going to need flight instructors anymore, either."

Marie smiled. "Don't be silly. But once you're up in the air, it probably doesn't feel much different, does it?"

Art grinned and patted her on the shoulder. "Marie, you couldn't be any more right. It feels exactly the same, and it will be a lot safer. Look, let me show you." He tapped a few keys, and the night skyline of New York City appeared. "Where would you like to go?"

The graphics were remarkably clear as the gorgeous skyline of downtown Manhattan magically wrapped itself around the windshield. Annette was amazed by how real it looked. The Empire State Building was off to one side, and the image moved slowly to the left as the plane banked. A slight thunk below their feet made everyone look down.

Art grinned again. "It's the landing gear simulation. The software programmers wanted to make the demonstration as realistic as possible."

The plane continued its slow bank, and in seconds, the 7,000-foot runway at LaGuardia airport filled their view.

"Will it be that easy?" Annette asked. It looked like an incredible computer game.

"To the user, yes. You will type in or talk in the details of the flight you wish to take, and the computers will do the rest. They monitor for other traffic, weather, requests, or commands from the air traffic controllers, just like a pilot would. If anything threatens to affect or interfere with their flight plan, they can immediately calculate the best course and action. Humans can't respond anywhere near as quickly." Art brought all the video screens to life. Maps, cameras, fight plans, and flight statistics filled the multiple software windows spread across the four large color displays. It was an impressive array of information.

"Amazing," Cliff said, as impressed as everyone else. "But what happens if the computer crashes?"

Art tapped a few other keys, and a configuration of four computers networked together appeared on the screen on the right. "The plane is equipped with four identical computers, three for backup. The chance of them all suffering a total failure at the same time is statistically less than zero."

"We saw you on TV a few months ago," Marie said, "but seeing it up close, it's just incredible. It's still hard to believe. Are these planes ready to fly?"

"No, not for a few years yet, and then there will be an extensive certification process that could take a few years, but it shouldn't be too long much longer."

"In my lifetime?" she persisted.

"Absolutely," Art laughed. "Within the next decade or so."

Marie got up out of her seat. "And you're sure they will fly?"

"The plane is basically a Freedom Four that we have lengthened and reconfigured." Art was beaming. "That was part of the plan to start with. Much more profitable this way, and all part of the master plan. The Freedom Five would fly tomorrow; it's the software and the tremendous computer infrastructure on the ground that's being developed as we speak that is the hold-up. That, and a few doubtful senators."

"Well, I've been a big fan for years, Art," Marie said. She had always liked the affable engineer.

"Yes, you have, and I'm so glad you came today. Can I call you up when I get these in the air? I'll take you up for a flight. I owe Harold that much, at least."

Marie looked shocked. "Me? In one of those?"

"Sure, why not?"

Annette could see Art was serious and decided not to comment, but it still sounded unbelievable. Would anybody really have the courage to get in a plane with no pilots?

Marie laughed and headed for the door. "I'll believe it when I see it, but if you still remember me then, I might just take you up on that offer."

Art followed her out. "Marie, I never forget a promise."

Chapter 10

A few days later, as Annette was getting ready to leave for work, the phone rang. She waved it off, but her mother caught her at the door. "It's your lawyer."

They hadn't talked in months. "Richard, hi."

"Hi, Annette." Richard sounded excited. "You remember Muti Hayan, our attorney friend? A contact of his says he knows where a blonde American teenaged boy is, a boy maybe sixteen or seventeen years old."

"Oh my God, is it Derek?"

Her mom raised her eyebrows at the mention of his name.

"Maybe. The contact thought he heard someone call the boy 'Ansour.' They're going to try and get a picture for us."

"It must be Derek!" She couldn't believe it. *After all these years!*

"I don't know. Ansour is not that uncommon a name, but it sounds like it could be." Richard was cautious, as always.

"That's fantastic news, Richard, fantastic!" Annette didn't want to hear any doubts. "So what do we do now?"

Richard coughed. "Muti's contact wants five thousand dollars to show us where your boy is."

Annette didn't care about the money. "Is he in Algeria?"

"Yes, on the outskirts of Algiers somewhere."

"We pay five grand, and he takes us to Derek?" Annette looked at her mother for a reaction.

"Yes, he'll show us where the boy is; then it's up to you on what to do. You won't have that many options, and not all of them will necessarily be legal."

"When will we get a picture?"

"I don't know. Hopefully today, but I don't know. I've pressed my contact, but he wasn't sure. Soon."

"Let me think about this, and call me as soon as you get that picture." Annette hung up and explained to her mother what was going on.

Marie raised her eyebrows, but her words were supportive. "That's a lot of money, but if it is true . . ."

"That's what crossed my mind. That would be cheap. I've spent a lot more than that on attorneys over the years. But there's no guarantee it's even Derek."

"But what if it is? What can you do?"

"I don't know. I'd better call Cliff."

Cliff picked up on the first ring, listened patiently, and then answered a few of her questions. "That's another country," he said, "and you know their laws better than I do, but your son is seventeen, you probably can't force him to do anything. He's an adult; all you could do; is ask him if he wants to come back."

Annette's mind had conjured up all sorts of ugly thoughts over the years. "He might not care about me anymore. He might even like living in Algeria."

A few days later, Richard faxed over a picture. The photo was from a distance and appeared to be on a soccer field. It was a little hard to make out, but it did look like it could be Derek. Tall, lanky, long hair. That night, after the girls had gone to bed, Annette, Cliff, Marie, and Val opened a bottle of wine and stared at the photo of Derek. Annette had dug out a few pictures of Derek from before, and they compared them, then and now.

Marie seemed pretty sure it was her grandson. "Look, same eyes, same nose."

Val wasn't sure. "I couldn't say. He sure is cute, though."

Annette had a magnifying glass out and scanned his face. He was smiling back towards the camera, his face frozen in time. "He loved to play soccer. Mansi bought him a ball before he could even walk."

"Okay, you all seem to think it's him," Cliff said. "Now what?"

"I think I have to pay, but I want to be close by in case Derek wants to leave."

"What?" Marie looked horrified. "Go there again?"

"Yes, Mother." She had thought it through a dozen times already. "If Derek wanted to leave, I would want to be close by and offer help. Maybe if he sees me, he will want to come, but if it's somebody else he doesn't know, he might not trust them."

"He might not even recognize you, Annette," Cliff warned. "He was seven. He might not trust you."

"I have to try, Cliff, I have to try."

"You know I'm on your side, but that country..." Marie's voice softened.

Annette remembered all the kids with guns. "I know, but if we travel with a bodyguard again, and stay out of the trouble areas, we should be all right."

Cliff raised his hand. "You told me how scary it was the last time you went. Are you sure you really want to do this? If he's seventeen and he wants to come home, he might just figure out how to do that, with or without you. Why don't you try to get him a message and see what happens?"

Annette had thought about that, too. "What if he needs money, or help? No, I want to be there, just in case."

Marie shrugged her shoulders. "I've had nightmares about that city. But I'll go with you."

Annette knew that at sixty-six years old, her mother would find it to be a long, hard trip. "You don't need to go this time, Mom. I've been there once. I'll be okay."

"You don't think you're going there alone, do you?" Cliff said.

Annette smiled at Cliff but turned to Val. "No, I thought I'd ask Val to go."

Val started laughing. "Algeria?"

Cliff slapped his hand down on the table. "I think I'm being set up... but I'll go with you."

"I was hoping you would say that," Annette said. She would feel much safer with him by her side.

"Yeah, well, what am I going to do? Sit here why you organize another all-female search-and-rescue team? My male ego can't allow that."

Annette rubbed his hand affectionately. "You don't have to come, Cliff. This is not your problem. You have your own life to live. I was fine last time; I'll be fine again. But do you think you would still like me as a brunette?"

Cliff grinned. "You're part of my life now, Annette. I love you, and if you need to do this, I need to go with you."

Annette leaned over and kissed him. "I love you, too, but this will take time and money. It wasn't cheap."

"I haven't gone anywhere in years, and I've got lots of time off coming. I'll take a few pictures and call it a vacation."

Marie laughed. "A vacation from hell."

Annette called Richard the next day with her decision. He was less than enthusiastic and tried to talk her out of it again.

"Muti said his contact thinks something big is going on," he said, "but he didn't know what. Let's test the waters first, have Muti deliver a message from you, see if Derek will even talk to you."

"What did he mean, something big going on?"

"I have no idea. Child slavery, prostitution, terrorism, who knows? You know how dangerous that country is."

Annette shuddered at the ugly words. "If I'm going to pay five thousand dollars, then I want to see him with my own eyes."

"The country is not much more stable than ten years ago. Annette, you could get killed."

She could hear his fatherly disapproval. "We went through this last time, Richard."

~~~

It didn't appear that much had changed at the Algiers airport. Customs and immigration appeared as stiff and distrusting as they had been years ago. Cliff was questioned twice about being a policeman, but when Annette added that a lawyer was waiting for them, the officers let them through. She could see that Muti had lost much of his hair, but he looked healthy. As always, he looked very neat and business-like in a jacket and tie. He had a different bodyguard, another big, burly young man who looked at them suspiciously.

Muti embraced Annette and gave her a light peck on each cheek. "Mrs. Ansour, it is good to see you again. I was expecting a brunette."

"It's Madison now, Annette Madison. It's great to see you. This is my good friend, Cliff Billings."

Muti bowed politely and offered his hand. "Mr. Billings, it is nice to meet you. Come, I have a car waiting for us."

Annette was anxious for news. "When do we meet this man?"

"Tomorrow night. Please come. We will talk in the car."

Inside the car, a driver was waiting with the motor running. The bodyguard opened the trunk, then stood back and scanned the people on the sidewalk. Cliff loaded the luggage in the trunk and followed Annette into the back seat. Muti climbed in the back as well and left the driver's seat for the bodyguard, who got in last.

The driver said something proudly about a new airport. Earth-moving equipment was hard at work, tearing open a huge tract of land west of the old terminal building, but as soon as they turned onto the freeway towards downtown, she was reminded of how dense and poor it was. It reminded her of Mexico. Half-finished buildings stood, with rebar sticking up, waiting for new floors, side-by-side with dilapidated shambles of the last few hundred years. Satellite dishes seemed out of place, but protruded from almost every roof or balcony.

Scores of armed men wearing several different types of uniforms seemed to be everywhere, watching and directing traffic and guarding entrances. Muti said it was normal. Guards were highly visible at their hotel. She kind of liked the El Aurassi with its oversized rooms and incredible views.

The meeting with the journalist was set up for the next afternoon. While Annette was disappointed that it couldn't be sooner, they both needed food and sleep badly.

Over breakfast, Muti retold the story and answered all of their questions. It was as Richard had said. "He heard I was looking for an American boy and called me. He said he can get close enough that you will be able to identify your son, but he would only meet me if you came. That way he thought he would be safe, that I wouldn't be selling him out."

"Selling him out?" Annette asked. "To who?"

"That I do not know, but he said it could be very dangerous." Muti paused and smiled oddly. "People are killed and disappear all the time. Journalists who get too close to the truth are a prime target. This meeting could be very dangerous."

"You sound more worried than ten years ago."

They were alone in the corner of the restaurant, and no one paid them much attention. Nevertheless, Muti was nervous and glanced around again before continuing. "I am. He thought they might be into child-trafficking."

"Jesus . . . I'm sorry, I don't mean to swear." Annette knew far too much about that ugly addition to the complex world of child abduction, and how some countries were turning a blind eye to much of the prostitution that too often ended up fatally for the young girls and boys involved. She shuddered at the ugly thoughts. "If it is Derek, what can we do?"

Muti's wry smile asked another question: "Legally . . . or otherwise?"

That was easy. "He took the boy with no regard for me or the laws of the United States," she said. "I say, fight fire with fire."

"Honey, we can't just go breaking laws here," Cliff warned in a loud whisper. "You could end up in jail."

Muti Hayan nodded. "We – you, especially – have to very careful. You don't want to be arrested by the police. The court system here is not as swift or as fair as that of the United States." He looked around at the other patrons again and then went on, "By 'otherwise,' I meant possibly taking the child yourself, if he will come with you. He is what, seventeen years old? Maybe he will come voluntarily if you can meet with him. That would not be illegal."

Cliff raised his hand. "Annette, we talked about this. There is no sense getting ourselves into trouble. If this is him, and we get a chance, it has to be Derek's decision. He's seventeen years old. He is a man and will have to want to come back."

Annette agreed. "Yes, he has to want to come home."

Annette and Cliff managed to stay awake until around five in the afternoon before falling asleep for twelve hours. It was dead quiet outside when they awoke early the next morning, and they thought it would be a safe time for a quick walk, but the armed guards finishing the night shift wouldn't let them go. It was too unsafe even at that early hour, so they did a few laps around the hotel. Between the big wide staircases that connected the various levels of the building and the short roads that led to the parking lot and the pool, they managed to make a few laps into a little hike.

Penned into the hotel made the hours drag, but eventually, at four o'clock, Muti pulled up. Annette had almost forgotten how badly deteriorated the Casbah was. Chunks of stone and brick were missing from both the road and from many buildings. Neglect and decay were evident everywhere. They parked on a street that had little traffic, but the café down near the corner seemed busy.

Muti checked his watch; it was a few minutes before five o'clock. He repeated the brief plan. "Our contact is a freelance journalist. He won't tell me who he is, but he said he would walk by the car. If he felt comfortable, he would go into the café but stop at the entrance for a moment and look up at the sky. We are supposed to go in and order coffee, and then he will join us."

They watched in silence as a few groups of young men wandered by and eyeballed the car. Annette knew trouble could develop quickly and braced herself, but the bodyguard made eye contact, and the boys quickly carried on. A few men staggered out of a side street, then headed off the other way. The street was quiet for a few long minutes. Then a lone figure emerged from shadows on the other side of the street and headed in their direction. The man walked quickly, glancing around nervously a few times. It was hard to tell what he looked like. He had the hood up on his light blue windbreaker, which obscured most of his face, but Annette could see a dark beard and black, horn-rimmed glasses. She wondered if they could trust him. Five thousand dollars would be a lot of money in Algeria.

Muti whispered, "That could be him."

They all stared as the man walked the last hundred feet to their car. As he passed, he looked directly into the car, and his eyes rested on Annette for a second. Without a word or a sign of recognition, he kept walking and headed straight for the café. At the entrance, he stopped and looked up at the sky.

"It's him," Muti said, turning to Annette and Cliff. "Everything is okay."

Annette reached for the door.

"Wait," Muti cautioned. "Let him get inside first."

As the man got within a few feet of the door to the café, a car slid around the corner and raced towards them. Machine-gun fire burst from two hands that reached out the windows, and the bullets tore through the man and splattered blood across the wall as he crumpled to the street.

Annette was stunned. "Oh my God, he's been shot!"

The car started to accelerate, then it suddenly slowed as it came abreast of Muti's Citroën. The three men with the black masks eyeballed everyone in it before the driver hit the gas and they zoomed off again. Annette was stunned, but there was no mistake in the three pairs of cold black eyes that had sized up everyone in the car.

Muti hissed, "We must get out of here, now!"

As they started to drive away, Annette pointed at the prone body lying on the sidewalk. "He's been shot. We have to stop! We can't just leave him."

"We have to leave. They might decide to come back for us. I think it's probably too late for him." Muti poked his bodyguard. "Okay, stop." The driver pulled the car up alongside the fallen man. The rapidly spreading crimson pool seemed to answer the question, but the bodyguard jumped out and checked. The man was twisted over on his back, and Annette had to look away as the bodyguard shook his head. The blood had started running over the curb in a thin stream.

"We are lucky they didn't shoot us," Muti said.

They started to drive away before the security man was fully back inside the car. The door slammed just as he pulled his head in.

Annette felt her heart pounding. "My God, what have we done?"

"We haven't done anything," Cliff said. "We don't know what that man was just killed for. He could have been into all kinds of things."

"What about my son? He was going to tell us where Derek is. Surely this man had some connections somewhere."

Muti looked apologetic. "I know nothing of this man. He contacted me."

"But what about Derek? Surely this man told someone else."

Muti looked at her sympathetically, but his voice wasn't very encouraging. "We will go to the police and tell them what we saw. Maybe they can find something in his notes."

Cliff had his arm around Annette and held her close. "First, let's get out of here."

The police asked dozens of questions about the murder, but after realizing how little the visitors knew about the dead man, they lost interest. The police captain ended the meeting by promising to contact Muti if any evidence of an American boy turned up, but he didn't seem very hopeful. The day before they left, they went back to the police station and found the same officer in charge.

He repeated the findings they had already been given. Nothing related to any American teenage boy had been found in the journalist's things.

Muti drove them to the airport and apologized several times for how badly things had gone. "I am so sorry. I thought we were so close."

"I sure never wanted anyone to die," Annette murmured. She felt awful. It was hard not to blame herself. She would feel at fault for the journalist's death for the rest of her life. No Derek, and another dead man. What a record.

"Many journalists have been killed or disappeared, and most of the sane foreign correspondents are long gone," Muti said. "This man, he lived in a dangerous world and knew the dangers. It is not your fault."

She wiped the tears away as they pulled up in front of the departures terminal. "I don't know if I can ever forgive myself, but thank you, Muti. Thank you so much. You got us close, and I thank you for all your efforts. I hope someday your country finds a more peaceful way to exist." She motioned to the heavy security around the airport terminal.

In Arabic, Muti said, "God willing."

That was one thing all faiths could agree on. "Yes, Muti, God willing."

They spent the night in Paris, and while Annette tried to find some joy in the city, the heavy presence of French security troops, many heavily armed with machine guns, only reinforced her gloom. She couldn't remember seeing so many police officers years ago when she had come with Mansi, but they seemed to be everywhere now. It wasn't just Algeria. The world had become a police state. Even Cliff had noticed.

They flew home the next morning through Washington Dulles, and as they sat and waited for their connecting flight to Orange County, a flight from Frankfurt disembarked at the gate next to theirs where a small crowd waited.

A few dozen U.S. soldiers, all young men and women, filed up the ramp to the cheers of the welcoming committee. Signs congratulated them on their service in Iraq. Annette thought about the gruesome pictures that appeared daily on the news and the mounting death toll of American military personnel. Many weren't much older than her Derek. Maybe, in some ironic way, she was lucky.

~~~

Cliff was glad to be back at work. California crime never ceased, but in contrast to what they had just gone through, it seemed somehow under control. They had speculated all the way home. The thought of human trafficking had been almost too much for Annette to bear, but the alternatives weren't much better. Drugs, murder, prostitution, terrorism, gangs . . . They were all deadly games. It was even possible the journalist had been working a few different sides, and maybe he was killed for double-crossing someone.

Years of dealing with distraught victims had taught Cliff a lot about human reactions and emotions, and he used a dozen plausible scenarios to assuage Annette's guilt. It wasn't her fault in any way. She had simply been reacting to what others had started, and it had been, as everyone had said from the beginning, very dangerous for everyone involved.

He decided to call an old friend of his in the FBI. Rick was stationed in Washington, D.C., but originally from Anaheim, and he usually stopped in to see Cliff when he was back in Southern California. They had met five years ago when Cliff had been taking a few courses at Quantico.

"Rick? It's Cliff Billings."

"Hey, it's Mr. Montana. How are you?" He sounded happy.

"Good. But I need a favor for Annette. She's right beside me. Can I put you on the speaker phone?"

"Sure."

Cliff touched one of the keys before he set the phone down. "You still there, Rick?"

"Sure, buddy. Hi, Annette."

"Hi, Rick, how are you?" Annette had met Rick a few times before.

"Great, thanks for asking. How can I help?"

Cliff explained, "Remember I told you about Annette's son, the boy who was abducted and taken back to Algeria?"

"Yeah, sure, I remember. Any progress there?"

"Progress, I'm not sure, but we went to Algeria a few weeks ago. Annette's lawyer found someone who had seen an American teenaged boy. We thought it might be her son."

"You went there?" Rick said with surprise. "What happened? Did you find the kid?"

"No, the guy who was our contact was killed right in front of our eyes, just as we were going to meet with him." Cliff would never forget that night, either.

Rick whistled. "Jesus. How was he killed?"

"He was shot by three guys in a car with machine guns. They went by us afterwards and pointed their weapons right at us. Scared the crap out of me. We're lucky they didn't decide to take us out, too. Shit, I didn't even have a piece." Cliff repeated the entire sequence of events as quickly as he could.

"This is quite a tale," Rick said. "I'm still surprised you went over there."

"I wish we hadn't. I feel responsible for that man's death," Annette confessed again.

"How can I help?" Rick offered.

"Is Algeria known for this kind of thing?" Annette asked. "Child-trafficking?"

"I don't think so. Certainly it's not high on their list of indiscretions. But that doesn't mean anything. Who knows what groups are operating inside that country and what they would do to make money or fund their cause."

They had talked about that ugly possibility a lot.

Cliff said, "After the fiasco in Algiers, we were wondering if anything new has ever shown up on her ex. Is it possible you can check his name for us again, see if he's involved in anything more than child abduction?"

There was a slight pause before Rick replied, "Sure. What's his name?"

Cliff spoke slowly and clearly, spelling out Mansi's first and last names. "He says he's Algerian."

Another pause, but they could hear keystrokes.

"Well, let's see what we have on your man," Rick said. "There are quite a few entries and exits into and out of the United States. He's been flagged a few times. Everything checked out, though. He's been in most of the countries in the Middle East and North

Africa, but nothing for ten years. He's disappeared. What did he do for a living?"

"He said he was in the oil business."

"Well, certainly most of the countries he has visited have oil, but many of them are on state watch lists. Who did he work for?"

"UniOil," Annette said. "It's a French company. What does that mean, flagged?"

"The CIA monitors travel in and out of a lot of the world's hot spots, and your ex has been to many of them. Someone thought his extensive travel itinerary dictated a closer look, but he turned up clean. But now ten years later, no one just disappears like that."

"What is his last movement?" Cliff asked. He wondered where the trail ended.

"Ah, he left L.A. for London in July of 1994."

"That's when he kidnapped Derek," Annette shuddered as she thought about the fear and hate they had seen on the streets of Algiers. "But I saw him a few weeks after that, when Mom and I went there."

"Yes, well, chances are Mansi Ansour was a fake I.D., anyway," Rick said. "But the Algerian government won't confirm or deny his citizenship either way. Sorry, but they just don't play ball."

"It's not your fault, Rick," Annette said, "thanks for checking."

"No problem. For what it's worth, he is on the States' watch list. If he ever tries to get back into the country, we will know."

"He was traveling through the Middle East and Africa when I met him," Annette said, sounding like she was trying to defend Mansi. "Maybe he has just stayed in Algeria all this time and raised Derek like he said. Maybe he has never come back to the U.S."

Cliff said what everyone was thinking: "Maybe . . . at least, not under that identity."

~~~

Mansi couldn't have been happier. For all the ten years Jill had been flying, he never had been flying with her. She had asked him years ago after she had first passed her test and received her license, but he wasn't comfortable in small planes and had never made the effort. He had no such qualms now. With almost 2,000 hours in a host of different U.S. Air Force aircraft, Jill Ruffe was not only a well-respected pilot, but an accomplishment he and the military were very proud of.

Mansi had been surprised when Jill had wanted to learn how to fly years ago, but after graduating with honors at USC and racking up almost 500 hours privately in the air, her timing had been perfect. The Air Force had been looking to increase the role of women in combat roles, and as one of only two female students at the Academy in Colorado Springs, Jill surprised everyone when she finished second in her course. Her recent promotion to captain was a reflection of her success at twenty-eight years old.

The rental clerk thought her military qualifications were "awesome," but because she hadn't flown one of the small props for eleven years, he made her take a checkout flight. Mansi thought it was ridiculous, but his daughter laughed it off. He made no protest and waited patiently. When she landed, the laughing flight instructor authorized her rental and gave Mansi a wink and a little advice: "Hang on."

Captain Jill Ruffe was qualified in dozens of military aircraft, single-engine, twins, jets, and props. She could fly the little four-seater upside-down if she wanted.

Mansi winked back. "I taught her everything she knows."

"Where were you up in a small plane before?" Jill asked as she walked around the plane.

"In Algeria, it was a Trainor too, but it was quite old and not well maintained." Mansi ran his hand along the fuselage. "But with you at the controls, I know I am in God's hands."

"God is my co-pilot," Jill said as she finished her inspection of the aircraft. She opened the door to get in. "Ready?"

Inside the small cabin, Jill went over some details and then turned the radios on. Mansi couldn't understand what they were saying at first, then he picked up the words *runway* and *hold*.

It seemed confusing, but he heard her reply clearly: "Roger, Long Beach Tower, two-five-two-Bravo to thirty-four, over."

"Hold at the marker, two-five-two-Bravo." The radio was staticky.

Mansi sat quietly and tried to take it all in. They were fifth in a line of small planes and had to wait as a few large commercial passenger jets landed. It seemed very busy, but in minutes they had worked their way up the line to the end of the pavement and were lined up next to go. "Is it like this everywhere?"

"Long Beach tower to two-five-two-Bravo-Bravo. You are cleared for immediate takeoff on runway twenty-five-Lima, over."

"Tower, two-five-two-Bravo rolling on twenty-five-Lima," Jill radioed as she pushed the throttle all the way in and released the brakes. "This is nothing, Father," she said. "You should see O'Hare."

The twin blade of the propeller pulled the plane down the runway with surprising speed. Mansi watched as the needle climbed past sixty miles an hour, and felt the small plane buffeted by the crosswind. In seconds they pulled free of the earth's gravity and seemed to be floating over the half-mile of unused runway. Jill scanned the skies before turning right and adjusting the trim. As they climbed, Mansi looked out the side window. They weren't very high yet, maybe a few hundred feet. He could see three other small planes taxiing and wondered how many aircraft must be landing and taking off at the hundreds of airports around the United States. Must be thousands.

"What do you think?" Jill said.

"I love it." The Trainor Jets neon sign flashed at them as they passed high over the corner of the huge building. A few dozen private jets were lined up in neat rows behind the plant. "The military has spent millions on you, and I get you to fly me for free."

"Do you have any idea what my mission is yet?"

"No. Just be patient, and continue to do well. As you know, other assets have come in for us, and we want to wait a while. Time is not important. Your time will come, trust me. For now, just enjoy the government's toys. You really love flying, don't you?"

"Almost as much as you, Father." She leaned over and kissed him on the cheek.

"So what does the Air Force want next for you?"

"Well, that's good news. Waiting might be good. There are a few spots open in a bomber course."

"Would that mean the B-2-B bomber?"

Her purpose might still be undecided, but the lists of targets had expanded far beyond anything they had ever originally planned.

"Maybe, but that could be years before I am qualified to command."

Mansi knew time answered all questions. "Everything settled with your mother?"

"Yes. Hank is selling the house and moving back east somewhere. The police say they have no suspects, but feel it was definitely a drug-related crime. Nobody has said anything about any file."

~~~

Annette sent the same basic letter each and every time. The paper would vary, but she always wrote the note by hand. This one was to her congressman.

> *Dear Mr. Cox,*
> *One more week has passed without the safe return of my son, an American citizen, who was taken almost ten years ago. I ask very little of my government, but in this matter I must be relentless...*

She had been writing Washington once every few weeks for ten years, but other than a few occasional and strictly official replies citing nothing but a lack of progress, she never heard another word through any channel about Mansi or her son. It was like they had vanished. She thought about Derek every day, trying to imagine what he must be like – how tall he might be, how handsome . . . But as her love for Cliff and Lisa deepened, her pain at her loss softened, and she prayed again and again, to an unknown god, that somewhere, somehow, her son was at least healthy and happy.

Part Two

Chapter 11
Present Day

A fresh-faced young man named Tony greeted Annette and her family in the lobby of the Trainor Jets offices at the Long Beach Airport. "This way, please," he said. "Mr. Trainor will meet us in a few minutes."

No more than twenty-five years old, tall, blonde, Tony answered a few questions and then flirted with Lisa and Darcy as he escorted them all down the short hallway and out the double steel doors to the tarmac. Two other male employees were towing an older-model Freedom Two jet across the apron.

The manufacturing plant always brought back a confusion of memories for Annette. She had gone there many times with her father, mostly to go flying, but over the years he had taken her all over the plant. It was just another day at work for the Trainor Jets aircraft manufacturing company and its 6,300-plus employees; and while her dad would have been retired by now, that could have been him driving the small but powerful Omega push-back tractor hooked to the front wheel of the silent twin-engine.

Many of the hangars and infrastructure hadn't changed in forty years, but the modern building improvements and renovations housed state-of-the-art high-tech manufacturing equipment that made aircraft construction a science today. For Annette, it was still all so unbelievable.

Rows of the new pilotless Trainor Freedom Five private jets were lined up in neat rows outside the hangar, and Annette counted a few dozen aircraft. Almost a squadron, her father would say. As they approached the huge building, the massive doors slid open and revealed a single white Freedom Five jet with no markings other than the black numbers on the tail, N500TJ. The stairs were folded down, and a red carpet trailed all the way from the door to the top of the steps. The royal treatment.

Her mother had been floored by the invitation and especially by Art's personal call, but she only agreed to a ride if someone else went with her. Art told her to bring the entire family and a few friends. Darcy and Lisa thought it was cool and signed on with their grandmother immediately, as did Val. Cliff had figured it was safer than a day patrolling the 405 freeway and said he'd go if Annette would.

Inside, the plane was even more luxurious than the other jets she had seen. The major difference, of course, was the absence of a cockpit. Instead of the normal pilots' seats, two beautiful brown leather ergonomic lounge chairs looked comfortable enough to sleep in, and the dazzling display of video screens was even bigger than the ones Annette remembered.

The young man checked his watch, and, as if on cue, they heard a car pull up and stop. A door opened. They heard someone get out, and an older man's voice said, "Yes, go pick up Joan. We're leaving at five." It was Art Trainor. They all turned as he came up the steps.

"Sorry to keep you waiting," Art said as he came through the door. Sporting his usual jovial smile, he even looked like he had lost weight, but he didn't seem to have lost too much enthusiasm as he exclaimed, "Wow, it's a beauty pageant! You, sir, are one lucky man."

"Except when the bathroom is busy," Cliff said with a grin. He walked over and offered his hand. "We met quite a few years ago when you rolled out the Freedom Four. I'm Cliff Billings." He pointed to the girls. "Lisa is my daughter. Of course, you know Marie and her family."

Art shook everyone's hand and even gave Marie a hug. "I do remember meeting you, and I'm glad you all came. I hope you enjoy your flight."

"It's beautiful, really beautiful," Annette said. She was surprised by Art's warmth as much as the plane. He had never hugged her mother before, and in a way it seemed oddly normal. They had only seen each other occasionally over the years at the roll-outs, but her mother had known Art since he was a teenager fifty years ago.

"I still can't believe this," Marie said to Art. "It sure isn't necessary. Just seeing this plane is incredible."

Art beamed. He might have lost the rest of his hair, but Annette could see he still had the same fire in his eyes. "It is incredible, isn't it?"

"It's so much bigger than the last one," Val said. She had even looked in the bathroom.

"Actually, the Freedom Five is basically the same plane as the Freedom Four," Art said. "We lengthened it and redesigned the interior to maximize the space. This airframe can now carry up to twenty passengers, the most in its class."

"It seems a lot more open up front," Annette said, nodding to the two seats in the nose.

Art turned to look. "Yes, it is. You might not remember, but in the Freedom Four, there was hardware and avionics inside cabinets on both sides of the cabin, and the cockpit even had a door."

"I remember. I sat in the pilot's seat," Cliff said. "It was kind of like on commercial jets."

"Yes, that's right. Well, now, improvements in technology have reduced the physical size of the electronics hardware, and we have relocated all the computers and avionics packages to other parts in the plane. I don't know if I told you before, but there are four high-performance computers on this plane, all independent, yet all networked together and in separate locations on the airframe. But none of them needed to be up here, so we gave the space back to the customer."

"It's long enough to practice putting," Cliff joked.

Art chuckled. "Don't laugh; guys do that."

"Really?" Annette thought he must be joking.

"The plane has a large luggage storage area behind the bathroom, and many clients will pull their clubs out when they are off on a golf weekend."

Marie shook her head. "Has Tiger Woods bought one?"

Art grinned. "No, not yet. He's not easy to convince."

"Who can afford to buy these?" Cliff said.

"Our client list is extensive and comes from all over the globe, companies and individuals. Most of our owners wish to remain as low-profile as possible, but let me just say they include business executives, celebrities, sports stars, and the government."

"A little short for basketball players," Annette observed. She had shown a couple a new home the other day, and she thought about the husband. He was six-foot-seven and asked about higher countertops and doorways. He would have stooped inside the plane.

Art nodded. "Yes, well, while this is the longest plane we have ever built, it's the same fuselage design as the Four, so six-foot-two is still the maximum interior height. Unless one moves up into something like the Boeing business jet, which is basically a converted two-hundred passenger 737 commercial jetliner, a little over six feet is the current standard height inside the main cabin of this class of business jet."

"You know, I noticed that," Cliff said. He stretched, and his hair brushed the ceiling. "I'm six foot exactly, and with shoes on, my head can just touch if I stretch."

Marie looked confused. "So somebody like Michael Jordan would always have to stoop when he walked around the inside of his plane?"

Art laughed. "Yes, Marie, but most people sit most of the time, so it's probably not much of a problem. I think he'll be okay."

"He can probably afford one of those Boeings," Marie said. "Is it too rude to ask how much one of these costs?"

"Interior design can change the price a lot, but the basic model is just under forty-five million."

Cliff whistled. "Wow!"

"Yes, it is a lot of money, but our main competitors, companies like Bombardier and Gulfstream, sell their jets for more, and they still need pilots to fly them, so our jets are a great deal." Art was always selling. "Without pilots to pay, the owner will save a bundle, and the plane will never be restricted by mandatory pilot rest hours. Some of our competitors also have designated rest space in the cabin for the crew for intercontinental flights. That takes up space and eliminates some privacy. Many of our owners like being totally alone."

Val laughed out loud. When everyone looked at her, she explained, "I bet all kinds of things go on at thirty thousand feet. Isn't there a mile-high club?'

They all laughed.

Art's reply got a few more chuckles. "Yes, well, we usually fly above forty thousand feet, so it's the seven- or eight-mile-high club. But what goes on in a Trainor Jet stays in a Trainor Jet."

"No cameras up there," Cliff said. "Probably all kinds of stuff goes on."

"No, there are cameras, remember – four on the outside and two inside. We can turn the ones inside on or off, and each portable LCD screen has a built-in camera, so two-way video communication and conferencing services are available in real time through satellites. It's all possible because of the incredible software programmers I have. They can do anything."

"Everything is run by computer these days, isn't it," Annette said.

"I just hope none of those computers ever gets sick," Marie said.

"We've never even come close to a serious problem," Art replied, "and the FAA flight certification program for the Freedom Five was the most intensive in aviation history."

Cliff sank into one of the soft, oversized leather couches that lined the walls in the rear section of the plane. "How long have these planes actually been flying now?"

"Three years. The first year, 2011, all we flew was freight. No passengers. After we passed flight testing and received FAA approval to start carrying passengers, we started selling planes and offering rentals through our rental and charter company, Fly America, in 2012. This is the five hundredth Freedom Five we have made, and we have had absolutely no problems with the other four hundred and ninety-nine."

"Has this plane flown already?" Val said.

"Yes, a number of times." Art smiled. "I wouldn't want anything to go wrong for my VIPs."

"I still can't believe you remembered," Marie said. "I had forgotten all about your offer."

"I should have called you a year ago."

"Nonsense. You must be very busy."

A man stuck his head in the door. "We're ready to go now, Art."

"Bill, come in and meet our guests."

The man entered the cabin. Ruggedly good-looking, with a tan, unlined face, he looked to be about forty years old.

He smiled pleasantly. "Hi. Bill Simpson, it's nice to meet you."

"Bill, let me introduce Marie Madison and her family. This is Val, Annette, Cliff, Lisa, and Darcy. Marie's husband, Harold, used to work for us, and he taught me to fly many, many moons ago."

"It's nice to meet you," Bill said as he shook hands with Marie. "Does your husband still fly?"

"Unfortunately, my husband died many years ago in an accident outside the plant."

Bill's face fell, and he stammered, "I'm sorry. Art told me that once. I didn't remember the name at first. I feel like a fool."

"Don't be. It was almost forty years ago."

"I'm still sorry."

Art changed the subject. "Bill is in charge of our computer engineering department, and it's his genius that made all this possible."

Annette didn't know much about programming, so she tried a joke to lighten things up. "I hope it's more reliable than my PC?"

Bill grinned confidently again. "It's foolproof, Annette, and we have backup systems for the backup systems."

"Glad to hear that."

"It was a pleasure to meet you folks. I think you'll enjoy your flight. I have to get back to the control center." He disappeared out the door.

Art sat down in the right front seat and pointed to the bank of computer screens. "This is the key to the plane," he said, holding up a small computer disk. He slid it into a slot on the control panel.

Art stared at the screen for a few moments until a message confirmed his status:

<pre>
         RETINA SCAN COMPLETE
         IDENTIFICATION APPROVED
</pre>

The computer displays immediately came to life, and a message on the top left screen asked: *DESTINATION?* Art typed in *CATALINA ISLAND*. A map popped up on the lower right screen, and a dotted line showed a route from Long Beach out to Catalina Island and back.

"How does that work?" Annette asked.

"This is still a prototype. It's not approved by the FAA yet, but there is a small camera in the dash over here, and it compares a scan of my eye to its list of authorized users. It's foolproof."

"I like the sound of that." Cliff said.

"Yes it's very secure." Art agreed. "I'll be glad when we install it on all the planes. It will eliminate the access cards too."

A soothing female voice requested their attention. "Please prepare for takeoff and fasten your seatbelts."

"You can change the flight attendant's voice to whatever you like, male or female," Art explained. "There are fifty different voices loaded, or we can customize one. Please take a seat, any seat. We're ready to go. Marie, would you like to sit up front?"

Marie shook her head. "No, I think back here is fine." She picked a seat in the cluster of four surrounding the coffee table. Lisa and Darcy sat down on one of the couches and buckled up.

"How about you two?" Art pointed at Annette and Cliff. "It's romantic."

"Go ahead," Val said, motioning as she took the chair across from her mother. "I'll check it out later."

"What about you?" Annette asked Art. "Don't you need to sit there to operate the computer?"

Art pushed a small button under the right middle screen. The LCD panel popped out of the dash. He held it up and tapped on the screen. It was wireless. "I'll sit in the back. There really is nothing to do, but I can enter any commands or access any program from anywhere in the plane. Never know when you might get a message."

"Isn't there a keyboard?" Cliff looked around the cockpit.

Art nodded. "There's a wireless one in the second drawer in the middle, but I prefer the touchpad on this screen."

Annette sat down in the left seat, and Cliff took the right side.

Views from the exterior cameras appeared on the far left and far right screens, and the images swiveled from side to side, front to back, above and below, as the cameras constantly panned the area around the jet. A soft whine from the twin engines was followed by the quiet whir of an electric motor as the steps folded quietly up and into the door frame. Annette found her seatbelt and buckled in.

Art sat beside Marie, the wireless screen in his lap. "Watch the main screen, Annette."

The screen opened a live satellite-image weather map. The skies were perfectly clear a few hundred miles in every direction. A small window was rolling through the different views on the outside of the plane, and another window contained their flight status and information, speed, altitude, and fuel. A checklist opened in a third window and started running through key functions as the plane's systems came to life.

Pivoting slowly, the jet turned right and rolled effortlessly out the open hangar door. At the taxiway, the plane stopped while the cameras checked every angle, left and right, front and back, above and under.

"The aircraft is equipped with twenty-two different sensors," Art said proudly, "including four extremely powerful zoom cameras that can see any place on the outside of the plane. Besides the camera on the tail, there are two cameras underneath, one near the front, and one near the back that can swivel three-hundred-sixty degrees. A fourth camera is just behind the pilot's windshield on the top of the aircraft. The computer programs can track and identify every object within five hundred miles – planes, cars, trucks, buildings, even birds."

An all-clear message flashed across the screen. The jet turned left and rolled down the tarmac. Annette looked to her right as they passed the long row of Freedom Fives parked on the edge of the apron. "I feel like I'm in a *Jetsons* cartoon."

"This is nothing like that," Art said. "This plane flies no differently from any other aircraft, and the technology is actually quite old. The Air Force has used drones for years. It was the freeway-in-the-sky technologies that made this all possible. Here, I'll show you." He tapped a few times on his screen. The camera's view of the tarmac ahead of them on the left screen was overlaid with a series of square neon-green boxes. The plane rolled directly into the center of the moving green lines that represented their path to the runway. "It's just like always being on autopilot, and they land jumbo jets on autopilot. Our system isn't that different. We just follow a pre-planned route."

Annette could see the grass of the field as they neared the end of the taxiway, and she felt the jet brake before it turned ninety degrees to the right. The end of the runway was straight ahead, and the plane stopped at the yellow hold line.

The onboard computer radioed the control tower. "Long Beach Departure, Freedom five-zero-zero-Tango-Juliet. Ready for takeoff on twenty-five-Romeo."

The response from the control tower was quick. "Roger, five-zero-zero-Tango-Juliet, hold for clearance, Charlie-seventeen on final."

"Why bother with the voice commands at all?" Cliff asked.

"That's only for now," Art explained. "Once automated computers are installed at every airport in the country; even the voice-activated software will become obsolete. The computer will instantly be able to update all weather data and all pertinent flight data and instructions without talking to anyone."

"Is there TV?" asked Lisa, looking around the spacious cabin. Four more even larger LCDs were built into different places along the cabin.

Art laughed. "Absolutely, and lots of video." He tapped on the touch pad screen, and a large, semi-transparent plastic sheet rolled out of the ceiling near the rear of the plane. It pivoted until it was at an optimal viewing angle for the two teenagers. "Forty-two-inch fully flexible displays for your viewing pleasure. There are two more, and I can put any software window or camera angle up there, too." A few more finger-taps brought up the forward view. The button at the end of the runway was a couple of hundred yards away. Annette had heard about these new electronic TV screens. As thick as cardboard and not much heavier, they could even be rolled up for easy transport. The color was as vivid and intense as any TV she had ever seen.

"What made you think this was all possible, Art?" Marie asked.

"I worked on the software programs for NASA back in the sixties and always felt that if they could guide a spacecraft to the moon, surely they could control planes in the atmosphere. After the advent of GPS, NASA opened the doors in the nineties when they decided to try and develop safer skies with a program called AGATE, which is short for Advanced General Aviation Transport Experiments. AGATE looked at dozens of new technologies and theories, and Trainor Jets has just taken it another step. Now, topographical maps, terrain warning systems, infrared night vision, high-resolution digital video cameras, microwave, and other global positioning data are all electronically mapped together and can position a plane within one cubic foot anywhere in the continental United States airspace. Anywhere. On the prairies, in the mountains, on the runway, at forty thousand feet."

"Isn't that what radar does?" Marie asked.

"Sort of, but not with this kind of accuracy." Art grinned. "The entire U.S. air space has been digitized on hard drives and is updated in real time for weather, traffic, and air traffic control instructions. The planes know exactly where they are at any given second, and the computer simply follows a digital map through the sky while sophisticated collision-avoidance systems protect the plane from every possible incident in the jet's immediate and significant airspace. Queuing, sequencing, separation, landings, and take-offs are now easily handled by computers."

"It is all still hard to believe, but computers are amazing. And that helps with air to air collisions too I guess? I remember the AeroMexico crash over Cerritos. It was awful. People on the ground got killed too." Annette said.

"Yes, that was awful. Traffic Collision Avoidance Systems, early TCAS systems were started back in the fifties, after the Grand Canyon disaster, but not mandated by the FAA until the 80's."

"But there have been air to air collisions since then." Cliff said. "I remember a DHL jet hit a Tupolev over Germany a few years back."

"Yes, the Überlingen mid-air collision .That was an air traffic controller error. Had the pilots listened to their TCAS instructions they would have been okay. Computers definitely would have saved those planes." Art said.

A deafening roar filled the cabin, and they all turned to look out the front window. A huge military transport floated past. The grey giant seemed to hang over the runway before bursts of smoke off the dozens of tires lay evidence to a perfect landing, and the U.S. Air Force behemoth disappeared down the runway.

Annette had never seen a plane that big in her life. "What was that?"

Art watched it race by, too. "C-17 Globemaster. Boeing used to make them here."

The radio squawked: "Five-zero-zero-Tango-Juliet, you are cleared for immediate takeoff on twenty-five-Romeo. Check in over the outer marker."

"November five-zero-zero-Tango-Juliet, rolling on twenty-five-Romeo," the onboard computer replied.

They rolled forward, turned onto the blackened concrete, and stopped. Annette swiveled around. Everyone was grinning, but no one said a word. They could all feel the plane shudder slightly from the torque as the engines revved up, then the brakes released and they raced down the runway. In seconds, the powerful jet was airborne and pulling away from the ground. Take-off was a lot faster, but it took her back to sitting beside her dad in the small plane she was a kid, and she wished again he was still alive and could see what incredible advances had been made in flying.

The video displays were constantly changing camera views, but the plane was perfectly centered as it headed into the ever-changing series of green boxes. Below, the 405 freeway was thick with traffic. As they started a slight left bank, downtown Long Beach swung into view. One of the cameras made a pass down the beach, and they could see Catalina Island glowing in the distance.

"Long Beach Departure, November five-zero-zero-Tango-Juliet, clearing the outer marker, over."

Annette thought the computer had the most perfect enunciation. "It's amazing!" she said.

The air traffic controller's response was much harder to understand in comparison, she thought. "Copy, five-zero-zero-Tango-Juliet."

The *fasten seat belt* sign clicked off. Art stood up and turned to Marie. "Come look at the view from up here."

Marie followed Art up to the front of the plane. Annette got up and let her mother sit down. The view was awesome. Ten thousand feet below, the Catalina Island airport looked far too small a strip of gray to possibly land on, and a few miles away, the boats bobbing in the harbor seemed happy and free.

Art set the flat panel down on the desk and opened the fridge. The small galley was exquisite in ebony wood and brushed stainless steel, and a well-stocked bar was visible through the self-locking glass doors in the top of the cabinet. "This calls for a little celebration," he said, pulling out a bottle of California champagne.

Annette got up and held the glasses as he poured. When they all had a glass, Marie raised her glass and offered the first toast.

"Here's to your success, Art. It's absolutely amazing. Harold would be so proud of you."

"Thank you, Marie, thank you." Art looked like he wanted to say more, but his eyes glistened in the awkward silence.

Marie smiled. "I felt like I watched you grow up with this plane. You have been talking about this day for a long time."

"Grow old, you mean?" Art said with a grin.

She laughed. "That, too."

"I did grow old with this plane. This plane took forty years – thirty years in concept, planning and design and ten years to build."

"Kids take less time than that," Cliff said.

"Yes, thank God for that," Art said, looking at Darcy and Lisa. "My son took twenty-nine years, but he finally got his law degree last year."

"Better late than never," Marie said.

"Yeah, boys . . ." He shook his head and laughed. "We just got him out of the house two years ago, too."

Annette saw Cliff's look, but Art had no way of knowing about her situation, and she wasn't going to bring it up now.

Art had to go to a meeting when they landed, but he insisted they stay and finish the second bottle of champagne they had opened. Left alone, they took a few more pictures and laughed at their good fortune. It was easy to imagine how incredible it would be to travel by private jet, and by the time they left, nobody even cared anymore about the absence of pilots. The quality and luxury swallowed them up as they talked about a life of travel and all the places one could go with a toy like that.

"Maybe we should rent one for our honeymoon?" Cliff said.

Her fiancé wasn't extravagant too often. "Okay, if we win the lottery."

"Art told us those smaller ones will be cheaper. I've saved a few sheckles."

"Okay, that's it, time to go," Annette joked. "You've had too much to drink."

Cliff had agreed to be designated driver, and he laughed. He hadn't touched the wine. "Drunk passengers coming off private jets? I never thought about that. Maybe I'd better run some security checks at John Wayne."

"Always the law enforcement angle, huh, Cliff?" Val kidded.

He grinned. "Never know what's going on behind closed doors."

~~~

Derek watched the entire flight from the control room at Trainor Jets. The systems and technicians monitored every function of every flight, but they liked to kid themselves that they were the Maytag repairmen of the twenty-first century. Derek had been working as a software programmer at Trainor Jets for five years, and nothing ever went wrong.

N500TJ stopped less than an inch from where it had originally been parked.

"Okay, that's the last flight today," said Bill Simpson. "How are we doing on the updates?"

"I figure another few days," Derek replied. Bill was his boss, but they had become friends in the last few years as Derek had proven his worth. Promoted a few months ago, he was now in charge of all flight-update software. "Then Sudesh will run the stress tests. We should be ready to upload within a week."

"Good. Let me know if anything changes." Bill patted Derek on the shoulder as he left.

"Sure." Derek had been working day and night on the update. Sudesh was his only concern, but his father had said not to worry; he would take care of the senior programmer. He waited until the VIP party had left the aircraft before cutting the video feeds. The two young girls had been hot. So many guests were celebrities, he checked the manifest to see who they were, but the names Madison and Billings meant nothing to him. On the flight plan, they were identified as personal friends of Art Trainor and not potential customers.

~~~

"Will you marry me?"

Cliff stared at Annette. "What? Marry you? Did I hear you right?"

"Yes, I'm proposing to you," Annette replied.

She had been lying awake for an hour, and the more she thought about marriage, the more she knew it was time. They had been living together for over eight years, and Cliff had asked her more than a few times. She had said no each time, citing a host of past and current issues, but he had never gotten mad or disappointed. He had said he was happy if she was happy. He had never let her down once, and he still treated her like a princess. She wondered what she had been waiting for. She loved him a lot and couldn't imagine a future without him. Third batter in her life or not, Cliff sure seemed like an all-star.

"Are you serious?" He kissed her. "Of course I'll marry you, anytime, anywhere."

"I'm sorry I made you wait," she said. Her mother would be delighted.

"Don't be sorry. I told you I'd love you forever."

He said the nicest things. "You're a doll, Cliff. You really are. I'm so glad you came into my life."

"And you mine, you hot little bride-to-be."

"Hot?" Annette pictured herself in a wedding dress. "I'm fifty-six years old, twice as old as the first time I got married."

"I like older women." Cliff kissed her again.

She could taste the garlic she had put in the chicken last night. "Stick with me," she said. "I'm getting older every day." She paused to think. "I don't suppose there's much need to have a long engagement?"

"Not unless you want to marry a retired guy." Cliff had talked about retiring in the spring.

Annette laughed. "Never thought about that this morning. Maybe I'll retire soon, too."

"Really? That would be nice. Still think you'd like to move someday?"

"Yes, I think a change would be nice. I've lived here for thirty years. Why?" They had talked about retirement and living somewhere else more than once. Vacations to the mountains had impressed her.

"Just thinking about my place up in Montana. We could go spend some time up there, once the girls are gone." Cliff had taken her to his old hometown twice over the years, when renters had moved out of his house. An older two-story three-bedroom, the house was a 1960s special and needed updating, but it was on a large, private lot on the aptly named Lakeshore Drive, and Cliff had been fortunate with stable, long-term tenants. Only a few blocks from the golf course, and with spectacular northern views of the lake, the ski hill, and the mountains of Glacier National Park, it was a hard place to leave.

"That sounds like a good idea." She had loved the feeling of being all alone down at the end of the tranquil lake or at the top of some trail with vistas for miles.

Cliff nibbled at her neck. "Will the girls approve of our union?"

"I think we had their blessing years ago." Darcy and Lisa often joked about their illegitimate parents who lived in sin. "Odd how life turns out. Wouldn't having my son back now make it the perfect dysfunctional American family?"

"Very dysfunctional. Twenty years is a long time. Who knows what has happened to him? Who knows what he would be like today?"

"I'm sorry, honey. I shouldn't have brought it up. Let's not talk about that now." While publicly she had all but given up on ever having Derek in her life again, she still had the faintest hope that someday, somehow, she would at least see her son again. "Let's talk about our honeymoon in Hawaii," she said brightly.

~~~

Cliff put his hands to his ears and watched as the American Airlines 757 came in for a landing. Barely a hundred feet up; the large jet cast a long shadow across the squad car for a moment before touching down a few hundred feet past the button. Telltale blue smoke marked the point of entry. The plane and its passengers were now, at least for the next little while, technically in his jurisdiction. He followed the perimeter road beside the rusty ten-foot-high chain-link fence that separated the field from the roar of the 405 freeway. There hadn't been many security breaches at the Orange County airport, and he sure didn't want any on his watch. It wasn't a beat he relished – usually it was too quiet – but airports were huge targets and required a lot of men to ensure the safety of the passengers and cargo.

A private jet, pure white except for the tail number and the large red letters, *FLY AMERICA*, floated by on its final approach. Cliff pointed at the plane. "That's like one of the planes we went up in."

"It's huge," Will commented as the sleek jet disappear down the runway. "Sure sounds sweet."

"Yeah. Pilots or no pilots, it was pretty damn incredible. Nicer than my house." He could still picture the gold fixtures in the bathroom.

"Something about it still scares me, though," Will said. "It seems like so many things could go wrong."

"I suppose, but our flight was as smooth as could be." Cliff had told everyone at the office about the incredible trip.

"Have you ever been in the Fly America office?" Will asked. "Maybe we should see how tight security is."

"That's a good idea. Let's go over to the rental office."

They drove up the west side of the airport, where the Fly America building looked busy. Inside, it looked similar to a car rental counter, but a wall of large LCD screens displayed everything from weather to onboard cameras to aerial navigation maps.

Cliff thought the young man behind the counter looked tired. "How's business?" he asked.

"Fine, Officer. Is there a problem?"

Cliff read the name off the clerk's company badge. "No, just curious, Bart. How many rentals do you do per day?"

"It varies, and business is getting better all the time. Right now we average about fifty flights a day. About half still fly cargo only, but the other half are paying customers."

"Do you run background checks on all your customers?"

Bart looked surprised at the question. "No, that would be impossible. We do check everyone's credit, but that's it. If they can afford to pay, I guess we'll rent to anyone."

"But everyone goes through a physical security check before boarding, right?"

"Yes, sir, absolutely. Everyone and everything has to pass through a metal detector to get access to the hangar area and to board a plane."

"And I guess everyone knows everyone else who is on the plane?"

Bart nodded. "Usually, although sometimes individuals will share a flight, just like sharing a cab, but they still all go through a security check."

"What about drinking? Do you check on that?"

Bart looked even more surprised. "Drinking? Do we check if people have been drinking before they board? No. Not unless they are really intoxicated."

"So, if someone is drunk, they can still rent a plane?"

"Yes, it's part of what makes our service attractive."

"What about if someone gets off drunk?"

"Is this a trick question?" Bart looked back and forth at the two officers as he searched for a reply. "That probably happens more than we know, but we can't police that."

"Drunks on any plane is a bad idea," Cliff said sternly. "It's something you might want to have management consider. Somebody comes off a plane drunk and then crashes his car on the way home, it wouldn't look good."

"No, sir."

"Can the drunk fly the plane?" Will asked.

"No, the flight is totally controlled here and at the Trainor Jets Control Center in Long Beach. Most of the time it's just a point-to-point rental."

Will nodded as if he understood.

"Anything we can help you with?" Cliff asked. He liked to leave with that invitation. You never knew when someone might spot a security problem.

"Nothing that I can think of Officers, unless you want to book a flight?"

"My wife said I could call you if I win the lottery."

They thanked Bart for his time and resumed their patrol up the west side of the field. Dozens of private jets sat inside and outside the hangars that lined both sides of the airport.

Will asked, "If you won the lottery, would you really rent one of those jets?"

"I don't know. It was a little unnerving. I mean, the ride itself was super smooth, and the plane is right out of *Lifestyles of the Rich and Famous*, but it sure seemed weird sitting right up in front of the cockpit like that. Would you?"

"I don't know, but I've thought about it. Trudy and I were thinking of renting one for our thirtieth anniversary; maybe fly up to Vancouver and back. How expensive are they?"

"Art told us it depended on a few factors and fuel costs, but it's over three thousand dollars an hour."

Will appeared shocked at the revelation. "Really?"

"You should have asked back at the rental office," Cliff said, turning back up Redhill. "Maybe you should wait until the smaller ones are converted. Art said they would probably rent for around a thousand an hour."

"That's more reasonable. We fantasized about flying to Vancouver and back, two hours each way or so, maybe four or five grand. I know that's still a lot of money, but for us it would be a trip of a lifetime. Trudy wants to join the mile-high club." Will grinned.

Chapter 12

Art had been to the White House twice before to attend formal state functions with his wife. Norman Kingston had been there on both occasions and guided the Trainors through some of the White House protocol, but he had lost his fourth campaign for office and was now living in Florida.

Art was here today at the request of the President of the United States, another old and good friend, Les Wilby. The general's youthful, charming, and sincere photogenic mannerisms had caught the voters by surprise. His unabashed and unparalleled military career spanned forty years, and his impressive, unblemished background had carried the Democrats to a unanimous vote of confidence at the national convention. With a popular vote of almost fifty-seven percent, the federal election was a surprise to many, but the lifetime soldier had won almost ten percent more hearts and minds than his Republican competitor. He was certainly the people's choice.

The Secretary of Defense, Bill Woutens, would also be at the meeting. A good sign.

Art was ushered into the Oval Office a few minutes after 10:00 a.m. He was surprised to see Norman Kingston having coffee with the President and the secretary.

The ex-senator stood up and stuck his massive hand out first. "Art Trainor, it's great to see you."

Art felt his hand disappear in his friend's giant paw. "It's great to see you, too. I didn't know you would be here."

"Les called me, thought I might be interested." Norman winked. "After all, I did introduce you two."

Art smiled. He owed his old family friend for a lot of things. "I'm glad you're here. Must mean good news?"

President Wilby answered, "Art, I'm glad you could come."

"It's an honor to be here, Mr. President." Art had shaken hands with Les Wilby many times, but it was the first time since the once chief of staff had been elected President.

"In here, it's Les, okay?" President Wilby said. "We're all old friends. Have you met Bill Woutens?"

Art turned to the face he only knew from TV. "No, I haven't had the pleasure. Good to meet you, Mr. Secretary."

"It's nice to meet you, Art," The Secretary was not a very big man, only five foot six or so, but he gripped Art's hand like a vise. "The President speaks very highly of you."

"I'm flattered sir."

Wilby turned to the serving cart and a young man who waited. "Coffee, Art?"

"That would be great, Mr. President. Black, please."

The waiter poured the coffee and handed it to Art. Wilby nodded a dismissal, and the man slipped quietly out the side door.

"Please, have a seat," said the President as he sat down first. "Bill, why don't you bring us up to date on NO LOSS? How's the program going?"

Art surveyed the room for a moment before turning his full attention back to the conversation. The oval office had been on TV since the sixties. Two white couches, both lightly embossed with gold trim, faced each other over the solid oak coffee table. The black leather chairs at both ends of the small setting provided for a total of eight places. Cozy and private, but room for a few very important opinions.

"Excellent, sir, excellent," said Woutens. "I think we're prepared to make a recommendation to proceed."

Wilby pointed to the reports on the table. "What were the results of the latest exercises?"

"Far better than the minimum requirements, Mr. President," Woutens said, picking up and handing copies of the report to the President first. "The computer pilots won decisively, sir. When the autopilot software flies the plane, the pilot can concentrate on killing the enemy. Everything you asked for, you got. The integration of the terrain-following radar and the air avoidance systems worked perfectly with the GPS-based satellites, but it was the video game technology that really opened the doors to true full combat automation and capability."

Art wanted to jump in, but the man was doing a great job.

Wilby smiled. "Explain that to me again."

"Art, you want to take that question?" Bill Woutens deferred.

"Computer games, sir," Art said with a grin. "Air combat video games have built-in parameters that define the capabilities of the enemy against the skills of the player. We employed that theory and programmed the flight performance characteristics of our aircraft into the computer, along with the flight characteristics of all known aircraft, enemy or not. The result was the computer could anticipate any and all moves of its adversary and the jets consistently made the single best move to defeat the enemy."

"How many of our planes were shot down in the simulation?"

"None, sir. Not one," Bill replied. He had opened the report to a page lined with numbers.

The President whistled softly. "Can you imagine? We would never lose another pilot."

Bill Woutens dropped his copy of the report on the coffee table. "Are you ready to move forward, Mr. President?"

Wilby looked out the window. A commercial jet was visible taking off from Reagan National Airport in the distance. When he turned around, Art thought he could see the answer in the President's eyes, but the commander in chief's words left no doubt. "Every pilot costs us millions, every death costs us more. We can't afford to wait."

Art knew there would be many critics, but it had been coming for years. Air combat would never be the same. Even the incredible military dominance that the United States had enjoyed in Iraq had cost American pilots their lives, in training and in combat. "I think you're making a good decision, Mr. President," Art said. "This decision will help ensure American air superiority through the middle of the century."

Norman Kingston concurred. "The United States will be years ahead of any other air force, and without the restraints and liabilities of humans, we can operate twenty-four-seven in any theater in the world. It gives us another level of capability at a greatly reduced price."

President Wilby's smile disappeared into a look of concern. "And we'll be able to keep this under wraps for now?"

Bill Woutens answered, "No one associated with the program has left Area 51 in over two years, and the morale has never been stronger. The men and women on this job all committed to five years inside. They're quite a remarkable bunch."

"Yes, I met some of them last year when I toured the facility," Wilby concurred. "But there will be far-reaching consequences from this technology, and we will need time to see how this affects long-term strategic planning."

Bill nodded. "Yes, sir."

The President turned to Art. "This country is going to be in your debt a long time, Art. Your dream and persistence will save thousands of lives, maybe even prevent future wars."

"Well, thank you, Mr. President. I sure hope so. It's also possible that flying as we know it could eventually become just a sport. Pilots will not be needed to fly planes, so flying will be for pleasure only, much like going for a Sunday drive. And if all commercial aircraft are flown by computers, there will be no cockpit for terrorists to take over."

"Yes, I see that," the President agreed. "But you know we're going to get one hell of a fight from the Air Force. We have thousands of trained pilots and hundreds more in flight school any given day. The commanders and the pilots will fight this conversion."

Bill Woutens answered politically, "You are right, sir, but their families will feel quite differently, and so will the voters."

President Les Wilby broke into a huge grin.

~~~

"Shit!"

Derek looked at the flashing lights behind him and then checked his speedometer. He was doing eighty. He pounded the steering wheel and raised his foot up off the gas. The needle dropped rapidly as he added brakes. He stayed in the center lane, hoping that maybe they weren't looking for him, but in a few seconds the police car had worked its way over and was right behind him. The officer in the passenger seat was pointing to the right. Derek threaded his way over to the shoulder of the freeway and found a safe place to pull over.

The driver, a male officer, got out and came around to the right side of the car. Derek lowered the window, and the cop leaned down and looked in.

"Going a little fast, son. Any particular hurry?"

"I'm sorry, sir. I didn't realize how fast I was going."

"Well, I know how fast you were going. You were doing eighty-four miles an hour, almost twenty miles an hour over the speed limit." The officer didn't sound very happy. "Driver's license and registration, please?"

"Certainly. Just a second." Derek dug out his identification and insurance and handed it to the officer. "I've never had a ticket before. Is there anything I can do? Do I get one chance?"

The policeman looked at the documents closely and smiled. "Sorry, son, it's the computers. Once we enter your license plate number in, it's too late. Excuse me for a minute. Wait here till I get back." He walked to the back of the silver BMW Z4 cabriolet and looked at the license plate.

Derek watched the officer closely in the mirror as he headed back to the police car. He could see the female cop nod her head and point at something in the squad car.

In a few minutes, the officer walked back to Derek's car. "Good news and bad news, Mr. Ansour. You used to have a perfect driving record, unfortunately you don't anymore." The officer handed a ticket to Derek. "You look familiar. You grow up around here?"

He shook his head. "No." He hadn't expected that question.

"Must be someone who looks like you."

Derek smiled in return, thankful for no more questions. "They say everyone has their double."

"Slow down. One of you will live longer."

"Yes, sir." Derek put the ticket in his glove box. He waited until the cop was back in his car before slowly pulling back into traffic.

~~~

Annette climbed the steps up to the podium. The association banner bearing the words *AMERICAN CENTER FOR MISSING CHILDREN* and signs announcing *Welcome Home Dawn* said it all. As the room filled up, Annette thought about the twenty years she had been coming to the meetings. Her first night had only been weeks after Derek had been taken, and now she was the chapter president and delighted to be witnessing the safe return of another child. She adjusted the microphone clipped to her lapel. "Good evening, ladies and gentlemen."

The crowd stopped talking instantly.

Annette looked around at all the eager faces. "What a turnout! Thank you so much for coming. We have a lot of exciting things to talk about tonight. Great news earlier today. Two more countries have signed the Hague Convention."

The room burst into applause. Each new country promised hope for someone. Most of the people in the room were victims in one form or another, and they all understood the relentless frustration the uncooperative nations represented. When the business part of the meeting was finished, Annette took the moment to make her own personal announcement.

"Okay, one last thing before we get on to tonight's star attractions. I have some personal news. I won't be here next month. I am getting married in three weeks and finally going on a honeymoon."

The applause was thick and sustained. Over the years, many of the women had become friends and knew about Annette's loss. They also knew that she had put her heart and soul into the ACMC. In her twenty-year association with the non-profit organization, a dozen more countries had signed the Hague Convention, and hundreds of children had been returned safely to their parents.

"Thank you," she continued. "It's my second marriage, and it took me a long time to trust men again." She paused for dramatic effect. "He is a thirty-year police officer, and I still ran a complete background check!"

The audience roared.

For Annette, at first, the group had represented hope, faint hope, but hope. Then it became therapy, and now it was her mission and part of her life. "But of course, the best news tonight is that Cindy Yaccine's daughter, Dawn, was returned last month from Algeria. Cindy moved here from Denver a few months ago, and we are delighted we could be here with them at this wonderful time."

The applause was deafening as Annette pointed to an attractive blonde woman standing near the side of the stage with her arms around a teenage girl. "Dawn was taken ten years ago, but Cindy never gave up, and today she has her daughter back. Please welcome Cindy Yaccine and her daughter, Dawn."

The girl shifted from one foot to the other and seemed quite embarrassed as all the women stood and broke into applause. A few flash cameras went off, and Dawn raised her hands defensively up in front of her face. Annette knew all too well that some children never fully adjusted, and she wondered what had happened to this pretty girl.

When the official meeting was over, Annette stopped to thank Cindy and Dawn for coming. Dawn didn't seem very happy, and Annette thought of Derek, wondering if he would have been happier if he had been allowed to return. "Thanks for coming, Dawn. You made a lot of mothers happy tonight."

"Maybe their kids will come home soon, too," Dawn replied. "My father thought it would be a good idea to get an education in the states."

"And he might be right." Turning to Cindy, Annette could see how happy she was. "It must have been quite a surprise for you to get that call."

Cindy laughed. "After ten years? I damn near had a heart attack."

Annette turned back to Dawn. "Are you glad to be back?"

"Yes. I like California."

Cindy tried to pull her daughter in for a hug, but Dawn resisted and pulled the other way. Cindy looked embarrassed. "We're starting all over," she told Annette. "It will take some time."

Annette could see the daughter's intensity. "I'm so very happy for both of you. I have a daughter, too. In fact, you look a lot like her. I can't imagine life without her."

"Your son was taken, right?"

"Yes, but it's been twenty years. I've kind of resigned myself to life without a son."

"Well, maybe he will want to come back someday," Cindy said, smiling encouragingly.

"My son would be twenty-seven now," Annette replied. "If he had wanted to, he could have come back on his own a long time ago." She still wondered why he couldn't have gotten in touch somehow. On her down days, she wondered if maybe he was dead.

"How old is your daughter?" Cindy asked.

"Twenty. She's graduating from university next year, pre-med."

"That's wonderful." Cindy turned back to her daughter. "Dawn wants to be a doctor, too."

"You'll have to meet my daughter. She can tell you all about it." Dawn didn't answer.

"My daughter wants to be a pediatrician, work with children," Annette told Dawn. "What kind of doctor do you want to be?"

"A research scientist, work with viruses, stuff like that."

"Well, that sounds interesting." Annette wondered if Dawn was just watching too much TV. She changed the subject. "Do you have other children?"

"Yes, a boy, Trevor. He's ten." Cindy looked at her daughter cautiously. "Dawn never even knew she had a brother until she got back. When she was taken, I was pregnant, but I didn't know it yet. He was born eight months later. I tell you, having that baby saved my sanity."

Annette was more than surprised. Cindy's history sounded a lot like hers. "Did the father know you were pregnant?"

"He didn't, but he does know about Trevor now. Dawn said she told him. I couldn't really stop her, and it's going to be a problem now. His father wants to see him."

Mansi had certainly known Annette was pregnant, but he hadn't seem to care about his unborn daughter. "What are you going to do?"

"I have a divorce and a sole custody order. There is nothing he can do."

"Be careful. Watch Trevor all the time."

Cindy nodded. "Once was enough for me. I watch them both like a hawk."

"My husband didn't want his daughter. All he wanted was his son. I guess I don't understand Islam."

"The Koran is very fair," Dawn said. "It offers more than Christianity, that's for sure."

"I'm sorry." Annette didn't want to get into a religious debate with the teenager. "I didn't mean that in a bad way. Did you study the Koran when you were in Algeria?"

Dawn looked back and forth between her mother and Annette before answering slowly. "Yes, everyone does."

Annette turned to Cindy. "Where in Algeria was your husband from?"

"From the capital, Algiers, but his ancestors were French."

"So was my ex-husband."

"Yes, so many Algerians have some French in them." Cindy flashed a quick but awkward smile. "And it appears they prefer their women blonde."

Something about Dawn intrigued Annette. "Yes, I think you're right. Here, let me show you something else." She dug in her purse for a picture. She found a recent shot of Darcy and handed it to Cindy. "Look. Dawn looks a lot like my Darcy. A lot."

Cindy looked back and forth between the photo and Dawn. "They do look a lot alike. How old is your daughter in this picture?"

"It was taken only a few months ago. She's twenty." Annette took the photo back and offered it to Dawn.

Dawn didn't appear to care until she looked at the picture. Then she managed a small smile. "She's pretty."

"Maybe you two are cousins?"

Dawn's face dropped. "I don't have any cousins."

"What was your ex-husband's name?" Cindy asked.

"Ansour. Mansi Ansour."

Cindy looked surprised. "Mansi? That was my husband's first name, too. M-A-N-S-I."

Annette had never heard of anyone else with that name. "Really?"

Dawn started pulling at Cindy's sleeve. "Can we go now, Mom?"

"Please stop that, Dawn. We'll go in a minute." Cindy grabbed her daughter's hand firmly and smiled at Annette as if in apology. "Maybe Mansi is a common first name, like John or something is here."

Annette looked at Dawn. "Is Mansi a common name in Algeria?"

"Yes, very common."

"It must be just a coincidence." Annette smiled and compared the photo to Dawn again. "You two sure look a lot alike. Dawn, do you have a picture of your father?"

Dawn shook her head. "No."

Cindy said, "She has a few at home."

"Mom, those are personal!" Dawn pouted.

"I have some older ones, too, from ten years ago, before he left."

Annette wasn't sure why she asked, but it seemed important. "Can you send me one?" She found a business card in her purse.

"Why? Do you think our exes are related?"

"I don't know what to think anymore, but nothing would surprise me. Maybe the men were cousins, and both families chose the same first name for some particular reason. I don't know."

"That would be too weird. But I'll send you a picture."

It bugged Annette on the drive home, and she knew it must be just a coincidence. When she got home, all the lights were out except in their bedroom, where she found Cliff in bed, reading.

"Hi, honey. I thought you'd be asleep."

"I was trying to finish this book. How was your meeting?"

"It was good, and . . . I had an interesting talk with Cindy Yaccine afterwards. She's the gal who just got her daughter back last month from Algeria. It was weird; her daughter looked a lot like Darcy."

Cliff laid his book down. "So?"

"That's not the most interesting part. Her ex-husband is from Algeria, and his first name is Mansi." As she spoke, Annette took her clothes off, folded them neatly, and slipped into a silky nightgown.

"That's quite the coincidence."

"Cindy said her ex was world-traveled and spoke a few languages," she said as she snuggled in beside Cliff. "He sounded just like my ex."

Cliff cuddled her and kissed her gently on the forehead. "Maybe your ex is guilty of polygamy or something, as well. Some say his religion allows it."

Annette asked the same question she had asked herself all the way home. "What are you saying? That Mansi has another family out there?"

"Why not? Hell, he lied to you and stole your son. Do you think he would call you up and tell you he was getting married again?"

"No, and it's not polygamy unless we were still married, but I don't expect anything he did would surprise me. Cindy is going to send me a picture of him from ten years ago."

"What if it is your ex?" Cliff asked.

Annette sighed. "After I get up off the floor, I have no idea."

"We're not going back to Algeria. We could have been killed last time."

"I know, and I love you for going with me. That was way above and beyond the call of duty." She cuddled closer.

"Some guys will do anything for love."

Annette kissed him. "That's why I love you, and that's why I'm marrying you."

"Just don't ask me to go back to Algeria." Cliff reached over and turned out the light.

~~~

"Slow down a little and get behind that truck," Mansi ordered. He was sitting in the back seat and had his rifle resting on the front headrest. The Port of Los Angeles never slept, and the tractor-trailer traffic at night on the 605 freeway was almost as heavy as during the day. It was a perfect spot.

Samzi edged their car in behind the row of semis. Mansi lined up the Saab in the crosshairs of the gun's sight. His powerful telescopic lens zoomed right in on the driver. He could see Sudesh chewing something.

"Say when."

"Steady, steady. Now!"

As the passenger window slid down, Mansi tapped the sensitive trigger gently. He could see the bullets shatter the side glass of the red convertible. The car continued straight for a few long seconds, then slid right and under a FedEx trailer. The car was pinned, and sparks started flying everywhere as it was dragged down the highway, leaving a trail of metal, broken glass, and assorted car parts streaming behind it. In seconds, flames shot out from the engine, and an explosion engulfed the car in a fireball.

The truck driver had slammed on his brakes as soon as the car hit his trailer, and he tried not to lock up the tires as he screeched to a stop. One lane over, Mansi and Samzi stared at the carnage. Traffic quickly slowed down on both sides of the freeway. As Mansi looked back and searched for any signs of life, another explosion totally encased the trailer in flames. He grinned as they sped away. There wouldn't be much left of Sudesh Pumeet or his car.

Cliff was glad the day was over. A high-speed chase early in the shift had started his day, and a corner-store robbery in Fullerton had ended it – except for the paperwork. He had looked forward to flopping on the couch and watching the first pitch of the playoff game; now he would be lucky to catch the last few innings. He was finishing the last report when his partner walked in. "Will, how did it go with Sandy?"

"Fine. She's pretty sharp." Will was breaking in a new officer. He sat down in the empty chair beside Cliff's desk. "Say, what was Annette's son's name?"

"Ansour. Derek Ansour. Why?"

Will flipped open his ticket book and turned it around so Cliff could see. "I pulled a Derek Ansour over for speeding last night."

"No kidding." Cliff scanned the ticket. "Shit. That's about the right age, too."

"Do you know when he was born?"

"Yeah." Cliff had memorized most of the details a long time ago. "Sometime in February. He'll be twenty-seven this year, so, let's see . . . He would have been born in 1987."

"February 13th, 1987." Will pointed at the birth-date on the ticket. "Quite a coincidence."

"I'll say." Cliff didn't know what to think. "If this is Annette's son, she'll be ecstatic."

"Well, then, I hope it is."

"What did he look like?"

"Good-looking kid. Long hair, looked like a beach bum. Look him up for yourself."

Cliff thought about calling Annette right away, but decided to wait and tell her when he got home. He ran Derek's name through the DMV computer and was surprised when the picture of a friendly-looking young man stared back at him. Dark hair down to his shoulders, tanned, intense black eyes. He looked like a surfer.

Cliff printed off a picture and stuffed it in his briefcase. He hoped the black-and-white photo was good enough. He was halfway out the door when he wondered if Mansi or Derek were still on a watch list. It had been twenty years since the kidnapping, but the FBI didn't take people off the list for no reason. His next call was Washington, D.C.

"Rick, its Cliff Billings, I was hoping I'd catch you. Burning the midnight oil?"

"Yeah, trying to get caught on some paperwork," Rick groaned, "it's been a long time, how are you doing?"

"I'm doing great Rick, thanks for asking and Annette is finally going to make an honest man out of me. We're getting married in a few weeks."

"That's great news Cliff, great news. You two were meant for each other."

"Thanks Rick, I think you're right, but that's not the reason I'm calling. Do you remember the story about her son?"

"The one that was kidnapped years ago?"

"Yeah, well my partner stopped one Derek Ansour for speeding the other day and it looks like it could have been him."

"Wow, after all this time, how long has it been?"

"Over twenty years."

"Has Annette met him?" Rick sounded concerned.

"No, in fact she doesn't even know yet, and I will tell her tonight, but I wondered about something. Would his father still be on the official watch list?"

Rick paused before answering, "Probably and that's a good question. Because it was a kidnapping, Derek's name should be cross referenced and on the list too. Hang on a sec."

Cliff could hear fingers tapping on the keyboard; then Rick answered his question, "Derek returned to the U.S almost ten years ago."

Cliff was stunned, "Why wouldn't Annette have been notified?"

"That's another good question, hang on let me bring up the notes on the file."

Cliff knew Annette would be devastated that her son hadn't looked her up.

Rick's voice was sympathetic, but official, "He was detained and questioned by immigration officers and the FBI. He was eighteen years old and he said he didn't want to contact his mother and he said his father had been killed in Algeria when he was eight. He said he hardly remembered either of them. Officially there was nothing we could do, he was an adult. Let's see…he was watched for another five years, but there was no sign of his father and he lived the normal life of a university student, so with nothing to go on, his name was finally taken off the list in 2009."

Cliff realized they couldn't watch everyone forever and in some ways it made sense, not that Annette would see it that way, "Thanks Rick, it's one of those good news, bad news things I guess. Annette won't be mourning the death of her ex, but if it really is the same Derek," there wasn't much doubt in his mind, "she's going to be awfully hurt, again."

When he got home, he was glad the girls were gone. "Honey, I'm home."

Annette answered from the master bedroom, "I'm in here."

"Are the girls home?" Cliff double-checked their bedrooms as he went by.

"No, why?" Annette came out of the walk-in closet.

"I don't know if it's just a coincidence, but last night Will Miller pulled over a kid named Derek Ansour." He had decided to tell her immediately, before anyone else showed up.

Her eyes went wide. "Derek?" she cried. "My Derek?"

"I don't know, but I think so. When was your son born?"

"February 13th, 1987."

Cliff pulled his notepad out of his breast pocket, flipped through the pages, and stopped at his notes. "February 13th, 1987."

A look of disbelief twisted her face. "Is it really him? What did he look like?"

"I looked up his driver's license on the computer. Good-looking kid." He handed her the photo. "What do you think?"

The photo was that of a young man, not a boy, but he did seem to have the same smile. The black eyes were as deep as she remembered. "I don't know; it's so hard to say. Why wouldn't he try to contact me?"

"I don't know, honey. Maybe it's just a complete fluke."

"Two Derek Ansours?" Annette started to sob. "Both with the same birthday, both with dark hair and dark eyes . . . It must be him."

Cliff had shared Annette's grief for years, but if this was a false alarm, it was an incredible coincidence. If it was really her lost son, there were a lot of questions that needed answers, "Wait, there's more," he knew Rick's information was going to hurt, "Derek returned to the United States almost ten years ago."

Annette's jaw dropped, "What? Why wouldn't the authorities have contacted me?" she started to cry.

Cliff pulled her close, "I wondered the same thing honey." He repeated what Rick had told him, "there was nothing they could do. He was an adult."

For a moment she sobbed on his shoulder and he just held her as close as he could. He could feel her body shaking, "But there is some good news."

She turned her wet face and stared at him with little hope, "What's that?"

"I've got his address," he said.

"You do?" Annette stopped crying instantly. "Where does he live?"

"Long Beach."

"Can we go see him?"

"I suppose, but I also have his phone number. Maybe you should call first."

"I'd rather see him in person."

"What if it's not him?" Cliff knew she would be heartbroken again.

"Life goes on. It's been twenty years. I'll be okay."

Cliff thought about the old adage, *Be careful what you wish for.* He wondered silently how Derek would react to such a surprise. "Okay, if you're sure."

Chapter 13

Bill Simpson loved his job and his office. He had joined Trainor Jets after hearing Art speak at a job fair. The futuristic technology had been more than inspiring and the chance to live in California too hard to resist. In ten years, he had worked his way up through the ranks from application programmer to systems designer, and at thirty-eight, he was the youngest department head in the company's history. The success of Fly America had paved the highway of his future and his career. It had doubled the department's payroll in a few short years. New hardware and software programs had found their way into every facet of the Trainor Jets aircraft manufacturing business, from accounting to maintenance, and soon, computers and programmers were essential to the efficient operation of every facet of the business.

Bill had been promoted to Senior Vice President of Computer Operations the previous spring, and while the other senior managers enjoyed the hardwood floors of the main building, the computer flight operations center was where he chose to have his office. Only two years old, the building was state-of-the-art in every way. The Plexiglas walls, suspended floors, and rich blend of color and natural light made it a surprisingly relaxing and comfortable place to work.

With workstations for sixty programmers, the main control room was usually a buzz of activity as the software technicians monitored every flight of every plane in the fleet. Fifty large video displays covered the two-story front wall and live pictures of jets landing and taking off were mixed together with streams of data and weather images from around the country. A large, 3D globe hung in the center of the room, and dozens of little holographic icons indicated planes as they inched their way across the U.S.

It was only a little after eight a.m., but one workstation was noticeably empty. Bill wandered over to Derek Ansour's desk. "Sudesh is late. Boy, that's unusual. Has he called?"

Derek looked up from his screen. "No, not that I know of."

"Did anyone call him? Maybe he slept in."

"No. Do you want me to?"

"No, its okay. I'll call."

Bill called from the privacy of his corner office, but Sudesh's phone rang four or five times before the message picked up. He figured Sudesh must be on his way, but left a message anyway. He put the phone down and thought about calling Sudesh's cell phone, but his own phone rang before he had a chance.

"Is this Bill Simpson?" The voice was all business.

"Yes."

"This is Sergeant Ted Randall with the Long Beach Police Department. Do you have an employee named Sudesh Pumeet?"

Bill's breath caught. "Yes, he's a computer programmer here."

"I'm sorry to have to bring you the bad news, but - we think he was killed in a car crash last night."

"Oh, no." The word *killed* rang through his head. *Jesus H. Christ.* His mind whirled. A minute ago, Sudesh had merely been late. "What do you mean, you think he was killed?" Sudesh had been a great employee and a good friend.

"His car was badly burned, but we found some identification and computer parts in a steel box in his trunk. His company I.D. tag was still legible. The autopsy won't be completed until tomorrow, but the body does seem to match the physical description on his driver's license. We went to his apartment, but it appears he lived alone. We need to contact his next of kin. Would you happen to have that information?"

Bill felt tears on his face. As far as he knew, the programmer had no relatives living in the United States. "I don't believe he has any family here. He moved here from India quite some time ago. I would imagine we have something in his file. The office staff are not in yet. Can I call you back?"

"Sure."

Bill hung up and stared at the wall for a few seconds. He was stunned. Other than his grandparents, he had never known anyone who had died. His heart went out to Sudesh's mother. He knew the young man's father had been killed in an airplane crash many years ago, and he knew Sudesh sent money home every month to his family in India. They would be devastated. He wiped at his tears and then realized how much his death would mean to Trainor Jets. They had a lot of other good programmers, but Sudesh was going to be a huge loss. He looked at his watch. It was a quarter after eight o'clock, and Art would be in soon. Better to get things in order here first. He headed for Derek's desk.

~~~

Derek looked up from his computer and saw the concerned look on his superior's face. Bill looked like he had been crying. His father had said it would probably take a few days to identify the body, but Bill looked shocked. *He must know.*

"Derek . . . I have some really bad news," Bill stammered.

"What happened?"

"Sudesh is dead," Bill whispered so no one else could hear.

"Jeez, that's awful. What happened?" Derek hoped he sounded terrified, but he knew he didn't care. After seeing death close up, it didn't scare him anymore.

"He was killed in a car accident with a truck on the 605 freeway last night."

"Wow. That's terrible. But that's a busy road with a lot of trucks on it."

Bill nodded. "I hate to bring up business at a time like this, but what about the update? Were you finished?"

"Yes, I think Sudesh was going to sign off on it today."

"Well, that's a bit of good news. Bring it to me. I'll look at it."

Derek turned back to his screen. There was no turning back now.

~~~

Bill went back to his office and closed the door. He knew Art would want to know immediately. Being a software programmer himself, Art had a fondness for all his computer programmers and was always stopping by the department to see what was new. He dialed.

"Good morning, Bill. Great day, hey?" Art answered.

"Actually, Art, it's not so great. I have some bad news. One of our guys was killed last night in a car crash."

"That is bad news. Who?"

"Sudesh Pumeet."

"Shit, he was a great kid. What happened?"

Bill repeated what the police officer had told him and reassured Art that from an operational standpoint, they would be fine.

"I drive that road almost every day," Art said. "The number of trucks is amazing. Poor kid. Do you have someone to replace him?"

"Yeah, I'll have to think about that for a while, but there are three or four programmers who are more than capable. Pat Johnston, Debbie Young, Derek Ansour, Eric St. Cyr. We can talk about it later."

"Okay. What about that update?"

"I talked to Derek already. It's finished, and apparently Sudesh was ready to sign off on it today."

"Well, that's a relief. Derek's a good kid."

"Yes, he is."

~~~

They had decided they would drive up in the early evening; hopefully Derek would be home from work. Cliff pulled up in front of the tall tower. The Long Beach waterfront high-rise was quite new and looked to be thirty or forty stories. He checked the address on his notepad and then turned the motor off. "This is it. Tenth floor, I guess."

Annette looked up at the stone and steel apartment building. "I'm scared." She reached for Cliff's hand and squeezed.

On the way over, they had discussed all kinds of possible explanations. "Are you sure you want to do this?"

"Yes. I need to know."

"Okay. Let's go meet this guy."

They walked over to the entrance and looked at the list of tenants. *D. ANSOUR* was the fourth name from the top.

Annette gasped. "Cliff, it's him."

"We don't know that for sure."

Inside the lobby, the elevator stopped, and a couple with a small dog got off. As the entrance door closed slowly behind them, Cliff grabbed it. He looked at Annette and held the door open. "We may as well just go in."

Annette peeked out cautiously when the elevator arrived at the tenth floor, but the hallway was empty. Cliff read the sign indicating the direction of the apartments and pointed to the right.

At apartment 1017, he held a finger to his lips and gently nudged Annette against the wall and out of view of the peephole. He knocked firmly on the door. The noise was surprisingly loud in the quiet hallway. At first they heard nothing, but as he raised his hand to knock again, they heard footsteps. Then an eye peered through the small hole.

"Yes, who is it?" The voice was short and irritated.

Cliff looked at Annette and shrugged his shoulders. They hadn't planned exactly what to say. "My name is Cliff Billings. I need to speak with you. It's important."

"What's this about?"

Cliff thought of something that should work. "It's about your father."

"My father's dead," the voice was cold.

Annette was surprised at the revelation that Mansi was dead, but it didn't faze her. She did wonder why her son wouldn't want to have a least one parent in his life.

Cliff tried another tactic, "It's about your father and your mother"

There was a pause, and then the door was unlocked and opened. Derek looked back and forth at Cliff and Annette. His eyes were cold and suspicious.

Annette's hands went to her face. "Derry, is that you?"

Derek glared at her. "Who are you?"

"I'm your mother," she cried as tears started pouring down her cheeks. "Don't you remember me? I'm your mother."

Derek backed up a step. "This must be some mistake."

"Don't you remember?" she pleaded. "I used to call you Derry. Your father was Mansi Ansour. I married him in 1986. You were born on February 13th, 1987."

"How do I know you're my mother?" Derek blinked a few times.

Annette was sobbing, and Cliff put his arm around her. "Can we come in?"

Derek looked awkward and glanced up and down the hallway before replying. "I'm actually quite busy at the moment."

Annette begged, "Derry, for God's sake!"

A door behind them opened, and a woman peeked out.

Derek grimaced and stepped back a few steps into his hallway. "Okay, come in."

He led them into the narrow entrance and closed the door. "What do you want?"

"Want? You are my son. What has happened to you all these years? I never thought I would see you again," Annette couldn't believe it, but it was him. At long last, after twenty years. *God, how he has grown. He's a man.* "Didn't your father tell you about me?"

"My father died a long time ago."

"I'm sorry to hear that." She had hated Mansi for years, and while she would never forgive him for taking her son, she had never wished him dead and just tried to forget him. "How did he die?"

"In a car accident."

"That's an awful coincidence. So did your grandfather." Her voice trembled at the gruesome memories. Car accidents had claimed three men in her life. No matter what Mansi had done do her, losing a father was never a good thing. "I know how painful that can be.'

He stared at her with cold eyes and growled, "How did you find me?"

"The deputy who pulled you over the other day was my partner," Cliff answered.

Derek looked suspiciously at Cliff. "Who are you?"

"Cliff Billings. I'm your mother's fiancé. We're going to be married in a few weeks."

"Are you a cop?"

"I'm a deputy sheriff in Orange County." Cliff could see Derek flinch. Even a lot of innocent people did that, but Derek immediately looked scared.

"How long have you been living in California?" Annette sputtered.

"Ten years."

"Ten years!? Why did you never call me?"

"It's been a long time. I don't remember you. It seemed too complicated."

"Complicated? I'm your mother. What's complicated? You're my son. I love you."

Derek scowled again. "This isn't a good time. I have a lot of work to do." He gestured at the desk and computer visible at the end of the hall.

"Work? What kind of work do you do?"

"I am a computer programmer."

Annette smiled. "That's a good career. Can we come in and sit down? I'd love to hear about your job and maybe get to know each other again."

"Maybe another time, but I'm busy right now." Derek hadn't moved and still blocked the hallway into the apartment.

"Okay, how about this weekend?"

Derek glanced at a calendar hanging on the wall. "I'm leaving on vacation on Sunday night. Maybe when I get back?"

"When is that?"

"In a few weeks."

Cliff could see the color drain from Annette's face in disappointment, and he wondered why the boy seemed so nervous. He couldn't see much of the living room, but he hoped the kid wasn't doing drugs.

"Derek, it's only Tuesday. Can't you find a little time later this week?" Annette reached for his hand, but he pulled away.

"I don't think so. I have an important computer program to finish before I leave."

"Wouldn't you like to see your sister?"

"What sister?"

"Her name is Darcy. She was born a few months after you left."

He scowled again. "I still don't have time."

"Please, Derek," Annette pleaded again. "We just want to get to know you."

"I can't promise anything, but if I have a little time, maybe I'll call."

"Okay, that's great." Annette dug into her purse. "Here, let me give you my card. That's my cell phone number. Leave a message if I don't pick up."

Derek took her business card. "I suppose you already have my phone number." He looked suspiciously at Cliff.

Cliff winked to answer Derek's question, but he wished he knew more about Derek Ansour. The young man was hostile, suspicious, evasive, and didn't appear to be very happy about seeing his mother for the first time in twenty years. Cliff had never worked with separation victims, but he knew from his psychology classes that anger was one of the most prevalent reactions when children were reunited with parents. He prayed that was all it was.

~~~

Annette didn't know what to think. Only hours ago, Derek had not existed, and then suddenly he was back but didn't want to see her. It was hard to believe. As they drove away, she thought about the fear in his eyes. He had looked surprised, for sure, but there was something more than that. He seemed anything but happy to see her. Cliff slowed down as they entered Naples. It was busy as usual, and teenagers filled the sidewalks.

"He sure didn't want to answer any questions," Annette said quietly.

Cliff stopped at the busy crosswalk as a pack of kids swarmed out and onto the road. "Did you see the way he looked at me when he found out I was a cop?"

"Most people give you a double-take when they hear that." Annette had witnessed all kinds of reactions when Cliff told people what he did for a living.

"I know, but he looked scared to me. I've seen it before."

"Scared? What would he be scared of?"

"That's a good question," Cliff said.

"Now you're scaring me."

Cliff reached over and squeezed her hand. "I'm sorry, honey. It's probably nothing, just me being a paranoid cop."

Annette still couldn't comprehend why Derek had never contacted her. "It's like he doesn't want to remember me."

"It has been twenty years. Give him some time. Things will change."

Lisa and Darcy were waiting at home, excited and full of questions, but after Annette told them what happened, they were confused and mad.

She phoned her mother next. Marie answered on the first ring; she had been waiting for the call. She was as dumbfounded as everybody else. Marie thought maybe Derek had been brainwashed, and Annette wasn't sure she was wrong. Val got on the phone next and asked all the same questions everyone else had, and Annette repeated her sad tale again before breaking down and crying.

Derek had called Mansi as soon as his mother had left. They met at the beach an hour later. "I knew who it was as soon as I opened the door. Shocked the hell out of me."

"All this time, now she shows up!" Mansi spat, furious. "What fucking bad luck."

Derek knew it was terrible timing, the worst. They had talked about a chance encounter years ago after he had first moved back, but as the years had gone by, they had forgotten about her. "She wants to see me this weekend."

"You told her no, right?"

"I told her I was going on vacation and that maybe I would see her when I got back."

"Let's hope that keeps her happy." Mansi stopped as a few bicycles sped by.

"What about her cop boyfriend?" Cliff had intimidated him.

"I hope that's just the coincidence it appears to be."

"He certainly gave me a second look. I could feel it. I bet you he runs me."

"So? You're squeaky clean. Everything he finds will back up your story. There's nothing to worry about. Did she ask about me?"

"Yes and I told her you had died in a car accident, just like you told me."

"Good. What did she say about that?"

"Not much," Derek stepped onto the warm sand, "So everything goes forward?"

Mansi looked out at the breaking waves. "Yes, I don't see any reason to stop now."

"What if she calls me again?" Derek hated his mother and hoped he never saw her again.

"Try to put her off, but if she gets in the way, you will have to kill her."

Derek thought about the small Beretta that his father had given him a few years after he started university. As much as he had never wanted to see his mother, he didn't want to have to shoot her. "I don't think that will be necessary."

"You never know. I'll see you on Sunday morning, and this time, stay home. Don't go out anywhere. Do you understand?"

His father's wrath he understood very well. "Yes, sir."

Annette hadn't slept more than a few hours. Wracked with questions, wracked with guilt, she had tossed and turned all night before finally getting up at 4:00 a.m. She just didn't know what to make of her son. So many questions.

Cliff shuffled down the hallway. "Hi, honey. You're up early."

Annette was at the kitchen table on her second cup of coffee. "I couldn't sleep. My mind is full of wild and crazy ideas. What happened that he never wanted to see me? I always imagined we would have a joyful reunion, but he sure wasn't happy to see me."

Cliff poured a cup of coffee, sipping at the hot black brew before answering. "It's been twenty years. Whatever his father told him, right or wrong; he's believed it for a long time. It will probably take a while for the truth to come out."

"At least I know he's alive, and for that I'm happy. Now, if I can get him to see me, maybe we can still have some sort of mother-son relationship."

Cliff headed down the hall. "We can talk about it more tonight; I have to get to work."

The girls got up shortly after and tried to get Annette to take the day off. Annette wished she could call in sick, but she had an appointment with a prospective buyer whom she had already shown a half-dozen homes to over the last few weeks. Today the husband was coming, hopefully to help make a final choice and write an offer.

~~~

Cliff had as many questions as Annette and wanted to talk to Will before they headed out on patrol. He found him in the locker room. "Will, you're just the guy I was looking for. Guess what? It was her kid."

Will stopped buttoning his shirt. "No kidding? What a coincidence. After that trip you took to Algeria years ago, the name just stuck with me. What are you going to do?"

Cliff would never forget the look of anger on Derek's face when he realized Annette was his mother. "We went up and confronted him last night."

"Really? What happened?"

"It's one of those be-careful-what-you-wish-for things. Derek wasn't any fun-loving kid. He was as cold as a repeat offender."

"He looked straight enough to me."

"Yeah, but something was wrong. Maybe it was just the shock of seeing his mother after all these years, but he sure didn't like me when he found out I was a cop."

"Yeah, that stops a lot of people in their tracks." Will put on his belt and checked the chamber in his gun before sliding it into his holster.

"I wonder if I should run him." As soon as the words left his mouth, he regretted saying them. Annette would be appalled.

"On your soon-to-be stepson?"

"Yeah, you're right. Well, I guess I'll let the two of them sort it out." He wondered what would happen next time they met.

"How old was he when he was abducted?" Will asked.

"Seven. His father took him on a holiday, supposedly to see his dying grandmother, and never brought him back."

"Annette must be all tore up."

"Poor thing, she had all but given up hope of ever seeing her son again, and now she finds him and he doesn't seem to care." It sure hadn't been the happy reunion Annette had dreamt of for twenty years.

Chapter 14

Annette wasn't sure how she managed to get through her day. Her mind kept drifting back to her son, and for once she was even glad when the buyers didn't want to write an offer. Her mother had come over and made dinner, but the food on the table wasn't the focus. They all posed the same questions over and over again, even managing to laugh as they speculated about what was going on with Derek. Darcy suggested he had been brainwashed and was a spy. Marie thought that Mansi had lied about how much religion had mattered. Cliff ended up defending Derek, suggesting that they were all overreacting and that maybe Derek just didn't remember her after all those years.

Annette didn't know what to think. "Let's just leave it a few days," she said. "Wouldn't it be nice if he called me?"

"Aren't you just happy to know he's alive and healthy? A lot of parents have difficult times with their kids." Cliff squeezed her hand reassuringly before getting up. "You'll win him back, you'll see."

"I sure hope so. He looked great. He must be popular with the girls." Annette had thought about everything, from his education to his love life. No matter what happened, he was still her son.

Cliff went into the living room and plopped down in one of the leather recliners, picked up the remote, and turned on the TV. "Let's see what else is going on in the world."

The set crackled to life, and a picture of the Trainor Jets assembly line covered the huge screen behind a female reporter.

"Look," Cliff said. "Trainor is on the news."

A female reporter addressed the camera and then her guest. "Good evening, ladies and gentlemen. I'm Tanu Tissii with LBN News live in Long Beach, California, with tonight's special guest,

Mr. Art Trainor, CEO and president of Trainor Jets. Good evening, Art."

"Good evening, Tanu. Nice to see you again, and good to be here." Art smiled at the cameras, then turned back to face the pretty reporter.

"Nice of you to give us a few minutes," Tanu said with a chuckle. "I remember our first conversations years ago. Looks like you were right."

"Yes, and business has been even better than we expected. Our confirmed order bank is over a thousand planes. That's four years production."

Tanu looked down briefly at her notes. "How many planes do you have flying today?"

Art grinned. "We're delivering number five hundred tomorrow."

Tanu turned to the private jet sitting in the background. "Your pilotless planes still have most people in disbelief. Is everyone nervous the first few times?"

"I'm sure they are, but after a few flights, they don't even think about not having a pilot on board." Art smiled at the camera. "I'll never convince everyone, but most people have no problem with trusting the cockpit to the four computers."

"It still seems pretty wild. How do you handle emergencies?"

"If there are any problems on board, we can take control of the aircraft from the ground, but in thousands of hours of flight time, we haven't had one incident. Not even a minor one."

"Yes, your statistics are amazing, but what if the computers failed? Could someone fly the plane?"

"Yes and no. The planes are all fly-by-wire, so they need some computer power to control the basic movements of the airplane. But that's no different than many other new planes these days. If the computers fail they are in trouble, but computers don't fail anymore Tanu, besides, we have a backup plan. The Freedom Five's unique wing design gives it tremendous glide range, if the unthinkable happened and the plane lost all power."

"Glide range?" Tanu asked.

"Yes, that's another incredible safety feature with the Freedom Five. It has the best glide ratio in the business, almost twenty-to-one. If both engines fail, the plane can glide over a hundred miles from forty thousand feet."

Tanu looked incredulous. "Have both engines ever failed at the same time?"

"Never, not even one engine, and our software is bulletproof, too. We've never had more than a level-one failure, and only a few of those."

"What's a level-one failure?"

Art held up four fingers. "We have four computers on board every plane, all running concurrently and independently. A level-one failure is in one computer only. We've only had that happen a total of four times in tens of thousands of flight hours. Statistically, that meets zero tolerance levels."

"We've got a little footage of one of your planes in action." Tanu turned to face the massive monitor behind her. "Let's have a look."

A window popped open in the corner of the TV screen. A video of a Freedom Five showed the inside of a plane. The cameras showed the absence of pilot seats and controls in the cockpit. Swiveling to the rear, the camera focused on the luxury interior of the jet. As the camera backed out the door, it was obvious there was no one in the plane.

The door closed, and the camera retreated to capture a picture of the plane as it taxied down to the end of the runway and took off. The next shot showed the jet landing, parking, and then opening the door. The camera zoomed back inside the plane. There was still no one on board.

Tanu addressed the viewers again. "It still seems like science fiction to me, but UAVs are the Air Force's favorite toy these days. No reason why the technology shouldn't spill over to the commercial market, too. CAAV's I hear they are calling your type of plane.

"Yes, I've heard the term," Art grinned. "We thought it would make personal jet travel much more affordable, and, substantially safer. Certainly our planes will never make an error in judgment."

"Your critics never thought you would be certified by the FAA. Now it looks like you've changed aviation forever. I understand your air taxi business is doing quite well, too."

Art beamed. "Thanks. Yes, I always thought this technology would change aviation. Companies like Fly America have created a new option for consumers. The air taxi market has been growing steadily over the years; it was always a matter of cost per seat, per mile. Now, with those costs cut in half, fares less than first or business class, and point-to-point service available in literally thousands of airports, it looks like that time has arrived."

"And I understand that you have worked out an agreement to use the planes for medical emergencies, too."

"Yes, we are very proud of that. We have a voluntary program with our owners. If they donate the jet for mercy flights, we donate the maintenance for those hours, and the tax write-off has been a bonus for the owners, as they provide a significant benefit to the community. With the support of our generous clients located throughout the country, we can have a plane ready at any airport in the United States within an hour."

"Do you expect the major airlines to start knocking on your door soon?" Tanu asked.

"I think some will. There is no doubt many of their first-class clients have chosen private jet travel in one form or another, from full ownership to air charter service, pilots or not. The events of 9/11 changed air travel forever, and the airlines have been struggling financially ever since. Another major terrorist incident involving a commercial aircraft, and half of the airlines will be bankrupt and gone."

Tanu turned back to face the cameras, a little grin on her face. "Well, I think I'll leave it right there for today. Thanks, Art, always great to have you on our show."

Art looked like he wanted to add something, but the picture changed to an automobile ad.

Marie shook her head. "No pilots! It still amazes me."

Cliff held up four fingers. "Just four little computers."

"I can't believe we were lucky enough to fly on one," said Annette, thinking about their flight. It had only been a few days ago, but it seemed like weeks now. "We trust everything else to computers, why not flying?"

Cliff nodded his head towards the hallway. "Are you still having problems with your computer?"

Annette smiled; her PC had given her fits a few days ago. "Yep. I was even wondering if Derek could help me."

"With that behavior of his? Don't count on it," Cliff repeated his previous advice. "Why don't you just buy a new one? They aren't very expensive anymore."

~~~

It was early the next morning when Mansi drove into the graveyard. It was cloudy and overcast, but as usual at that hour, there was no one else around. He got out and walked through the first few rows of graves, but he didn't pay much attention to the dead. As far as he was concerned, there just wasn't much history laid to rest here – nothing like Algiers, where graves hundreds of years old validated a struggle a thousand years old. A large grey tombstone had been decorated with bouquets of fresh flowers no more than a few days old.

Samzi was waiting for him and got right down to business. "Is there reason to be worried?"

Mansi had thought it through a few times. There were only a few days left, and other than Annette's sudden appearance, nothing else had gone wrong. "I don't think so. I think it was just bad luck."

Samzi started down the slope. "I don't like luck."

Mansi followed; he was still confident they had everything under control. "Derek says he can handle her."

"And if she becomes a problem, can he take care of her?"

"He will do whatever he needs to."

"Good. What about Jill?"

Mansi's smile returned. "She keeps getting one promotion after another. Her time is coming, too."

~~~

Annette had agonized all day, but despite Cliff's warnings and her own misgivings, she decided to call Derek. Surely he could find a few minutes to talk to his mother on the phone.

The phone ran three times before he answered. "Hello."

"Derek . . . it's your mother."

He didn't say anything for a few seconds, but when he did, his voice was cold. "What is it?" His anger seemed to seep through the phone line.

She tried not to let his reluctance deter her. "How is your schedule? Do you think we can get together this weekend?"

"No, I don't think so." He sounded exasperated. "I told you, I'm going on vacation."

Annette couldn't believe he could say no so easily. "I can't say that I'm not terribly disappointed. Please, even for a few minutes?"

"I told you, I have a lot of work to finish, and I'm leaving on Sunday. I just don't have the time."

"What time is your flight?"

"Eight-thirty at night."

She thought of a favor most people appreciated. "How about I drive you to the airport?"

Derek sounded surprised, but he declined. "Thanks, but no thanks. I want to have my car at the airport when I get back. But I thought about it, and I do want to see you, too. I'll call you when I get back, I promise."

Annette jumped on the chance. "Okay, but you promise, a whole day, just you and me?"

"Sure, whatever, but I have to go now, okay?"

She tried to keep the conversation going. "When are you back? Where are you going?"

"London. I'll be back in a few weeks."

"London? I went there with your father when we were dating years ago."

A pause. "He never told me much about you."

"There are probably a lot of things he never told you."

Derek cut her off, and they ended the conversation.

That night, she dreamed of Derek as a child. He was playing with his small model airplane and laughing. She woke up happy, sure that things would get better.

Cliff had to leave early; he was working security at John Wayne Airport again. Fridays were always busy for Annette, with half the day taken up by broker previews of the new listings. She was delighted when she saw a home that was ideal for one of her clients. Weekends were usually her busiest time of the week, and she wouldn't have much time to dwell on her son.

~~~

Derek met his father at the beach. They both wore sweats and looked like they were out for some early morning exercise. "It's an old test card," Derek said. "It was supposed to have been destroyed. It is programmed and ready to go." Derek handed his father the small, flat computer disk.

"This thing can fly a plane?" Mansi looked at the back of the disk. There were no markings on either side. "It looks like a hotel key of some kind."

"It's not that different. It only contains authorization commands, but once this card is inserted into the control panel, the plane's computers will do the rest. Here's your technician's pass." Derek pulled a sealed plastic I.D. card out of his other pocket.

Mansi examined the Trainor Jets identification card. His own face smiled back at him, but the name on the identification was now Adam Marks. "Perfect. Is the program loaded?"

"Yes, it will go off at twelve o'clock Pacific Standard Time, noon." Derek had calculated the most effective time based on maximum traffic in the target zone.

Mansi slipped the disk into his pocket. "You'll be in Algiers by then, and I'll be in Canada."

"Yes, and our journey finally over."

Derek didn't think Trainor would ever discover what had happened. The moment the operating disk was destroyed on Meyers' plane, the program would cease to exist. He had buried the binary code in the constant flow of data between the automated radar and traffic control computer systems and the 500 other aircraft that shared the same operating system and the same network. Connected by the infinitely microscopic measures and seemingly endless streams of data transfer, the software confused the command recognition interface by inserting an extra character randomly into the entry field.

"Good, then this is it," said Mansi.

"I'm glad I'll be gone before anything happens."

"I'll see you in a few days, my son. May God be with you."

~~~

The thump woke Annette. She peeked out from under the covers and asked, "What time is it?"

Cliff was standing there looking at her, and the Sunday paper was lying on the bed. "Eight-thirty. You slept in. That's good. I'm sure you needed it. I'm going to get the car washed. I'll be back in an hour or so." He bent over and gave her a kiss. "There's a fresh pot of coffee brewing. I'll see you in a while."

Annette got up and went out to the kitchen. The girls were still asleep, and the house was quiet except for the gurgling of the coffee machine. She poured herself a cup and climbed back in bed. As she sifted through the thick *LA Times*, the name *Trainor Jets* jumped out at her. There was an article about how well the company was doing. The writer had nothing but good things to say about the company and its success, and how key Trainor Jets had been in reviving the entire Long Beach area. Not only had the new technology put the aerospace industry back in the news, but Trainor's work force had grown to over 6,000 employees in the last four years and had helped foster a new mini high-tech boom. Long Beach was thriving, property values were on the rise, the city was hopping, and once again, it was a great place to live.

Annette read the entire article, thinking about Derek living in Long Beach. But that made her question his hostile behavior, and soon she was dwelling on him again. The phone rang, and while she knew the chances were almost nonexistent, she still hoped that he would call.

"Good morning."

"Hi." It was her mother. "How are you?"

"Fine."

"Did Derek call?"

"No. I guess I'll just have to wait until he gets back."

Her mother was still furious that Derek had been so heartless. "Why don't I go see him with you? Maybe if Cliff wasn't there, he might be more receptive."

"Thanks, but I have an appointment in Seal Beach this afternoon. I was thinking about stopping by after I'm done . . ." Cliff had counseled her against it already.

"If he's leaving tonight, wouldn't he be home packing?"

"That's what I was thinking."

"All he can do is say no again."

Her mother meant well, but the comment hurt. "Thanks, Mom."

"I'm sorry, but really, what can it harm?"

Maybe if she went by herself, Derek would open up a little. "You might be right. I love him. Surely he can understand that."

By the time Cliff returned, she had made up her mind.

He tried to talk her out of it. "I don't know, honey. It doesn't sound like a good idea to me. Why don't you call him first? Maybe he's not home."

Annette had thought about that, too. "I don't want to give him a chance to put me off. If he's home packing, we should have at least a few minutes to talk."

"You would think so, but he has said no twice now."

Annette hoped she wouldn't hurt Cliff's feelings. "I know, but maybe if he sees it's just me, he'll feel more comfortable."

"That's possible. He didn't seem to like me."

"Why don't you come with me this afternoon? You wouldn't have to come up. I only have the one home to show, and after I'm done, we'll go by Derek's. I won't stay long, and then we can go out for dinner at that Italian restaurant you like." Annette knew that would entice him.

"Bellini's? Okay, you win." They had been there a few months ago, and Cliff had loved the classy decor and the delicious Italian cuisine. "What time is your appointment?"

"Four."

"Okay. I'll wait in the car and listen to the game on the radio."

"I promise I won't take long if Derek is home and will see me." After twenty years, even a few minutes with her son would be great.

Chapter 15

Cliff parked on Ocean Blvd right in front of Derek's apartment building. He turned the Jeep engine off. "I'll be right here, waiting for you."

Annette opened the door, then decided she needed some love first. She leaned back into the SUV and hugged her future husband before kissing him. "I could be back in a few minutes."

"If you're gone for a longer than a few minutes, its probably good news."

"Well, if I'm not back right away, you'll know he's been hospitable to some degree."

"If he decides to serve any appetizers, call me."

Annette laughed. Cliff knew how to make her relax. "I won't be long."

A young man in running gear was leaving as Annette approached the entrance, and he held the door open for her. She thanked him and entered the lobby. She checked her watch. It was almost 5:30, and she wanted to be leaving by 6:00. She didn't want Cliff to get too hungry – he would get cranky – but that gave her a half hour or so alone with her son.

The elevator stopped at the tenth floor. The hallway was empty. She walked slowly, gathering her courage. When she stopped in front of Derek's apartment, her hand was shaking as she raised it, but she managed to knock firmly twice.

Almost immediately, she heard footsteps, then his voice. "Who is it?"

"Derek, it's your mother. I need to see you before you go."

His eye glared at her through the tiny hole in the door, then the deadbolt slid back and the door swung open swiftly. "What are you doing here?" he demanded.

"I was hoping I could catch you, just for a few minutes. You dyed your hair, and cut it."

Derek's hair was now much shorter, more businesslike; and light brown. He seemed surprised and looked at himself in the hall mirror for a second, but he didn't answer her question. "I told you the other night that I was busy. I'm leaving tonight."

Annette started to cry. She just couldn't help it. "Please, just a few minutes, I promise. Can't we talk for a few minutes? It's been so long!"

A couple came out of another door a few apartments down the hall. The man looked concerned and asked politely, "Is there a problem?"

Annette tried to smile as she wiped at her tears. "No, it's okay."

Derek stepped back into his apartment and motioned his mother in. "Okay, come in. But just a few minutes, that's all. Then I have to go." He directed her to a denim-covered couch in the living room and sat down in the matching chair facing her.

The room was sparsely furnished, with only one small round table and one mountain landscape picture behind the couch. A wooden bookcase under the window was more junk storage than books. The Sharp flat-screen TV looked like an older model, but the picture was crisp and a soccer game was on. Derek turned it off.

"Why the change in hair?"

Derek glanced at his image in the mirror again. "Just a change, that's all."

Annette decided to change the subject. "Are you really good at computers?"

"I have an MBA in Computer Science."

"Can you fix my computer?"

Derek looked at his watch. "What's wrong with it?"

Annette was glad he would talk about anything. "It keeps locking up. I'll be halfway through something on the internet, and it will freeze up. The program just quits responding, and then I get one of those 'Send the error to Microsoft' messages."

"What operating system is it?"

"Windows XP."

"Why don't you upgrade? Windows XP is over ten years old. They don't even support it anymore."

Everyone told her that. "I know, but usually it runs fine."

"Do you have a lot of files on it?"

"No, not now. I back them all up on DVDs." After she had lost a few files, she had learned to save all her correspondence. It was ironic, she thought. Most of the stuff she wanted to save was related to finding Derek.

"Why don't you reformat the hard drive and reload the programs?" Derek suggested. "It's easy to do."

Someone else had suggested that to her, but she kept hoping there was a better solution. "You think that would that fix it?"

"Probably. It's an easy way to correct a lot of conflicting hardware problems, without having to edit any DOS files. It doesn't take that long."

"Well, maybe sometime you can come down and visit me and show me how."

Derek didn't say anything.

She was going to have to pry every word out of him one at a time. "Why didn't you ever call me? Do you know how much I've worried about you?"

"Worried about me? You didn't worry about me before. Why do you care now?" Derek was angry, and she was startled by the hatred in his eyes.

"What do you mean? I've always cared about you. You are my son. I love you."

"Then why did you want to give me up for adoption?"

"What? I never wanted to give you up for adoption. Where in the world did you ever get that impression? Is this what your father told you?" Had Mansi lied about everything?

"Yes, and I remember; you never liked me."

"That's not true, Derek. I loved you. I even went to Algeria a few times looking for you." Her voice cracked as she started crying again. What had Mansi told their son? How could she convince him it wasn't true?

Derek looked out the window.

She would always hate Mansi for what he did, but she had never seriously wished him dead. "You said your father was dead, and while he did leave me and kidnap you, I am sorry to hear that. Everybody needs a father. How long ago did he die?"

"Ten years ago. Just before I moved back to the states." His eyes returned to hers.

"Why didn't you call me then? Weren't you curious about me at all?"

"No." His gaze was cold and unsympathetic.

Tears ran down her cheeks. Her face was wet, but her throat felt parched. "Can I have a glass of water?"

He gave her an annoyed look before standing up and going into the kitchen.

She heard the water running, and in a minute he came back with a tall glass. When she reached for the water, her fingers touched his lightly. "You have to believe me. I never wanted to give you up. You went on a holiday with your father and he never brought you back. He kidnapped you. I even went to Algeria twice to try and find you. I never thought I would see you again."

"That's not what I remember."

"Then your father twisted your memory. I never, ever wanted to give you up. Your father said he was taking you to see your grandmother." Was that a lie too? Was Derek's grandmother even alive?

"He took me because you didn't want me, because you didn't want to be my mother."

"That's just not true. I always wanted you. I want you now. All I want . . . is to have a normal mother-son relationship. Please just give me a chance." As she leaned forward to reach for his hand, she accidentally bumped her glass, and some water splashed onto the wooden coffee table. "I'm sorry. Do you have a towel?"

Derek didn't seem to care. "Don't worry about it. It'll dry."

A phone rang, startling Annette. Derek looked at the cell phone ringing on the counter. "I have to get that." Picking up the phone, he went into the bedroom and closed the door.

Annette picked her glass out of the puddle on the table and looked around for a coaster or a napkin. The coffee table had a small drawer, so she opened it. Inside was a pile of computer magazines, but something else grabbed her attention. Sitting neatly in the middle on top of the stack were what appeared to be three passports. The top one was Canadian. She glanced at the bedroom door. She couldn't make out exactly what her son was saying, but she heard her name and wondered who he would be telling about her visit. A girlfriend maybe?

She reached down and picked up the passports and opened the Canadian one first. It took her a second before she realized what it said. It was her son's picture, with his lighter hair, but the name read Mark Adams.

~~~

Inside the bedroom, Derek had his back to the door and tried to keep is voice down, but it came out louder than he intended. "Mother just showed up."

"What?" his father exclaimed. "You have to get her out of there. You have to get on that flight."

Derek knew the clock was ticking. "We're just making some small chitchat. I'll push her out the door in a few minutes."

"Do whatever you have to. It doesn't matter at this point. Kill her if you have to."

Derek grimaced at the thought. "I don't think I'll have to do that."

"If she suspects anything, she's better off dead. I told you that before."

"I'd better go. Don't worry, it'll be okay. I'll ask her to leave right now." Derek checked his watch. He was running out of time quickly.

"Get her out of there before she asks too many questions."

"Yes, Father."

~~~

Annette flipped through the other two passports. One was U.S., the other Algerian. Both had Derek's real name in them. She closed the drawer just as Derek entered the hallway.

He stared at her. "What are you doing?"

She held up her glass in defense to his question. Her hand was shaking. "My glass was wet. I was looking for a coaster."

Derek glared at the coffee table. "I don't have anything like that."

She stared back at him before she replied. "Why do you have a Canadian passport with the name Mark Adams in it?"

Derek ran over and opened the coffee table drawer. The passports were back where she had found them, the Canadian still on top. "It's none of your business."

"Are you involved in something illegal?"

Derek moved over towards the hallway closet and looked around his small apartment as if for an answer.

"What's wrong?" Annette asked. "Cliff is a police officer. I know people aren't supposed to have fake passports. What is going on?" She could see he was scared, but of what?

Derek reached into the closet and pulled out a gun.

Annette was shocked. "What are you doing?"

Derek's hand was shaking as he pointed it at her. "You already know more than you need to know. I can't let you go."

He was so close she could see the inside of the barrel. "Know what? All I know is you have a fake passport. What are you going to do, kill your own mother?"

"You didn't want me then, I don't need you now." He raised the gun a few inches and aimed it at her head.

"Derek, you keep saying that, but it's not true. I loved you then, and I want to love you again. You can't kill me. I'm your mother. I love you."

Derek sneered. "You never loved me."

Annette started crying and tried to stand up.

Derek shoved her back down. "Sit down!"

"Have you no conscience?" she demanded. "My God, what did your father do to you?" She couldn't die at the hand of her own son, could she? Was that to be her fate? Was this to be the ugly end to her sad life?

"My father loved me," Derek insisted. "It was you who deserted us. It was you who didn't want us anymore." The gun wobbled in front of Annette's face.

"Why would I be here today if I never cared about you? Why would have I gone to Algeria twice to try to find you?"

"I don't know and it doesn't matter now."

Annette saw the barrel lower a few inches. "I even brought some stuff from my two trips to Algiers so you might believe me." She pointed to her purse, then reached down and picked it up. "I have some pictures. Look."

She dumped the contents of her red purse out on the coffee table. A half-dozen photographs spread across the table. One was a photo of Derek as a small boy, sitting on Annette's lap, holding a toy truck. Two other pictures were of Annette in Algiers.

His eyes scanned the photos, and she thought she saw a hint or recognition before he looked up. "I told you, I don't care. It's too late."

"Too late for what? What is going on?"

"Too late for anything. I'm going to bring glory to the family name. If father were alive, he would be very proud of me. Maybe someday you will understand."

"Proud of what? What are you going to do?"

"Never mind." He pulled back the safety.

Annette cringed. "Derry, I have done nothing. I'm your mother. You can't kill me."

A few tears ran down his face, and he pointed the gun to the side. "Shit! Why did you have to show up now?" He backed over to the closet and came out with a large roll of duct tape.

"I'll probably regret this," he said. "Get on the floor." He pushed the cold barrel of the gun up against the side of her cheek.

Annette slid off the couch and sat down on the carpet. Derek spun the tape around her torso a dozen times, pinning her arms to her side. He taped her mouth, leaving her nose and eyes uncovered. Then he pushed her over on her side, grabbed her legs, and wrapped the remainder of the roll around her torso until it ran out. Taped like a mummy, she could hardly move.

She watched helplessly as he closed the drapes and turned off most of the lights. He disappeared into the bedroom but was out in seconds, a carry-on suitcase and a briefcase in his hands. Annette stared up from the floor. There was absolutely nothing she could do. She could hardly even move. Derek swore as he took the passports out of the open drawer. He threw them in his briefcase and slammed it shut. Grabbing her feet, he dragged her to the far side of the room.

"This time you will never see me again, I can promise you that. Just forget you ever had a son." He laughed bitterly. "Besides, once you see what I've done, I doubt you'll ever love me again."

He took one last look at her, picked up his bags, and walked out.

Outside, parked on the street, Cliff was enjoying the game. The L.A. Angels were up by three in the bottom of the eight. His stomach growled, and he hoped Annette would be down soon. He checked his watch; it was 6:10. Things must be going okay, since Annette had been gone for well over half an hour. That was really good, he thought. Hopefully they had found some way to accept each other. He turned his attention back to the game. It had been a close one, but the Angels had scored five in the top of the ninth, and it was the Orioles' last at-bat.

The game ended on a pop-out to center. As he turned the radio off, he saw a BMW appear at the top of the parking ramp. Barely slowing down, the driver pulled into traffic and squealed the tires as he sped away in the new car. Cliff wished he was on duty. *Nothing like a good chase.*

He looked at his watch again; it was now almost 6:30. His stomach growled again. It was way past his feeding time, so he decided to call Annette's cell phone. Even if things were going well, Derek must have to leave soon, anyway. Her phone rang five times, and just when he thought it was going to go into voice mail, it stopped, and he heard a muffled cry.

~~~

Upstairs in the apartment, Annette worked her bound body across the carpet. She could only move a little at a time, contracting and then extending to gain a few inches. The phone startled her, but she recognized the ring tone. It was a new jingle she had just programmed in a few weeks ago. She rolled over onto her other side and managed to slide over to the coffee table. She sat up and leaned forward. Her phone was face-up where she had left it when she was searching for the pictures. When it rang again, she saw Cliff's number in the small display. She leaned over and tried to push the *send* key with her nose, but the phone slid sideways. She laid her face down on the table and rolled her nose on top of the small phone. This time she managed to push the *send* key. She tried to yell, but only a vague mumble escaped her throat.

~~~

At first, Cliff wondered if his phone had crossed channels with someone else, but he saw Annette's name displayed on the caller I.D. He looked up at the apartment tower, wondering what the hell was going on, but then he realized who he had seen drive away. It had been Derek speeding off. He jumped out, ran to the front door, and pounded on the manager's button a half-dozen times.

A voice barked back through the scratchy intercom. "What is it?"

"I'm a police officer. There might be an emergency in 1017. I need to get inside right now."

"I'll be down in a few minutes." The man sounded tired and unconcerned.

Cliff looked at his watch as the seconds ticked by, trying to figure out how long it had been since Derek had driven away. Finally, the elevator light stopped at the L. The doors opened, and a middle-aged man in dark sweats and a torn old white T-shirt came out. He had a big ring of keys, and he opened the door a few inches. "Can I see some I.D.?"

Cliff held out his badge, hoping the man wouldn't ask what jurisdiction an Orange County deputy sheriff had in Long Beach. "Do you have keys to 1017?"

The man took a quick look at the badge and then backed away as he opened the door wider. "Sure."

Cliff ran to the elevator. "I might need you to let me in."

"Do you have a search warrant?"

Cliff grabbed the man by the arm. "No, and we might not have time. It could be a matter of life and death."

Cliff pushed the button for the elevator, and when the door opened, he hustled the manager in. On the tenth floor, the manager pointed to the right. Cliff ran down the hall to 1017 and banged on the door. He could hear a thumping.

"Annette, Annette, Annette!" He pounded on the door again and then turned to the manager. "Open it up."

The manager juggled his keys. "Wait a minute and see if someone answers."

Cliff leaned forward and put his ear against the door. The thumping shook him. "Open this door right now," he ordered.

"You're supposed to have a search warrant."

Cliff grabbed the keys out of the man's hands. "I don't have time for that. My wife is inside. Something could be terribly wrong. Which key is it?"

The manager took the keys back. "This was your idea, not mine." He found the right key, inserted it, unlocked the door, and stepped back. Cliff turned the knob and pushed, but it didn't move. He leaned into it with his body. The door reluctantly opened, and a pair of bound legs became visible. The manager looked shocked and jumped back. Cliff pushed the door open a little more. "Jesus Christ!"

Annette's wild eyes stared at him from under a mask of gray tape.

Chapter 16

Derek slowed down as he neared downtown Long Beach. He'd had the sports car doing seventy before he realized it. Getting stopped now would be disastrous. He reached for his phone and called his father.

Mansi answered on the first ring. "What is going on? Are you on the way to the airport?"

"Mother was snooping around and discovered my Canadian passport. I panicked and tied her up."

"What? I told you to kill her."

"I couldn't. I tried, but I couldn't." Derek turned right onto the 605 on-ramp. As he merged, a California Highway Patrol car passed him. The officer in the passenger seat looked over and smiled. Derek let off the gas and slipped in behind.

"Where is she now?" Mansi demanded.

"At my apartment. I'm on my way to LAX. I tied her up really well with duct tape."

"If she gets loose, she could ruin everything," Mansi hissed. "What does she know?"

"She doesn't know anything. All she knows is that I have a Canadian passport."

"Does she know what name it was?"

Derek hesitated, and then, for the first time in his life, he lied to his father. "I don't think so." Derek prayed his mother wouldn't remember his alias and that he would be long gone before she ever got untied.

"Good. But it won't matter once you're gone. Just be cool at the airport."

"I'm on my way. I will see you in Algiers in two days." Derek hung up.

Ahead, the patrol car was signaling right and heading for the next off-ramp. He floored it as soon as the police car disappeared, and in minutes he could see the jetliners coming in for landing on the multiple runways at LAX. Traffic started bunching up just before the 105 off-ramp, but he got off at the Century Blvd exit and slowed down so the cars behind would pass and leave him momentarily alone. He had one last thing to take care of, and the grass beside the off-ramp looked perfect. As he rolled down his window, a quick check in his rearview mirror showed no one was behind him, so he threw the gun over the chain-link fence into the low bush.

~~~

Cliff pulled the tape off Annette's face and mouth carefully. "Are you okay? What the hell happened?"

Annette's heart was pounding. "I thought Derek was going to kill me. He has a gun."

"I knew this was a bad idea, but why the hell would he want to kill you?"

"I opened a drawer by mistake. Inside, there were three passports. One was a Canadian passport with his picture, but someone else's name." She tried to picture the passport and his photo. "Mark . . . Mark Adams, I think."

"A fake passport? Why would he have a fake passport?"

Annette winced as the tape was pulled off her ears and out of her hair. "I don't know, but something is going on. He said that it was too late, that he was going to make his father proud, and when I asked him what he meant, he said that I would know soon enough."

Cliff pulled the rest of the tape off her upper body, gathering it in a sticky ball over her head as he unwound it. "Shit! What kind of mess is he in?"

The building manager defended Derek. "We have never had a problem with him before. He's as quiet as a mouse."

Cliff pushed the man toward the door. "This apartment is under my control. I'll get you a warrant soon, okay?"

"Whatever you say, just get me my warrant." The manager left and closed the door.

Annette stood up. "Cliff, he freaked out when I asked him why he had the Canadian passport. I couldn't believe it when he pulled out the gun."

"I have to call this in. Who knows what he's involved in."

Annette still didn't want to believe that her own son was involved in something illegal, but the look on Derek's face had been pure venom. "Whatever it is, it was important enough that he thought about killing me for it."

Cliff shook his head. "I hate to be a told-you-so, but I knew he wasn't going to be glad to see you. I should never have let you come up here on your own."

"Oh, I almost forgot. He cut his hair and dyed it light brown."

"I know. I saw him drive off. Shit!"

"Who are you going to call?"

"Will's on the desk tonight. If Derek is making those kinds of threats, he could be involved in some kind of terrorist plot. We need to stop him from getting away."

"Terrorist plot? Why the hell would he be involved in something like that?"

"I don't know. Why are any of those fanatics involved? Some misguided beliefs, hatred for the West, nobody knows. But in Derek's case, all the facts support it." Cliff ticked off the reasons on his fingers. "He said that you wouldn't love him when you saw what he had done. He might have killed you. He's Algerian. He's got at least one fake passport, maybe more. He's on the run. He sure fits the profile."

Annette closed her eyes and felt the hot tears on her cheek. "But he's my son."

"I know, honey," Cliff said as he dialed. "But Timothy McVeigh was somebody's son, too."

~~~

"Airport Security. This is Will Miller."

"Will, its Cliff. Annette's kid just about killed her a few minutes ago. He has a fake Canadian passport with a different name – Annette thinks it was Mark Adams." Cliff realized he was talking fast and tried to slow down. "Derek said that he was going to make his father proud, then he tied Annette up and took off. He's been running at least thirty minutes, and he's probably trying to get out of the country. Apparently he had a flight to London out of LAX at eight-thirty tonight. This could be a code red."

"Code red? Are you sure about this?"

"He damn near killed Annette. He's got a fake passport, he's got a gun, and he made some sinister threats. You're damn right I'm sure."

"What do you think he's involved in?"

"I don't know, but remember, this kid's father abducted him and took him back to Algeria. Oh, and he's cut his hair short and dyed it light brown."

"Okay, I'm on it. Are you on your cell phone?"

"Yes, and I'm calling the Long Beach police next. I need a crime scene team at his apartment. Call me if you get anything." He ended the call just as the official Department of Motor Vehicles photo id of Derek appeared on the screen on his cell phone. A computer updated version would follow. *CODE RED! CODE RED! CODE RED!* flashed repeatedly.

~~~

Derek found a spot on the second floor of the massive LAX parking lot close to the overhead causeway to the international terminal. He grabbed his bags and ran, hoping he would be seen as just another late passenger. But it didn't matter; people were hustling in every direction and nobody paid any attention to him. Inside the terminal, he slowed down and concentrated on his breathing, no sense attracting any undue attention.

It was busier inside the massive Tom Bradley International Terminal than it had looked, but there was only one couple ahead of him in the business-class line. He waited patiently for a few minutes, glancing about casually and trying to appear as disinterested as possible. Police officers were everywhere.

In a few minutes, the ticket agent finished with the couple ahead of him and waved him up. "Good evening, sir. Where are you flying this evening?"

"Good evening. I'm on flight 1101 to Paris at eight-thirty." He handed her his Canadian passport and his ticket.

"Thank you." She looked at his ticket and then his passport. Her eyes blinked a few times. When she looked up, she smiled pleasantly. "Yes, Mr. Adams. Let me check your flight."

Derek saw two officers on the other side of the terminal walking in his direction. He turned back to the agent. "Is the flight on time?"

"Yes, sir, it is," she replied without looking up.

The two policemen stopped beside Derek. One stood back a few steps with his hand resting on his gun. The other officer addressed Derek and the ticket agent. "Excuse me. May I see this man's passport, please?"

Derek felt his heart start to race. He turned and ran.

"Stop! Stop right now!" the officers yelled. "Stop, stop or we'll shoot!"

Derek turned at the warning, stumbled, and slammed into a bystander. They both tumbled to the ground, but he jumped to his feet and was off again. He headed for the exit doors, but two more policemen cut off his escape. He paused, looking frantically for another exit, but the officers tackled him and threw him to the floor. In seconds, the scuffle was over. Derek struggled in vain as he felt the handcuffs snap closed on his wrists.

~~~

Annette's ears hurt from the being taped so tightly, but other than the red marks across her cheeks, she was fine. "No, I'm okay," she told the two Long Beach police officers who had answered the call. "I don't need a doctor."

Cliff had explained what happened. "I believe there's a lot more to this than his attack on her," he added.

One of the officers had a pad out and took notes. "What else do you think he's involved in?"

Annette answered, "He said he was going to make his dead father proud, that I would soon know a lot more, and that I wouldn't want him as a son anymore."

The officers exchanged looks. "That sounds pretty vague."

Cliff added, "Except that he had a false passport."

The taller of the two men agreed. "You're probably right, but it doesn't sound like something for us. You said your partner has already called Homeland Security?"

Cliff looked at his watch. "Yes, about twenty minutes ago."

"Yeah, I got the alert." The officer nodded and then addressed Annette. "Do you want to press charges?"

Annette shuddered at the question. It was her son. She looked at Cliff for help.

"You have to, honey," Cliff said. "He tried to kill you. God knows what else he's capable of."

She had never been so frightened, first for her own life, and now for her son's. "But he's my son."

"He's already committed a very serious crime. He has a fake passport. That's a federal offense. There's no going back now."

She realized Cliff was right; it was already too late. Derek was in serious trouble already. "What do I have to do?"

"You'll have to come down to the station and sign the complaint. Then we can issue a warrant for his arrest."

"You said he had a gun," said the second policeman. "Can you describe it?"

"It was a hand gun, a pistol. A small one." Annette had stared down the black barrel for several minutes.

The officer pressed, "Would you recognize it if you saw it again?"

Annette could almost see the gun shaking in his hand. "I don't know. I couldn't believe what was happening. I didn't really pay attention to what it looked like. But I don't think he would shoot anyone."

"He might not be able to shoot you, his mother, point-blank," Cliff warned, "but the fact that he pulled the gun means he might shoot someone else."

The first police officer motioned toward the door and said, "Let's go. We need to let the lab go over the room."

Cliff followed Annette out. "I have my car outside. I can drive her over. Where's the station?"

"Downtown. Pine and Fifth."

~~~

Mansi was fuming and drove far too fast, but he didn't care. A speeding ticket wouldn't be a problem. Next time he returned to see Dawn, he would have a new name and a new driver's license. It took him less than half an hour to make it to Derek's apartment, and he was dismayed to find a Long Beach black-and-white parked outside. He parked a half block away and checked his appearance in the mirror. He had dyed his hair blonde, and with his glasses and baseball hat, he hardly recognized himself. He pulled out his 9mm Beretta, checked the clip, and twisted the silencer to make sure it was on tight. Then he slipped it back in his belt and pulled his sweater down to cover it. He looked back at the police car, got out, and started walking toward the tower.

Mansi hadn't taken three or four steps when he saw the police officers come out of the elevator, and right behind the police, he recognized Annette. He hadn't seen her in twenty years, but it was definitely her. He dropped his head, turned in at the next walkway, and headed for the lobby of the neighboring high-rise. With one eye on the reflection in the window, Mansi reached for the keypad and pretended to push a few numbers. He stood back and watched patiently as the police got in their car and drove away. He figured the big sandy-haired guy who opened the Jeep's passenger door for Annette had to be her fiancé, the cop Derek had mentioned. He faked another attempt on the keypad and then walked away, not looking in Annette's direction and keeping his back to her. He heard the Jeep start up behind him as he reached his own car, and just after he got in and closed the door, he heard it pull out. He started his car and waited until they went by, then he pulled in behind them.

~~~

"He must have been trying to leave tonight," Cliff said to Annette as they drove. He was positive Derek had been ready to leave the country for good when Annette showed up. As if in answer to his question, his phone rang. He dropped the small phone into the cradle and pushed the speaker button. "This is Cliff Billings."

It was Will, and he was excited. "Cliff, they got him!"

"That's fantastic news." Annette would be safe. "Where did they catch him?"

"At LAX. He was trying to get on a flight to Paris. What the hell is going on?"

"We have no idea, but it smells really bad."

"Will? It's Annette. Is he okay?"

"Hi, Annette. I didn't hear anything about injuries. Where are you two now?"

"We're on our way to the Long Beach police station to sign a complaint. Where is Derek now?" Cliff turned onto Pine Street.

"He's being held at LAX."

~~~

Mansi followed at a safe distance, wondering where they were going, but then he saw the half-dozen squad cars parked in front of the police station. "Shit," he muttered, slamming his hand on the steering wheel. Getting close enough to eliminate Annette was going to be impossible. He should have killed her years ago.

～～

"Can this wait?" Annette pointed to the police station as Cliff pulled over to park.

"Why?" Cliff didn't turn the engine off.

"I want to go to LAX and confront him. Maybe we can help find out what he's up to."

Cliff shook his head but began backing up. Rolling the window down, he reached under the seat and came out with a portable red light.

Annette had never seen the light before. "I didn't know you had one of those."

"They were issued after 9/11. Never know when an off-duty deputy sheriff needs to get somewhere in a hurry." Cliff reached outside, put the light on the roof, and flipped a switch on the lower part of the dash. The light started flashing, and the siren pierced the night.

～～

Mansi couldn't believe it. Derek had made a mess of everything. He waited until the Jeep turned the corner and was out of sight, then he reached under his belt and took out his gun. He opened the glove box and threw the gun inside. Things were spiraling out of control, and killing Annette probably wouldn't make any difference now.

Chapter 17

Derek was dragged out of the terminal by four unhappy police officers who threw him into the back of a squad car. His head hurt from where he had hit the armrest, but when he complained, they just laughed. It was a short ride to the police station and it was busy inside. He was surprised at the collection of characters crowded into the waiting room, but nobody paid any attention as he was taken directly into the back hall and down into a small, windowless room with a large mirror that covered one wall. Three wooden chairs, one with arms, and a heavy metal table were set in the middle of the room.

He was shoved into the lone chair, and his handcuffs were clipped into the thick metal eyelet on top of the table. He tested the weight of the table, but he couldn't budge it. Escape hadn't been something they studied.

One of the officers read him his rights. They started asking him questions, but he did exactly what he had been trained to do and asked to call his lawyer. One of the policemen found the business card in Derek's wallet and dialed the number for him. The officer held the phone to Derek's ear. When the phone answered, it was a recording, but the attorney's voice promised a quick return call, so he left a message.

The officers tried to intimidate him with descriptions about how he would be treated by the other inmates. Derek shuddered at their crude threats. Prison had never been something he had even remotely considered. They went through his bags and found his cash, almost over 10,000 dollars in fifties and hundreds. The bundles of bills lay in a thick stack on the table beside the passports. He told them hookers didn't like credit cards. They laughed like friends.

After fifteen or twenty minutes of badgering, two FBI agents showed up. "I'm FBI Special Agent Phil Housely. This is my partner Alex Romero. You are in a spot of trouble, young man."

Phil looked like he was in his early fifties and was the older of the two agents. Derek thought he looked more like a lawyer than a cop. His double-breasted dark brown suit, stiff white shirt, and splashy checked tie were in contrast to his partner, who was dressed much more casually in a sports jacket, jeans, and open-collar shirt.

"Where's my attorney?"

"I don't know. What did he say when you called?" Phil slid his right hand through his thick gray hair and pulled a pair of reading glasses out of his inside jacket pocket.

"All I got was his answering machine."

Phil looked at his partner, who hadn't said a word.

Alex was probably forty or so, but his dark brown hair was rapidly thinning. He turned the chair backwards and pulled it close to the table. "Why don't you just tell us the truth? If you're innocent, it doesn't matter."

"I thought I didn't have to answer any questions until my attorney was here."

The agent smiled. "You don't, son, but if it's the truth, it's the truth, and the judge will go easier on you if you cooperate from the get-go."

Derek thought through his story one more time. It was simple, but he had to make it believable.

A uniformed officer opened the door. "The kid's lawyer is here."

Derek wasn't impressed when the attorney walked in. Short and overweight, with thick glasses, the man looked more like a clerk than a lawyer, but he had no choice. Mansi had assured him that the man could help with just about anything legal.

"Hi." The man sat down and slid a business card across the table. "I'm Bezzi Tazrit."

"Can you get me out?" Derek said.

"I don't know. They haven't charged you yet because they're waiting for an Interpol report. Is there anything else I need to know about?"

"No, this passport thing was just a foolish mistake on my part."

"What about this attempted murder of your mother?" Bezzi took out a notepad.

"My mother is nuts. I haven't seen her for years. She freaked out, wouldn't let me go. I panicked, that's all, and it was only tape." It was her word against his.

"She says you had a gun."

"That's all bullshit, too. I've never owned a gun."

Bezzi nodded. "If they don't come up with anything, I can probably get you out on bail. It's not going to be easy, though, and the judge might set a fairly high amount, but I think we'll be fine financially. Significant funds have been in place for a long time."

"I want to get out of here as soon as possible. Right now, if I can." Derek knew many things had been in place for years, but he didn't care about the details.

"Let me go see what's going on with the Interpol report. It's early in Europe. Maybe I can get this moving a little faster."

"Make it happen, and make it happen fast." Derek and his father had only briefly discussed what might happen if either one of them was arrested. There was no real plan.

"It'll be easier if you answer some of the FBI's questions."

"Will you be here?"

"Yes, and if you don't want to answer any particular question, don't. We can talk about those issues one-on-one later. Okay?"

"Okay."

Bezzi nodded to the FBI agents, invisible through mirror, but waiting outside the door. The doorknob turned immediately and the tall agent entered.

Phil sat down in one of the empty chairs. "Okay, everything you say is being recorded and can be used against you in a court of law. We have already read you your rights, but you understand all this, right?"

Derek looked at Bezzi for confirmation. The attorney nodded.

"Tell me why you had three passports?" Phil pulled out a small notepad.

Derek stuck to the story he had concocted. "As I'm sure you know by now, the other two passports are real. I have dual citizenship, but neither Algerians nor Americans are always welcome in the world, so I just felt much safer traveling this way. Canadians are no one's enemy and everybody's friend."

Phil nodded as if in agreement. "Okay, but why use a false name?"

"That's what was available." That sounded weak, but he couldn't think of another plausible reason.

The agent held up the arrest sheet. "Why did you try to kill your mother?"

"I told the police that, too. She's lying. Ever since she found me last week, she won't leave me alone. I panicked and tied her up so I could get away from her. She was hysterical."

"The Long Beach Police are drawing up a warrant for your arrest," said Housely. "If there's something else, now is the time to tell us."

"I don't know why you're taking her word. She hasn't seen me in twenty years, and she flipped out. She wouldn't let me go."

"What did you mean by all those threats?"

"What threats?"

"The ones you made to your mother. The threats you made about something that might happen."

"I told you, I didn't make any threats." Derek prayed the wheels of American justice would turn quickly and he could be out on bail in a few hours. "I haven't done anything wrong."

Housely smiled. "Is the work you do at Trainor Jets confidential?"

"I guess, but it's pretty basic. I'm just a computer programmer."

"So is my son. Are you a software designer, or service and support?"

"I'm a systems designer." There was nothing they could find.

"That's great. What do you design?"

"Flight Integration Navigation Execution Systems. FINES, for short."

"That sounds pretty cool."

"It is." Derek remembered what his father had told him about the good-cop, bad-cop routine, but all his employment information would be on the table anyway.

"I've called Trainor Jets. They know you're under arrest."

Derek pictured Bill Simpson. He must be shell-shocked. First, Sudesh's death last week, and now his arrest. Bill would feel lost. Derek had worked hard to be a model employee and easy to get along with. "I hope I don't lose my job."

Phil smiled. "You've already committed one serious crime, Derek. If you tell us what else is going on, maybe we can go much easier on you. Who knows, maybe you can be back at work in a few days."

~~~

The flashing lights and screaming siren cleared the six lanes of traffic very effectively, and Cliff hit almost a hundred miles an hour in some places as he raced up the freeway. Annette clung to the door handle, less scared of the high speed than terrified by their wild attempts to guess what kind of trouble Derek was in.

Cliff braked hard at the off-ramp, squealing the tires as they pulled onto the city street. With the lights and siren still wailing, the thin Sunday-night traffic scattered, and Cliff stomped on the gas for two blocks before making a hard right and screeching to a stop in front of the LAX police station.

They jumped out and ran. "He sure has a lot of explaining to do," Cliff said as he opened the heavy glass door for Annette.

Annette thought that was an understatement. "I just hope that whatever he has planned, we can stop him in time."

They were taken into a private meeting room. A man in a white shirt and bright yellow tie was on the phone. Tall, with grey hair and thick reading glasses, the man smiled as he hung up the phone.

The police officer introduced Annette and Cliff. "These are the kid's parents."

Cliff stuck out his hand. "I'm Deputy Sheriff Cliff Billings, but I'm not the father. This is Annette Madison. She's the mother, I'm her fiancé."

"Special Agent Phil Housely." Phil shook Cliff's hand first, but he directed his questions at Annette. "He tried to kill you? His own mother?"

"Yes and no. He threatened me with a gun, but he didn't actually try to kill me. He just tied me up with duct tape."

"Where is his father?"

"I haven't seen him for twenty years. Derek told me that he died in car crash ten years ago."

Phil turned to Cliff. "Are you also the deputy who called in the Red Alert?"

"Yes. Something is going on here, and the kid's past made me very nervous."

"I will stay out of the attempted murder charge, but until we get the results back from Interpol, he won't be going anywhere." Phil agreed.

Someone knocked on the door, and another man walked in. Housely introduced the younger agent. "This is my partner, Alex Romero."

Alex was short, but what he lacked in height he made up for in size. He was stocky and looked like he had been lifting weights for years. "Can we start from the beginning?" he said.

Annette looked at Cliff, who shrugged. "I haven't seen my son since was kidnapped by his father twenty years," she began. "Last week I found him by a complete fluke, but he didn't want to see me. He was hardly even civil." She paused. "Today, I decided that I would drop by for a few minutes. I just wanted to ask him a few questions."

Phil was taking notes. "Go on."

"At first, he didn't want to see me, but he let me in, and we talked about a few things. It was going okay. Then I spilled some water on his coffee table. I asked him for a towel, but he told me not to worry about it. Then his phone rang, and he took it into the bedroom. I opened a drawer looking for a coaster; that is when I saw the three passports."

The agent looked down at the three passports on the table.

Annette nodded and continued, "The Canadian one was sitting on top, and that seemed really odd to me, so I opened it. I was shocked."

"Is that when he caught you?"

"Yes, and when I asked him what was going on, he pulled the gun out."

Phil shook his head in disbelief. "Not many people could kill their own mother."

"Good thing for me. Then he told me that he would never see me again, but promised that I would soon know more than I wanted to."

"He says that you made it all up," Alex said. "He says that you've been bothering him, that you wouldn't let him go. He says that's why he panicked and tied you up."

Annette was floored. "Made it up? He threatened to kill me!"

"You don't doubt her, do you?" Cliff asked.

"No, but other than her story and this Canadian passport, we don't really have much on him."

"I understand." Cliff nodded. "How long can you hold him?"

Phil shrugged his shoulders. "As you know, possessing a fake passport is a serious federal offense, especially these days, but unless there is some other evidence, I'm not sure. He'll probably get bail in a few days."

Annette didn't know what was appropriate. "He almost killed me. He tied me up."

"As I said, that's a different charge. But if something else comes up, or if he tells you something, maybe we could hold him longer."

"Did he tell you where he worked?" Annette asked.

Alex pointed to the employee I.D. card on the table. "He's a computer programmer at Trainor Jets in Long Beach. They make private jets."

"What? Trainor Jets?" She picked up the I.D. card.

"It's a small world," Cliff answered the agent's look. "Annette's father worked there years ago."

Phil raised his eyebrows. "Is it possible there's some connection here?"

"I don't know, but they never knew each other, and my father has been dead for almost forty years, long before Derek was born." Why hadn't she asked him about where he worked? *What a coincidence.*

"We've contacted Trainor Jets already," Alex said. "They're beefing up security and running system checks."

"Can we see him?" Now that she would be safe, she had a million questions to ask him.

"Sure."

They were led down a long corridor and through the double steel security doors that led into the holding room. Derek sat on the single bunk in the narrow cell. He looked thoroughly dejected, and her heart went out to him. He was still her son, even if he was in jail, and even if he was guilty.

~~~

His father had been right; he should have killed her. The police had told him that he was going to be charged with attempted murder, but that was the least of his problems. He needed to get out on bail as quickly as possible, and when he heard voices coming down the hall, he hoped it was his attorney with some good news. The steel bolts of the holding room door slid back with a heavy clunk, but to his dismay it was his mother, her boyfriend, and the two FBI agents.

Derek snarled, "I told you I didn't want to see anybody."

"You've got no choice pal, and your mother deserves some answers," Cliff barked. "What the hell are you involved in?"

His mother's tone was softer. "Derry, we can help you if you let us. What is so terrible that you would want to kill me?"

Derek looked down at the worn concrete floor. He hated his mother. She had deserted him as a boy, lied repeatedly, and had no idea about a leading pure life. She was just another American whore. How many men had she slept with? He had never wanted to see her once in the ten years he had lived in Southern California. For him, she had ceased to exist. For her to have him caged like this was the ultimate disgrace. His father would demand the ultimate sacrifice.

He repeated his lie to his mother as if he were pleading, as if he she didn't understand. "I never tried to kill you. I tied you up because you were hysterical. I had to catch my flight, and you wouldn't let me go."

"Derek, that's not what happened. Why are you lying? If you tell us the truth, maybe we can help you."

He wanted to laugh. There was nothing she could do to help him now. It was far too late. "I don't want your help, can't you figure that out? Are you stupid, woman?"

Annette stumbled back a step, almost falling. Cliff had to grab her. The FBI agents gave him a threatening look, but they didn't move.

"Derek, I love you. Something is going on. I still love you, and I still care about what happens to you."

"You never loved me before. Why would you fucking care now?"

"I keep telling you, that is not true. Your father lied to you. I loved you then, and no matter what is going on, I still love you now."

"Bullshit."

Of all the scenarios and outcomes they had evaluated and planned for, having to deal with his mother's lies and questions like this had never been remotely considered and should never have happened. It had been such a fluke, but it was obvious now that he had made the wrong decision in the critical moment. Surely his lawyer could get her out of his face.

"Did your father tell you that your grandfather worked for Trainor, too?"

Derek stared at her. All Mansi had told him was that his grandfather had been a boring middle-class factory worker. "My grandfather . . . your father?"

"Yes, he worked there for twenty years and was a shift manager in the wing section."

Why hadn't his father told him that? It probably didn't really matter, but it was pretty incredible. He closed his eyes for a moment and tried to shut out the problems. One thing was clear. "I know my rights, and I told you, I'm not answering any more questions."

"What if it's just me?" Annette asked. "Would that be better?"

"No."

The FBI agents took them back to a private waiting room, where two small televisions were perched on a shelf. One had CNN on; the other showed Derek sitting on his bed. They had taken off his handcuffs and shackles, and he sat hunched over, his elbows on his knees and a scowl on his face. Everyone had been shocked by his angry outbursts and wondered if Annette was luckier than she realized. Maybe he did hate enough to kill.

Alex said it for all of them: "There is obviously a lot of hostility there. I guess one of the questions is, why?"

"He sure has some issues with you," Phil agreed.

"Yes, it seems his father told him all kinds of lies about me." She dabbed at her tears.

"Where did this car accident that killed his father happen?"

"He didn't say."

"We can check it out."

Annette nodded, "Who knows what is true. What happens now?"

"We can probably hold him for forty-eight hours. The phony passport will require an Interpol check, and that takes time, but if he's clean, he could get bail. He could be out in the next day or two."

"We were on our way to sign a complaint against him," Cliff said. "Hopefully the Long Beach Police can get out a warrant in the next few hours. Will that help?"

"Yes. Have them send it over right away. The more charges, the better. If we can convince the judge there's something larger going on, we can hold him for quite a while. The new terrorist laws give us new powers to detain and question suspects."

Annette didn't know what to think. "Is there anything else I can do?"

"No, not right now," Alex said. "But leave us your phone number, and we'll call you if something comes up."

They thanked the agents and the police for their help and left. It was past midnight. As they were driving away, Annette's stomach growled, and she managed to laugh. "I'm sorry, honey. I promised you dinner. You must be starved. We'd better get something before we go to Long Beach."

Cliff was more than starved, so they pulled into a Burger King before hitting the 405 freeway south. They ordered burgers with fries, and Cliff asked for Italian sauce on his. She laughed and apologized again, but the custom order was cooked fresh. It was tasty and amusing. Cliff finished her burger when she gave up on it.

"Mansi or somebody must have brainwashed him," Annette mused. "There's no other answer."

"He sure has some incredible misunderstandings about you," Cliff agreed.

"I guess that's why he never wanted to see me."

"I think that's only part of it."

Downtown Long Beach was deserted, and Cliff parked right in front of the police station. "You ready?" he asked.

She had no choice. The desk sergeant took them back to see the lieutenant on duty. He had the complaints all ready to go. After a thorough explanation, the officer slid the paperwork in front of her. "You understand that the district attorney might choose to prosecute this as a lesser offense, but for now, we'll charge him with attempted murder."

Annette asked a few other questions; then signed all the forms. "Not an easy thing to do, signing your child's arrest warrant."

"No, I'm sure it's really tough," the lieutenant said as he separated the copies. "Okay, that's it. We'll send a copy of the complaint over to LAX right away."

"Thanks for all your help, Officer," Annette said.

Cliff yawned as they got back in the Jeep. "That warrant will help keep him in jail for a while."

Annette was exhausted, too. "A few days ago I was ecstatic that I had finally found my son," she said sadly, "and now I've just signed an attempted murder complaint against him."

Cliff headed for Ocean Blvd. "And that might not be the worst of it."

Annette shivered. The possibilities were all too unreal. "What is the FBI doing now?"

"They're probably running checks on both Derek and your ex-husband. Maybe they can find some connection. I think he could be planning some kind of terrorist attack."

The mother in her had to defend her son. "But he's an American citizen. Why would he want to do that?"

"He's also an Algerian, a Muslim, and so is his father."

"That's kind of stereotyping, isn't it? I thought you weren't supposed to make those kinds of snap judgments."

"You're right, honey," Cliff said, but he didn't sound convinced that he was wrong, "Let's just wait and see what happens."

She didn't say anything, but her mind was spinning out of control with everything that had happened. What other explanation made any sense?

~~~

The name TAZRIT displayed on the caller ID screen surprised him and probably wasn't good news. "Yes, what is it?"

"This is Bezzi Tazrit. I'm sorry to bother you in the middle of the night, but I was instructed to call this number if anything ever happened to Derek Ansour. And he has just been arrested at LAX."

Mansi wanted to scream. One of his worst fears had been realized. He sat up, wide awake. "What has he been arrested for?"

"He was caught using a fake passport trying to leave the country, and apparently he tried to kill his mother." Bezzi told the man what he knew.

"Can you get him out on bail?" The contingency he had hoped would never happen, but had anticipated.

"I don't know," said Bezzi, sounding tired. "The police haven't charged him with anything yet."

~~~

The phone jarred Art from some odd dream about flying, but he was a light sleeper and sat up immediately. Joan grumbled as she turned over and looked at the clock on her side of the bed. It was two o'clock in the morning. "It's the middle of the night. That can't be good news."

The caller I.D. display answered his wife's question. It was Bill Simpson's home number. He reached for the cordless handset on the nightstand by the bed and managed to catch it before its third ring. "Bill, what's going on?"

"Sorry for calling you at this hour, Art, but something really bizarre just happened. Derek Ansour has been arrested trying to leave the country with a fake passport after he apparently tried to kill his mother." Bill sounded very dubious but worried.

"What? Derek?" His programmer? Art pictured the quiet young kid. "That's nuts!"

"Yeah, but it's true. The FBI called a few minutes ago, and they're on their way to our Long Beach offices right now."

"What for?"

"Apparently he made some threats of something big happening, something that would bring glory to the family name. The FBI wonders if it has anything to do with our jets."

Art headed for his closet. There would be no going back to sleep now. He tried to imagine what the FBI thought they could find. "Tell me that's not possible."

"It's not possible, but they want to have a look at our operation anyway."

"Let them look, we have nothing to be worried about." Art pulled on a pair of black cotton pants and a yellow dress shirt. Hopefully he would be back in a few hours.

"No we don't. I'm going to the office to meet the FBI," Bill said. "I'll call you as soon as I know anything. Awful coincidence though. First Sudesh, now Derek."

"Yeah," Art was trying to connect the dots himself. "I'm on my way in too."

"Okay, I'll see you there."

~~~

Annette was dead tired. It was almost three o'clock in the morning when she turned out the light. She crawled in beside her future husband and wrapped her arms around him. He was more than just her man. "Aren't we supposed to get married in a few weeks?"

Cliff snuggled close. "We are. We still can. Everything is pretty much all arranged."

"What about Derek?"

"Why? Were you going to invite him to the wedding?"

Annette laughed. "I hadn't thought about that."

"Who knows – with a good attorney, he might not have to do time." They hadn't talked about jail too much. Cliff did say if his crimes were unrelated and nothing else happened, a judge might well turn him loose on bail.

"It's still hard to believe. Last week Derek was nonexistent, and then he was a miracle. Now he's a criminal?" There had to be some other logical explanation.

"I don't know, honey. We'll see. Try to get some sleep. It's going to be a hectic day tomorrow."

"Tell me everything is going to be all right. Tell me this is just a bad dream." She pushed back into Cliff's arms a little more.

"I wish I could, honey. I wish I could."

~~~

Even in Los Angeles, traffic died down to almost nothing in the dead of the night, and Art made it to his office in twenty minutes, half the time it normally took from his home in Rancho Palos Verdes. On a really busy morning, it could take over an hour. There were normally only six employees on duty in the control room at Trainor's Long Beach head office on the night shift, but he could see there were a lot more technicians than that hunched over their computers. Bill must have called some other programmers in. Usually most everyone would say hi, but only a few looked up as their fingers danced across their keyboards and their eyes scrolled through line after line of software.

Bill was standing beside two young men in recently pressed dark suits who were sitting in front of computers filled with programming code. He smiled when he saw his boss. "It looks like this has nothing to do with us."

Art felt himself let out a deep breath. "That's great news."

Bill looked quite relieved, too. "Yes, I'll say so." He turned to the two young men. "Art, this is Tim Batterson and Charlie Demori from the FBI."

The agents were probably in their early thirties, young enough to understand some of the technical aspects of the software, but that's about as far as their computer knowledge was going to help them. The one-of-a-kind integration of automation and navigation into a live interface represented tens of thousands of hours of code and baffled many industry experts. Art wondered if the two FBI agents would even know where to start looking.

"Sorry to drag you two out in the middle of the night," Art said. "Hopefully this is all just a bad coincidence."

"Yes, sir. We hope so, too," they replied in unison, as if on cue.

"Nothing out of the ordinary?" Art asked Bill for clarification and reassurance.

"Everything looks fine so far," Bill replied. "I've given them access to all our programming, but to this point, everything looks good."

Tim Batterson stopped typing. "There are millions of lines of code here, so it's a little premature to give you the all-clear, but yes, so far we can see nothing irregular."

Bill elaborated, "We have no security breaches at any of our facilities. We've run diagnostics on all our aircraft, and nothing seems out of place. We checked all our in-house systems, and manufacturing is looking at their platforms right now. I don't know what else to look for."

"Is there anything else Derek could have gotten access to?" Art asked.

"I checked his log-on. He never logged into anywhere he wasn't supposed to."

"Have you looked at the traffic scheduled for today?" Art looked at one of the large computer screens. A list of flight data was constantly being updated.

"Yeah, it's not that busy a day today," said Bill. "As you know, there's the World Business Congress Summit Wednesday in Washington this week, so we have a lot of flight plans filed for D.C. for tomorrow, but traffic is relatively light today."

"Not a time for anything to go wrong," Art muttered. He had already lost two of his best software programmers in one week.

"We could reload the software on the planes," Bill suggested, "which would take hours to complete, but of course all the planes would have to be on the ground. That would be almost impossible in the short term."

"No, I don't think that will be necessary. Derek's arrest probably has nothing to do with us." Art sure didn't want any doubts hanging over Trainor Jets. Hopefully it was just a sad domestic issue. "It's sure hard to believe he threatened to kill his mother."

"You know I worked with him for five years. He never seemed like the violent type."

"I wonder what the hell he was doing with a fake passport?"

"Yeah, that's pretty wild. I mean, who gets a fake passport?" Bill shook his head in disbelief. "That's a pretty serious crime on its own these days."

"Yes, and that bothers me the most."

"If we could focus on the task at hand, gentlemen?" Tim said.

"Sorry." Art turned back to the two agents. Both were clicking through pages of data. He doubted they would know a problem if they saw one.

Tim seemed to be in charge. "So if anything happens to any of these jets, you can take control from here and land the plane?"

"Yes, that is correct."

"Even if there is a terrorist on board, and he wants to redirect his flight?"

"Even then. We simply override his authorization and land the plane wherever we want."

Tim turned to his partner. "We'll keep running through the software, but tell Washington that so far we can't find anything out of the ordinary."

"How many planes do we have in the air?" Art thought he could see a few dozen of the tiny jets moving slowly across the holistic 3D image of the earth that seemed to hang in the center of the room.

Bill's touched a few keys, and a window with flight status appeared. "Twenty-two."

There would be dozens more in the air by nine o'clock that morning, and hundreds going to the convention in D.C. on Wednesday. Art said a silent prayer as he got up. "I'll be in my office. Call me if anything changes."

Chapter 18

Mansi was exhausted. He had driven around for several hours, wondering if he should proceed with their plans. Around 3:00 a.m. he checked into a motel not too far from Long Beach Airport. He showed his British Columbia driver's license to the clerk and paid with Canadian cash for two nights. Inside the room, he checked his suitcase to make sure he had no incriminating evidence that could identify him as Mansi Ansour. After he said morning prayers, he collapsed on one of the twin beds.

He should have killed Annette ten years ago when he had killed Linda, but Hashim had wanted to give Darcy a chance. Jill had turned into such a formidable asset that Hashim fancied the idea of another girl, and even speculated that maybe girls were better soldiers for an army that fights the West. They had discussed how they would take Darcy a few times, but when Mansi had driven by and scouted Annette's house, a squad car had been parked next door on a regular basis, and he had never gotten any closer.

What he should have done was killed Annette and taken Darcy as a baby. Then none of this would have happened, and Derek would be on his way to Algiers right now. Darcy would have just finished her years of training and been on her way back to the States. He would have his third sword. He prayed for forgiveness. He prayed that his weakness ten years ago would not cost him success tomorrow, and he prayed his son would do what he had promised his father he would.

~~~

Annette turned to look at the clock again. It was ten till six o'clock. She hadn't slept more than a few hours, but the night was definitely over. She kept replaying the evening's shocking turn of events in her head over and over. It was so hard to accept. Absent from her life for twenty years, Derek was suddenly back, and in ways she could never have imagined.

Cliff had fallen asleep shortly after they got home. She had listened to his slow, steady breathing and tried to use it to hypnotize herself back to sleep. It hadn't worked. Every time his chest rose and fell, she silently thought, *I love you*, and then found herself thinking, *I need you*. Cliff had been in her life for ten years, and soon he was going to be officially and legally the man in her life, her second husband and the fifth close relationship with a male in her life. She prayed he would never leave; she just couldn't take that. But his patience and support had been obvious since they went to Algiers ten years ago. Cliff was a great guy and loved her. She could see and feel that, but had to remind herself that she had felt the same with both Paul and Mansi. Men came into her life with such promise and joy, but they could be gone instantly and leave nothing but anguish and sorrow.

Cliff's words from years ago haunted her, and she realized how right he had been. He had cautioned her on how people change and that she should not expect to have the normal mother and son relationship they'd had before. Had he seen the future? What would her father think of Cliff? What would her father think about his grandson working at Trainor Jets? What a small world.

Her father's funeral had been on a wet day in October thirty years ago. Mack Trainor had been the first speaker, and she never forgot his kind words. "Love never ends," he had said. She remembered Val standing beside their father's grave and crying endlessly, but at nine years old, who understood such things? For a while, Annette had wished she were dead, too. Her mother had amazed her. Marie never cried. How had she been so strong?

When she focused her tired eyes on the alarm clock, it was now 6:40. Had she slept?

As she pulled herself out from under the covers, Cliff stirred and mumbled, "Did I have a terrible nightmare?"

"No, honey, that nightmare was real," Annette said as she turned the radio on. The weather report was finishing. It was going to be another nice day. "Are you sure you still want to marry me? Who knows what kind of criminal I have for a son."

Cliff turned over and pulled her on top of him. He nibbled on her neck and then kissed her gently. "Who better to protect you?"

"Thank God you were there yesterday."

"I should have gone upstairs with you. Thank God you didn't get hurt. I would have never forgiven myself."

"I'm sorry. It's my fault. I shouldn't have gone in the first place."

"Then Derek would have gotten away."

"God, you're right." That hadn't occurred to her. "If I hadn't gone, he would be gone." She got out of bed and shivered as she headed for the bathroom.

Cliff got up, too. "I'll call in and get some time off. I have a feeling today is going to be a busy day."

"Thanks, honey. I sure hope they can find out what Derek is up to." Did she really want to know? Could she deal with the truth?

"I'll call the bureau, too, and see if they came up with anything last night." Cliff slipped on a pair of sweats and a t-shirt and headed for the kitchen.

~~~

Derek didn't sleep for more than a few minutes at a time, tossing and turning on the hard, narrow bunk. He was worried about his immediate fate, but he was more concerned about disappointing his father, whose fury he knew all too well. He prayed throughout the night that he would get out on bail in the morning. Then, he hoped, he could get to Mexico, where his Spanish should help him escape. The guards came in around 7:00 a.m. with a few pieces of cold, dry toast and a glass of warm orange juice. He wolfed it down, and then they shackled both his arms and his legs. They let him sit in his cell, unable to move, for over a half hour before they came back and got him. He figured that was just part of their pitiful techniques that his father had already warned him about. "They will try and mess with your mind," Mansi had said, "but don't worry – the Americans would never actually hurt you."

Bezzi was waiting at the courthouse. Derek was surprised that after such a short night, his attorney now looked so sharp. His suit was well tailored, and he spoke with a grace that seemed out of place given his earlier demeanor. "The police have nothing back from Interpol yet, so I believe they are going to charge you with kidnapping and possessing a false passport for now. They could add other charges later."

"Will I get bail?" The charges meant nothing if he could get out.

"I don't know. Maybe if I can get the charges reduced. We'll see in a few minutes."

The bailiff called Derek's case first, and Bezzi grabbed him by the arm and helped him stand up to address the court.

"Bezzi Tazrit representing Mr. Ansour, your honor."

The judge looked down through her oversized glasses at Derek first, and then she glared at Bezzi. "I don't believe I've seen you in my court before, Mr. Tazrit."

"You haven't, Judge Herrmann." Bezzi thought the woman looked far past retirement age. Many worked for years after they turned sixty five.

"Well, there's always that first time." The grey haired justice turned to the prosecutor. "Good morning, Mr. Shenley. What do we have?"

The prosecutor stood up. His boyish face suggested he was in his forties, but his advanced male-pattern baldness added fifteen years and made him look much older. His worn brown jacket and wrinkled pants didn't help his fading appearance. He looked down at his notes before speaking. "We would like a postponement of the arraignment, your honor. The arrest was only twelve hours ago, and we have not had a chance yet to fully evaluate the evidence we have."

Derek turned to say something to his attorney, but Bezzi cut him off with a sharp look and a quick finger to his lips before he had a chance to utter a sound.

"How long do you need?" the judge asked the prosecutor.

"Another twenty-four hours, your honor."

Judge Herrman turned to Bezzi and Derek. "Sounds reasonable to me. What say you, Mr. Tazrit?"

Bezzi held up a stack of papers. "Your honor, my client has no priors of any kind and is a fine, upstanding, law-abiding young man. He is not a criminal, and I believe the charges sound much worse than the facts. He is an American citizen and willing to answer to all charges. All we ask, your honor, is that we proceed with the arraignment today, as planned, and if it should please the court, allow him to post bail."

"That sounds reasonable, too." The judge turned back to the prosecutor. "Mr. Shenley, anything else?"

The district attorney read from the arrest sheet. "Your honor, the defendant was caught trying to use a false passport to leave the country, and, in a separate incident, assaulted his mother, purportedly making threats that could only be interrupted as evil, grand, and very sinister. His actions are viewed as suspicious, to say the least, and not the behavior of someone with nothing to hide. I urge you to allow this short postponement so we may have a chance for further and sufficient investigation."

The judge looked down at her copy of the complaint for a few minutes, then banged her gavel once. "The charges are serious crimes, and the defendant attempted to flee at the airport. I am going to grant the prosecution's wish. The arraignment is postponed for twenty-four hours. I'll give the FBI a little latitude under our new laws."

Bezzi dropped his stack of documents on the table. "But your honor, the prosecution has no evidence that my client made any threats. It's his word against hers."

"Except for the fact that she isn't charged with two serious offenses," the judge replied. "Sorry, Mr. Tazrit. This case is remanded for another twenty-four hours."

Bezzi started to protest again. "But your honor, the FBI—"

"Did you not understand me, Mr. Tazrit?" she cut him off sharply. "You are done here today. Bailiff? Next case!"

The two guards grabbed Derek, but he couldn't believe what was happening and struggled with his captors. "Your honor, what about my rights? I'm entitled to due process!"

"And you will get it, Mr. Ansour."

The guards turned him around and dragged him out of the courtroom.

~~~

Marie and Val were over at Annette's house just after 9:00. Annette had another pot of coffee on and did her best to answer all their questions, but they were just as shocked and dumbfounded as she was. Lisa and Darcy didn't know what to say. Just a few days ago, they had been excited about having an older brother; now they were terrified of what he might be.

The call from the FBI shut everyone up. Cliff looked pleased. "No bail. They're going to hold him another twenty-four hours."

Annette shivered at the painful words. "Can we see him again? Maybe if we all go up, he'll open up a little more."

Darcy wasn't enthusiastic. "I don't even know him."

"He should remember me," Val said. "I babysat him for seven years."

"He should remember his grandmother, too," said Marie, sounding hurt.

"He might get violent again," Cliff suggested.

Darcy looked back and forth between her mother and Cliff. "He'll still be behind bars, right?"

Cliff didn't smile. "Maybe for a long time."

Annette didn't know what to wish for anymore.

They all drove up to LAX together. The five women were all hopping mad, yet they all wanted to believe that it looked worse than it was. He was family, one of them. He was their little Derry.

The police were surprised at Cliff's female entourage, but after a few jokes, they were taken down the hall and into the last interview room. Annette couldn't tell if the paint was grey or green and thought it smelled like urine. Heavy mesh and steel bars covered the high windows. A half-dozen folding chairs waited for them on one side of the table, and Derek sat shackled and handcuffed to the other side. A large ring secured his hands in front of him, and for extra measure, two officers stood on either side of him.

Marie gasped. "Derry, my God! It is you?"

Derek looked at his grandmother but never said a word. Darcy and Lisa remained by the door, and Cliff put his arms around the girls. Annette sat down in the closest chair and pulled it up to the table so that she was directly across from her son.

He sneered at her. "Ganging up on me now?"

Annette had decided she didn't care how rude he was going to be. "This is your family, Derek – your grandmother, your aunt Val, your sister Darcy, and soon your stepsister Lisa."

"You don't have any idea about my family."

Marie was fuming. "We are your family, Derek. I changed your diapers. I saw you walk for the first time."

Derek growled at his grandmother. "That was twenty years ago. You are not my family anymore. I have a new family, one that loves me."

"What do you mean, you have a new family?" Annette's mind raced with questions. "Do you have a new mother, too?"

"No . . . but I have others who care about me, family that has always wanted me."

Annette was surprised at the mention of others, but somehow not shocked. "I don't know what other family you might have, and I don't know what lies Mansi told you, but I never wanted to give you up. Never. Your father kidnapped you."

"Bullshit! After Darcy was born, you didn't want me anymore."

Darcy looked terrified and stuck close to Cliff's side.

Annette tried to reason with him. "That's not true. Your father took you to see your grandmother and never brought you back. I told you that last night. I have tried for years to get you back. We love you, and no matter what has happened, we're your family, and we want to help."

Derek looked back and forth between the three generations of women, glaring at each one but never looking at Cliff. "It's too late. I have a new life, a new family. I don't need you."

"You should be nice to us," Annette said. She and Cliff had wondered if Derek was full of false bravado and might eventually crack. "We can help you if you tell us the truth."

"I told you the truth. You want to help me? Get me out of here."

Cliff asked, "Why were you going to Paris?"

"I was going on vacation."

"You told me you were going to London," Annette said.

"I was, after a few days in France." Derek seemed exasperated, but he answered her question. "I was flying to Paris, but then I was going to London for most of the trip." He looked at her as if she were stupid.

"By yourself?"

"Yes. I told all this to the police. I like to travel alone. I meet people easily," Derek grinned, but looked unsure.

"Really? That's interesting," Cliff said. "The FBI told us you seemed to live a relatively quiet lifestyle. They say you hardly went out. That doesn't sound like someone who socializes much."

"How would they know how I lived? I was out a lot."

"Credit cards, bank accounts . . . The FBI says you never spent any money. This is L.A. You can't go anywhere without money. New procedures and new technology have answered all those basic law enforcement questions about you. By now, they've probably even interviewed your neighbors and co-workers. Your life is not invisible here." Cliff's voice was not quite a threat, but it implied a lot.

Derek glared at him. "I always use cash when I'm out. It's easier."

"Really? And which bank account did all that cash come from?" Cliff said. "The FBI told us your bank account shows very few cash withdrawals."

"My uncle sends me cash. He wants me to save my money."

"Your uncle? Or your father?" Cliff asked, his voice full of distrust.

"I told you, my father is dead."

"Tell us how to get in touch with your uncle. We'll see if he corroborates your story."

Annette took Cliff's hand and squeezed it. He was being the cop, and she had wanted to try a softer side today. "Leave it for now, Cliff."

"I've been through this with the FBI a few times," Derek said. "Get me out of here, and maybe I'll be willing to talk to you, but right now I'm not going to answer any more questions. Guard . . ." He turned to the guard on his right. "I'm through with my guests."

"No, not yet," Annette said. "We'll talk about something else, okay?" Annette had hoped for some kind of reconciliation and didn't want it to end on another ugly note.

"Get me out of here, Mother, and we will have lots of time to talk." Derek glared at Cliff again. "Without him."

Annette wondered if she could bargain her way to a few more minutes. "What if Cliff leaves the room? What if it's just us, right now?"

Derek shook his head. "Not today, but that's a good idea. Don't bring him next time." He banged his hands sideways, motioning as if to shoo his guests away. "Do I have to listen to this? What about my rights?"

The older of the two guards moved to the door and slid his key into the lock. "Okay, folks, I guess that's it for now."

Annette hesitated as the others turned towards the door, and she touched Derek's shackled hands in sympathy. His skin felt hot. "I'll come back tomorrow, if that's okay."

Derek's voice cracked, and he sounded weak. "Don't bother. I'll probably get bail and get out of here tomorrow."

"I'll call. If you get bail, maybe we can get together and try again."

On the way home, they all couldn't stop talking. Marie just couldn't believe the cute little seven-year-old boy she had helped care for was now a grown man full of hate and lies. She figured for sure that he had been brainwashed, or was under the influence of some kind of drug. Darcy didn't want to believe that he was her brother, and Lisa decided she didn't want a brother. Val couldn't believe the change in her nephew, either; he had been such a happy kid twenty years ago.

~~~

Art decided to stay until mid-morning. If everything was okay, he'd go home early and take an afternoon nap. He sat in on Bill's meeting, along with the two FBI agents. Everyone was shocked at the charges against Derek, but the more they looked at the software systems, the better they felt. Nothing looked unusual, and all systems and aircraft were performing perfectly.

Art asked, "What about the update we loaded last week?"

"We've run it through every test we have, and we think it's fine, Mr. Trainor," said Eric St. Cyr, who had been given a promotion to team leader that morning.

Bill seemed confident that nothing was wrong. "Art, we'll continue to stress-test the software today, but right now it looks like all systems are go."

"Good." Art stood up slowly; his back was bothering him again. "I guess there's no reason to cancel my trip to Washington." He had meetings with a few Germans who were eager to see his planes fly in Europe.

"No reason at all," Bill agreed.

"Let's just pray that this is the crazy aberration it appears to be."

"Yes, sir.

Art headed for his office. It sure wasn't the start of the week he had planned, especially a few days before the convention.

~~~

Mansi slept fitfully until the bright sunlight wouldn't be denied and the small hotel room started to heat up. He checked his watch. It was almost 9:30 a.m., and his last day in America for a long time.

He had planned on getting up early, but it didn't really matter. Jill was in place, Derek's situation was disappointing but manageable, and Dawn was in her American-education phase. He reckoned they were looking for him, so he decided to forgo the trip up to Los Angeles to the mosque to see his brothers. Allah would understand.

He wrote a short letter to Derek, then pulled a pair of surgical gloves out of his suitcase and put them on. Unzipping a small inside pocket in his overnight bag, he delicately pulled out a tiny brushed aluminum tube. Slowly, carefully, he twisted it open.

Holding his hand under the bottom part of the tube, he turned it upside down. A vial about an inch long dropped into his palm. The aluminum container was no bigger than the end of a pencil. A small line identified the end with the lid. He had dispensed the deadly liquid a few times before, but took no risks and handled the poison with extreme care. Odorless and clear, it was lethal instantly if taken orally, but even a small amount absorbed through the skin could cause death. He twisted the cap clockwise – it was reverse-threaded as the last line of protection – and the tiny cap spun around seven or eight times before it came off. Inside was a little dropper. He unscrewed it even more carefully, then dabbed the letter to his son in a number of places, just a drop in each spot, before setting the single sheet of paper on the table to dry.

The dropper and poison went back into the vial as carefully as it had come out. After he had tightened the cap and checked it twice, he slid the deadly vial back into its sleeve and put the pen back together. He could barely see the wet spots on the letter as they quickly dried and faded before his eyes. When it was completely dry, he folded the page and slipped it into the envelope. He addressed it to Derek, then slipped the white envelope into a larger one that was addressed to Bezzi Tazrit.

Checking his appearance in the mirror in the bathroom, Mansi thought his casual dress was perfect. A Nike sweatshirt, an Anaheim Angels baseball cap, and a pair of sunglasses changed his appearance dramatically from the crisp business attire he normally wore. The traffic moved quickly, and he was in Los Angeles in less than twenty-five minutes. On the fringes of Bel Air, built for a textile merchant in the fifties, the restored home was an impressive office. He checked his appearance in his rearview mirror and hoped he looked like a courier. *Kulla & Hedda & Tazrit, Attorneys at Law,* was written in gold lettering across the heavy wooden door, and the mail slot was on the side of the building. He hustled up the steps, dropped the envelope in, and hurried away.

~~~

Derek tried to sleep during the afternoon, but the guards at the jail seemed bent on giving him grief. Every time he dozed off, one would come by and bang on the bars, grinning at his displeasure and ignoring his complaints. His mind swirled with a dozen scenarios. He knew he should have killed his mother, but his thoughts kept drifting back to his father, and he wondered when and if the message would come. They had never talked about something like this, yet the options were ultimately the same if he couldn't get out. Mother or no mother, he had already promised his own life.

His father had provided bail money for a variety of reasons, although getting out of prison had never been discussed, because getting caught had seemed so highly unlikely, but no matter what had happened so far, Derek still thought he had a chance.

There was only one real piece of evidence, and that was the disk that contained the software program. If it was destroyed along with the Meyers aircraft, they could never prove it was him. And killing Sudesh had been a brilliant idea. Maybe the defense could create as much doubt around a student from India as the prosecution would a boy from Algeria. He closed his eyes and thought about what it would be like to be on the stand, testifying in a trial.

He loved the television show *Law and Order* and watched reruns all the time. But being questioned by some hard-ass attorney frightened him, and confronting his mother in a courtroom could be dangerous. Who knew what she would say? It could be explosive, and he couldn't afford to lose his temper in front of a judge or have his mother break down on the stand. He had to remain cool and detached, and he had to maintain his innocence.

Once again, his father had been right. He should have killed his mother.

~~~

By the end of Monday afternoon, Annette didn't know much more than she had known in the morning. There was some good news. The FBI had called, and Derek had a clean Interpol sheet, but there were no answers that seemed to make sense. They talked themselves in circles, but the only thing they knew for sure was that Derek's behavior defied all logical explanations.

When the mail came, Annette saw it was more advertising and bills than anything else, so she just threw the small pile on the table, intending to sort it later. One hand-addressed white envelope slid out from between the glossy brochures. It was addressed to her.

She turned it over. It was from Cindy Yaccine. She ripped it open and found a folded letter inside. When she pulled it out, a picture dropped face-down on the table. She picked up the small photograph and turned it over. Mansi, a younger Cindy, and a little girl who had to be Dawn stared back at her. Mansi's hair was lighter, and he wore glasses, but it was definitely him. "Oh my God, it's Mansi!"

The girls rushed from the bedroom. "Where?" Darcy asked.

Annette shook as she held the picture up for them to see. "It's Mansi."

Darcy looked confused. "I don't understand. Who are they?"

"I don't know, but I think your father has another family. That girl, Dawn, might be your half-sister."

Darcy was amazed. "Is this other family Derek was referring to?"

Annette thought the same thing. "Must be. I wonder if there are any more?"

Lisa compared the picture to her future stepmother and stepsister. "The girl does look like you, Darcy."

Dawn Yaccine was maybe six or seven in the picture, a cute little girl with pigtails. Annette dug through her purse and found her cell phone. After a couple of keystrokes, Cindy Yaccine's phone number popped up on the small display. Her hands shook, and she tapped her fingers impatiently on the counter before someone answered.

"Hello?"

"Cindy?" Annette could feel her heart pounding. "It's Annette Madison from the Centre."

"Oh, hi, Annette. Did you get my letter?"

"Yes, Cindy – it is the same guy! This is the same guy I married, Mansi Ansour. I'm sure of it." *Was she sure?* It looked like him, his eyes, smile, and posture.

"There must be a mistake," Cindy said, sounding shocked. "He told me he had never been married."

"Derek said Mansi died ten years ago," Annette tried to make it all add up. "What year did you get meet Mansi?"

"When did you meet Mansi?"

"In 1989, just after he moved here from Paris. He was so charming. He swept me off my feet. We got married in1990, but Dawn's father is still alive, or he was a few months ago."

Annette's eyes welled up with tears. Her voice cracked as she said, "Mansi left me and took Derek in 1988. He could have come right back and started all over. The story about his death might be a lie too."

"This is crazy. There must be some other explanation."

Annette didn't know what to believe anymore. "And something else has happened," she said. "Since I saw you last week, my world has gone crazy. My son Derek – he's back."

"That's great news."

"I'm not sure about that." She choked on the words. "He tried to kill me."

Cindy gasped. "What? Your own son tried to kill you?"

"Yes, and now he's in jail. But there's more. Derek told us that he has another family."

Cindy gasped. "And you think he meant Dawn?"

Annette looked at the picture again. "Yes, I do."

Cindy started to cry. "I was just so happy to get Dawn back. This is almost too much. You really believe that your two children and mine have the same father?"

"He kidnapped both kids at seven and brought them both back at seventeen." Annette knew it sounded crazy, but after what had happened so far that week, nothing seemed impossible anymore. "But wait, there's more."

"More?"

"Yes. Derek was caught by the police with a fake passport, and he made threats about doing something really big and making his father proud. He said I wouldn't want him anymore. The FBI thinks Mansi might be involved, too. They could be terrorists."

"Oh my God!"

Cliff got home a few minutes later and was stunned. Now, more than ever, he was sure something big was going on. "Jesus Christ! What the hell is he planning? How many kids does he have? I'd better call the FBI. Maybe they can trace Mansi through Cindy."

"Poor thing, she's in almost the same position as I was," Annette said. "All she wanted was her child back. Who knows what else is going on? Especially if Mansi is still alive?"

Cliff picked up the phone. "It could be the break we're looking for. I'm sure Mansi never thought you would find Cindy and Dawn, let alone Derek. Maybe they can tie them together through DNA."

"That could prove it, couldn't it?"

"Yes." Cliff knew the two women's testimony would be enough reason to order the tests, but the results would be conclusive. "They'll test Darcy, Derek, and Cindy's two children. It shouldn't take that long." He picked up the phone and dialed.

"This is Phil Housely."

"Phil? It's Cliff Billings. I think we may have another lead on Mansi Ansour." Cliff went through all the similarities between the two kidnappings.

"I'm bringing the files up right now. Okay, got them." Phil paused, then whistled softly. "Damn. You could be right. I can order DNA tests, but that could take a few days."

"I understand." A few days would be incredibly fast. "Will you need samples from Annette?"

"No. We'll need a sample from Derek and Annette's daughter, and samples from the Yaccine children. I'll get on it right away."

"Sounds fantastic. Anything else we can do?" Cliff wished he could be an official part of the investigation. "Is there any other news on Derek?"

"No, and nothing else you can do for the moment. We are trying to verify his story about his father's death, but getting information out of Algeria is almost impossible. I'll get this other alias out, and maybe we can find something under Yaccine."

"Let's hope so." Cliff had no idea what he hoped for. Not many scenarios offered a chance for Annette to get her son back into some kind of normal life.

Mansi spent Monday evening at the motel watching TV, flipping back and forth to see if there was anything about Trainor Jets on the news channels. Not that he expected there would be. Even if Derek had talked, it might never be released to the media. It was also possible that he could be walking into a trap. A live report from the Washington Convention Center showed the final preparations that were underway for Wednesday's opening festivities of the huge international business convention, and that made him smile. He knelt down to say his evening prayers and immediately felt guilty. Years of decadent Western living and dedication to his cause had weakened his ability to observe the foundations of his faith, and he prayed for the day when he could once again have the pillars of Islam back in his life.

He decided to go for one last reconnaissance drive to make sure there were no road repairs southbound on the 405 that could slow him up in the morning. He drove down to John Wayne Airport first. Traffic was not that busy, and neither was the airport. Police were at the entrances to the terminal, which was normal, and he could see a few officers inside by the metal detectors and x-ray machines. That looked normal, too. He pretended he was looking for someone and stopped in front of the double doors, where he looked up and down the sidewalk. It didn't take more than a couple of minutes before a police officer tapped on the passenger window. Mansi touched the power button, and the tinted window opened quietly.

The black female officer leaned in the window. "You can't park here."

"I'm waiting for my wife," Mansi said. "She should be out in just a minute." Mansi nodded towards the glass doors of the terminal.

The officer shook her head. "You'll have to go around. I can't let you park here, not even for a few minutes."

"Why? What's going on?"

"Just normal procedure, has been for a long time. Listen, sir, I don't have time to debate this with you." The officer took out her ticket book.

Mansi smiled apologetically, raising his hands in a defensive gesture. "Okay, sorry. No problem."

Another car pulled up behind Mansi and caught the officer's attention. Mansi drove away without a word and headed around to the back side of the airport, where most of the private aircraft operations were. The security seemed as light as ever, and he saw only one Orange County Sheriff's car on Redlands Avenue, headed away from the area. Satisfied things were normal, he drove back to Long Beach and the commercial side of the airport. The entrance to the Trainor Jets facilities was on Lakewood Blvd, and things appeared normal there, too.

Two guards stood inside the booth at the entrance gate; one looked like he was drinking coffee. Mansi continued on for a few miles, swung through a residential neighborhood, and then headed back for a second look. He stayed in the right lane so the plant would be on his immediate right. As he approached the beginning of the Trainor property, he could see the white maintenance trucks parked up against the chain-link fence. When he drove by the security gate itself, he casually but purposefully looked the other way. Derek had told him there were security cameras trained on the entrance twenty-four hours at day.

~~~

Derek felt like he had been in the cell for a week, but it was just over twenty-four hours. He had scanned every inch of the room and still couldn't tell if the paint was blue, grey, green, or just dirty. The tile floor was grey and old, but it was better than his room had been when he first went to Algiers. Here he had blankets and three meals a day. There, he had not been given more than a sheet for the first few months, and food only when he was good and obeyed his teachers. He could survive this easily.

There was no clock, and the guards had taken his watch, but the sun had just gone down. He thought back to last night. *What a catastrophe.* This was not any contingency they had planned for. His father must be furious. He didn't know who to be more scared of. He hadn't slept last night, and he doubted he would sleep tonight, but he would pray. While he had lived a Western lifestyle, he had still managed to worship Allah each and every day, and he hoped his prayers would be heard tonight. He tossed and turned on the small bunk. His body was physically exhausted, but his mind was on overdrive.

None of the training had prepared him for the stress of failure like this. He had always agreed that he was prepared to make the ultimate sacrifice, but somehow he had never believed it would be necessary. What made it more painful now was his mother's claims that she still loved him. Were all his fears and beliefs built on lies? And if so, what other falsehoods had his father perpetrated to ensure his loyalty?

~~~

"Look up 'dysfunctional,'" Annette said. "My picture is there."

Cliff laughed. "You're as normal as they come dear, but that ex of yours is anything but."

"You can start your own first wives' club." Val said.

The five women and Cliff talked all evening about Derek and what might happen next. Annette was terrified of the worst scenarios but tried to focus on a best-case basis. Derek was alive and looked healthy. Happy? Maybe not, but she could help change that. If there were no other charges or evidence, Cliff even thought jail time might be avoided if Derek cooperated with the police. He outlined many of the different work programs available for first-time offenders.

Annette decided to take half a sleeping pill when she realized it was two o'clock in the morning and she was still awake. As she counted off her love to Cliff, she prayed nothing else happened tomorrow; she didn't know if she could take it. A few days ago, all she had wanted out of life was a happy family. She almost giggled out loud when she thought again of the term *dysfunctional family*. It had been complicated enough just a few days ago, but now her children had more siblings from other mothers. One brother was in jail, and the father was a kidnapper, at least – who knew what else.

Part Three

Chapter 19

It was still dark when Mansi turned into the Holiday Inn and parked in the back of the lot. He checked his revolver one last time and made sure the silencer was on tight. His bomber jacket had a large inside pocket that fit the small gun easily. It was impossible to detect and easy to get out. At the front of the hotel, a few taxis were parked off to one side, waiting for a fare. The driver was disappointed when Mansi gave him the address; the Trainor Jet offices were only a few miles east. Mansi had the man drive past the entrance, and, after making sure the coast looked clear, he exited at the far corner.

He walked back toward Lakeview Ave, offering a silent prayer that Derek hadn't talked. If his son had been broken, years of planning could all be over in a few fast seconds.

Like clockwork, the black Honda Accord came round the corner, on time as the driver usually was. Mansi had cased the entrance more than a few dozen times, but the reliable young technician had never been late more than a few minutes.

As the car turned into the employee parking lot, Mansi sat down on the bench at the bus stop and checked his watch. The next bus wasn't due for fifteen minutes. Traffic was still very sparse, and there didn't seem to be any suspicious vehicles or activity.

In a few minutes, a white Trainor van pulled out of the main gate, turned left, and headed towards him. Mansi scanned the street one last time. It was deserted. He stepped onto the street and the crosswalk. The young man driving smiled at Mansi as he stopped at the intersection. Mansi waved and walked over to the driver's door. His right hand reached inside his jacket as he approached the van.

The man powered down the window. Mansi pulled his gun out quickly and fired two shots. The bullets struck in the middle of the driver's forehead, and he toppled sideways and backwards into the van. As the vehicle started to roll forward, Mansi grasped the door handle, jumped in, and pushed the dead body out of the way. Looking around, he saw no traffic and heard no cries of alarm.

The Holiday Inn was only a few miles away, and in minutes he was parked beside his car in the back lot. The sun was just peeking over the horizon, and there were no other cars in the overflow parking lot. He got out and opened the rear doors of the maintenance van. Just as Derek had described, there was a panel door under the computer console, and as Derek had promised, it was basically empty inside. Just a few cables and easy access to the back of the computers. Plenty of room.

Mansi opened the trunk of his car. Inside were a couple of blankets and a large duffel bag. The van was parked so it blocked the view from the hotel, and after he looked around again for any curious eyes, he dragged the heavy canvas bag out of the trunk and slid it into the back of the van. It just barely fit in the space under the control panel.

He laid the blankets down on the tile floor at the back of the van. He wrapped the body up in one of the blankets, then dragged the dead man out the side door and loaded him into the trunk of his car. Another quick look around showed he was still alone. A pool of blood had formed, and brain matter had splattered across the passenger seat and on the interior. The back spray from the small-caliber bullet was fairly minor, and the body hadn't had a chance to bleed much yet. Paper towels and a sprayer cleaned the mess up pretty well. A few squirts of air freshener, and in seconds the van smelled like oranges.

A new set of black floor mats and seat covers improved the look even more. It wouldn't pass any thorough inspection, but it should do for his purposes. He put on the white Trainor jacket that Derek had given him, with the I.D. badge already clipped to the pocket. One last look around confirmed everything was done, so Mansi locked his car, jumped into the van, and headed south on the 405 freeway.

It only took about twenty minutes to get to the John Wayne Airport. When he pulled into the parking lot, he was happy to see only a few cars scattered around, just like on the days he had scouted the location. He parked under the trees at the far end of the narrow lot, where there was a good view of the front doors of the Fly America office, and settled down to wait. In a few minutes, a navy-blue Jaguar XKE pulled up in front, and a middle-aged man got out, a man Mansi recognized from a photograph. Bernie Meyers was the founder and CEO of Nationwide Publishing and was well known for his aggressive style in life and in business. His picture and name were in the papers constantly. Bernie left his sports car running and went inside.

Mansi watched as the clerk slid some paperwork across the counter. Bernie signed in a few places, shook the clerk's hand, and headed out the front door. He got back in his Jag and drove up to the security gate. One of the guards had Meyers open the trunk, while the other one used his stick mirror to check under the car. The guard hardly glanced at the two small travel bags in the back of the exec's car before closing the trunk and waving Meyers through.

Mansi drove over to the Fly America building. After checking his appearance in the mirror, he grabbed the Trainor work order and headed up the sidewalk. Inside the office, a large banner covered one of the walls, reading: *FLY AMERICA – AND LEAVE THE FLYING TO US.*

"Good morning," Mansi said, handing over his manifest. "I have a scheduled upgrade this morning."

The clerk scanned the paperwork. "Yes. Bernie Meyers, two-six-eight-Sierra-Sierra. He told me he was expecting you. FYI, he just got here, and he has filed a flight plan and is due out at eight o'clock."

Mansi smiled. "It won't take that long. It's just routine maintenance, fifteen, twenty minutes tops."

The clerk signed Mansi's authorization. "Where's Chuck?"

"Holidays. Two weeks off."

The guards made Mansi get out of the van and open up the back door, but it was nothing they hadn't seen before, and after a quick search under the van with their mirrors, they signed him in. He drove as fast as he dared down the service road. The private-services side of the airport would start to get busy soon, and he wanted to be long gone. At the end of the road, he turned left and drove around to the business side of the hangar, where the huge sliding doors were open.

Pulling up beside Meyers' jet, he did a quick survey of the hangar. It looked like they were alone. He hurried to the steps of the plane door. "Mr. Meyers? Adam Marks from Trainor Jets."

"In here," a gruff voice from inside the jet commanded.

Mansi climbed the few steps and stuck his head inside the jet door. "Good morning."

Bernie gave him a busy look. "I hope this won't take long?"

"No, sir, not long at all."

"Good. Come on in."

As Mansi entered the beautiful cabin, he was almost sorry he had to destroy something so nice. The interior was done in shades of blue, with dark wood and a nautical décor that was complete with life preservers. It reminded Mansi of a ship's cabin.

Myers was stretched out on one of the rear couches, reading the morning's *Wall Street Journal*. Sixty-five years old, Myers was a short, round man. "They're all yours," he said, pointing to the computer screens in the nose of the plane.

"Thanks." Mansi turned his back to Meyers and set his silver briefcase down on the round coffee table between four captain's chairs. Inside, there were a small set of stainless steel computer tools, some high-capacity data disks, and a pair of surgical gloves. He pulled the thin gloves on slowly, taking a few seconds to make his complete and final assessment before he crossed the point of no return.

"What do you need those for?" Meyers asked.

Mansi smiled and turned to face the computer screens on the dash. "All this high-tech equipment." His hand slid inside his jacket and around the smooth handle of his gun. "I wouldn't want to leave any fingerprints."

Mansi turned back to face Myers and fired three times. The silencer muffled most of the noise, but the bullets struck the man inches apart in the left side of the chest, and he collapsed sideways onto the couch. His eyes fluttered a few times as a small triangle pattern of holes started seeping blood. He never made a sound or took another breath.

Mansi looked outside the jet; the hangar was still quiet. He ran down the steps to the rear of his van. Opening the rear doors, he popped open the panel door and pulled the duffel bag out. It was heavy, and he had to struggle to carry it up the steps, but he was careful and tried not to bump it on the door. After setting it down by the couch, he sat down in the left front seat in front of the four video screens. Inside his jacket pocket, he found the computer card Derek had given him, and he inserted it into the slot on the panel.

The computer's voice was silky smooth. "Good morning. Destination, please?"

A window opened on the center screen. A cursor was blinking in the open box. Mansi typed in *DEREK*.

The computer confirmed. "Washington, D.C.?"

Mansi typed in *YES*.

"Passengers?"

Mansi looked at Bernie Myers. He chuckled as he typed *ONE*.

The computer went down a checklist. "Departure time?"

Mansi looked at his watch. It was almost 6:30. He entered 7:30. The computer acknowledged the request with a message: *Flight plan submitted.*

He waited anxiously as the plane's computers communicated with the weather and air traffic control servers. In less than fifteen seconds, they confirmed the request: *Flight plan approved.*

He picked up his briefcase and ran out the door and down the steps. Outside, he pushed the small, recessed switch on the side of the plane. The steps collapsed inward, and the door folded up into the plane behind him. As he drove out of the hangar, Mansi saw a few people going to work. There were hundreds of hangars, charter companies, and freight forwarders in the airport, but it was still very early, and no one paid any particular attention to him.

The security guards were a little surprised he was back so soon. "That was quick," one of them remarked.

"Yeah, just a small data upgrade. It doesn't take long anymore. Those new computers are really fast."

As he drove away, he checked his watch. *Right on schedule.* He turned onto Redhill Avenue and headed for the John Wayne Airport passenger terminal. He had a plane to catch.

~~~

Annette stretched her neck to see the alarm clock. It was on Cliff's night table, and they had turned it off, but she woke up early just the same. It was over three hours since she had crawled into bed, but it only felt like a few minutes. Maybe she would have a nap later.

Cliff turned over and wrapped his arms around her. "Did you get any sleep?"

"Not much." She wiggled closer. "I keep wondering how many other women that bastard has out there, and if he's kidnapped their children, too."

"You think there are more wives and kids?"

"Why not? He did it twice. Maybe he married three times." The words were barely out of her mouth when she thought of another girl. She pushed Cliff away and sat up. "Shit! I just remembered a girl who came back from Algeria just after I joined ACMC, twenty years ago."

"Twenty years ago? And you think she could be another one of Mansi's kids?"

"Yes." It was coming back. "I remember being so hopeful when I found out she had also been kidnapped by an Algerian father."

"Do you remember her name?"

"No, but . . ." She could almost picture the teenage girl.

"Will she be in the files at the Centre?"

That was a good idea. "Yes, I think she should be."

"That should be easy, then."

"Maybe not. The older files are all in storage. It might take some looking. There are hundreds of boxes in those lockers." She hadn't been to the storage locker for months, and it was getting to be a quite a mess. Boxes had been taken in and out over the years, and some had been misplaced.

"I wonder if he is even dead. It sounds too convenient." Cliff thought her ex was capable of lying to anyone, even his own son if need be, although Derek could be lying about that too.

~~~

Mansi parked the van at the terminal and slid the gun under the seat. He had worn gloves and but wiped the van down anyway. They would find it soon enough, but it wouldn't matter. He changed out of the Trainor Jets uniform and put on a white sweatshirt, blue jeans, his Angels baseball hat, and sunglasses – his best casual tourist look. A web-generated return ticket and one mid-sized carry-on bag allowed him to go straight to the gate. The security guard gave him a look, but after carefully comparing the picture on his I.D. to his face, he handed the documents back without a word. Mansi put a few things in the tray and passed through the metal detector without a peep. The gate for Seattle was down the concourse to the left, and when he got there, the flight was already loading.

The boarding agent scanned his passport through the machine. "Thank you, Mr. Marks."

"Thank you."

The plane was only about two-thirds full, and he was glad when no one sat beside him. It was time for prayer.

~~~

Bill was in the office at just after 7:00 a.m. He was exhausted. Driving in as the sun was starting to rise wasn't that unheard of for him, but usually he had six or seven hours sleep, and often he would leave early and hit the club for a workout before his day officially began. Last week, he had thought about taking some time off, but that would be out of the question for quite a while. Monday's business had been normal, but that had not answered any questions. For years, life at Trainor Jets had been almost perfect, and now, in just a couple of days, it had gone from paradise to panic.

Two of their best programmers were gone. Even if Derek was not guilty of anything more than bad behavior, he would need to be replaced, too. He had called in extra software technicians again, and they would continue to run diagnostics on their aircraft and systems, but so far, all were operating as perfectly as ever. The 30,000-square-foot, highly sophisticated Long Beach flight control data center was his pride and joy, and he loved working there. Converted from the old administration building, which had moved to its new offices on top of Plant Four, the renovated four-story had been gutted, saving the classic fifties gothic architecture and the thick skin of the massive stonework. Replacing the inner floors had been an architect's dream. A blend of space, light, and color, the results dazzled most first-time visitors. Conservative and classic on the outside, the solid block walls opened into a blend of steel, glass, and wood that reflected the fundamental technology that was the essence of the Trainor Jets. Extremely pleasing aesthetically and impressive to the naked eye, it was the software that ran through the powerful computers that was exotic and super high-tech. With live footage from airports, domestic and foreign television, security updates, flight status, weather, and onboard cameras, the screens contained a sea of data and unlimited capabilities.

Art had kept the center in the latest of the latest hardware, and the U.S. government had provided access to data and video from literally around the world, but it was the integration and compatibility of the various sources of mega-information technologies that was the unseen genius of Trainor Jets. The company still had critics, but the enormous financial success of Fly America and Trainor Jets had made the company more than a household name. They had made aviation history.

Hundreds of flights were scheduled today, and it promised to be one of the busiest days in a long time, but one or two hundred additional flights per day was not a problem for the center to manage. The company planned to grow much more than that in the next few years as they expanded to Europe and, finally, to intercontinental capabilities. He scrolled through the list of flights scheduled around the country. Over four hundred departures and arrivals were already approved, and the list was growing by the minute as aircraft logged onto the system and their computers automatically requested flight plan approvals and instructions.

The sea of data was neatly displayed and easily sorted. The rows of planes could be sorted by variable: location, tail number, name, departure, arrival. He typed in *N111TJ*, and Art's plane's stats popped up in an expanded window. Three camera views were available: runway, aircraft exterior, and aircraft interior. Art almost always left the planes' on-board cameras on. Bill clicked on the runway view. The jet was just rolling onto the black runway. It turned to face the long strip, and he could see the heat resonate from the twin engines. Looking down, he opened a window with engine performance indications. When maximum power of over 15,000 horsepower was reached, the computer released the brakes, and the jet accelerated down the runway. Bill loved to watch planes land and take off – any plane, not just theirs, but especially theirs.

As Art's plane disappeared out of view, he tabbed over to the live feed from Orange County Airport in Santa Ana. A view of the main runway was accompanied by audio from air traffic control. The runway was empty, but a row of different jets could be seen along the taxiways that paralleled the east-to-west runway.

The computerized voice was clear and easy to understand. "John Wayne Ground Control, this is November-two-six-eight-Sierra-

Sierra. Flight plan number one-four-three-six-five for Washington, D.C. Request permission to taxi, over."

Bill found the plane on his screen. N268SS was Bernie Meyers – not someone he personally knew, but a well-known and very successful businessman from Newport Beach.

The ground controller replied, "Copy that, November-two-six-eight-Sierra-Sierra. You are cleared for taxi on Delta taxiway. Please hold at the ramp."

"Copy, John Wayne, November-two-six-eight-Sierra-Sierra on Delta, hold at ramp, over."

"Confirmed, two-six-eight." The controller's accent was definitely harder to understand than the Freedom Five's clear voice.

Bill grinned. No one had ever complained they couldn't understand the computers. They had focused on the enunciation of the voice software, and it was perfect. One could tell it was mechanical, but it was English at its clinical best.

Another controller said, "American one-seven-five-six, you are clear for takeoff on runway nineteen-Romeo, clear to go."

Bill clicked on another window, and a different view of the airport appeared. An American Airlines Boeing 757 raced down the runway, pulling up long before the end of the pavement, the twin Rolls Royce turbine engines more than a match for the short, 5,700-foot strip. The jet seemed to be going almost straight up as it crested the end of field, but then the nose came down as the plane flattened out for its noise-controlled departure out over the Back Bay and Newport Beach.

"John Wayne Departure Control, this is November-two-six-eight-Sierra-Sierra, holding at the marker, ready for takeoff on runway nineteen-Romeo."

Bill saw the Trainor jet holding at the end of the taxiway. Real-time. It was almost surreal. Most of the audience wouldn't know the different private jet manufacturers and wouldn't necessarily be aware that there were no pilots on the private plane turning onto the runway. He grinned.

"Roger, November-two-six-eight-Sierra-Sierra. You are cleared for immediate takeoff on runway nineteen-Romeo."

"Copy that, Departure Control, away on runway nineteen-Romeo."

Bill watched for a few more moments as the Freedom Five gathered speed and took off, before clicking to another screen. The report showed the takeoff was, as always, perfect. At just above sea level, and with a headwind of fifteen miles an hour, the plane was designed to lift off in a maximum of 4,000 feet. N268SS must have had a light load, as it used only 3,800 feet.

~~~

Art had tried to talk his wife out of going to Washington, but she wouldn't hear of it. Joan loved flying in the Freedom Five as much as he did. She had liked the pilots before, too, but she appreciated privacy more than personality, and she loved the sleep she could get on the longer cross-country trips. She adored Washington and had looked forward to the trip, so if everything was okay and Art was going to D.C., so was Joan.

They had taken off from Long Beach at 7:37 a.m. PST, and were scheduled to arrive in D.C. at 4:10 p.m. EST. The forecast was good for much of the country, and visibility would be unlimited for most of their trip. Reports of a strong jet stream should push them across the country even faster. It was a perfect day for flying.

A beep from the computers caught Art's attention. He turned away from the incredible view and clicked on the incoming message. "Good morning, Bill."

Bill's face popped up on one of the video screens. "Good morning to you, too, Art. How's the weather?"

"Perfect. As smooth as could be." Art looked out the window. The dusty desert was far below, but the skies were as clear as water for a hundred miles. "Blue skies in every direction. Perfect. Anything going on there?"

"No, just touching base."

"I take it there's nothing new on Ansour?"

"No, not a word," Bill said. "I guess no news is good news."

"How's traffic?"

"It's getting busier by the minute, but no problems whatsoever."

"Good. Let's hope it stays that way. How many of our planes are in the air?"

"Let's see . . . two hundred forty-two so far, and we have three hundred ninety-four different aircraft scheduled to be in service at our peak today at three fifty-seven p.m."

"That's what makes our planes so damn good – no down time. Our birds are always in the air." A window on his computer screen started blinking at him. He had an incoming video call from Norman Kingston. "I have to go. I'll talk to you later."

After disconnecting, he moused over and clicked the *Accept* button.

Norman's smiling face appeared. "Hi, Art. Am I interrupting anything?"

"No, not all. How are you?"

"I'm great as always," Norman said with a laugh. "And I've got Les on another line. Can I link him in, too?"

Les? Les Wilby? "President Wilby, sir?"

"Yes, he wants to say hello."

"By all means, log in on." Another window popped up, and Art quickly accepted the invitation. He hadn't seen Les Wilby since the presidential inaugural ball in January of 2013. They had never socialized outside of a few official events, but he had known Les now for thirty years, and he had been the right kind of guy from the beginning. "Friendly, fair, firm," had been Wilby's mantra, although it had been his positive attitude and negative views on war that had captured the nation's hearts. A soldier who hated war and who championed the day civilization outgrew the need for violence and hatred; he had won in a landslide.

"Hi, Art," the President greeted him. He was sitting in the Oval Office and had a small stack of correspondence on his desk. He looked happy and joked, "Another high-flyer on his way to Washington?"

"Good morning, Mr. President." Art had had countless video conferences over the years, but he would always remember this one. "Should be an exciting week."

"Yes, I'm looking forward to it. Not my speech though." He laughed. "But there will be lots of decision-makers in town, and I'm sure we've all got a few meetings we're looking forward to. But hey, that's not the reason I called. Look at all the letters!"

Art didn't think there were more than a few dozen envelopes and letters, but then the President turned around and pointed to a white cardboard filing box on the credenza, full of letters. "I get a box like this almost every day supporting our No Loss program. Widows, children, other pilots . . . it's heart-wrenching stuff."

Art had read a few of those types of letters before. They were heart-wrenching. Young women, widowed in their early twenties, often left with two or three infants. Parents whose son was lost in a training accident, pilot error, but dead nonetheless. "Is that good, sir?"

"It's good in the twisted yin-and-yang way the world works." He pushed at the pages open on his desk. "All these people support our program for all the right reasons, and it's all your doing. Your determination will save thousands of lives. We will be in your debt forever."

Art had heard similar appreciations before, but hearing it casually from the President like this was quite an unexpected honor. "Well, thank you, sir. You are too kind. I had a lot of help, including you, sir."

"Yes, well, looks like we both win. Listen, Art, we've had a cancellation for dinner on Friday night. Norman and Sheila were already coming, and they suggested you and Joan might like to join us at Camp David. It will be a great place to unwind after a busy week at the convention."

Art looked at his wife, who was already nodding. They had never been to the President's personal retreat before. "That would be wonderful, Mr. President."

"Great. Nicole and I look forward to it. I'll let you two go now, and we'll see you on Friday."

The picture clicked dead.

~~~

Cliff put out cereal, made toast, and poured two glasses of orange juice. He hadn't eaten much more than Annette in the last two days, and he virtually inhaled a bowl of corn flakes before she came out. He hoped she was hungry too; she needed to eat. "Here, baby, it's all ready. Coffee, too."

She definitely looked tired, but when she smiled, he could see she was okay.

"Are you ready to go?" She asked as she pulled her thin blue jacket from the closet.

"Yes, but aren't you hungry?" He thought she had lost a few pounds in the last few days.

"Thanks, honey. I guess I could use a cup of coffee."

"Yes, day two of no sleep." Cliff filled her favorite mug and handed it to her.

"Me or you?"

"You. I know I slept for a bit, somehow." He couldn't have slept for more than a few hours either, but she had tossed and turned all night.

"I know, I was jealous. But I just couldn't sleep. I thought about Derek and what has happened. It still doesn't make any sense."

One thing Cliff knew for certain was that, eventually, Derek would have a lot of explaining to do. Whether his new step-son to be would serve time was another question, but his flight, resistance, and denials would not bode well in the hands of justice. His future would depend on how well he was perceived in court. It could mean the difference between no time, or years in a prison cell. Cliff wondered which side of the bars he would end up on.

The phone rang and startled them both. Cliff picked it up. "Hello?"

"Good morning, Cliff, this is Phil Housely with the FBI." It was one of the agents they had met yesterday at the LAX jail.

"Morning, Phil." Cliff looked at Annette as he answered. He could see she had hoped it was the district attorney. "Did you get my message?"

"Yes, you said something about other wives, in addition to Yaccine?" Phil said.

"Yes."

"Do you have a name?"

"No, not yet." Cliff immediately felt unprofessional. "But Annette remembered meeting a woman about twenty years ago whose daughter had been voluntarily returned by her Algerian father. The circumstances surrounding her return were very similar to Dawn Yaccine and to Derek. Annette thought nothing of it then, but the timing of her return parallels the others. We're going to her office to look for the file this morning."

"Twenty years ago?" Phil whistled. "And you think Mansi was her father, too?"

"Well, maybe. She has just returned, about ten years after Derek came back. The girl before would have been about ten years earlier. All three were returned by their Algerian fathers, purportedly to go to American schools. It's like he had a ten-year cycle."

"All for what purpose?"

Cliff laughed. "That's the million-dollar question. Your guess is better than mine."

Phil was serious. "We will have to question Dawn if the DNA matches."

"Yes, I suppose." That sounded like a good idea to Cliff. Dawn had said she hadn't had any contact with Mansi since returning, but she could be lying too. "Nothing makes much sense yet."

"That's for sure."

"Anything new with Derek?"

"I'm taking him back to court in a few minutes."

"Annette is getting madder by the moment." Cliff wondered if Annette really wanted the attempted murder charge to be filed. "But she's still not sure if she wants to see him go to jail."

Phil's words echoed both men's concerns. "As you know, any one of these factors on its own is not that alarming. But all added up, this situation gets worse by the minute."

"There certainly is more here than meets the eye."

"It appears that way," Phil agreed. "I'll call you later if I find anything on any Mansi Yaccine, Mansi Ansour, or any other Mansi."

"Thanks." Cliff hung up and repeated everything to Annette.

"I really want to try and talk to him again," Annette said. "Can we offer Derek some kind of a deal? Maybe reduce the charge if he comes clean on the passport?"

Cliff chuckled. "You've been watching *Law and Order* too much. That's the district attorney's job. Don't count on Derek opening up anytime soon. It could take a long time, weeks, months; not a few days."

Annette sat down in one of the kitchen chairs to put on sneakers. "Will he do time?"

Cliff thought Derek belonged behind bars just for the way he had treated his mother. "I don't know, honey. If Long Beach decides to prosecute on some kind of lesser assault charge, and if he shows remorse, the judge might be lenient. After all, he never hit you or really caused you any bodily harm. But the passport charge is federal, and that is going to be tougher to explain away, especially as he made those threats and was caught trying to get out of the country."

"Next time I pray for something, I'm going to be more specific," Annette said. "This sure isn't what I had in mind."

Chapter 20

The FBI agents had shown up just after Derek had finished his cold food. He hadn't slept much on the hard bunk, and the thin blankets had left him shivering, but he tried to remain optimistic and had prayed throughout the night that good things would happen in the morning – maybe even bail. The leg irons and handcuffs chafed at his skin as he struggled to walk. He could hardly shuffle more than a few inches at a time, so after he had shuffled halfway down the corridor, the two FBI agents grabbed him by the arms and dragged him the rest of the way. They shoved him into the back seat of an unmarked gray Ford and grilled him again on the short drive over to the courthouse for his morning appearance.

Phil looked through the steel mesh that portioned the back seat. "Your father is now wanted for impersonation and personal fraud charges. It seems he has at least two identities, two lives, and two families. What can you tell us about that?"

"Nothing," Derek said stoically. "My father divorced my mother a long time ago. I've never met any other family." *What do they know?* he wondered. Tariq had told Derek that he had more than one sibling out in the world and that Mansi had married more than one beautiful American blonde. At first Derek hadn't wanted to believe it, but how would the Americans know?

"Like father, like son," Phil said. "Are there more than two criminals in the family?"

"It's all going to come out, Derek," said Alex. "Why don't you just tell us now?"

"If it's true, it still has nothing to do with me."

"Where there's smoke, there's fire, and son, there's a lot of smoke around you and your father. Hang on." Alex turned the corner sharply.

Hands cuffed in front him, Derek fell over sideways and banged his head on the window. "You trying to win me over, or kill me?"

Phil laughed as he watched Derek struggle to sit up. "Either way, it doesn't matter to us, but if you come clean now, before we get to court, we'll tell the judge to go easy on you."

"I told you, I didn't do anything."

Phil gave Derek a tip to toe look, "Yeah well all we know for now, is that none of your clothes are explosives."

Travel security was constantly being revised and improved, but so were the terrorists. From shoes to underwear, the airport inspectors checked everything.

Bezzi was waiting for his client in the courtroom and he looked pleased. The Interpol reports had come back clean. Other than the new charges being prepared against his father – identity fraud, possibly polygamy and desertion – there was nothing to give evidence to any of the prosecution's claims of possible terrorist activities. Derek's case was called first, and after the assistant district attorney conceded they had no other new evidence, Judge Herrman granted the defense's request for bail.

"These are very serious charges, Mr. Ansour, and you have already tried to leave the country once," she said, frowning at him. "So I agree with the District Attorney and find a serious risk of flight, but bail will be granted in the amount of five million dollars."

"Your honor, that seems a little excessive," said Bezzi. He was shocked, but his tone was very respectful. "My client is simply a computer programmer. This is far above his means."

The judge's wry smile left no doubt as to her personal feelings. "The law-abiding citizens of Los Angeles hope so, Mr. Tazrit."

"But your honor, there is no victim here, and much of the evidence is hearsay."

"No buts, Mr. Tazrit. If your client cooperates at trial, we can see about reducing the bail then. Trial is set for three weeks today." The judge banged her gavel down hard, and the bailiff grabbed Derek firmly by the arm. He wanted to scream.

~~~

There had been dozens of children returned during Annette's twenty years with the ACMC, but not many had been from Algeria. In the United States alone, there were tens of thousands of kidnapping cases and illegal abductions every year, family and non-family, domestic and international. Many were parental disputes, and quite often the child was found or returned quickly, but long-distance displacements to countries on the other side of the world had a poor rate of recovery. She tried to picture the girl from years ago but couldn't. The one thing she did recall was how happy the mother was, and how quiet the teenager had been. It had been Annette's first experience with a reunion and something she had talked about with her counselor. Anita Sanchez had been a big help to Annette in understanding the emotions of loss. Maybe she would call her up later and tell her everything that had developed in the last week. What would she say?

The storage room was on the third floor of an old four-story building in Santa Ana. It wasn't the best area of town, but the site was owned by a member who had offered the space for free, so the non-profit association had taken it gladly. Cliff groaned when he saw the large room and hundreds of boxes, but the cartons were numbered, and it didn't take long to find several stacks from the late eighties. They went through the files slowly and carefully, one box at a time, wanting to be sure they didn't miss anything. A few hours later, they were both totally discouraged.

Annette sighed and sat down on the floor. "They're not here." She had been positive that they would be. There were quite a few boxes from 1985 and 1990, which they figured was the approximate time frame, but none contained the files they were looking for.

"It sure looks that way."

"Damn it." *Now what?* She had been sure they would find the files.

Cliff started stacking the cardboard containers back against the wall. "Well, who knows? It might have been a wild goose chase, anyway."

"Let's call the district attorney's office," she said, checking the time on her watch. It was 9:50. "They should be there by now. They might have records."

"Yeah, well, I happen to know their record storage isn't the best, either, but we'll call them as soon as we're finished."

Annette picked up one of the boxes and carried it over to the wall. "You're my hero, Cliff Billings. You really are."

Cliff stopped and gave her a kiss. "Some guys will do anything for love."

~~~

Mansi managed to sleep for an hour on the two-hour flight up to Seattle, and he felt refreshed when he woke up. He even had time for one last prayer. Whenever he flew, he tried to get a seat on the plane's east side. That way, he could turn to face Mecca. He closed his eyes and prayed for his son to have strength and to do what he must. There was no other choice. Derek's life had been given a long time ago.

The flight attendant tapped him lightly on his shoulder. "We'll be landing shortly, sir. Make sure your seat belt is on."

Mansi turned back to the aisle and opened his eyes. He smiled at the pretty young lady. She was blonde and looked to be about the same age as Jill. "I must have fallen asleep. Are we almost there?" He snapped his seat belt buckle together.

"We've just started our descent. Captain Ross says we'll touch down a few minutes early." She smiled and moved on down the aisle.

"Great." Being early was always a good sign.

His rental car was pre-arranged, and in a few minutes he was out of the massive Sea-Tac airport and doing seventy on I-5, the main north-to-south interstate highway that ran all the way from Mexico to Canada . . . and freedom.

Traffic was moving pretty well for the middle of the morning, but it was steady and there were lots of trucks on the two-hour drive to the border crossing. Depending on the wait to get through customs, Mansi calculated he should make the Vancouver International Airport somewhere around one. By then, Washington should be a war zone.

~~~

Bill was glad the morning had settled to its normal busy pace. He was drinking too much coffee but figured he could probably catch up on his sleep tonight. Air traffic was increasing by the minute, and the Freedom Five flights were arriving and departing as scheduled. Other than weather delays, most of the planes were within minutes of planned flight times. Hopefully today would be as problem-free as yesterday, as problem-free as most days at Trainor Jets.

He pulled up the main flight activity screen. There were now 205 planes in the air, over forty percent of the fleet. He watched as the main flight data fields were updated. Two hundred seven airborne. Two more planes had just taken off. His phone rang.

"Bill, its Melody." Melody Barnes was one of Trainor Jets' senior client relations managers. "We've got a problem on Bernie Meyers' plane. I just got a call from his office, and they can't seem to reach him. I've tried but haven't been able to contact him, either."

"Have you tried the emergency frequency?"

"I've tried a half-dozen times. Nothing."

"I'll be right there." Bill punched off his speakerphone and walked out into the main control room. An emergency was unheard of.

Melody had the first cubicle in the row of workstations outside his office. She had worked at Trainor Jets longer than he had and was his and everyone's favorite client manager. She had managed minor and major customer problems, from simple late arrivals to missed tee times, and could soft-pedal, back-step, and massage any overwrought temper tantrum if and when needed. In her early fifties and a grandmother with the patience of two saints, Melody was the perfect woman to handle a client who was drunk or belligerent. She seemed able to calm clients with a quiet, easy going, and persuasive manner that was worth far more than they were paying her. Bill looked over her shoulder at the flight information. The aircraft itself was operating perfectly.

Melody shrugged her shoulders. "Nobody answers."

"Try one more time."

Melody turned back to her screen. A static picture of a Trainor jet blinked in the video window. "Mr. Meyers, this is Melody Barnes at the Trainor Jets customer service center in Long Beach. Please respond. I repeat, please respond. It's extremely important."

There had been only one medical emergency on board a Trainor jet. It had been about six months ago, and there had been nothing they could do. The man had had a heart attack at 40,000 feet. The plane had been rerouted and landed within a half hour, but it had been too late to save the victim. According to the autopsy report, the 74-year-old man had been dead within seconds of hitting the cabin floor.

No answer from N268SS.

"Okay, go ahead and activate the camera." Onboard cameras were installed on all the planes, one in the rear and one up front. They were used for conferences or during video phone calls, and their use was usually at the client's discretion. Melody tapped a few keys, and a picture of the interior of N268SS appeared on screen.

Bill almost choked when he saw the slumped body of Bernie Meyers. Three dark red blotches were visible in the center of his chest.

"Mother of God!" Melody crossed her heart.

"It looks like he's been shot," Bill said, his heart racing. He had never seen a person who had been shot before Was he still alive?

"It looks like he's dead."

Sudesh, Derek, now this, Bill thought. *What is going on?*

"Let's get this plane on the ground as quickly as possible," he said. "I guess there's a slim chance he's still alive." He noticed the large blue duffel bag on the floor of the plane's cabin.

"Look at his chest. It's not moving," Melody said, zooming the camera in quite close. They should have seen his chest rise and fall, but it was eerily still, and his face was frozen in a shocked expression.

"I wonder if this has something to do with Derek," Bill said.

"That crossed my mind, too, but why?"

"What's that?" Bill pointed to the duffel bag.

"I don't know. Sports equipment?"

"Yeah, maybe." He didn't think Bernie Meyers looked like the athletic type. "Art is going to flip when he hears this."

Melody looked sympathetic but said nothing.

"Get me Art, and send it into my office." Bill looked around. A few other technicians had looked up. They must have heard what he had just said. He hurried in and closed the door behind him.

The video feed came on-line. Art was sitting in the right swivel chair up front in the nose of the aircraft. He mugged for the camera. "What's up?"

"Art . . . this is going to sound pretty wild, but Bernie Meyers was not responding to any form of communication, so we turned on the video feed. It looks like he has been shot and is dead."

Art's expression instantly changed to concern and fear. "What?" He set his book down. "Dead? Are you sure? Is this what Derek meant?"

"We don't know anything yet. We got a call from Bernie's office that they had been unable to contact him. We only turned the video feed on a minute ago."

"Have you called the police?"

"No, I called you first."

"Well, you'd better call the police and get his plane on the ground as soon as you can."

"Where should we put the plane down?" Bill looked at the electronic maps on the main wall for the location of the plane. The highlighted red blip was crossing the southwestern border of Missouri.

"Ask the police."

Bill checked the flight data screen. "His plane took off from Orange County Airport. I'll call the sheriff's office there and see what they want us to do."

"What is the closest airport we can get him into?" Art said.

Bill typed in a few commands, and a stream of data rolled across the screen. "St. Louis."

"Okay, but call Orange County first."

Bill brought up a list of the nation's airport police departments and scrolled down to John Wayne. His call was answered on the first ring.

"John Wayne Airport, sheriff's office. Deputy Will Miller speaking." The voice was all business.

"Deputy Miller, my name is Bill Simpson. I'm a Vice President at Trainor Jets in Long Beach. I believe someone has been murdered on a plane that took off from your airport a few hours go."

"Murdered? How do you know that?" the officer asked.

"We have a video link on board the plane, and I can see a body that looks like it has bullet holes in it. Do you have internet access?"

"Yes, of course."

"Good, you can see for yourself." He instructed the deputy on how to sign in to Trainor Jets' secure website to view the camera feed from inside Meyers' plane.

"We're not sure when it happened," Bill continued as he looked up at the digital clocks. It was 10:32 a.m. PST. "The plane took off three hours ago, but we just discovered him a few minutes ago."

After seeing the video feed, the deputy advised him to land the plane in St. Louis. "I'll have the local police meet it there," he assured Bill.

~~~

Annette called the district attorney as soon as she got back in the car. She had met Barry Midstrom a few times at official functions with Cliff. Hopefully he was as good an attorney as he was a politician. Her story might sound a little far-fetched, but she was sure there had to be some connection between Mansi, his two or three ex-wives, and Derek's behavior.

"Can't you search by his first name?" she asked. "Maybe he used the name Mansi before, too."

Barry listened to her theory patiently, but his answers weren't encouraging. "Annette, I can't even promise you we can find the files. You're talking about paper files from twenty or thirty years ago. A lot of that old stuff has been recycled lately, and nothing was cross-referenced very well back then, so searching for another Mansi might be almost impossible."

"Can you search by nationality or age?" She had seen Mansi in Algeria and heard him speak French; some of his lies were true.

He shook his head. "My search capabilities are limited."

"Can we help you look?" She pictured another few hundred boxes in a dusty lock-up somewhere.

The exasperation in his voice ended that idea. "Annette, some of those records would have been shipped out for storage a long time ago, and honestly, the off-site storage facilities have been plagued with problems over the last ten to fifteen years. The paper was starting to break down, so they tried scanning files onto CDs, but that didn't work too well. Many of the different conversion projects have lost files. The ones you're looking for might not even exist anymore."

"How long will it take you to find out?"

"A few weeks."

"Weeks?" She groaned in disappointment. If it was the same Mansi, it could mean a lot to Derek's defense. "It's really important, Barry, really important. Isn't there some way to speed things up?"

"I know this is very important to you, but so are many of the other hundreds of requests we get. Unless there is some kind of emergency or court order, there's nothing I can do."

"It is an emergency. My son has been arrested and could be charged with some very serious crimes. Finding out about his father might save his life." Two days ago, she had been pleading for her own life at Derek's hands, and now she was begging to save his life. "He has made some sinister threats about making his father proud . . ."

The district attorney sighed. "I'll see what I can do. It will still take a day or two."

"That's great, Barry."

"No promises."

~~~

It only took Bill a few minutes to get an emergency landing approved at Lambert Field, the St. Louis International Airport. The air traffic controller promised to clear all inbound and outbound flights and would have the emergency rescue vehicles standing by. Bill had reassured him that all they probably needed was one ambulance, but the man figured they'd better be safe than sorry.

Seconds later, Melody was logged into the computers on Meyers' plane. Bill watched over her shoulder as she checked the flight information. The original scheduled arrival at Ronald Reagan National Airport was two and a half hours away, but fuel wasn't a problem. They could land with what they had on-board.

Melody typed in *STL*, the code letters for the airport, and hit the enter key, but the computer didn't accept her entry and flashed an error message.

UNABLE TO PERFORM REQUESTED ACTION
PLEASE CHECK ENTRY AND TRY AGAIN

"What the hell is that?" Bill had never seen the software reject a command before. Wrong codes usually resulted in a different type of error message.

"Maybe I made a mistake." She typed the letters slowly and deliberately and touched the enter key again. Same message.

"What the dickens?" she exclaimed and switched to the one of the plane's other three onboard computers. The same error message flashed again.

"Check the other two." Bill felt sweat trickle down the inside of his armpits. He had never seen that message before; normally, mistakes were immediately identified and highlighted so the errors could be repaired. If an error was detected, the four powerful onboard computers were designed to work independently, concurrently, or in any combination of the four. Each box contained the same hardware, same software, and same capability. With redundant processing to the third level, any one of the computers could fly the plane. As an added safety precaution, the custom-built hardware was encased in individual carbon-steel hardened boxes spread throughout the airframe, so as to provide controls even in the event the airplane was physically damaged in one area. Software and hardware, the system was bulletproof.

Melody tried the other computers but got the same error message.

"Maybe St. Louis is stacked up," Bill suggested, trying not to sound too worried. He knew something was wrong. "Maybe the system is rejecting you. Try again."

Melody tried again. Same error message.

"Are you logged in under our master I.D.?"

"Of course," Melody said. "I don't know what else to do. I've never seen anything like this before."

"Neither have I. Try another airport." *Stay calm. There has to be some mistake.*

Melody tried Cincinnati but got the same response.

"Shit." Everything else on the aircraft was operating perfectly. It had to be something simple that the utility program would find and repair. "Okay, let's run diagnostics on CPUs number one and three. I'm sure we'll find the problem. That will take about twenty-five minutes."

"Procedures call for one CPU at a time. Why two?"

"Procedures call for one computer at a time for maximum safety, but if Meyers is still alive, we have to get him down as soon as possible. If a bug has affected only one computer, and it's the last one we test, testing all four could take an hour and forty minutes. He'll be dead for sure by then, and closing in on D.C." Bill pointed at one of the large video screens that displayed a map of current national commercial air traffic. The eastern seaboard was extremely busy, as usual. There were thousands of flights in the air. "I'd better call Art back."

He went into his office and shut the door. A few taps on his keyboard, and a window opened up on his screen. A map showed a tiny icon of Art's plane over northeastern Oklahoma, not too far behind Meyers. He typed in the call letters N111TJ, and in a few seconds Art's face appeared on his screen.

"Well, what did the police say?"

"They told us to land Meyers' plane in St. Louis. But we have a bigger problem."

"What now?"

"We can't redirect it anywhere. We have a Class Five failure on Meyers' plane. We can't take control of the aircraft."

"Class Five?" Art was visibly dumfounded. "You mean you can't control the plane?"

"That's correct." Bill could hardly believe it himself. "We have tried all four computers, nothing. The plane is flying perfectly, but the computers won't allow us to change destination."

"This must have something to do with Ansour. What did he do?"

"I don't know. We don't even know what's wrong with the plane yet, but this would seem like quite a coincidence."

"How are you going to fix the problem?"

"We're not sure." Bill checked a few data screens. Melody had the first two systems ready to come off-line. "I'm ready to start the diagnostics on CPUs number one and three, which will take about twenty-five minutes. I'm sure we'll find the problem. Then we will disable the other two CPUs and land the plane. We have lots of time."

"Two CPUs at one time? Isn't that a bit risky?"

"Art, I made that call, but Bernie Meyers might still be alive. If diagnostics finds something wrong on the first two computers, we could still land the plane safely with a fully functioning backup computer in reserve."

"Okay, that makes sense," Art said. "I leave that decision to you. Do the police know you can't control the plane yet?"

"No, they're waiting for me to call." Joan had come over and sat down in the other chair beside her husband. She didn't say a word, but Bill could see the worry on her face.

"What about the rest of the fleet?" Art put his arm around his wife reassuringly, but his words were anything but calming. "Anyone else reporting any problems?"

"No, not a thing. But I was hoping you would try your plane for me, make sure this is just a one-off. I don't want to alarm anyone else."

Art looked at his wife, but she didn't appear to understand. He turned back to the camera. "Have you tried redirecting any of our freighters? Surely there are a few of those in the air."

"Yes, Melody has tried some of them, and they were fine, but all the passenger models have the upgraded hardware and the newer software. It wouldn't harm to try, and I'd rather ask you first."

"You want me to try and land my plane somewhere else?"

"Yes. Make sure the bug or whatever hasn't affected you. Maybe I'll call a few other clients after you."

"Is our plane okay?" Joan asked.

"Let me try now," Art said. "We're approaching St. Louis, too." Art tapped at the keyboard on the dash in front of him. "I'll try to get a landing approved."

Bill watched as Art's request for landing was approved almost instantly. Estimated time of arrival changed from two hours and twenty-seven minutes to eleven minutes, and the engines on the Freedom Five twin jets powered back as the plane began a gradual descent. West of the International Airport, and with runways over five miles below their cruising altitude of 41,000 feet, it would be a long spiral down into the landing pattern.

"Everything is working fine here," Art said. "I'm going to change back to D.C."

The flight status data on Bill's main screen changed immediately, and the airspeed on N111TJ started to accelerate. In minutes, the aircraft had returned to its cruising speed of 570 miles an hour, leveled itself out, and settled back into its original flight plan.

"Nothing wrong here," Art said.

"Okay, that's good to know." Bill was relieved but not surprised. Security was just too good.

"I have another call coming in; I'll call you back in a few minutes."

"Okay, thanks, Art."

At least the other aircraft were okay. Bill opened the window into his electronic day-timer and found the name of the police officer he had talked to a few minutes ago.

The man answered on the first ring. "Airports. Deputy Will Miller."

"Mr. Miller? It's Bill Simpson from Trainor Jets. I'm afraid we have another problem. We are having technical difficulties and can't land the jet."

The agent's demeanor changed immediately. "Ten minutes ago, you told me you could set it down anywhere."

"Yes, sir," Bill admitted, "and we should have been able to, but something is wrong with the software."

"I'm going to have to report this to Homeland Security. Can you fix what's wrong?"

"Oh, I'm sure we can, sir. You must know we never have any problems."

"Seems to me that you have got a big one right now," The officer's tone was chilling, but Bill was confident they would find the problem quickly.

~~~

Art clicked open the waiting window, "Norman, hi, what's up?"

Seated in the left front seat of his own Freedom Five Jet at cruising altitude thousands of miles away; his old friend sounded almost jovial. "I hope I didn't put you on the spot back there."

The weekend was a long way from his mind now. "No problem, Norman. We're looking forward to it. How's your flight today?"

Norman beamed as he turned and looked out at the clear blue sky behind him. "Just fine, son. We got out early and hope to be on the ground by a little after three. What time do you arrive?"

"After four. But listen, I'm in the middle of something at the moment, so I'm going to have to be quick." Art decided it was best not to say anything. No sense in alarming anyone yet. "Was there anything else?"

"Not really, but I wanted to tell you personally how delighted Les is that you and Joan are coming this weekend. It should be a lot of fun."

"We're honored by the invitation. Camp David . . . wow. Have you been there before?"

"Yes, a few times," Norman replied. "But don't worry, it's low-key, and the President likes to hang out in jeans."

Art did, too. "That sounds relaxing. We look forward to it. But I'm going to have to go. I have a problem that needs my attention."

"Nothing serious, I hope?"

Who knew, at this point? "No, I don't think so."

"Good. Let me know if there is anything I can do. We'll see you in D.C."

Art watched the video screen go black and disappear.

"What now?" Joan asked. "Do you think the computer will find the problems?"

"They bloody well better." In the final analysis, safety factors had been the FAA's main concern in the lengthy flight approvals for the pilotless Freedom Five, but Art had insisted on a statistically zero tolerance level of performance, and all four computers had never once made more than one minor mistake – and that had been on only one CPU. High wind and electrical storms, possible collisions, wind shear, snow, rain, loss of one engine, loss of both engines . . . They had put the three test airframes through rigorous training from Florida to Alaska, in January and in July, and in thousands of hours of testing, planned maneuvers or emergencies, the computers had not made one error in judgment.

A plethora of data streamed across cyberspace, millions of bits by the second as the transponders, GPS systems, onboard computers, and communications equipment on each and every plane airborne in the continental U.S. sky was updated with destinations, speeds, positions, reports, estimates, calculations, changes. Merged by the Trainor Jet software into a precise understanding of where every plane in the sky was, and where it was en route to. Any changes were constantly updated to each and every Freedom Five's flight plan accordingly. Man simply wasn't capable of analyzing the data fast enough in some time-critical situations, and at billions of bytes per second, the computers anticipated more possible scenarios per minute than the pilots could contemplate in a lifetime.

All of their other aircraft appeared to be operating perfectly, and Art's own estimated time of arrival was even five minutes ahead of schedule. Whatever the problem was with Meyers' plane, it had to be something small. The problem certainly wasn't in any of the flight systems. Cruising at 40,000 feet, its twin engines were humming as smoothly as could be.

~~~

Melody had beeped him. A general from NORAD was on the line.

"Is this Bill Simpson?" The weathered voice commanded respect.

"Yes, it is."

"This is General Bart Allison. I understand you have a jet out of control and headed towards Washington, D.C.?"

"Yes, sir, but we are trying to correct the problem as we speak."

"And if you can't, what will happen?"

"I'm not sure, sir. It has a landing slot approved at Reagan National at five after four Eastern Standard Time. The plane will probably fly on and land as scheduled."

"Are you sure about that, or you think?"

"I don't know, General." It sounded logical. "We have never had a problem like this before."

"That's not very encouraging, Mr. Simpson. I'm scrambling two fighters to ride shotgun. If this plane looks like it might endanger anyone, we will be forced to shoot it down."

"Lord almighty." *That could ruin Trainor Jets.* "Hopefully that won't be necessary. We have almost two hours and twenty minutes before the jet reaches Washington, and I have my best programmers working on the problem. I'm sure we will be able to fix the glitch long before then."

"I hope so. I want you to call me back every ten minutes with an update. Do you understand?"

"Yes, sir."

The first two computers on Meyers' plane were almost finished with the diagnostics, but the utility software hadn't found any problems yet. It was ironic to think they would be hoping they would find something wrong, but code was relatively easy to fix. Bugs, viruses, and other malicious programming would be another thing entirely. He called the FBI next.

"Phil? This is Bill Simpson at Trainor Jets. I have some disturbing news. As of a few minutes ago, one of our jets is out of control. It has a possible dead man on board, and it is headed for Washington, D.C."

"What? Say that again."

Bill ran through the details.

"Have you reported this to anyone else yet?"

"Yes, to the Orange County Sheriff's Department. They called Homeland Security, and I just got a call from a General Allison." He wondered how long it would be before the story was picked up by the press. "But I thought you should know."

"Do you think that Derek was part of this?"

"Derek and/or Sudesh, I don't know. But it certainly does seem suspicious."

"How many other planes do you have in the air right now?" Phil said.

"Two hundred and eighty-seven." Bill checked the fleet status screen again.

"Where are they headed?"

He slid the wireless mouse over the flight-tracker screen to reach the destination fields, not surprised that over half the entries were the same. "A lot of them are on their way to Washington, D.C., for a global business conference. The rest are scattered around the country."

"Are you going to ground those other jets?"

"No, not necessarily. We've checked out some of the other planes, and nobody else seems to be having a problem."

"Bill, I'm dispatching a team of agents to your offices right now. You are to cooperate with anything they ask. You understand? They will be there in ten minutes." It was an order, not a request. "Lock your doors and don't let anyone in or out."

"Yes, sir."

Bill looked around at the busy command center. Never in his wildest dreams had he imagined an FBI team would someday take control.

Chapter 21

Derek had been back in his cell for a half hour when he heard footsteps running down the hall. The two police officers hardly said a word. They handcuffed him, didn't bother with legs irons, and ran him down the hall and into the interview room.

The two FBI agents were waiting, and they didn't look happy. Phil shoved Derek into the chair. He stumbled and banged his forehead into the table. "Hey, watch it! You could have broken my nose."

"Your nose is going to seem like the least of your worries," said Alex Romero as he pulled up one of the chairs on the other side of the table. "Someone has been murdered on a Trainor Freedom Five jet, and Trainor says the plane is out of control. What do you know about that?"

"Murdered? How would I know anything about that? I've been locked up for over two days." He glanced at the clock on the wall. It was only 10:50. The program wasn't supposed to start until 11:00. Something must have happened.

"This is what you planned, isn't it? This is what you told your mother was going to happen, isn't it?"

Derek could smell the two cups of coffee on the agent's stale breath, and he sat back as much as the restraints would allow. "I don't know what you're talking about."

"There are just too many coincidences for you not to be involved."

"I told you, I haven't done anything, and I certainly had nothing to do with any murder or any problem with a plane. Maybe it was Sudesh Pumeet. Maybe he did it." That sounded like a better story every time he repeated it.

"Why do you say that?"

"Because I know it wasn't me. Maybe somebody wanted Sudesh dead after he did the job." His father had calculated long ago that Sudesh would make a good scapegoat when and if needed. "You know, tie up loose ends."

"Maybe that was you. Maybe you wanted him dead so you could finalize your plans."

"There you go again. I don't have to put up with this bullshit again, and I'm not going to answer any more questions without my attorney."

"You know, Derek, everything has changed now that someone is dead. If you're tied to murder or terrorism, they will throw the key away."

"I'm not a terrorist, and I'm an American citizen. You can't do that." Their threats were meaningless. God would do what was right.

"Listen to me carefully, son. This country doesn't tolerate terrorists anymore. If you happen to die deep inside one of our jails, it's no sweat off my back. Sometimes justice is done outside the courtroom, you know what I mean?" Phil leaned over the table as he threatened.

"Funny, for once I couldn't agree more," he muttered. They would never understand.

"Funny?" Phil pulled Derek's chair out from under him, causing him to fall on the floor. "How's that for funny?"

A sharp pain stung his right hip where he had landed. "Get your jollies pushing around defenseless people? I told you, I didn't do anything." He tried to roll over and sit up.

"Do you really expect us to believe this is all just a coincidence?" The agent grabbed him roughly by his jumpsuit and sat him back up in his chair.

"Believe what you want, but I never had anything to do with this."

"Do you think we're stupid?" Alex sneered. "Your supervisor gets killed a few days before you get caught trying to flee the country, the software you worked on doesn't work, and there's a murder on a Trainor Jet. You're guilty, kid. It's just a question of what the charges will be."

"You have nothing."

"And you don't have five million dollars."

When the phone rang, Annette hoped it was some good news for a change. Maybe Barry had found something already, but it wasn't the district attorney.

"Annette, this is Will Miller. It might just be a freak coincidence, but it sure doesn't look good. Someone has been murdered on a Trainor Jet, and the plane is out of control and headed to Washington, D.C."

"Oh my God." The words were almost incomprehensible. "Who was murdered?"

"Bernie Meyers, the CEO of Meyers Entertainment. They own a bunch of TV stations across the country. They think he has been shot."

"Shot?" For all the speculation, she had still maintained that Derek couldn't be involved in anything really sinister, but one ugly coincidence after another was making that reality harder and harder to deny. "And what do you mean, the plane is out of control?"

"Apparently, Trainor Jets can normally take control of all their planes from the headquarters in Long Beach, but not today. They tried to land it, but it won't respond. It's still flying and on its original flight plan to Washington, D.C., where it's scheduled to land around four p.m. eastern time. Turn on the news. Meyers' own network, METV, is running the story."

"That's awful." Annette turned on the TV as Cliff came into the living room. Clicking through the channels, she found METV.

A company picture of a smiling Bernie Meyers was on the screen in the background, and a middle-aged female reporter was describing the situation. "Bernie Meyers, the CEO of Meyers Entertainment, the corporation that owns this TV station, has apparently been shot and killed on his private jet." She went on to say that the plane was still in the air and would not respond to commands to land.

"I have to go, Annette," Will said. "I'll call you back when I know more."

"Thanks, Will."

The station cut to a commercial, and the phone rang again. Annette looked at it for a second before picking it up. She wasn't sure she could stand any more bad news. "Hello."

"Annette, this is Phil Housely."

"Hi, Phil."

"Have you heard about the murder on the Trainor jet?"

"Yes. We're watching it on TV right now."

"Did they mention a suspicious package on board?" Phil asked.

"No. What do you mean, a suspicious package?"

"There's a large duffel bag on the plane. Meyers' office and wife say they have never seen the bag before. It's possible it's some kind of bomb."

"Bomb? This must be what Derek meant . . ."

"I don't know that."

"Have you talked to him about this?"

"Yes, but he still insists he knows nothing. Would you be willing to come up here and try to talk to him again?"

"Yes, I guess so." What could she say that would make a difference?

"Great. I'm going to send a helicopter for you."

"A helicopter?" She had never been up in one before. "That won't be necessary. We can drive."

"That will take far too long, and we don't have a moment to spare. It looks like we have one murder already. Go to the Costa Mesa police station. They'll have a chopper standing by."

The racy black helicopter was sitting on the pad when Annette and Cliff arrived, the blades already spinning. Two officers helped them climb in, buckle up, and slip the headsets on, and then closed the door. In seconds, the pitch of the propeller changed and the helicopter lifted off, rising vertically until they were well over the treetops, then the nose tilted forward, and the five-passenger Bell Jet Ranger raced off.

~~~

The control room was dead quiet as the entire Trainor support staff watched the diagnostic program finish its analysis on the first two computers on Meyers' plane. When the progress bar reached one hundred percent, the display rolled through a series of lists of files that had been scanned and analyzed. Then the results popped up in a summary message. They all gasped.

<center>NO VIRUS FOUND
NO PROBLEMS FOUND
NO REPAIRS NECESSARY</center>

Bill slammed his palm down on the table in front of him. "That's not possible!" He had personally overseen the requirements of their utility program, and it had been designed not only to detect viruses, worms, Trojan horses, and any alien code, for that matter, but to repair the errors or changes immediately. The program contained the entire software code, and a complete copy of up-to-the-second current data was available through the Trainor Jets network and the high-speed GPS link. Theoretically, the program could rewrite code or repair any errors without ever having to shut any part of the system down.

Melody checked a few other screens. "Maybe it has fixed our problem," she said. She brought up the DESTINATION selection window and typed in *STL*.

UNABLE TO PERFORM REQUESTED ACTION
PLEASE CHECK ENTRY AND TRY AGAIN

Bill couldn't believe what he was seeing. "The bug must be in the other two CPUs."

Melody connected the first two computers back on-line, then let her boss make the decision.

"Okay, let's take number two and number four off-line," Bill said. He knew he was running out of options.

Everyone held their breath while Melody changed the configuration on the plane's network, but the twin turbofan engines didn't miss a revolution, and the jet continued on at its high-altitude cruise speed of just over 585 miles an hour, mach .782.

Bill headed back to his office. "I have to call Art and Homeland Security. They are not going to be happy."

~~~

"You have to be kidding me," Art said. He felt sick to his stomach. Years of one success after another had never prepared him or his staff for disasters. He could see the worry etched onto his vice president's face from thousands of miles away. "So, what now, Bill? We wait another twenty-five minutes?"

"Art, we are absolutely at a loss for answers. There must be some kind of bug in one of the two other computers. There is no other explanation."

"I sure hope so. There are no other computers. What did the police say?"

"Homeland Security is involved now. I talked to a General Bart Allison at NORAD a few minutes ago." Bill was in his office all alone, but he dropped his voice anyway. "If we can't fix Meyers' plane and it threatens other lives in any way, they said they would have to shoot it down."

"What? It's a little early for that, isn't it?" Art didn't lose his temper very often, but he heard himself nearly shouting. "You have to fix it, Bill. You have to find some way to fix it. We can't have one of our planes shot out of the air. We'll never sell another plane. You can figure it out, I know you can."

"I'm trying."

"If all else fails, why don't we leave it? See if it lands on its own?" Bernie Meyers sure looked dead. Why not just let it land in D.C.?

"That works for me, but I'll have to talk to Homeland Security."

"I'm leaving our line open. Let me know the minute anything changes."

"Yes, sir." Bill's face disappeared from his screen, but Art could hear the urgency in his sharp tone as he ordered the staff to try a few other possible solutions.

Art had already dialed in and checked the status on Meyers' plane himself again. Everything did seem to be working properly. The computers were controlling all of the plane's systems and functions, adjusting flaps, power, even cabin comfort. Inside, air temperature was seventy degrees Fahrenheit. Everything about the flight was as planned and it was two minutes ahead of schedule.

Joan hadn't said a word until now. "Should we turn around?"

"I don't want to. We're more than halfway." He had a lot of important meetings scheduled for the week. The European Aviation Safety Agency was sending members of its review panel to the business conference, and their input was critical to the future of Trainor Jets overseas. The delegates had said they were looking forward to the VIP flights he had scheduled for Thursday morning, and that usually convinced even the most dubious of his skeptics. They had to fix this problem now, or that was not going to happen.

"Is our plane still okay?" his wife asked.

"Yes, I think so, but let me check a few things." The staff would be testing each and every possibility, but he decided to have a quick look, anyway. Art hadn't designed software for years, but he still knew his way around an operating platform

He logged onto the support center's main computer. System traffic was thick, as was expected. With electronic communications between the FAA, air traffic controllers, weather stations, TV networks, the amount of information available was almost unlimited, but few planes utilized much more than navigation and air traffic control instructions. The Freedom Five's computers were networked together into a main server that monitored every function on every plane. All the programs seemed to be executing perfectly. There weren't any hardware conflicts, and the security software utility had just cleared all zones for potential problems.

"Who are those guys?" Joan said, pointing to the video feed from the Long Beach command center. The four men who got off the elevator were all in dark suits, with trim haircuts and muscular physiques. No one was smiling.

"I think that's the FBI. Looks like the two guys from yesterday."

~~~

"Hi, Tim," said Bill. "Sorry to see you back so soon." Bill had been called when the men arrived at the gate.

"Yes, maybe we should have stayed," Tim Batterson said. "I've left two men at the front gate. Have you secured the building?"

"Yes. We have a private security force, and they've locked all the gates. The only way in and out is through the main entrance you just drove through." Bill pointed to a few of the video screens on the main wall where security cameras panned the property. Art was visible on one of the screens. "Mr. Trainor, who you met the other day, is watching and listening to us right now. He's on his plane over the Texas panhandle."

Tim nodded at the video displays and cameras that faced the control room. "Looks pretty busy."

"Yes, it is," Bill said. "As you know, we track and control every plane in the United States from here."

"Phil Housely briefed us on the way over," said Tim. "You have a jet with a dead man on it, and you can't land the plane, is that correct?"

"Yes, sir."

"Do you think this is some kind of virus?"

Charlie Demori, the other agent who had also been there a few days ago, was taking notes. The other men stood at the two entrances.

Bill couldn't see any guns, but they all had bulges under the left armpit of their jackets and looked ready to use them. "I don't know."

"Is it some kind of sabotage or a terrorist attack?"

"I don't know that, either."

"Is it possible it's some kind of industrial espionage? Phil told me about your two programmers. Was someone murdered to get information?"

Art had always worried that someone might try to steal the proprietary software that Trainor Jets had developed. It was one of the first questions he had asked Bill when Derek had been arrested.

"Anything is possible," Bill said. He shrugged his shoulders and looked at the camera.

"Who would do that?" Charlie asked.

"I don't know," Bill said. "Maybe one of those two programmers, Derek Ansour or Sudesh Pumeet? Maybe they turned on each other."

"Well, we don't have the luxury of time to sit here and guess what's going." Tim looked at his watch. "How much time before the first jet gets to Washington?"

"Just under two hours. It's estimated to arrive at five after four, D.C. time. We've analyzed two of the plane's four computers, but they appear to be okay. We're running diagnostics on the other two computers that will be completed in nineteen minutes."

"Okay, but in the meantime, keep checking other aircraft for problems," Tim ordered.

"I've got most of our programmers looking at the CPUs on Meyers' plane."

"And you think you'll find the problem?" Tim didn't sound convinced.

"Yes, the bug must be in those two boxes. There's no other reasonable explanation."

"But you've checked all your other planes?"

"No, not all, but quite a few of them."

"Don't you think you should?"

"Yes, but it's a matter of priorities, and I only have so many technicians. Most are working on Meyers' plane."

"Okay . . . I understand the realities of resources." Tim was respectful but firm. "But if you can't fix it real quick, they'll all have to land soon. Okay?"

"I understand, but it's also not just up to me. The people who own those planes will make their own decisions. I can't force them to do anything." It was ironic. After 9/11, Art had been appointed to a government committee tasked with designing new provisions for dealing with terrorists on jetliners, recommendations that would be implemented by the airline industry, commercial, charter, and private. At the time, he had whole-heartedly agreed that getting any compromised aircraft on the ground as fast as possible was always a priority. The longer the plane at risk was in the air, the greater its chance of being a catastrophic loss. This time, it was his business and his life that was at stake, and the thought of grounding his fleet was frightening.

"Can't you just take over the planes and land them all?" Tim asked.

"Actually, yes and no." Bill waved his arm at the command center. "Once again, even if we have to log on and take over each flight, it will take quite a while. You can see how many technicians are available. We could have the problem with Meyers' plane figured out before too long, if . . . I don't have to take too many people away from that job to land planes."

"Have you called in any extra staff?"

"Yes, a few minutes ago, and we've got five more programmers dialed in from home," Bill said. Twenty-three technicians were logged on. That normally would be more than plenty. Much like an air traffic controller, each technician could normally handle multiple planes at any one time, and with the jets spread across most of the country, sequencing landings shouldn't be too much of an issue.

"What is your back-up plan?" Charlie asked.

"GAL." Bill hadn't thought it would ever come to that. "It's a glide program. GAL is short for Glide Assisted Landing. It's an engines-off safety feature for emergency landings."

"How does that work?"

It had been a long time since Annette had been in the air anywhere over Los Angeles, and she had never been so close to the ground or gone so fast. Cliff leaned over and pointed to the speedometer in the center of the dash. She could see that they were doing over 150 miles an hour. The pilot had told them it would take less than fifteen minutes to cover the thirty-five miles from Costa Mesa to the Los Angeles International Airport.

They followed the 405 freeway north, and as they came up on the Long Beach Airport, the pilot took the helicopter up quite a bit higher, and she found herself looking down at the top of the Trainor Jets manufacturing plant. It looked much bigger from above, and seemed larger than a few football fields. A number of small planes were visible moving around on the taxiways, and one was on its final approach. Annette watched as it touched down. The little plane bounced twice and then settled into its roll. She wondered if it was a student pilot.

The Pacific Ocean was on her left, and she looked past Cliff at the new skyline that had emerged in the last decade. There were a dozen new high-rises along the beach, and she hardly recognized the once-so-familiar skyline of downtown Long Beach. She tried to spot Derek's apartment but could hardly even remember what it looked like. As they slid past the city and Long Beach Harbor came into view, she thought about the article on terrorism and shipping they had seen. There literally were tens of thousands of containers stacked in countless rows, and dozens of trucks shuffling around the huge storage yards. Security looked like it would be an enormous task.

The hills of Palos Verdes seemed to tower over the helicopter, but its meager peak was actually only 500 feet higher than their 1,000-foot cruising elevation. It was hard for Annette to even focus on what she might say to her son. The jet engine, the props, and the constant chatter on the headsets were overwhelming, so she just closed her eyes and prayed that her son hadn't been any part of the man's death.

A sudden rise jolted her back to reality. When she opened her eyes and looked down, she could see a KLM 747 coming in for a landing on one of the runways at LAX. It was an incredible perspective high above the city and the airport. The Pacific Ocean disappeared in a milky horizon, and it brought back memories of her trips to Algeria years ago. She had been so optimistic flying in, and so terrified flying out. Now she was terrified, and not sure if she even wanted to know the truth.

There were jets in the approach circuit around Los Angeles Airport, and she could see the multiple landing lights of a few jets on final approach as they lined up for one of the four east-to-west runways. It was far busier than Long Beach had ever been, and she said a silent prayer that the air traffic controllers saw their little helicopter. Once directly over the airport, the pilot carved a steep turn down to a landing grid on top of the LAX police station. A small welcoming party waited.

Phil Housely grabbed Annette and Cliff as soon as they were clear of the rotors. He had to yell to be heard over the roar of the helicopter's turbine engine. "It looks like the situation has escalated. They might have to ground the fleet."

"Has something else happened?" Annette's mind raced with nightmares, and she stumbled on the stairs that led down into the building. Only Cliff's quick hands saved her from falling down the steps.

"No, but they haven't been able to fix the computers yet, and NORAD doesn't want to take any chances."

They were taken to one of the interview rooms where the other FBI agent they had met yesterday, Alex Romero, was waiting. He was on the phone, and when he looked at her, she could sense it wasn't good news.

"Fighters have been scrambled," he said. His words terrified her. "NORAD says they'll shoot the plane down if they have to."

Chapter 22

Phil led Annette and Cliff down the hallway, past the noisy cell block and back to the same small, cold room where they had talked to Derek the day before. It was empty and quiet after they shut the heavy door. Annette wondered if anyone was watching behind the large mirror that covered most of one wall. Her son must feel like an animal. Phil answered all their questions the best he could, but Annette could hear his frustration. "We have no idea if he was involved in any of this, so anything you can get out of him will be a big help."

"I don't know that he will even be happy to see me."

Noises from the outside hall caught their attention, and as they turned to the door, her son was brought in. Hands cuffed, legs shackled, he looked tired and definitely not happy to see her. The two guards fastened him to the table and chair with the heavy clamps.

"What do you want?"

"Derek, what have you done? Are you responsible for what's happened?"

Derek rolled his eyes in exasperation.

"Answer her," Cliff said, banging his fist on the table. "People could die!"

Derek glared at him. "People die all the time. I told the FBI, I didn't do anything."

His hostility continued to amaze her, but Annette tried to ignore it. "Derek, if people die, you could be charged with murder." Thoughts of jets crashing into buildings were just too frightening to say.

"You say you love me – then believe me. I keep telling you, I didn't do anything."

"You tried to kill your mother, and you have a fake passport," Cliff said. His menacing manner was more threatening than anything Annette had seen in him before. "If they find evidence that you're connected to this murder, you could get the death penalty."

"This is America," Derek sneered. "My attorney will get me out of here. I am innocent."

"You'd better hope so, because let me tell you, our regular scum-of-the-earth prisoners don't like terrorists. Jail will seem like a fate worse than death. Maybe, if you're lucky, somebody will want you for a girlfriend. You know what I mean?"

Annette stared at Cliff. *Was this what it took to be a policeman?*

"I'm not afraid of death," Derek bragged. "I'm not a coward."

"If you're not a coward, then tell us the truth," Cliff said. "Face the truth like a man."

"I keep telling you, I had nothing to do with this. That is the truth."

"Is your father really dead, or is that just a lie too?" Cliff knew most criminals would lie about anything to save their skin.

"You can believe whatever you want, but I didn't do anything." Derek glared at Cliff.

"If you didn't do anything, maybe you can help," Annette suggested.

"Help? How can I help?"

"Just tell us what's going on," Cliff snarled. "Tell us what you're planning to do."

Her son turned away from her fiancé the best he could, but the solid clamp didn't allow him to turn his shoulder more than few inches. "Get him out of here. I'll only talk to you if he's gone."

Annette grabbed Cliff's hand before he could say anything else. "It's okay, honey. I'll be okay."

"Okay, but I'm right outside if you need me."

Annette waited until Cliff left the room. She knew he would be watching. "Can you fix what's wrong with that plane?"

At first, Derek didn't answer. He looked over at the mirror. "I don't know what's wrong, but they have some really good programmers at Trainor. They might not need me."

"But so far they haven't been able to fix the problem. If you could help them fix it, maybe the FBI would consider dropping the charges." She glanced at Phil.

"We don't usually make deals, but anything is possible." The FBI agent smiled, as if he could make it happen.

Derek closed his eyes for a few seconds. She prayed he would say yes. When he opened them, she saw a faint smile.

"Okay, I'll try to help," Derek agreed. "But I want all the charges dropped before I start."

Phil chuckled. "If you're not guilty, why do you want the charges dropped?"

"That's my offer," Derek said. "Take it or leave it."

"Phil, if he can save that jet from crashing, I would certainly drop my charges," Annette said. He was her son. What else could she do?

"I don't know what's wrong, so I can't promise that I can fix anything," Derek reiterated.

"You're asking a lot, son," said Phil, "but it's not my job to say yes or no. I have to call my superiors. Give us a few minutes." Phil headed for the door. "Annette, why don't you come with me."

In another room, Annette and Cliff listened while Phil discussed the offer with his bosses in Washington. He hung up and repeated part of the conversation. His superiors suggested they call Trainor and see if Trainor Jets even thought Derek could help. They didn't want to say yes, but if lives were at stake, they wouldn't say no.

~~~

Art had watched the FBI on one monitor and scanned the navigational software code that directed Meyers' jet on another. All the real-time updates were still being received and complied with, and the plane was making normal minor adjustments to trim and power. Estimated time of arrival was still 4:05 EST. The Windows-based system appeared to be operating perfectly – every system, every program, every command – except for commands to change the landing.

Bill came on-line in a second window on top of the lines of code. "Art, Derek's mother is on the video phone. She says she thinks she can get Derek to help us, but he wants immunity."

"If he can help save us, I don't care about immunity. That's the least of our problems." They had all their available programmers working frantically on the problem already. Would one more make any difference? He clicked to maximize the window to full screen. "But why is his mother calling?"

"She says she knows you. Can I patch her in?"

She knows me? He didn't usually forget those things, and Derek had been one of his favorites. Where would he have met Derek Ansour's mother? "Sure, I guess so. Where is she now?"

"At the LAX jail. Just a second."

A woman's face popped up on his main video screen. Art could hardly believe his eyes. "Annette Madison? Derek is your son?"

"Hi, Mr. Trainor. Yes, Derek's my son. Ansour was his father's name. I'm so sorry."

"Why didn't you tell me this before?" Art was absolutely stunned. He felt like he had known the Madison family all his life, but he never knew Annette had a son.

"He was kidnapped twenty years ago by his father. I never knew he was even alive until a week ago and he never told me worked for Trainor Jets." Annette started to cry. "I'm sorry."

Phil Housely stepped into the picture behind Annette. "Mr. Trainor, none of that matters right now. What matters is whether he can help."

"Yes, of course," Art said, wondering if maybe Sudesh was the guilty one after all.

Phil took over. "Mr. Trainor, if Derek is willing to try and help, Annette is willing to drop her charges. If he is innocent and not guilty of any other crimes, he could get probation for his passport offense. That's probably the best I can do. The FBI does not like to make deals like this, so the question is, would it even help? I sure don't want to cut this guy loose for nothing."

"Bill, you'll have to answer that," Art said. "Could Ansour help?"

Bill was in his office with his new team leader. "Derek was a good software engineer, but we have a lot of great programmers," he said. He turned from the camera. "Eric, what do you think?"

"I don't think it could hurt," said Eric St. Cyr, "but we already have two dozen technicians on-line, and they can't find anything."

"If he is innocent, why does he need a deal?" Bill asked. "Why wouldn't he want to help?"

"That's what we think," Phil said. "He says he just wants to protect his rights."

"It won't matter if the diagnostics find something on the last two computers," Art said. He hoped the bug, or whatever it was, would be found and fixed shortly, anyway. "Shouldn't we wait before we start making any deals?"

"Absolutely," Tim agreed. "If you can fix it, we don't need to make any deals."

~~~

The constant muffled chatter never ceased as the police officers made their way up and down the hallway, laughing and yelling. It was a very busy place. The FBI had shackled Derek back in the same room, and Alec, the younger agent, waited inside. There were probably a few others behind the mirror watching his every move, too, but it didn't matter. He couldn't move, and he wasn't sure what, if anything, he could do.

"What part of the software did you work on?" Alex asked.

"Flight Integration Navigation Execution Systems – FINES for short."

"Oh yeah, you told us that before. You computer guys have an abbreviation for everything."

It would be incredible if they gave him some kind of deal, but after planes started crashing, they might renege. Maybe, if he managed to save one or two of the jets, they might believe his innocence, but saving any of the planes was going to be a big problem. He had designed the ghost program in a loop that should be impossible to detect. Somewhere between a backdoor and a worm virus, his program had been quite simple. "They try to make them catchy," he replied.

"So, did you have a specialty?"

"I was a navigational integration specialist." That was in his files. He didn't volunteer that the digital data of the entire continental United States airspace stored on the planes' hard drives also included a lot of land data and details, including roads, bridges, tourist attractions, shopping centers, and government buildings.

"You had access to how the plane flies?'

"No, not really. I had access only to how the information was analyzed and interfaced."

"You didn't write the software?"

"I didn't write the software program, but I do help maintain it." Derek knew that the FBI must be very suspicious, but he felt more confident about his work than his troubles.

The software had been stored on the disk used to authorize and activate Meyers' plane, and then downloaded to the other Freedom Fives through the lightning-fast satellite communications network. Designed to confuse the input commands of the plane's four computers, the program simply put one hidden extra character into every destination field, causing each and every command to change direction or airport, to be misunderstood and rejected by the computers.

When the clock reached 12:00 PST, the host computer, Meyers' jet, would send the activation signal to the network, and in seconds, every Freedom Five jet would change its course to Washington, D.C. Derek had selected the longitude and latitude of two hundred of the most important buildings, locations, and monuments, and the software inserted the target's location as the beginning of the runway. They would vector in as if they were headed for Reagan National, and then, with two minutes to go, they would change course directly for their specific target. Many of the bigger buildings had multiple jets directed at them. The White House had four jets targeted on it. Congress had six planes assigned to it. Bridges, highways, museums, monuments . . . The city would never look the same. Any jet that tried to change direction before 3:00 p.m. EST would automatically lock in on their D.C. target early.

It had been hard to speculate with his father on how many Freedom Five jets would actually hit their targets. Certainly the U.S. defense systems would be quicker to respond than they were years ago, but would ten percent get shot down, twenty percent, or more? Either way, dozens of the private jets would probably get through, and the damage would be significant. Casualties could be in the thousands, and property damage would be in the billions.

"Isn't that part of the problem? Navigation?" Alex asked.

"I don't know exactly yet." He had no idea how to stop it. When he had written the program, he had never thought about wanting to interrupt it once it had started. If he could save somebody, though, maybe he could work his way out of his own jam yet. "But it doesn't sound like it. Other than the one problem, you guys said the plane was flying perfectly. Sounds to me like navigation is working perfectly. Maybe it's the fly-by-wire, the flight control software."

~~~

The staff in the control room went dead silent as the digital clock clicked down and the diagnostics program on Meyers' second two computers finished its analysis. Bill was sure it would be some rogue virus, maybe attached to one of the live weather data uploads, or maybe the heavy air traffic control system had contaminated a file. That had happened before.

Another window opened.

NO VIRUS FOUND
NO PROBLEMS FOUND
NO REPAIRS NECESSARY

They gasped in disbelief and shock. The summary details of the test showed no errors, no problems. Both computers were operating perfectly, far below capacity, and well within all design limits.

Bill was stunned. "How can that be? There has to be something. Melody, try landing again."

She brought up the destination window and tried *CVG*, the call letters for Cincinnati, but the computer rejected the change of destination.

"There are no errors in all four computers?" Tim Batterson asked. "No bugs, nothing?"

Bill sighed heavily. "I don't know, Tim. If it was a bug, we would have found something like a corrupted file, at least. It has to be software sabotage." They all thought they had designed a foolproof security system, both in the initial design phase and in maintaining integrity in the programs and the databases. "It could be some kind of ghost program."

"What's a ghost program?" Tim asked.

"A free-floating program that uses data gathered from files and erases itself as it goes. I've never seen one, but apparently they are almost impossible to detect." The software was well protected from common viruses, but malicious hackers kept finding new ways to access company files and steal data. Bill talked about intellectual property theft and prevention constantly to his staff.

"So, we're nowhere?" Tim asked angrily. "After all this time, we're nowhere? Is that correct? You still can't land this plane anywhere?"

Bill nodded reluctantly. "We'll keep looking, but yes, that is correct."

"Then we absolutely need to get the rest of your planes on the ground immediately."

~~~

Art typed up the alert message personally and emailed it to Bill. He felt powerless thousands of miles from the command center, but there certainly wasn't anyone else responsible. His name was on the door, and it was his dream and his reputation that would be severely damaged. He offered a silent prayer that the Trainor Jets clients would understand the need for the inconvenience. Hopefully it would all be over shortly.

"Okay, here's the message I want to send out to the entire fleet of Freedom Fives," he said. "I don't want to cause any panic, so the message is going to ask for owners to voluntarily change their destination."

It was simple, compelling, and hopefully not too frightening. Panic and fear wouldn't help the situation. It was sure to cause anxiety amongst some of the owners and passengers, but hopefully things would be resolved soon. The email went to each and every Trainor Jet Freedom Five in the air and on the ground, even the planes not in service. To alert the passengers, the message automatically opened a software window and sounded a soft bell. It read.

A VIRUS MAY HAVE INFECTED THE AUTOPILOT SOFTWARE ON YOUR AIRCRAFT. AS A SAFETY PRECAUTION, ALL FLIGHTS ARE REQUIRED TO IMMEDIATELY REDIRECT TO THE NEAREST AVAILABLE AIRPORT.

"Okay, Mr. Trainor," said Tim. "Let's get you on the ground, to start."

"Going there right now." Art opened up the flight window on his main video screen. His scheduled airport and landing time were displayed.

WASHINGTON, D.C.
ETA: 4:07 P.M. EST

Art checked his position. The closest major airport was Cincinnati. They were less than fifty miles south. He typed in *CVG*. Nothing happened for a few seconds. When the response came, he couldn't believe his eyes.

UNABLE TO PERFORM REQUESTED ACTION
PLEASE CHECK ENTRY AND TRY AGAIN

Had he mistyped? He tried again, with the same result.

The FBI agent was staring at him through the thousands of miles of cyberspace, waiting for an answer. Bill looked lost.

Art tried again and said, "It won't let me change. We're still headed for D.C." He switched over control to the plane's number two computer and tried to redirect again. Same response. He tried all four different computers and received the same response. He felt panic clutch at his insides. He closed his eyes and tried to think of some possible explanation.

"Try another airport," Bill suggested. "Maybe Cincinnati is stacked up."

"Okay." Art was feeling less optimistic by the second, but typed in *IND*. "How about Indianapolis?"

The same error message came back. No change allowed.

"No, it won't let me change," Art said. He could see the worry spread all over his wife's face, too. She looked ready to break out crying. He typed in *BNA*. Nothing. "I tried Nashville, too. Nothing."

He flipped back to the other window. It still showed D.C. as his destination. Something was wrong, though. Why wasn't the airport listed? He brought up another screen.

38.890 DEGREES NORTH
77.005 DEGREES WEST

"What is that?" Joan said.

"The landing coordinates for Reagan National Airport, I think." *What else could it be?* He brought up another window and copied in the coordinates. The answer stunned them both.

THE SUPREME COURT

ELEVENTH STREET NE

WASHINGTON, DC 20543

The Supreme Court? The building? He typed the coordinates manually to double-check. The result was the same. He kept trying but it was to no avail.

Tears began flowing down Joan's face. Art tabbed to the videophone window. His hands were shaking, but he couldn't stop it.

"What is it, Mr. Trainor?" Tim Batterson said.

"Uh, Tim, we're in even bigger trouble. I think my plane has redirected itself to land at the Supreme Court."

"What? How did that happen?" An incredulous expression tore at the agent's face as he punched at the keypad on his cell phone. "Are you sure?"

"I don't know how it happened. I checked five times. I'm checking again as we speak. Bill, you check, too."

Art could see Bill typing furiously on his keyboard. When his vice president looked up, Art knew he hadn't made any mistakes.

"Shit, Art, this is crazy!" Bill shrieked.

"This changes everything," Tim said as he cupped his hand over his cell phone. "Has this affected all the other planes, too?"

Art hands shook as he logged onto Meyers' jet.

Chapter 23

Bill double-checked the landing coordinates on Meyers' plane one more time. Tim and Charlie were right beside him. There was no mistake. It wasn't landing at the airport, either. Meyers' jet was set to land at the White House in one hour and twenty-five minutes. Art's plane would hit the Supreme Court two minutes later. There could be no doubt now. This was certainly no software bug. This was definitely a planned attack.

The color drained from Melody's face. "Oh, my God. N118PV is headed for the Capitol Building!"

Someone else yelled, "So is N378CD!"

"Are you absolutely sure?" Tim asked.

"Yes, sir," Bill said. He had double-checked and double-checked. There was no mistake.

"Are all those jets headed for Washington?"

"I don't know."

The control center buzzed with the sound of fingers on keyboards as the technicians checked the other aircraft.

"Do you think reprogramming, trying to land, made this happen?" Charlie said.

"I don't know," Bill said, "but it looks that way."

"If this bug did this," Tim ordered, "you have to stop the others from redirecting."

"Melody, send out a message to all planes to stop any attempts at redirecting immediately." Bill opened a window on one of the fifty-inch screens on the main wall. The live map of the United States was covered in thousands of little blips representing all the air traffic in the country. A few clicks hid all the other planes and left nothing but the blinking yellow lights that represented the Trainor Freedom Five jets. As they watched in horror, planes were visibly turning towards Washington. Bill brought up the fleet destination tracking window. Tim was looking over his shoulder and dialing. The White House, the Capitol, FBI headquarters, the Justice Department, the Executive Offices, the Treasury, the Pentagon, the Supreme Court, the Federal Triangle complex, the Washington Monument, the Jefferson Memorial, the Lincoln Memorial, the Smithsonian, every major government office, museums, shopping centers, bridges, and even Arlington National Cemetery were listed.

The FBI agents were still calm, but there was terror in Tim's voice. "Phil? It's Tim. This is a code red. Repeat, this is code red. There are now dozens of Trainor jets targeted to hit D.C. The White House, the Pentagon, every building and every tourist spot you can think of. Shit, even our head office. The Air Force is going to need every plane it has."

Bill stared at the outbound message. Owners were sure to panic.

STOP REDIRECT IMMEDIATELY.
STOP ANY ATTEMPTS TO REDIRECT YOUR AIRPLANE. THE VIRUS MIGHT BE IN THE NAVIGATIONAL CODE AND COULD AFFECT YOUR AIRCRAFT'S DIRECTION. DO NOT ATTEMPT TO CHANGE DESTINATION. IF YOU HAVE ALREADY INITIATED A CHANGE, THE AIRCRAFT WILL FLY ITSELF AS WE WORK TOWARD A SOLUTION.
PLEASE REMAIN CALM AND ALERT FOR FURTHER MESSAGES.

The technicians managed to contact quite a few of the planes before the owners had attempted to redirect, but Bill watched helplessly as the number of planes headed for Washington increased by the second. One by one, they were redirecting themselves, and some were not too far away from the capital.

"The Air Force doesn't have that many fighters on alert," Charlie said. "This is going to be worse than 9/11. This is going to be a catastrophe." He shook his head. "How close is the nearest jet to D.C.?"

"Jesus, just a few minutes," Bill replied. Lights and LCD panels were flashing all over the wall. Bill looked up as a flight statistic window re-sorted its data based on estimated time of arrival.

N477WF had just taken off from Reagan twenty minutes ago. It had been the last departure before they had canceled all Freedom Five flights, and it had turned around and was coming back. It was less than fifteen miles away from hitting the Capitol Building. "Oh, my God."

"What can I tell NORAD?" asked Tim desperately.

"I don't know, Tim. I don't know." Bill felt like he was going to be sick. "We'll have to put him into a GAL landing."

"They can't let that jet get much closer." Tim switched to his cell phone. "General, I've got some more bad news . . ."

"Tell me again how the glide program works?" Charlie asked.

Bill had seen it work personally during certification trials in the Mojave Desert. "We have to shut down the engines, and then a fifth computer will take over and glide the plane in for landing. It's never been done with people on board, but it worked flawlessly in testing."

Charlie rolled his eyes. "Testing? Jesus!"

It sounded incredible, but it was all they had. It had been designed as the last line of safety if both engines were lost; they had never thought they would need it for complete computer failures. If the computers were powered down, the engines would shut off, and the multi-million dollar luxury suite in the sky was turned into a 39,000-pound glider. The plane would find an airport in its database, calculate the best path through the sky, and aim for the runway. All radar functions would continue to work, but any avoidance tactics were out of the question.

The computer and programs were not much different from the main network system itself. Hard-coded into a small, independent computer that had its own auxiliary battery, the software would dead-stick the plane in, just as a pilot would. Literally falling from 40,000 feet would be quite unnerving, but no different from any other plane that lost all power.

Another bell went off, and he heard Melody cry out, "Sixty seconds!"

"Oh, no," said a technician as he pointed at one of the TV monitors. "Look!"

A news crew was filming a green camouflage military Humvee. The truck was a few miles away from the camera, but it was easy to see the missiles on the roof. Bill couldn't make out if there were soldiers inside, but then the turret turned slowly to one side, and two surface-to-air missiles exploded out of their tubes and disappeared before the camera operator could react.

"Holy shit!" Bill heard himself gasp.

The camera raced to catch the speeding projectiles, and did so just as the two rockets hit the two engines on a Freedom Five jet. In a one-two punch, the rockets blew the jet to pieces. A fiery red ball of flame quickly disappeared into a cloud of black smoke, and chunks of burning plane plummeted to the ground.

~~~

Art heard Joan's sobs before he realized he was crying, too. Live news and instant communications had carried the horrific images around the world before the burning wreckage even hit the ground. It had happened so quickly that even with the powerful zoom lenses of the network, it had been impossible to read the tail numbers on the plane.

"Oh, my God," he heard Melody cry out from halfway across the country. He could see the shock on everyone's face at the command center. Squawking one-sided radio conversations went unanswered as everyone tried to comprehend what had happened.

"Jesus Christ," Tim Batterson muttered.

"Why did they shoot that plane down?" Art barked over Bill's headset. "They just killed a bunch of people!"

The FBI agent started talking on his cell phone. "General Allison? Tim Batterson. What happened?"

Everyone was quiet as the agent nodded a few times. "I understand . . . Yes, sir . . . I'm not sure. Just a sec." He held his hand over the phone and repeated his conversation to Bill and the staff. "The plane was on a glide pattern that came in over the White House. It was just too close, and they couldn't take any chances. He says we have five minutes before the next one gets too close."

"We have to put all the planes into GAL landings right now," Charlie ordered. "At least, the jets closest to Washington."

Art had already checked the latest stats. They had no other options left.

"There is one other major consideration, though," Bill warned Tim. "These planes will only have one chance, so all other air traffic will have to be cleared, and it's better if the airport has automated landing systems. GAL wants to lock on to the ground computers to guide the aircraft in, and once the software selects the airport, it totally commits the plane. Remember, the engines are shut down, and they have limited battery power to control the flaps as the plane glides in. And we only get one landing attempt per plane. There are no go-arounds."

"Another thing," Art added. "The GAL system might not pick an airport. If one is not available within a typical seventy-five radius, the system is designed to search its database and identify roads, fields, any long, flat surface." Art remembered the success of the testing in the Nevada desert. They had closed major sections of a stretch of highway, and it had been a test of nerves as they followed the Freedom Five in a chase plane, but the pilotless jet had landed dead-center on the two-lane highway and stopped within 2,700 feet. "With this many jets coming down at once, they could end up in big and small airports, roads and highways, even huge parking lots."

Tim shook his head. "I'll get the FAA to re-route traffic."

"Yes, and just so as you know, some airports will have quite a few of our jets wanting to land, so we'll have to stagger the planes. We don't want them all trying to land at the same time."

"Okay, so you stack them up, land them one minute after the other," Tim said. "Anything else I need to know?"

"Bill, what else?" Art said. He could see that Bill wanted to add something.

"No, that's how it will work, but it won't be very efficient. It's not like aircraft in a pattern with power to maneuver. Our planes will be gliding from five miles up and approaching from every direction and angle. We won't be able to control any of that. You've just seen that. We can't predict their descent trajectories, and we'll have to shut them down systematically, one at a time."

Tim was taking notes. "All the jets that don't have any traffic conflicts, they could land immediately, right?" he asked.

"Yes." Bill looked at Melody for another answer. "Where would be the best place to land Meyers' plane now?"

She tapped a few keys before replying, "Cincinnati. But it's still out of range. We'll have to wait fifteen minutes or so."

"Okay, let's get going on the rest. Melody, log on to the closest planes first. If they won't do it themselves, put them into a GAL landing as soon as they get close enough to an airport."

Tim stared at the wall. A mass of blipping icons were converging on the nation's capital. "Do you know who is on those planes?"

"We have a list of passengers," Art said. He knew at least half of the owners casually, and he hadn't paid much attention or cared who was actually flying today –but the Kingstons came to mind. "There are some very important people on those jets."

"That's what I figured. Do you have the list?"

"It'll be quite a few pages," Art said as he brought it up on his screen. It was arranged alphabetically. He rolled down through the hundreds of names. Sports stars, celebrities, movie stars, business tycoons . . . most were household names.

"Should we make the deal with Ansour now?" Tim asked.

Art hoped they weren't making a deal with the devil. "We have nothing to lose."

~~~

Annette was paralyzed as she stared at the incredible pictures. She had never heard of the men on the jet who had been killed, but it was an awful way to die – on TV, in a fireball, for the world to see. She could imagine how devastated the families must feel; millions must have watched the unthinkable happen. But she was mortified what it meant for her own family. If her son was involved, there were now five people dead. He could be a murderer, and maybe even more. Things just seemed to be getting worse.

The door flew open, and Phil ran into the room. He was on his cell phone. "How many planes . . . shit. Okay, right now." He hung up. "Every Freedom Five jet is now out of control and headed to Washington," he told them. "Hundreds of planes, and they are targeted on half of downtown. The White House, Congress, the Pentagon, you name it."

"My God!" Annette exclaimed. It was far worse than any nightmare. "What are they going to do?"

"They have an emergency program that can apparently glide the planes in. They're going to try and implement that." Phil shrugged his shoulders.

"What about Meyers' plane?"

"On all the planes. They found out that trying to change direction triggered the bug, and the planes all plotted new courses for targets in D.C." Phil nodded at Derek on the other side of the thick glass. "They want to take his deal."

Annette was numb. It was great news, but the developments were frightening.

Phil flipped through the channels on the TV, stopping at CNN. The reporter was summing up the new developments. "There are three hundred ninety-six Freedom Five jets that could be in trouble. The Air Force has scrambled squadrons of planes across the country to ride shotgun and shoot down the out-of-control jets if necessary."

The TV image switched to an Air Force base, with a perspective through a fence at the end of a field. The picture was clear enough to make out the two F-15 fighters roaring down the runway. Two more could be seen on the taxiway, getting ready to take off next.

"Come on," Phil said, grabbing Annette by the hand. "We don't have time for this."

They rushed back into the interview room.

Derek was smug. "So, do we have a deal?"

"Mostly, yes," Phil said. "Your mother is willing to drop her charges. The Bureau is willing to recommend a much lower bail, ten thousand dollars, and they will recommend probation or community service for the passport offence. You could be a free man."

"I need to talk to my lawyer."

"Derek, there is no time for that," Annette said. "They need you to log on now."

"Okay, but I want it in writing on FBI letterhead. And this means no other charges, either, right?"

"What other charges?" Phil asked.

"I don't know, Mr. FBI, but this deal includes no other new charges."

"I can't give you a free pass if you've committed other crimes. Are you guilty of something else?"

"No, but I don't want to be tricked into some false deal."

"Based on everything we know right now, there will be no other charges if you help. If they find you are connected to Bernie Meyers' death, that's a different story."

Annette watched as Derek looked back and forth between the two agents.

"I didn't have anything to do with that."

"Can you save those people?" Phil asked.

"I told you, I don't know."

"If you did this, you can probably fix it," Phil said. "Is that what this is? Be the hero and then walk away? Is that what you want?"

"You want my help, or not?"

"Derek, please," Annette pleaded. "If you are innocent, you have to help." She was flabbergasted and found herself getting angrier by the second. In one breath, her son claimed his innocence and his willingness to help, but his hostile demands were not signs of cooperation. "There are hundreds of lives at stake."

"I told you yes," he snapped. "But get it in writing."

"Okay, we'll be right back," Phil said. He took Annette by the arm and pushed her to the door. "Annette, why don't you come with me?"

Outside, Phil unclipped his cell phone and called his superiors. "A few of those jets are less than five minutes from restricted Washington, D.C., air space. We might be too late already, but if somebody else dies, he won't be going anywhere." He turned away and started barking orders into his phone. "Okay, get the computer set up. We'll take him into the back office."

Cliff came out of the observation room. He took Annette's hand, pulled her close, and kissed her softly on the cheek. "You are one brave, compassionate lady. I hope Derek realizes that one day."

Annette smiled weakly. She didn't feel brave; she felt terrified. She had seen the venom in her son's eyes when he tied her up. Now she could see his hatred and his fear. "I hope I'm doing the right thing. I feel like I'm betraying my son."

"You are absolutely doing the right thing. If Derek is innocent and can reprogram those jets, you will have helped save lives, and you will have helped him help himself. That's definitely doing the right thing."

"What's happening now?"

"Washington is in a state of panic. Everyone is comparing it to 9/11." Cliff pointed to a crowd of officers watching one of the TVs at the end of the hall.

"Let's go take a look," she said.

"Are you sure?" Cliff rubbed her shoulders.

"Yes. I want to see what's going on." They went back into the observation room, where the TV was perched on a ledge in the corner. A male reporter, young, black, and obviously scared, was live at the Washington Mall, on the east side close to the Capitol Building. People were streaming out of all the buildings. Thousands of cars had jammed the roads, and people were even driving across the grass of the long park. A view west towards the Washington Monument was almost unrecognizable; it looked more like the chaos at a crowded drive-in theatre as the terrified drivers chewed up the turf and headed in dozens of different directions. The reporter was talking about the traffic and the pandemonium. Twice, people running by bumped into the man and almost knocked him over.

"My God, Cliff, a lot of people are going to get killed in that panic," Annette said.

"You're probably right, but how do they stop it? This isn't something they can hide from the public, and you can't control a crowd like that."

"Will Derek be charged with those offenses, too?"

"Honey, I have no idea. I just hope he can fix one of those computers. This will be a blood bath if he doesn't."

"He must be pretty smart to be working there," Annette said. She knew little about the inner workings of computers, but she had struggled over the years with a host of her own home computer hardware problems and software glitches, most of which she had been able to fix. "I wonder what kind of supercomputers are on these planes."

"I don't know. Probably some high-end custom box."

Annette thought about what Derek had told her last week. "Why can't they just reformat the hard drive and then reload the software?"

"I don't know, honey, but I'm sure it's a lot more complicated than that."

"Before Derek tied me up, I asked him about my computer. That's what he told me to do. He said sometimes the simplest solutions are the best solutions."

"Honey, this must be a very sophisticated computer."

"Is it? But remember last week when we saw that show about Trainor? Those planes can glide for miles. Why don't they go on glide and then reformat the computers? Couldn't they fix the problem that way? That's what Derek told me to do."

"I'm sure they've thought of every possibility, Annette."

Annette got up and headed back to Derek's interview room. "Let me go ask him."

The guard let her into the locked room. Alex was walking in circles around Derek, and he looked up in anticipation. "Are we ready to go?"

"Phil hasn't come back yet, but I had another question." She sat down across from her son. "Remember on Sunday night when you told me how to fix my computer?"

"Barely."

She would remember every detail of the night for the rest of her life. "You told me to reformat the disk drive. What kind of computers are on those planes?"

He thought for a moment. "Well, they're not that different from a typical computer, but they use new hyper-fast data chips called quantum chips. They're designed to interpret enormous amounts of information and predict possible scenarios even in the most complex simulations. Quantum computing uses sixteen-bit processors called Qubits, and something called parallel processing. Why?"

"Doesn't sound like your average PC."

"It's not that different to the user, and they do use similar hard-drive technology."

"So, why couldn't they do that for these planes?"

"Do what?"

"Reformat the hard drives?"

"Reformatting would wipe out the operating system and all the software programs," Derek replied. "How's it going to fly?"

"Couldn't they reformat the drives as the plane glided down, and then reload the programs necessary to land the plane?"

"The plane's engines would be shut down."

"So? I thought those planes could glide for miles. How long would it take to format the hard drives and reload the basic programs?"

"I'm not sure . . . maybe half an hour."

"How long will they have for gliding?"

"It depends on their altitude and the wind conditions, but a jet at forty thousand feet will have . . ." Derek closed his eyes as he did the calculations. "About thirty-five minutes. If they're higher, more."

"Is that safety-landing program stored on the main disk drives?" Annette wondered if she knew more about computers than she thought.

"No, it's hard-coded on a separate board."

"That means it can't be erased, right?"

"Yes."

"So if you erase the hard drives, the landing program would still be there? It should still work?"

"I don't know. It's never been done, but if something goes wrong, the planes will be doomed."

"They're doomed now." Annette paused to let the statement sink in. "Will it work?"

"I don't know. That wasn't my area of expertise."

Phil came in with a smile on his face. "Okay, let's go. It's all ready. We've got a web cam, too—"

Annette cut him off. "That's great. And while you were gone, I talked to Derek about a possible solution."

"What kind of solution?"

Annette repeated her idea.

"Let's get Derek on-line first," Phil said as he unlocked the handcuffs that bound Derek's hands to the table. "Then we'll ask Trainor if your idea makes sense."

~~~

Art heard the fighter before he saw it. A deafening roar filled the cabin, and then the F-15 Eagle appeared on the right side of his plane. He swiveled his seat around to see it. The camouflaged smoke-grey jet was probably less than two hundred feet off their right wing, and the pilot was easily visible. He waved a black flying glove. Art waved back.

A moment later, a voice squawked over the radio. "N111TJ, this is Major Sid Linden with the United States Air Force. Are you okay?"

Art thought that was a silly question. "Physically, yes, we're fine, but you probably know we can't control our plane. We're going to go into an emergency letdown in a few minutes."

"Yes, sir, I understand that. I am instructed to stay with you until the situation is resolved." The voice was sympathetic. The unsaid message was anything but.

"I hope that will be very soon, Major."

"I hope so, too, sir."

"What happens if they can't fix the problem?" Joan said, terrified. "Will he shoot us down?"

"Not if GAL works."

The Air Force jet slid back a few hundred yards and out of their view. Art checked his main screen again. They were only two minutes away from being close enough to the airport and able to initiate the emergency landing. He had decided to go first. He had to prove it worked.

The Freedom Five jets were scattered all over the country, but most of them were on the eastern seaboard, and many were getting close to Washington. He pulled up a list of the tail numbers to see who was on board. Scrolling down, he recognized them all: Martin Dickers, left-fielder for the Houston Astros; Nancy Femet, the outspoken CEO of Hewlett Packard; Dan Ziworski from the Los Angeles Kings; and his good friends, the Kingstons. Norman had been one of the first to buy a Freedom Five. The rest of the list was a who's who of other wealthy, successful, and famous faces from around the globe.

Art highlighted the ex-senator's plane, and the details popped open in a separate window. Norman's jet was two hundred miles northwest of D.C., and only twelve minutes from hitting the Pentagon. *Shit*

He called Bill. "Norman Kingston is really close. What are you doing for all those jets that are getting too close?"

Bill looked up from his computer screen. "We've got three jets waiting for traffic to be cleared from National and Baltimore right now. We should be able to start the GAL letdowns in a few minutes."

"Good. Norman Kingston is on one of those jets. Have you talked to him?"

"Yes. He's scared, but he's okay."

Art had double-checked all his coordinates. It was now or never. "Okay, Bill. I am going to institute GAL in five seconds."

Art looked at his computer screens. Cincinnati International Airport was now within range. He had to show the others that the procedure would work. "I'm sixty miles east of Cincinnati. This is probably the best chance we're going to get. Here we go, gentlemen."

The computers made Art enter his password three times, and warnings flashed each step of the way, but when he tapped the enter key to go ahead and initiate a GAL landing, nothing happened. Not a thing. The engines burned on, and the plane continued its course. A message flashed onto the main screen.

> UNABLE TO PERFORM REQUESTED ACTION
> PLEASE CHECK ENTRY AND TRY AGAIN

Art tried again, and then again. Nothing. He logged onto Meyers' jet. Same message. Nothing worked, not even the emergency program. *Shit*

Bill repeated the procedure at his end, too, and got the same error message. "It's even affected the GAL software. All the operating and navigational software must be fine. The plane changed course, but it won't let us make any changes."

Art could see the terror in his vice president's eyes. "So this thing," Art said, "this bug, creates a problem with the navigation command structure." If they could define the modules that were infected, they should be able to solve the problem. It was obviously something small, because in every other way, the jets were operating perfectly.

Joan offered another faint hope. "You still have that programmer coming on-line. Maybe he'll be able to help."

Chapter 24

At first, the reports had been vague and conflicting, but when the truth about Washington broke, Mansi could almost feel the sense of panic that swept through the airwaves. He had wanted to be through the border before any shooting started, but his instincts told him it wouldn't matter. The reports were full of conjecture, but it didn't sound like the authorities had any idea what was really happening or who was behind the attack.

He took a few deep breaths as he pulled up slowly. He had chosen the Blaine truck crossing because it was the commercial entry and usually busy. Closing it for any reason would be a major nightmare for both countries. So far, traffic was slow but steady. Did the authorities know more than they were revealing? A multitude of paranoid and unanswerable questions worried him as he approached the United States and Canadian border. But only one man knew his alias, and that man was thousands of miles away and knew nothing of Mansi's whereabouts. He should have nothing to worry about.

At first the wait had looked daunting, but the stream of tractor-trailers moved through the five open booths fairly quickly. When the green light finally flashed to signal that it was his turn, he took a few deep breaths to calm his nerves as he pulled up to the waiting border guard.

The immigration agent, a young black man, looked down at the car without any recognition or concern. "Passport?"

Mansi passed over his Canadian passport. The guard found the photo and held it out to compare. "Where have you been, Mr. Marks?"

"Seattle, on business." He did his best to sound tired.

"And what kind of business is that?"

"I work for an American company that sells construction materials in Canada. I was at a sales meeting."

"Which company is that?"

"Master Construction Supplies."

"Okay, just a minute." The guard stepped back into his booth.

Mansi knew his passport was being checked, but it didn't matter. Vladimir's documents had never failed in forty years. It took only a few seconds before the man returned.

"Do you travel through here a lot?" the guard asked.

"I just started with the company, but I don't think so. Maybe three or four times a year."

"Will you always drive?"

"I would imagine. It's pretty close." Mansi pointed to the radio and turned it up a bit. The reporter was describing the mayhem in Washington. "Quite the news about the planes, huh?"

The guard nodded. "What are they saying now?"

It was ironic. All the expensive modern security measures taken by the Western nations to combat terror and crime, and when a major emergency broke out in the capital city of the United States, the citizens were better informed than the Canadian Border Services. "Apparently they shot one jet down, but there are more in trouble."

The guard looked shocked. "Really?"

"Apparently they are getting too close to restricted airspace."

"I've read about those planes. Good thing they're not up here." The guard shook his head in disbelief and then handed his passport back. "Welcome home."

"Thanks."

Mansi pulled away from the row of booths slowly and into the merging traffic on his left. He had memorized the route a long time ago. Less than a mile up 176th St., he turned left onto Eighth Avenue, and in minutes he made a right onto the on-ramp and the 99 freeway that led north to Richmond and the Vancouver International Airport. The distant mountains that seemed to define British Columbia glistened in the brilliant sunshine. In some odd way, it reminded him of his home. Snow was often visible on the Tell Atlas Mountains in the winter. The white peaks were quite a paradox to the rich aqua of the Mediterranean Sea.

He turned the radio back to CNN. It would all be over by the time his flight even took off. Derek had done his job well. How many planes would be lost didn't even matter; one or one hundred, a few people or a thousand, the damage was done and the rewards already accounted for. He switched channels, hoping to hear more Wall Street news, but the reporters were focused on Washington and the hundreds of jets still in harm's way.

No matter how it turned out, he still needed twenty-four hours to get to Algeria and safety. On the freeway, he checked his speedometer frequently. No sense getting a speeding ticket now, and the airport was not much more than a half-hour drive from the border. If everything continued to go well, he would have two and a half hours until his flight departed. Perfect timing, unless the Canadians closed their airports, but something told him that wouldn't happen.

Licensing and trade disputes had kept Trainor Jets out of Canada, and no Freedom Fives would be within hundreds of miles of Vancouver. There would be no operational reason to restrict air traffic in or out, and while the situation in the U.S. would affect many Canadian flights, the question was how much it would affect other carriers and international flights.

Mansi was betting on Air France and had booked an Airbus A380 nonstop to Paris. In the event that the Canadians sympathized with the Americans yet again and closed the airport to all flights, his contingency plan had him driving east until things settled down. He would be just another salesman driving across the flat, endless Canadian prairies. He pushed the pedal down and sped up to 120 kilometers an hour. That was only ten over the limit, and he was still being passed by most of the traffic. Ahead in the distance, he saw a KLM 747 on a long, gradual climb from west to east. That was very encouraging on two accounts. They were still letting flights depart, and KLM was owned by Air France.

~~~

Annette watched the live news reports with Cliff on the TV inside the soundproof observation room. Derek was hard at work in the room right beside theirs, visible through the large one-way window. The police had supplied a seventeen-inch wide-screen laptop, and his hands were a blur as he typed. Alex sat beside him, watching, but there was no way he could follow the flurry of keystrokes. Annette checked her watch. There couldn't be much more than a few minutes left for some of the jets.

The scene on TV switched to a reporter standing in front of the icon of Wall Street, the famous charging bull. A crowd had formed, and horns, voices, cars, and sirens could all be heard in the background. The reporter, a pretty young black woman, was already speaking. "The Dow Jones Industrials dropped almost eight percent in the first few minutes after news of the attack on Washington broke, but trading has been stopped here and at all the other American stock exchanges. Everyone remembers how the economy went into a downward spiral after that tragic day in the fall of 2001." She fell silent, then nodded as she re-focused. "Stand by. We are going to take you to FAA headquarters in Washington, D.C."

A picture of an older man standing behind a bank of microphones appeared. The Federal Aviation Administration emblem was visible on the wall behind him. He was in the middle of a briefing. "While this threat only affects the Freedom Five computer planes made by Trainor Jets, as a precaution, the FAA has ordered all air traffic cleared in the airspace surrounding the hundreds of airports on the East Coast that are affected. All other flights are being redirected to airports out of the area. No new departures or arrivals are being allowed at any airport east of the Rocky Mountains, but airports on the West Coast will continue to operate as usual. The FAA, on the President's orders, wants the world to know that this problem will be resolved as soon as possible and once again does not affect any other type of aircraft, commercial or private."

A male reporter's voice cried out, "Is it true they have scrambled fighters?"

The man closed his eyes momentarily before answering. "As a precaution, and as a last resort, Homeland Security has scrambled fighters."

Another male reporter asked. "Will they have to shoot down any more planes?'

The FAA official blinked a few times but answered clearly. "Not if they don't have to, but if any of those jets gets too close to Washington, or puts others at risk, that is one option. I have to go. That's all I have for now. We'll let you know more when we know more."

The TV switched to a picture of downtown Washington. A well-known face, Andy Sworken, a D.C. reporter for years, had his back to the jammed streets as he swept his hands over the unfolding nightmare. Traffic was at a standstill, and tens of thousands of people were running in every direction.

He sounded terrified. "As you can see, Washington, D.C., is in full panic. Officials still maintain that the jets will never hit any targets, but nonetheless, they have ordered an immediate evacuation of the city to be on the safe side."

A flurry of different camera views showed scene after scene of the endless masses of people literally running for their lives. Then, with no warning or explanation, the image switched to an Air Force base and video of fighters scrambling into the sky.

Annette stared at the TV in horror. Was her son really responsible for all this?

Phil opened the door. "Okay, we're set."

They rushed down the hall to the lieutenant's office, where the video conference call with LAX had been set up. In addition to the screen on the commander's desk, there were five nineteen-inch displays mounted on the side wall. Annette recognized the Trainors' faces first, on the top right screen. The brilliant blue sky in the cockpit window visible behind Art and Joan made her think of her own flight less than two weeks ago.

Bill was surrounded by a half-dozen people, four men and two women, including the two male FBI agents. They all listened while Annette spelled out her plan.

"Shut down all the computers on purpose," she said. "The plane should go into GAL. Reformat the hard drives as the plane glides down."

"I thought the plane wouldn't respond to any commands," Phil said.

Annette frowned. "Oh. Isn't there a way into the operating system?"

"There is a way, isn't there, Bill?" Art asked.

"Yes, I guess there is, but you just tried GAL, and it didn't work."

"I thought the program was designed to activate automatically in the event of total power failure," Annette said.

"It is," Bill replied, "but with all that's happened so far, we don't know that the GAL program will work the way it was supposed to, either." There seemed to be little conviction in his shrug.

"Do you have any other choices?"

"I don't believe we do," said Art, "not at this point. Would we even have enough time to reload the software, Bill?"

"If her idea works, the reformat shouldn't matter. GAL will land the plane somewhere, and then we can worry about reformatting the computers."

"Why don't you try it on the Meyers' plane?" Annette said. She hadn't thought about not getting the computers back up and running, but they were right; it might not matter. "If he's already dead, he won't mind."

"That's a good idea," Bill agreed.

Cliff squeezed her shoulder. "Annette, you are full of good ideas."

"They're both good ideas," Art said. "We should have thought of this before. I think we have nothing to lose. As far as I'm concerned, it's a go. Bill, what do you think?"

Annette felt Cliff's arms wrap around her in a hug. He had a way of holding her that made her feel safe. *Good ideas.* That was the wrong term, but maybe her solution would work. If it did, and they saved those innocent people, maybe they could save her son, too.

"Okay, we'll try it," Bill said, turning to Melody. "Let's get Meyers somewhere he can't do too much damage in case something doesn't work."

Annette wondered what Bill meant. "What will happen if the GAL program doesn't work?"

Bill met her gaze steadily. "The plane will fall out of the sky."

~~~

Derek had designed the program to be used once and to be virtually impenetrable. Only a complete shutdown of every Trainor Jet would cut the execution loop that ran through the network millions of times per second, but he had to admit, reformatting all the disks would have the same effect. He scrolled through line after line of code, but he really didn't know if he could do anything else. Even if he knew where to look, the ghost program was impossible to detect and impossible to stop. It had been configured to take control of the airplane when one of two scenarios occurred. The first trigger event was if the aircraft tried to change its destination. The second trigger was at 3pm EST, when most of the planes would be just over an hour's flying time from Washington, D.C. Once executed, the ghost program would remain undetectable and would be theoretically irreversible. It had never occurred to him that someone would reformat the hard drives while in flight.

The GAL software program had been part of the system he had never worked on or had much access to. He knew it was the plane's ultimate doomsday solution, but they had always figured it wouldn't matter. If Meyers' death hadn't been discovered, the planes would have started crashing into Washington before anyone knew what was happening, long after the point of no return. The GAL software would have been too late to save most of them.

He could feel the FBI agent watching his every move, and there were sure to be others on the other side of the mirror, as well, maybe even his mother. Who would have thought she would have come up with the idea? It was ingenious and might just work, and it was so simple he couldn't believe someone else hadn't thought of it. But he had an even better idea that might save a few lives – maybe even his own.

~~~

"Five minutes," Bill said, "and we can try the procedure on the Meyers jet, General." He knew they were desperately running out of time, but Meyers' jet was still over twenty miles outside the glide range to Nashville Airport.

"Nineteen aircraft have now become thirty-four, Mr. Simpson," Bart Allison said from his command center somewhere deep inside the mountain in Colorado. "Seven are approaching thirty thousand feet. We're running out of time. Who's on those planes?"

"I forwarded all that to you, sir, but bear in mind that sometimes there are unofficial passengers." Bill checked another screen. *Shit.* "It's now thirty-six planes. Two more have started their descent."

Bill watched as the general looked down at his computer screens for a moment. He tapped a few keys, then looked back up at the video camera and Bill. "Norman Kingston and Sammar Zeggan. Jesus Christ."

Bill looked down. "Yes, I know. Norman and Sheila are personal and lifetime friends of the Trainors." Bill had met the Kingstons dozens of times over the years, but he had never heard of Zeggan. "But I don't recognize the other name."

"The son of the President of Algeria," said the general. "Plays for Barcelona. Obviously, that's not what's important now, but Algeria is in some very critical talks with the White House."

Bill looked down at the flight status of Norman Kingston's plane. The jet was now at less than 30,000 feet and on its way into a landing pattern set for the massive white stone building tucked in neatly behind the Capitol Building. There were twenty-five minutes before it crashed into the Supreme Court, and Zeggan's jet had about thirty seconds less before it zeroed in on the Pentagon.

~~~

Derek had only barely logged on to N412LN when Phil Housely rushed into the room. He handed Derek a piece of paper with some writing on it. "Try to save N339HT. He's twenty-four minutes out."

"Try what?"

"I don't know," Phil said. "But he's some VIP from Algeria."

Derek pulled up the plane's manifest. His mouth dropped. It was hard to believe. His father had never talked about who might end up as collateral damage. "Sammar Zeggan?"

"That name mean something to you?" Alex was sitting right beside Derek and looking over his shoulder.

"He's the son of the president of Algeria. He's also a professional footballer."

"Well, save his ass, and you'll be a hero."

Mansi had called Sammar's father, Rami Zeggan, the best leader the country had ever had. However, the new president was not popular with the Americans, as he continued to nationalize much of the petroleum industry, eliminating billions in U.S. oil companies' investments. Saving the president's son would be a gift from God and would show the FBI that he had helped.

Maybe this was his ticket to freedom. But how? His mother's plan? Even if it did work, Zeggan's plane was running out of time. He had to try a potential shortcut, a way he could harness the power of all four CPUs. Maybe he could even improve on his mother's idea.

Bill saw the flight statistics change by the second as more and more Trainor Freedom Five jets were starting to power back and slow down, beginning their long, slow descent into the Washington, D.C., area. There were now fifty-four planes already lining themselves up for landings. A warning flashed across his screen, and he heard the verbal warning echoing from a dozen programmers' terminals around the control room. A few small sirens wailed in protest.

"Possible air to air collision . . . probable air to air collision . . ."

Bill instantly knew what had happened. He was not only running out of time, he was running out of air space. Many of the jets were coming in from the west, and they were all on the same automated course as they swung into the patterns and control of the ILS. The onboard computers still tracked the trajectories of all the traffic within hundreds of miles, and unless one changed course, two Trainor Jet Freedom Fives were now going to collide in four minutes. One was Norman Kingston's plane.

Meyers' plane was still three minutes away, so they had no other choice. Art discussed it with Bill and then called Norman personally with the devastating news. Waiting another few minutes to use Meyers as a test would be too late for the Kingstons and the Tambellini family.

The Kingstons seemed remarkably calm to Art. "The probability of collision is statistically one hundred percent, Norman. You are both heading for the same piece of sky. You know the technology; the GPS is accurate to one meter. Unless you do this, you will collide in less than two minutes at nine thousand feet, ten miles west of downtown D.C."

"Good Lord, first we're going to crash into the Capitol Building, and now we're going to kill a family of six?"

Art didn't want to believe it, either, but the positioning system had proven to be so accurate, it was almost guaranteed. "Well, if for some reason you actually do somehow miss each other, you will be inches apart and headed for Washington and your targets. The air force will have no choice, and they will shoot you down anyway."

"Sounds like we're between the proverbial rock and a hard place, Art," Norman said. "What about this family, the Tambellinis?"

"They're hysterical, but it doesn't matter. They're going to have to do this too, if it works."

"I always liked being at the forefront of technology."

"You did, sir." Art didn't know how to answer. If it didn't work, they might all be doomed. "But we're going to be right behind you. We're just waiting to get closer to an airport. You're close to a half-dozen suitable airports, and you have no time left."

"And we don't have any other choice but to try this emergency landing?"

"Not really. Crash, or be shot down." Art could hardly believe the options. "But we have every confidence it will work. You remember how excited I was when we talked about the testing results years ago? Not one failure."

"I remember." Norman turned away from the camera and talked to his wife. Art couldn't see their faces, but he saw Sheila's head nod a few times.

Norman swiveled his chair back around and addressed the dash camera again. "Okay, Art. We trust you, and we have no other choice. Let's do it."

"Norman, I never wanted to put anybody at risk, least of all you. I wish there was another way." Art saw the digital readout. They were less than twenty miles away, less than ninety seconds from collision.

"Me, too. But we have faith that this GAL program is going to work and we're going to float to the ground like a butterfly, so let's get at it." Norman motioned impatiently.

Bill was watching, the FBI was watching, and who knew who else was watching. "Okay, Senator, here we go. I'm going to have Bill shut all your computers down simultaneously. That will cause the engines to shut down, and you will go into a glide. It will be quiet, and you will feel yourself start to descend, okay?"

"Which airport will we land at?" Norman asked.

"We don't know. There are dozens of airports in Virginia, military and civilian, but it doesn't matter. The software will pick the best one, and everyone will know you're coming in."

Norman and Sheila nodded in unison. "Okay."

"Watch your video screen. It should show the status of the reformat process, which tells us that everything is okay there, but once your plane has locked onto an airport, that doesn't really matter. You should be safe and just glide in. Okay?"

Norman offered a silly grin as he agreed. "I've believed in your autopilot software since day one, Art. I'm sure it will work just fine."

Art had sat through a few dozen GAL simulator landings. They had been eerie, but the program had set the plane down as gracefully as a pilot would have. "Thanks, Norman. Okay, here we go. Bill, start the shutdown and reformat procedure now."

~~~

Bill closed his eyes for a moment. He felt a pounding in the back of his head. So much was happening so fast.

"It's NORAD," said Tim. His remarkably calm voice pulled Bill back into the control room. He looked up at a bank of video screens.

General Bart Allison's picture came up on one of the four large screens. He stood in the middle of a command bunker somewhere. Dozens of video screens of all sizes covered the walls behind him, and soldiers in blue uniforms could be seen manning the workstations. "What the hell is going on there?" the general said. "I've got one minute before I have to shoot down the distinguished ex-senator from California."

"Give me thirty seconds, General, please," Bill said. He kept remembering the fireball in the sky again and again. "I'm starting the emergency shutdown on the Kingston's plane right now." A series of screens warned him not to shut the jet's computers down. Finally, the last exit screen popped up. "Okay, here we go."

He pushed the last enter key, and the room froze as all the images turned to black. Even the video feed of the Kingstons' plane was gone. For a few long seconds, there was silence, and then a message flashed across the dozens of screens monitoring the results.

GAL EMERGENCY PROGRAM HAS CONTROL
COMPUTER FAILURE GAL HAS CONTROL

The room burst into cheers and applause. Bill felt a wave of joy and a rush of pleasure the likes of which he had never felt before. Nobody else was going to die. They were going to be okay. He switched over to a window that showed the trajectory of Senator Kingston's jet. It was turning south and lining up for the long, steady descent into Richmond area. They wouldn't have enough time to reformat the disk drives and load the necessary software, but it proved the system worked. GAL had found the Richmond airport, locked onto the incoming flight pattern, and was working its way down to its final approach. "Let's see . . . estimated time of reformat, twenty minutes and forty-one seconds. That won't matter. Estimated glide time, six minutes at current fourteen-hundred-feet-per-minute rate of descent. You see that, General?"

Bart Allison had looked away from his camera and leaned over the shoulder of one of his technicians. He smiled when he looked back up. "I do, Mr. Simpson. Good work. Now, what about all those other jets? What about Zeggan? He's almost out of time, too."

"Yes, sir. He's next, and then the rest. I think we can save them all."

"Well, that's wonderful news, Mr. Simpson. We'll continue to monitor things from here, but excellent work."

"Thanks, General." Bill turned to face the technicians who awaited his instructions. "Okay, it works. Eric, send out the good news. Tell everyone we're going to talk them through the procedure one step at a time, closest ones first. Everyone will initiate the reformat procedure and GAL landing immediately, or we will dial in and do it for them."

The room burst into a loud, raucous cheer, but silenced quickly when Tim Batterson raised his voice and shouted, "Okay people, we have almost four hundred planes to get on the ground, and they need our full, undivided attention right now."

Bill sat down at one of the terminals and listed the flights by distance and time from Washington. At almost ten miles per minute, they were all getting closer by the second. They prioritized the flights, called the already terrified owners, and started to talk them through the forced landing. Bill looked at Sammar Zeggan's jet. The icon was flashing red. It was past Richmond and less than three minutes from the no-fly-zone that surrounded the nation's capital. The collision alarm went off again.

Melody shouted, "N441BC is on a collision course with N290BT. They both went into GAL and are gliding into Baltimore."

Bill couldn't believe it. "How much time do we have?"

"Less than five minutes. Both planes turn onto the downwind leg within two seconds of each other. It will be awfully close."

~~~

Derek couldn't believe what a whiner Sammar had turned into.

"Okay, Sammar," Derek announced, "I have orders to put you into an emergency free-fall landing."

The young star was almost hysterical. "This is an assassination plot. The Americans are trying to kill me."

Derek watched the speed bleed off and the trajectory change. The message confirmed the success.

> GAL EMERGENCY PROGRAM HAS CONTROL
> COMPUTER FAILURE GAL HAS CONTROL
> RICHMOND INTERNATIONAL AIRPORT
> ETA: 4:15:52 PM EST

Derek figured the president's son should be okay, but he had lost a lot of respect for the European star. Sammar had screamed at him several times like it was Derek's fault, and the two scantily clad girls crying in the background were evidence of the Algerian's lifestyle. Certainly not what Allah had in mind. But it would mean a lot to Sammar's father if he could save just this one plane. This was a chance to prove himself in many ways.

~~~

Annette stared at the images on the TV as she switched channels, but it was a lot of the same footage. She stopped when she recognized a reporter standing outside the Trainor Jets manufacturing plant in Long Beach. Numerous security guards could be seen at the gate, and two police cars, red lights flashing, blocked the entrance to the plant.

The reporter had her back to the massive plant as she talked. "The heart of the Trainor Jets command and control is normally here, behind this well-patrolled gate and inside the top three floors of this top-secret facility. For the last two years, hundreds of thousands of Freedom Five flights have been planned, executed, and managed without so much as an error message, but today, suddenly all that went wrong. Nothing is known yet as to the cause of this unprecedented, massive, and deadly failure, but what is known is that thousands of people's lives are in imminent danger...."

At that moment, the station cut the reporter off as it switched to a feed of a camouflaged green and black Army Hummer parked in a small stand of bushes. A soldier standing in the Hummer could be seen through the telephoto lens of the camera. The man had his face up against the eyesight of a turret-mounted rocket launcher and was tracking something across the sky. The cameraman zoomed back and panned the sky. It surprised Annette how far away the camera was from the truck, but when the camera found what it was looking for, she gasped. By now she recognized the shape of the Freedom Five. It was still quite high, but as the camera worked its way in closer, the world could see that it was descending in a slow, wide left turn.

The cameraman swept the skies for another few seconds before zooming back in close on the military Humvee. It was a few miles away, at least, but remarkably clear. She watched as the gunner turned slowly. Then, without any warning, the picture flashed to a photo of a private jet. A red *Breaking News* banner raced across the bottom of the screen, flashing an ugly message for the world to see:

JETS COLLIDE ~~~ JETS COLLIDE ~~~ JETS COLLIDE.

The picture on the screen zoomed out, and another jet could be seen turning in towards the first one. In seconds, the two Freedom Five jets ran into each other and exploded.

"Oh, my God," a reporter cried in disbelief. "Two jets have collided over Virginia."

"Shit!" Cliff pounded a fist on the wall. Shouts, screams, and a lot of cursing could be heard throughout the station.

Annette felt the room spin. As she reached for something to hang onto, everything went black, and she collapsed.

~~~

Plane after plane had started GAL descents. Art wasn't too worried about the ones further out, but there were over a hundred planes within two hundred miles of D.C. that were still in a lot of danger. Sequencing them in without losing any more was the new challenge, and one they would have little control over. Once the engines shut down, the GAL system had no ability to consider or communicate with other traffic. The software picked the best airport in range first. If none were within gliding distance, then the computer would assign a secondary location to attempt a landing. That usually meant a road. Every student pilot prepared for engine failure and knew the procedure didn't allow for any second chances. A software window opened, and he smiled. It was Norman and Sheila, and they were going to be okay. For the moment, that's what mattered. "Thank you, Norman. You are a brave man."

"I told you I trusted you, Art," Norman boasted. "This thing is working like a charm, isn't it?"

"Yes, it is. You are on final for Richmond." Art glanced over at the flight information. The plane even had the wheels locked and down. "Thank God, or somebody, for all this modern technology."

Sheila waved. "Art, this is one incredible plane. I can't thank you enough."

She's thanking me? She was so gracious. A bright flash on one of his other screens caught his eye. The image of the fireball stunned him.

~~~

Bill felt sick at the sight of the burning wreckage. A minute ago, they had been elated. The idea had worked, and they had already saved dozens of airplanes, including Senator Kingston, but many were still locked onto targets in downtown Washington and waiting for landing opportunities. Others had started their GAL descents.

The TV reporter's frantic voice was describing the scene. "The two planes are gone. Oh, my God. They are both gone."

The footage rolled again. The planes had exploded together in a fiery blast that blew both planes to pieces. The fireball seemed to hang in the sky for a few seconds, and then a few bigger sections of the cabin plummeted to the earth, trailing streaks of fire, smoke, and carnage. Another explosion and plumes of thick black smoke left little doubt as to the fate of the passengers.

It had happened in seconds, before anyone had a chance to respond – not that there was anything left anyone could do. Alarms had gone off when the Air Force threatened to shoot down N217PL unless it immediately put GAL into motion. The command center had wanted to wait a few more minutes, but there were too many other planes and too many potential conflicts. N217PL was a family of five, and N199JJ was two executives from Microsoft.

"Oh, my Lord," Melody's hands covered her mouth in horror.

"We lost both of them." Bill felt sick.

The FBI agents looked as shocked as he was.

"Jesus!" Tim asked. "You can't predict that?"

"Not until the approach computers recognize both aircraft are on the same heading. GAL doesn't transmit its intended flight path and it doesn't see any other traffic. It just picks an airport it can reach." There were far more potential problems in reality than had been seriously considered in the GAL software development. They certainly had never envisioned a mass catastrophic scenario like this.

Chapter 25

Annette felt cold. Then she heard voices. Everything was blurry, but she recognized Cliff's face. She wondered why he seemed so far away, but then he leaned closer and she could smell the cola on his breath.

"Honey, are you okay?" he asked.

She was lying on a couch. Cliff had a cold cloth on her forehead. She pushed him away and she sat up. "What happened?"

"You passed out a few minutes ago. Are you okay?"

She looked around the room. A TV was on in the corner. Pictures of the pandemonium in Washington flickered across the screen. She was in the same office as earlier. She could hear the fear in the reporter's voice.

"The two jets were apparently gliding in for the Baltimore airport when they struck each other. Eyewitnesses say both planes disintegrated instantly, and pieces of burning metal have fallen across a few square miles of eastern Virginia. There are unconfirmed reports of injuries on the ground as well, but we caution that those are just preliminary reports. Back to you, Neil."

Annette sat up and looked around. Phil was in the next room talking to Derek. She turned and looked back at Cliff. "Two of the Freedom Fives collided?"

"Yes, and they're worried that more could hit each other. But the good news is, your idea worked. It worked perfectly, but they have a lot of jets to reprogram, and some are really close to Washington."

"We can't win, can we?" Annette said. She was glad her idea had helped, but if more people died because of her suggestions....

"We don't even know what the game is, honey," Cliff reassured her. "But your idea is going to save a lot of people, hundreds, so let's just see what happens, okay?"

The newscast switched to another shot of the beltway around Washington. It was at a standstill, and abandoned cars could be seen stopped in the middle of the freeway. People were walking, running, pushing, and climbing over cars to get out of the city. Everyone looked terrified.

Cliff picked up the remote and changed the channel. The view was from the inside of a private jet. A dark-skinned young man in a blue Nike sweatsuit stood right in front of the dash camera. Two attractive blonde girls were visible behind him, crying.

The voice was from the man. "This was an attempted assassination. The American government has fabricated this whole emergency in order to kill me."

"Who's that idiot?" Cliff said.

The TV reporter cut in and answered Cliff's question. "Sammar Zeggan is one of the top soccer players in the world and son of the newly elected Algerian president. Relations between the U.S. and the North African country have been strained for the last few years. While this is not likely an assassination attempt, it would not bode well for U.S. business interests in the fledgling North African democracy if he were to die in this American-made jet."

"This is the plane Derek was trying to save," Annette said. "Apparently the president of Algeria is promising to kick the American oil companies out if his son dies."

For a moment, an image of Derek at Huntington Beach as a toddler, laughing in the surf, flooded her mind. The mother in her wondered if this could be her son's last chance, but the incredible pictures of the planes blowing up burned in her brain and erased any logical hope. She had no idea of what would happen next, but one thing seemed for sure: her prayers weren't being answered.

~~~

It didn't take long for Derek to talk Bill into letting him try his networking idea. Zeggan's plane would land at Richmond a few minutes behind the Kingstons', whether the reformat worked or not. There just wasn't enough time, even with the four CPUs. He was sure it would work, and it did. *Amazing!* He watched the four CPUs eat up the hard disk. And it had been his mother's idea; that was the most incredible part. But it didn't matter now how many planes they saved, or how many people died. Numbers were never the primary goal.

"That's awesome, Derek, awesome," Bill said. He had watched from Long Beach. "I will send you a list of planes where that might help. Six or seven minutes instead of twenty-five will make a big difference. Maybe some of those planes can regain control before, say, ten thousand feet. That would make the military happy."

"How many?" Alec said. He was on the phone behind Derek. "How long?"

"I'll be right back," Bill said and clicked off.

Derek watched the flight path of Zeggan's jet. It was at 2,000 feet, and the landing gear was down. The progress bar was moving quickly, but reformatting and reloading would take another four minutes – sixty seconds after touchdown.

Alec wrote down two tail numbers on his notepad and tore off the sheet of paper. He handed it to Derek. "Here, check these out. NORAD says they're attempting to land on the beltway."

Derek wanted to laugh. They had kidded about that at work occasionally – saved by technology, but killed when the jet touched down on top of a semi-trailer or a station wagon full of kids.

N402NT was a couple from San Francisco, no one he recognized, and N392GC was a charter out of Sea-Tac. Seven City of Tacoma officials. Both had less than two minutes before they landed on the busy freeway that surrounded Washington. Derek couldn't do a thing for the planes or the innocent life about to be randomly and rudely interrupted from above. The planes were lining up for a straight section of the road, but the freeways were clogged with traffic, and clearing the road was out of the question. *Perfect.*

"There's not enough time for my work-around," Derek said, pointing to a screen that showed the ticking clock. "I'll try to save someone else, but you'd better have them clear the highway right now."

"Hell, there's not enough time to clear the road, either," Alec said. "Will that jet just land whether the road is clear or not?"

"The engines are off, remember?"

A window popped open on his screen. A list of tail numbers showed planes that had not started the GAL program yet and still had sufficient altitude to complete the process. There were fifty-two. He wondered what the outcome would be for the other 340-odd planes. A few more would certainly be lost before they were all safely back on the ground. "I'm going to log on to this one, okay?"

"Ah, sure." Alec turned his attention back to his cell call.

Derek kept Zeggan's flight performance in one window while he dialed into the first jet on Bill's list. Sammar and his two friends were sixty seconds from touchdown. Derek wondered what his father would say about the kid's political outburst. That certainly had never been part of their plan, and he hoped it wouldn't hurt his father's relationship with the president of Algeria. The important fact was that he had helped saved the president's son.

~~~

Art had watched his friends landing, as had most of the staff at Long Beach. Their jet had touched down beautifully and rolled about half way down the runway before stopping dead-center. He was happy, but still terrified.

"Norman, you have to get out right now," he said. "Get out of the plane."

Norman and Sheila looked relieved and confused. "Sure," Norman said, "but . . . what's the problem now?"

"There's another Freedom Five right behind you." Art prayed different fuel levels and load levels would make enough difference to the roll-out the jet would need. If not, Zeggan's Freedom Five would plow right into the Kingstons' jet. The GAL program had only been written to land and stop, as quickly as possible, and it had no power to move. Pushback trucks were on their way, but the powerful little United diesel tractors were not built for speed. "It could run right into you. You have to get clear of the jet right now."

~~~

Phil had told Annette the great news. Derek had found a faster way to improve the reformat, and they should be able to gain control of a lot of the jets long before they got too close to the ground. That sounded good for a change. Her son had done something good. She felt like smiling, but his fate was far from settled. A number of people were dead already, and lives were still in jeopardy. No matter who Derek saved now, there were still many questions that needed answers.

The TV caught her eye. A Freedom Five was flying very low. She could see the tops of office buildings. When the picture retreated, she could see that the jet's wheels were down and it was coming in for a landing, but the wide angle of the camera showed a frantic freeway below. A female reporter in the news helicopter following the jet was describing the scene. "The roads are still clogged, and there is nowhere to go. It appears that many of the drivers can see the jet coming down . . . Oh, my God, it's going to hit that bus . . . Oh, my God!"

The white jet looked huge as it came in for landing. Its wide wingspan threw a quick, eerie shadow across the smallish yellow bus, before its front nose gear plowed through the roof. The bus started swerving around, but the weight and force of the jet was irrevocable. The two hung together for a few seconds, half-flying, half-driving, half-car, half-plane, but as gravity pulled the full weight of the plane down, the bus twisted underneath into a mass of crumpled metal and exploded into flames. The picture cut to black.

The anchor desk returned, and a still photo of the jet just before it hit the bus had replaced the live footage. The reporter started recapping what he knew. "This is the second jet to hit a local highway. The first jet hit the 95 Capital Beltway bridge over the Potomac a few minutes ago. We have camera crews on their way to the scene, and eyewitness reports are preliminary and conflicting, but apparently four cars were hit and there are a number of injuries. This is all unfolding as we speak. First responders have only just arrived on the scene, and there is a lot of panic and confusion." The picture changed to an image of burning cars. Smoke and metal obscured the shaky image, and it was hard to tell how bad it was, but then the photographer moved back a few steps, and the wreckage of the plane was clearly visible.

"God, Cliff," Annette murmured. A moment ago, she had thought they were all saved.

~~~

Bill knew things were out of his control. His programmers were scrambling to get the planes down safely, but events were unfolding so quickly they could hardly keep up to the requests and emergencies. Five planes had been destroyed or crashed, and many people were dead and injured. It was a catastrophe he could never have imagined. Some news was good; Meyers' jet had landed safely at the Nashville airport. The police and ambulance were waiting. Maybe Bernie was still alive, but it didn't look good.

The cameras were still on, and Bill watched as the two police officers entered the plane. They looked around somewhat timidly at the ghost aircraft first before proceeding into the cabin.

A female paramedic followed the policemen in and rushed over to the slack body, but in seconds she was shaking her head and frowning. "He's been dead for quite a few hours." she said.

One of police officers unzipped the duffle bag and appeared startled. He zipped it back up and motioned to the paramedic. "Okay, you can leave."

She nodded and left without a word.

"Jimmy, look at this," said the officer as he unzipped the bag again and opened it up so it was easy to see inside. Bill could see the distinctive logo from five hundred miles away.

Jimmy was a red-faced man in his late forties or fifties, and he looked like he could boil over. "Oh my lord, it's a freaking nuke!"

The officer nodded. "Yes, and Russian, by the looks of it."

Jimmy started backing towards the door. "It's probably radioactive, Frank."

Tim tapped him on the shoulder. "Bill, who else can see this? I want this feed cut right now."

"Okay." Bill looked around the command center. "Do you really think it's a nuke?"

"I don't know, but it's a matter of national security," Tim said. "There's enough going on. For now, until we know, let's just keep it quiet, okay?"

Bill had no choice. He restricted and installed a password for the audio and video feeds from Meyers' plane, but he watched long enough to see the two officers quickly exit and close the door behind them. "This is just unbelievable," he muttered. "Does this mean the Russians are involved in all of this?" *First Sudesh, then Derek, now the Russians?*

Tim shook his head. "Your guess is as good as mine."

~~~

Traffic was slow around the airport, and there seemed to be extra police everywhere. Mansi was glad to see other flights landing and taking off when he turned off the freeway. The runways were almost due west, and the jets roared over his car as he got closer.

The deafening roar was Allah's music to his ears. Inside the rental car return, the TV was turned on to CNN. Five planes were reported down, but many more were still in danger. The attendants hurried him through the check-in procedure, and in minutes he had his receipt and was headed for the terminal. The first-class line was empty, so he walked straight up to the Air Canada ticket counter and handed the agent his ticket and passport.

The Air Canada ticket agent smiled politely. "Good day, Mr. Marks," she said. "Traveling with us to London?"

"Yes, is everything okay? I heard about the private jets." TV monitors all over the waiting area had the story on.

"Yes, sir, but it doesn't affect us. It's only those computer-controlled planes, and all of the trouble is back east." The agent pointed at one of the TVs in the concourse. "I think they've found a way to save most of those people."

"That's good news." He couldn't care less. The damage had been done, and the money had been made. "You have pilots on your planes, right?"

"Of course, sir. Of course."

"Good." Mansi smiled. "Will we still be on time ?"

"Yes, sir, but you need to go straight to customs. Security is backed up." She handed him his documents and ticket.

"I'll go straight there." He was confident that he had left no trail, but the sooner he was out of the country, the better.

~~~

Derek kept the software window that showed Zeggan's jet open. Saving the others was now no more than a few dozen keystrokes each, but if anything could help his situation, it would be this one plane. He had been horror-struck when he had found out who the passengers were, but the obnoxious athlete might just turn out to be his savior – first with the FBI and police, and then later, who knew what power the president of Algeria could bring to bear.

Derek had gotten tired of Sammar's ranting and turned the audio feed off. He didn't tell them that he was still watching, and they didn't seem to know, because the girls pulled out a small white packet of cocaine. In minutes, they were all giggling again.

Derek could see the buildings going by through the window of the jet, so he changed views to the outside forward view of the camera. It was startling to see the pavement that close. Big white numbers, *34*, identified the runway and direction. In seconds, the plane landed and started its roll-out. Derek could see something white down at the end of the runway, and as Zeggan's plane got closer, he realized what it was. Another Freedom Five jet was stopped in the middle of the runway.

"God have mercy," he murmured. There was nothing he could do.

"Is that plane going to hit that other one?" Alex asked.

"I don't know, but there's nothing we can do."

"You can't stop it?"

"No, Mr. FBI agent. Remember, there is no power except for flaps and brakes. The plane will stop in the least amount of space it can."

~~~

Art could see Norman and Sheila running for the police car. Thank God they were safe. They had left all the cameras on, and he flipped back to the rear view. The other jet's landing lights were visible, and it was racing down the runway towards the Kingstons' parked jet. The Freedom Fives could stop in less than 3,000 feet, but he had no way of knowing how far down the strip the Kingstons had gone. His video flashed. It was Bill.

"Art, I have some incredible news."

Art looked back at the other screen. The jet had gotten much closer, but it was hard to tell how fast it was going from the straight-on angle.

"Good news, I hope."

Bill hesitated. "No."

"What, then?" Had they lost another plane? He looked at Kingstons' video feed again. The jet was filling up the screen.

"The duffle bag on Meyers' plane," Bill said. "They think it's an atomic bomb."

~~~

It was hard to keep up with the stream of TV reports. As far as Annette could tell, at least five planes had crashed or been shot down. Twenty-seven people were reported dead. The anchorman still sounded panicky, but as the images switched from one airport to another, planes were landing, and people were being saved. In one report, two F-15s could be seen flying low over the top of a landed Freedom Five and wagging their wings in salute .

The scene changed, and she could see an older couple jumping into a police car. The black-and-white pulled away in a hurry, burning the tires as it tore off down the pavement. The cameraman turned in the other direction, and it was obvious what they were scared of. Annette stared in horror as a Freedom Five roared down the runway and slammed into another Freedom Five jet that was stopped in the middle of the faded, broken white center line. The explosion covered both planes in flames and pushed the screaming wreckage hundreds of feet down the tarmac.

~~~

The TV images were horrific and nonstop. Even Art's plane had been captured on film as it came in for landing. Art had tried most of the big-name channels available through the satellite, but there were no reports about an atomic bomb. The slight jar of the landing gear brought a cry of relief from Joan, and she wrapped her arms around him.

"We're safe, Art," she said, looking out the porthole window as the landscape rushed by. "GAL worked."

Art could feel the brakes working overtime as the emergency systems procedures endeavored to get the plane stopped as quickly as possible. "Yes, that's one piece of good news, isn't it?"

~~~

Bill Simpson stood up on the platform and clapped his hands loudly. The room fell silent. "First, thank you, thank you, thank you," he said. "You are all heroes. Real heroes. You've saved hundreds of lives. I know we lost some planes, but it's over. Every Freedom Five is now on the ground or back under control."

A burst of applause and cheers made him smile. He continued, "I have no idea how we're going to handle this, but we'll deal with the clients one at a time. Melody has volunteered to be the liaison to the press, who are camped outside our gates and calling every phone we have, as you know. Officially, I believe our files show we lost a total of seven jets. We have the passenger manifests, but we don't know how many other people might have been killed."

Chapter 26

Cliff was used to the way many crises often ended: sometimes with a bang, sometimes with a whimper, but the agony of the senseless loss of life was always hard to fathom. Seven planes, forty-five people in all. A nation paralyzed by fear. He had been there and knew the feeling personally and professionally, but he had never expected to be witness to tragedy on this scale. To think his fiancé's son was responsible was almost unbelievable.

They left the station shortly after the crisis was over. The FBI had taken Derek off to a new cell somewhere else, and there was nothing they could do or add. The FBI knew all Annette did, although Cliff wondered if the authorities knew something they weren't telling. Phil had been tight-lipped when Annette had asked about Bernie Meyers and the bomb.

Annette sat beside him in a lost slump. She had cried a bit and looked numb. It was hard to know what to say. Cliff had called home and told the girls and Marie and Val to pack a few bags. The media were sure to track Annette down, and it would be a circus. He had made arrangements for a big house out in Riverside, where they knew no one and no one knew them.

～～～

The FBI interrogated Derek off and on until almost midnight before they left him alone. They didn't feed him, and despite his attorney's pleas, they continued to pound him with questions and accusations, threatening anything and everything to get him to crack. They even had an Algerian-born agent who spoke Arabic and talked about life in Guantanamo Bay, but Derek stuck to his denials and did what Bezzi had told him to do: not say a damn thing.

He hoped his father would be proud of him. While the mission had not gone exactly as planned, he knew that the attacks had struck deep into the heart of the American psyche, and the stock market's reaction alone would have netted millions to fund future operations. That had been the main purpose, and in that he had succeeded. But saving Sammar Zeggan only to have him die on the ground would cast a shadow over their operations. Money wouldn't buy the President a new son.

He lay awake most of the night, wondering what his father would say. It had all started with his mother. If she had never shown up, he would be in Algeria, watching the news on satellite TV.

~~~

Annette and Cliff had sat up together until 3:00 a.m. before even trying to sleep. They split a sleeping pill, and at first Annette didn't think it would work. Cliff dozed off in minutes, and the last time she looked at the clock, it was almost four o'clock. What had happened and what was yet to come still scared her to death, but eventually the drug blanked out her overworked mind and exhausted body. She woke up about 7:00, dazed, not sure where she was. Her head hurt. Cliff wasn't there. They weren't at home. They were somewhere strange and the half empty bottle of Tequila sat on the dresser as another reminder of what they had tried to shut out.

A note from Cliff was on the nightstand beside her. He had gone out to get some breakfast. She wasn't sure if she could eat, but her stomach growled at the thought of coffee. She got up and put on clothes. They would have to get some more clothes today. She thought the house was okay; but the cheap furniture was well worn and looked like it had been there a long time. Cliff thought it was fine for a few days, but she hoped they didn't have to stay too long. Just knowing it was a safe house gave her the creeps.

For a moment, she thought about turning on the TV, but the news would undoubtedly be covering the aftermath. The repeated footage would be hard to take. She went into the bathroom and brushed her teeth. Her eyes were bloodshot, and she wondered if she had looked this bad twenty years ago when Derek had been taken. At least she'd had youth going for her back then. Only a few weeks ago, she had been enjoying the thought of the girls moving out and her parenting days pretty much over. Now she had no idea what horrors the truth about her son would reveal.

The door opened, and Cliff came in, his hands full with a tray carrying six cups of coffee and a brown bag that instantly filled the room with the smell of fresh bread. Her stomach growled again.

"Hi, honey," He set the food down and leaned close for a kiss.

"Hi, honey yourself." She gave him a kiss and a big hug. Even though he couldn't change anything that had happened, having him beside her had been such a comfort. They talked a lot about what would happen next and speculated on what Derek would face. FBI had not given him his freedom or pressed new charges yet.

Cliff brought the idea up first, but it sounded better the more they talked about it.

"We had talked about retiring in a few years, anyway," he said.

"Are you sure we can afford it?" Annette had looked at their finances a few months ago.

"I think so, especially if we live up in Montana. But yeah, I think we should sell this house and buy a condo. Let the girls live in it for now, and it can be our tie to Southern California. Then we can move back anytime."

"It'll be a good investment, and we had been talking about moving out, anyway."

"It's getting to be winter in Whitefish, but it's a cozy place with a big fireplace."

"It'll be the first time I've never lived close to my mother," Annette said. "I hope she'll be okay."

"We'll be back in a few years after this dies down. Besides, she'll be busy keeping an eye on the kids."

"And we can come back all the time, if we're retired." *What will I do all day?* She wondered.

Her cell phone rang, and she looked down at the dial. Who was calling her at this early hour?

Then she thought of Cindy Yaccine. Annette had forgotten to call her back last night. "Cindy, I'm sorry. I forgot to call you back."

"It's okay. Gosh, all this stuff about the jets, it's been really scary. We were terrified and were glued to the TV. Did you watch it?"

Annette blurted it out: "The police think my Derek had something to do with it." She started crying.

"What?" Cindy exclaimed with shock. "With all those jets?"

"Yes, Derek was a computer programmer at Trainor Jets." Annette tried to control herself. "They think he might have done this."

"That's incredible, Annette, absolutely incredible. Did the police find out anything about Mansi?"

"No, not yet, and they are trying to find out if he still alive," Mansi's name made Annette stop crying. "Nothing would surprise me now."

Cindy's anger piqued. "That bastard. I got your message about the DNA tests. I can make it tomorrow."

Annette had forgotten all about the appointment at the county lab. "I don't know if I can take any more surprises, but hopefully it will help answer some questions."

~~~

Breakfast had been the same cold toast Derek had been served the last two days, but he was hungry, so he ate the dry bread. He demanded the police let him out again, but they laughed and never even answered. He yelled a couple of times that he wanted to talk to the FBI, but the guards had no idea when that might be. When they came in just after nine o'clock and told him his attorney was here, he prayed he was somehow on his way to freedom.

They shackled Derek up even tighter than the last two days, reducing the links between his legs so he couldn't manage much more than a shuffle. Instead of turning right down the hall, though, they went left and into the first door. It was a different meeting room than he had been in, and a row of six booths were separated by glass from the chairs on the other side. It looked like something he had seen in a cheap TV movie.

Derek was surprised when Bezzi slid a letter under the thin opening at the bottom of the partition. "What's this?"

"It was dropped off at our office Monday night." Bezzi said quietly as if it was still a secret, but the one page letter had already been inspected and dusted for fingerprints by the police. "The FBI want to know is it from."

The seal on the envelope had been broken. Derek unfolded the single sheet. It was his father's neat handwriting. "It's from my uncle."

"Is that the person I called when you were arrested?"

"I guess, I wasn't told about any of that."

"Where does he live?"
"In Algeria, but he travels a lot."
"He must be close to drop it off at my office."
"I don't know."

> Derek,
>
> It saddens me to hear of your unfortunate situation. However, I know you will do what is right – right for a man of honor, right for a man of God. Please accept this letter as my sincerest best wishes for your future, for your life in your new world. May God be with you.
>
> Allah is great.

"What does he mean by 'do what is right?'" Bezzi asked.

Derek read the letter again before replying. "To stand up and face whatever is in store for me. No matter what happens in life, my family always wanted me to be strong." That was true.

"Is there any way to get in touch with your uncle?"

Derek had no idea what Bezzi knew, didn't know, or guessed. His father had told him that the attorney client privilege would protect him, but denial was always the safest option. "Not that I know. I haven't seen my uncle since I left Algeria ten years ago."

"The FBI thinks your uncle might have had something to do with yesterday, too, and they are pursuing him and your father… with everything they've got. If either one of them is involved; their lives could be in danger. Are you sure there's nothing you want to tell me?" Bezzi's tone was as uncertain as his knowledge of the facts.

"I have told you the truth. My father is dead and m y uncle is not involved. I know it looks bad, but I can't help you or the police. What happened to the deal I made with the FBI?"

"They say they are going to charge you in all those deaths," Bezzi said, looking down at some notes he had on his scratch pad. "The desk sergeant told me the FBI was coming to move you."

Derek thought it would be ironic if they decided to send him to one of the ghost interrogation prisons the FBI or the CIA had tucked away. He didn't care. He wasn't going there. The deal had never really mattered after Meyers' plane had landed. It wouldn't be long before they identified the disk, and probably within a few days they would figure out how he had done it.

"What about my deal?"

"Your deal is done, Derek. They aren't going to let you out until your innocence is proven."

"I thought I was innocent until proven guilty." Mansi had told him that American justice wasn't much better than Algerian.

"Technically, you are, but depending on the charges, you might or might not get bail now. If you do, it's probably going to be much higher than it was."

Five million was already far too much. Any more was just a second death sentence.

"Can you call my mother and my attorney for me?"

"Yes, sure."

"Tell my mother I want to talk her with Bezzi present. Ask her if she can come today."

Derek didn't want to spend another day behind bars.

~~~

Phil relayed Derek's message to Annette that it was very important he talk to her, although he hadn't been specific. She had been surprised, but happy that he had called her for anything, so she quickly agreed. Cliff had to go to work for a few hours, but Val volunteered to drive up to the jail with her.

Bezzi Tazrit was waiting for her and went into the private room too. They sat down in the small wooden chairs on one side of the table. They weren't very comfortable, and not designed for long conversations. The unpleasant mix of odors bit at Annette's nostrils. It would be a nasty smell to wake up to for the rest of one's life.

Two big guards dragged Derek into the room and sat him down across the table. He winced, then tried a small smile. Annette thought he looked as exhausted as she was. He probably hadn't slept much, either – who had? He still had the orange jumpsuit on, and she wondered if the police would let her go to his apartment and get him a change of clothes. She wished she could hug him.

"Are you okay?" she asked.

Bezzi didn't say a word and pushed his chair back a few feet.

The shackles had restricted Derek to a small shuffle, but she could see that something was different in his demeanor.

"As okay as I could be, I guess." He smiled for a moment, but the anger in his look had faded.

She thought he looked thinner. "Are you eating?"

"No, not much."

"Try to eat. You'll need your strength."

"Food is not why I called you."

It had sounded motherly. "I'm sorry. What was it that you wanted to talk to me about?"

Derek had asked to speak to his mother with his attorney present. Val had rive up with her and was in the waiting room being happily entertained by a few of the officers on duty.

A police siren suddenly wailed in the distance. Derek looked up at the small, high window as the sound disappeared in the distance. He grinned quickly; then turned to looker his mother in the eyes. He stared for a few long seconds and then quietly said, "I wanted you to know that I'm sorry for all the pain that I've caused you."

Annette felt her throat tighten. "It wasn't your fault."

"Well, maybe, maybe not, but I realize that my father lied to me. He wanted me to never contact you." Derek looked like he could cry. Pausing, he looked up at the window again. He sniffled, then turned back to her and continued, "So he made me hate you and hate America."

"I should never have let him take you to Algeria without me." Annette had never forgiven herself.

"He would have taken me anyway. I was all part of a long-term master plan. You were just the unlucky woman he picked to bear his son. I was just your unlucky egg." Derek's eyes met hers for a few long seconds, but he couldn't or didn't want to hold her gaze. He looked down at the table.

"I honestly thought he loved me," Annette said. She had loved him, especially the first few years.

"I thought he loved me, too."

"He used everybody, Derek." She paused. She wanted the truth. "Can you tell me what happened to you in Algeria?"

He looked at the guard standing outside the door, lowered his voice and leaned closer. "I'm not going to repeat this in court."

"The police are probably taping this conversation." Annette looked around.

"They can't do that, attorney client privilege. That's why Bezzi is here."

"This room is secure and off limits," Bezzi nodded. "But even if they are listening, they couldn't use any of this conversation as evidence."

"I don't really care anymore."

"The courts will go much easier on you if you cooperate." Annette wondered if he would be grilled endlessly later anyways." Is your father really dead?"

Derek ignored her question. "Twenty years ago," he said softly, "when I left, I was taken to a training camp in Algiers. There were dozens of children there. We were all abducted kids, citizens of countries from around the world, and we were trained to be warriors for the future of Algeria."

"Warriors against who?" She pressed the phone against her ear so hard it hurt.

"The United States, Western Europe, their policies, capitalism, greed."

"And the plan all this time was to attack Washington, D.C.?"

"For me? No. They never had a hard target in the beginning. Father used to say, 'See what the intelligence develops. Suitable targets will identify themselves.' Those were his words."

"How did you pick Trainor Jets?"

"That was kind of a fluke. I was a computer programmer. I did an accelerated program at USC, then went to Cal Tech for my master's. Father never told me my grandfather worked at the Trainor Jet plant, but he did seem to know quite a bit about the company, and he was ecstatic when Art made me an offer."

"Art Trainor?"

"Yeah, Art offered me a job, and I took it."

"Art's company, you mean?"

"Yes, but Art himself, too. I went to a job fair during my last year at Cal Tech and met Art there. Apparently he has been going to the big job fairs for years. He has a degree in software programming, too, all the old stuff, and we got along great. I told him about going to the Freedom Four roll-out as a kid, and he was impressed I knew so much about his company and his dreams."

"Yes, I remember that show you went to." Both Mansi and Derek had been mesmerized by the size, grandeur, and luxury that the private jets had represented. A few weeks later, her son was gone. For all the years she had speculated what and where Derek was, never once had she thought he would return so close to home and cross her path in so many ways. "And the plan to crash all those planes and kill all those people, who planned that?"

"I never knew what the target was until a few weeks ago. I just did what I was told."

"But why? Why did your father do all this?"

"Father has always hated the United States."

"Why?"

"That goes back a long time."

Annette shrugged. "You're not going anywhere."

Derek caught the humor. "My great-grandfather, Sadat Nasser, was a cook at the French embassy in Algiers during the 1930s. He had an affair with a French diplomat's teenage daughter, who got pregnant. The girl's father was livid, especially when he found out that my great-grandfather was married and already had two children. The diplomat only agreed to let the infant live if the daughter would go back to France immediately after the child was born, and never see my great-grandfather, or her son, my grandfather, Yassi Nasser, again."

A love vendetta from eighty-five years ago? "That's tragic. Did she love him?"

"Yes, but he was twenty-five and already had a family. She was eighteen and had a charmed life waiting for her back in Paris. So she left the baby with my great-grandfather and returned to France."

"A mother leaving her child? That must have been really hard to do."

Derek stared at her for a moment before replying. She hoped she had offended him again. She thought about her dad again. "Do you know your grandfather?"

"No. He's dead, but I'll get to that. In the 1930s, Algeria was beginning another struggle for independence. When the Second World War was over, my grandfather Yassi was fourteen, and his older half-brother Kadar was seventeen. Both had been involved in the resistance against the Nazis."

"You've been fighting for generations, haven't you?"

"Yes, we have." Derek smiled proudly. "A few years after the war, my great-grandmother wrote and offered an opportunity for her son to go to school in England. Most Algerians put a high emphasis on education, so Yassi accepted. He didn't know his mother, but they ended up liking each other and apparently got along well."

Annette hoped she would have the same luck now. "Well, that's a nice part of the story."

"Yeah, well, don't get excited. It doesn't last. Grandfather lived in London for six years and returned to Algeria in 1954, a trained economist and ready to help his country. He found a good job with the French government and married his old girlfriend, my grandmother Shalla. But then his half-brother Kadar and his wife were killed by the French in 1956 in a freedom rally. They left one child, a seven-year-old son, Hashim, my cousin. My grandmother happened to be pregnant, but they didn't have any kids, so they adopted Hashim. Mansi was born a few months later in 1957. The problems got so bad with the French that Yassi quit his position in 1959 and went to work for a company that built fishing boats."

Mansi had told her that. "This is quite a story," she said.

"Yes, well, there's more. Yassi also got involved in the PLN, which was the freedom movement in Algeria. In fact, he was one of their leaders. When the war ended in 1962, Yassi was a hero and hired by old friends in the new Algerian government. In a senior role, he was the second in command in the Foreign Office at age thirty-three."

Annette had never thought the conversation would take them back to a foreign government fifty years ago.

Derek continued, "Yassi stayed in touch with his mother, who still lived in Paris, and on his first business trip to Washington in 1964, he met his mother for the first time in ten years since he had left London school."

Annette liked where this was going. She didn't say anything but tried to compare this old reunion with hers. Derek's great-grandmother must have been fifty by then.

"Her father, Yassi's grandfather, is now eighty-something, living in Washington and still a diplomat of some kind for the French government. He found out that Yassi had been getting money from his daughter for years. He had no other heirs and his daughter was going to get everything, and he didn't want Yassi to get any more of his money, but the final straw was when the CIA discovered Yassi was buying and selling guns for other African freedom fighters."

Annette thought of all the genocide and atrocities that had plagued Africa in the last fifty years. It was human misery at its worst. Wars had killed millions of parents and orphaned millions of children. Was this what this was all about?

"Your grandfather was a gun-runner?" she asked.

"He did many things. I don't know it all." Derek shrugged as if it weren't important. "But my great-great-grandfather, Laurence Magne, had Yassi killed."

"He killed his own grandson?" Fact or fiction or fantasy, she had no idea what to believe any more.

"Yes."

"Jesus!"

"He had nothing to do with it." Derek smiled weakly.

"What?" Annette tried to remember all the details. "Your father told me his father died during the war."

"He did. The Western war of oppression." Derek shrugged his shoulders again. "He was murdered on Friday, August 13th, 1965, by the CIA."

How much had been a lie? Just about everything?

Derek went on. "At first his death was just another unexplained airplane accident."

"Your father died in a plane crash?"

"Yes, in an old Trainor 252 to be exact."

Why was she surprised? "What happened, those are pretty reliable planes?"

"It wasn't an accident. He was shot down by a CIA missile."

"This sounds more incredible by the second Derek, how do you know all this?"

"A few years after my grandfather's death, a letter arrived for my father from his grandmother in Paris. Her father had told her the truth on his death bed, and she decided to tell her grandson the truth about what really happened to his father."

"She must have felt awful." Annette couldn't imagine the guilt the woman must harbor, giving up her only child only to see him murdered years later by his own grandfather.

"My grandfather wasn't innocent either."

"What else was he involved with?"

"He had built a financial network for different efforts in Algeria, investing in the American stock market under the guise of non-profit organizations and then skimming the profits to supply rebel leaders with weapons."

"A sophisticated gun-runner."

"I think of him as freedom fighter."

She knew little of the dozens of struggles that faced Africa, but the recent ugly history of Rwanda, the Congo, Darfur and the human genocide and suffering had been well documented on TV and was still all too real.

"Why attack the United States now?"

Derek shook his head. "This has been planned for a long time. My grand's education in London changed his views on life. He knew education was the key to power, and power was the key to controlling men. Yassi started and funded the private school education for Mansi, his cousins, and a dozen other young Arab men in a small school on the south side of Algiers. The curriculum included a long-term plan to influence events worldwide."

"Why?"

"To capitalize on the market. We fund our causes with the losses of Western investors."

"This is all about money?"

"No, but making money is just as important as succeeding with the attack. The attack provides the statement; the money is the fuel that feeds our war. We probably made millions when the U.S. markets fell after word of our attack. Millions of U.S. dollars. It's a business."

"Jesus. Who's we?"

Derek smiled. "I can't say."

Annette wondered if she could ever trust him. There was so much to comprehend, let alone the problems he was facing. His story was incredible, but did any of this new past even matter to her? He was her son. "You've had a lot to go through," she said. "Maybe the courts will see that."

"Ah, the courts. I'll probably be charged with murder."

"Forty-five people lost their lives."

"More people die from alcohol-related car accidents every day. More people die from over-eating every day. The number means nothing. Maybe they will have better luck in their next life."

How he could be so callous? "What about their families that still need those people in this life? What about them?"

"That happens in a war. There are always innocent people killed. 'Collateral damage,' I think, is the U.S. military term."

"We are not at war."

"Really? Then why do the Americans have armies all over the world? If it's not a war, it sure the hell is a police state, and the Americans are the police."

"If this is a war, have you won? Did these deaths really bring victory? What have you won?" Annette could still picture the TV images of the jets blowing up.

"Respect. The ability to fight another day."

"Not for you, and there is no respect from me. Your story is incredible, but nothing justifies what you have done."

"That's your opinion. There are others who would disagree." Derek shrugged. "I just wanted you to know enough to know that it had nothing to do with you."

It was the nicest thing he had said since they had met just ten days ago. "Thank you, but why won't you tell this to a judge? Maybe they will give you a break if you help bring in some of the others. Would you help us find them?"

"No."

Annette was disappointed when Derek ended their conversation a few minutes later, but it seemed like he had finally been honest. "I'll see you soon," she said, putting her hand on his.

Derek got up pulling his hand away with a jerk. "Who knows where I will end up? Don't hold your breath."

Chapter 27

The brand new black stretch Mercedes S600 was surrounded by six men, and Mansi counted at least two dozen men up and down the street. A small squad of motorcycle cops sat on one side of the ramps, and four other armored Mercedes Benz automobiles completed the official motorcade. Rami Zeggan, President of the Republic Algeria, Head of State, former Secretary-General of the United Nations, former Minister of Education, and still a loyal member of the Front de Liberation Nationale political party, never traveled lightly.

The two cousins were searched thoroughly at the compound gates by the well-armed and well-dressed security guards. Almost uniform, the muscular men all wore the same dark suit, white shirt, a black tie, and they moved with a military efficiency and determination that wasted no effort. When they reached the top floor, Mansi was surprised to see a restaurant. There had been no sign or even street number on the building. The view of the Bay of Algiers was stunning.

Mansi had not seen Rami Zeggan for twenty years, long before his rise to power, but Hashim had told him what the papers didn't. He recognized the loud laugh and thought how quickly things could change. His father had been one of Rami's early confidants. Who knew where Yassi might have gone if he had not been killed.

The President had put on a lot of weight since the days they used to run in the streets, but an exquisite custom-tailored two-piece Italian Baroni took years off his image.

"I cannot begin to express my sorrow for what happened to Sammar," Mansi said. He had been shocked to read of the death of the three passengers. "We had no way of knowing he would charter a Freedom Five airplane."

Zeggan seemed at peace. "His death had nothing to do with you, Mansi. He is dead because he lived the life of an infidel. It was Allah's will, as was your son's destiny. There is no greater honor. Your father was a hero, you are a hero, and your son was a hero"

"Thank you, President Zeggan. Derek was eager to do his duty and his bravery has ensured we have funds to keep the project alive for years."

"Yes, well, that is another matter." Zeggan's words were an order, not a request. "Hashim has kept me abreast of many of your activities. The Americans think you might still be alive, so I think it is time Mansi Nasser retired."

His youngest daughter had just been returned to study in America. Would she be as talented as her sister? "What about Dawn?" Mansi asked.

Hashim's answer was to be expected. "Chances are she has been discovered and will have to be forgotten or even eliminated. We have already moved the school in case the Americans trace any of our children back there. Good thing we changed our tactics too."

"I am very sorry Derek was caught. He has caused our program lot of problems." Mansi wondered what his son had told the Americans before dying. Torture was hard to resist.

President Zeggan summed up the government's position. "You have been a great service to your country Mansi and we have made hundreds of millions over the years. Algeria will forever be in your debt, but President Wilby is furious. Forty-five people were killed, and there are millions of dollars in damaged property. He wants blood and has threatened to send in their Special Forces. We don't want that."

Mansi pictured American commando units hanging off the sides of U.S. Blackhawk helicopters, guns blazing. That would start another revolution. "No, sir."

"So I need to give him some satisfaction," Zeggan said.

Mansi glanced at his cousin. Had they just been told they were expendable? The stairs were blocked by a half-dozen men, and they all had guns of one type or another. Many were the sub-compact Uzis that so many of the Western-trained special forces around the world preferred.

The president laughed at Mansi's look of concern. "Don't worry. I told you the country was in your debt. I have prepared a new identity for both of you and staged your death in a way that will end all questions. In a few minutes, two men we selected to impersonate you, two traitors, will leave in your car. You will leave in another car waiting out back. Five miles down the road, there will be nothing left of the infidels or your car but small pieces scattered down the highway. Identification will be impossible, even with DNA."

~~~

Art had been surprised the weekend at Camp David was still on. He had a lot of damage control to do back in Long Beach, but there was no place better to start than at the top. The FBI was still in control of the command center in California, and software technicians were still trying to figure out exactly what had happened, but some things were already clear.

It was obvious as soon as the helicopter landed at the presidential retreat that the agenda had changed. Instead of the dozen or so guests who had been invited, it was just Art and Joan and Norman and Sheila Kingston. The dinner table conversation centered around the catastrophe.

"You're telling me the software worked flawlessly, even the landing program?"

"Yes, Mr. President, we think the program was somehow attached to the input instructions code set. A ghost program that was impossible to detect confused the input commands, and the computer just rejected what it couldn't understand. The planes were all networked together, and at one o'clock in the afternoon, the computer on Meyers' plane sent out a signal redirecting the entire fleet to targets in D.C. Yes, everything worked except for security."

"To some degree, I'm surprised that hackers haven't caused more damage than they have. Technology is getting a lot better, but so are our enemies. We might not be able to admit anything in court, but Derek's confession told us a lot about who and what we are dealing with. I have already spoken with President Zeggan of Algeria, and he assures me that they will find out if this Mansi character is still alive. I have even lent them some assets to help locate him. We'll get the bastards who did this."

"I hope so, Mr. President, but with those two programmers dead, we might never know the whole truth of how they did this."

"You might be right," the President said. "I will continue to condemn this horrific act, but what congress decides to do with you and your Freedom Fives, I don't know. Will Trainor Jets survive?"

"It doesn't look good. Besides insurance claims, we will undoubtedly have hundreds of clients suing us."

"Well, it's not all bad news," Wilby assured him. "We know your technology worked perfectly. I am going to continue supporting No Loss. Saving pilot's lives and saving billions of dollars is still the way of the future, there is no question. Oh, and there is other good news – the atomic bomb turned out to be a fake."

"Really?" Art had wondered why he hadn't heard anything about it on the news. It sure had looked real. Was the President trying to reduce the worries of the beleaguered nation or telling the truth? He would probably never know. "That is good news."

"Yes. We didn't need to have the finger pointed at Russia. Things are testy enough with the Kremlin these days as it is." President Wilby got up and walked over to the window. The sun was shining and it looked warm outside. "The United States has enemies both international and domestic, and as you know, we've had more than one homegrown terrorist. But this woman, Annette Madison, is a homegrown hero. No question. I don't care if it was her son, if she hadn't confronted him or come up with her idea to reformat those computers; you might still have planes out there."

"I agree, Mr. President," Art said. He hadn't talked to Annette since the disaster had ended, and he certainly hadn't thanked her properly. He owed her his life, as did many others. "I'm going to have to find some way to thank her."

"I have an idea. Let's call her together. I want to thank her personally, too. Do you have her phone number?"

~~~

"Annette? It's Art Trainor."

"Art," Annette said. She had read the name on the display before answering the phone, "Hi"

Art's name brought a look of surprise from Cliff and he turned the TV down.

"How are you doing?" Art asked.

What a question. "I'm okay, but I'd sure like to forget the past week. I am so sorry for what my son did. I'll never forgive myself."

It had been an awful couple of days. The story would be on the front pages for a long time, and life for her had, once again, changed forever. This time it had been her son.

"Annette, don't say that," Art said. "If you hadn't intervened, it might have turned out far worse. You have nothing to feel guilty about. I think what you did was remarkable. Not many parents could keep their cool like you did and find a solution that saved probably saved thousands of lives. I think you're a hero."

"I'm not a hero, Art." Annette could still the pictures of the jets blowing up and the stories of the innocent lives lost. Her son had been responsible for the deaths of all those people. "I just did what any mother would do. I know what he did was wrong, and the pain he caused will haunt me forever. I have no faith that any God will or should forgive him for that, but part of me still loves him."

"You are a very compassionate woman, Annette. Try to have some faith that you did the best you could. None of this was in your control."

"I know, but it's still difficult to accept."

"Well, there's somebody else standing beside me who wants to thank you, too."

She didn't really want to talk to anyone else. "I'm really kind of wiped out and would rather not," she said. "Is it Sheila? Tell her I'll call her later."

Art chuckled. "Actually, it's not Sheila. It's the President of the United States."

President Les Wilby? You're kidding, right?"

Cliff looked up, just as surprised as she was.

"Not at all. Here he is."

There was a slight pause, so Annette covered the mouthpiece and quickly whispered, "It's the President of the United States."

Cliff nodded and smiled. Not many people ever got a personal call from the President.

"Annette Madison, this is Les Wilby," said a voice used to commanding. "Thank you for taking my call."

What do you say when the President catches you at home in sweatpants? "Mr. President . . . This is an honor."

"It is my honor and pleasure, Annette. Art told me how you helped. You saved hundreds, maybe thousands of lives. You are most definitely a hero."

Art was on a second line. "Annette, you saved a lot of lives including Joan's and mine. If there is ever anything we can do, and I mean anything, I want you to call me, okay?"

Annette didn't know what to say but thanks. "Mr. President and Art, you are both far too kind. After all, it was my son who was probably responsible for all those deaths."

"We might never know who was responsible," President Wilby said. "But I do know that things might have turned out much worse, and for that the United States government wants to offer its thanks and whatever help it can. I understand you are being looked after and have a place to stay? Those reporters can be pretty tenacious."

"Yes, Mr. President. Thank you for asking."

~~~

Derek never touched his food. He hadn't felt very hungry the last few days, and the cold food did nothing for his appetite. While the other prisoners in his block ate, he wrote a short letter to his mother.

> Please forgive me. I have only tried to be a faithful son and a willing servant of God. I have gone to a better place. Whether I am rewarded as Islam and Father have promised, or whether I die a coward, you will never know, and maybe I won't, either. I am sorry that you had to go through all this. That was never part of the plan.
> I was convinced you hated me, and soon I hated everything my father hated, and that included the United States. I was never meant to be a normal son. I was meant to be a warrior, and I was. I was convinced I would die a hero, a martyr, like my grandfather, and I believe I succeeded beyond anyone's expectations.
> I'm not sure what is true anymore, and I have many questions that remain unanswered. Perhaps we will meet again in another life when things can be different.
> I think you probably were a great mother.
>
> Your son in paradise,
>
> Derek

He folded the single page neatly, creasing it so it would stay flat, and wrote *Mother* on it. He opened his Koran and pulled out the letter he had received from his father. He replaced it with the letter he had just written to his mother, leaving her name visible when he closed the cover. He unfolded his father's note and read it again. As he did, tears started running down his cheeks. When he was finished, he crumpled the letter into a ball and stuffed it into his mouth. It was dry and hard to swallow, but in seconds it was gone. He lay down on his bunk and stared at the greasy ceiling. The poison would only take a few minutes.

Epilogue

Annette was devastated by Derek's death. Horrified at what he had done, murderous at what his father had done, and anxious for answers, she only felt more guilt when she heard about Derek's suicide. Tormented about having let him go two decades earlier, she couldn't stop crying for days. The funeral service was discreetly hidden from the press by some clever maneuvering by Cliff's friends at the Orange County Sheriff's Department. The body was released late at night and shipped out under the cover of darkness. The cremation was only attended by Annette, Cliff, Marie, and Val. A non-religious service, Annette focused her final words on her son's happy childhood and how wonderful a young boy he had been. No quotes from the Bible or the Koran, no conjectures about what might have been. Few words seemed appropriate or offered any kind of consolation.

    A burial and gravestone didn't seem right, either, so Annette chose to have her son's ashes spread across the Pacific Ocean, just like his grandfather's. Perhaps their souls would meet, perhaps some God would forgive her son for what he had done; Annette had no answers. Cliff's love and support had been awesome, but it was her old friend and colleague, Anita Sanchez, who really helped open up the floodgates.

    Shortly after the burial, Anita visited Annette four days in a row. Soon, the crying had turned to laughing as they remembered all the struggles that they had been through over the years at the American Center for Missing Children. For all the trauma Annette had dealt with; there were still thousands of mothers whose children had vanished, and that reality always put things in perspective. Her own son's future had been taken from her hands, but Anita reminded her how many mothers and children Annette had personally helped, how many children she had been instrumental in bringing home, and how much her contributions had meant to hundreds of families. Anita reminded her of how much she had to be thankful for.

No one blamed her but herself, but unlike the loss of her father and her fiancé, she realized she still had a lot to be thankful for, and Anita reminded her more than once of the family who loved her and still needed her. Darcy and Lisa had somehow gone from giggling teenagers to young adults in one week and had never been more helpful. Her mother and sister had always been there for her and still were. Cliff still wanted to marry her.

Dawn's DNA had matched, but the files on the woman and her daughter from twenty years ago couldn't be found. Annette felt sorry for Cindy Yaccine and spoken to her a few times. The FBI had been tough on Dawn, but apparently the teenager knew far less that Derek had. They hadn't heard anything about Mansi or Derek's uncle.

They had initially put the wedding off indefinitely, but after a few weeks of mourning and self-pity, she realized that she had to go on with her life, and that included marrying the one man who had never let her down. She knew it was only a piece of paper, but the more she thought about it, the more she wanted to be Mrs. Cliff Billings. She wanted to start a new chapter in her life, and Anita only repeated what she knew and what she had been telling others for years. She had to move on. Life was full of the wrong choices. No person alive lived without some remorse. Everyone made mistakes; forgiveness had to be part of life.

They kept the details of their wedding quiet, so she was stunned when Art had called and offered the use of a private jet for their honeymoon. A Freedom Four with two pilots on board would take them wherever they wanted to go. She had tried to decline, but he wouldn't hear of it.

When they arrived at the executive side of John Wayne Airport, she was once again amazed at the luxury of the executive jet. The interior was decorated in a mixture of sandy-colored fabrics and leathers, with a long couch upholstered in a muted floral pattern that ran down one side opposite a table and four chairs.

The table and woodwork throughout the cabin was a butterscotch-swirl mahogany from Honduras, and the rich tan glove leather had been handpicked in Italy. With flowers, small pieces of art, hidden lighting, and soft music in the background, it was nicer than Annette's living room. The rear of the jet was even more decadent, with a custom-made bed laden with a checked chocolate brown duvet, lavender silk sheets, and matching toss pillows. The little love nest also included two chairs in front of an electric fireplace and an LCD screen that hung down from the ceiling. Cliff had joked about joining the mile-high club, but Annette wasn't sure. It all looked a little too much a setup to be truly romantic, but it was gorgeous and tempting.

Art Trainor had insisted on being one of the pilots, saying he needed to remember what flying was all about. Through the intercom, he talked about his excitement at seeing the two military jets.

"Sorry to disturb you two love birds," he said with a chuckle, "but you not may ever see anything like this again. There's a B-2 Bomber off to the port side."

Cliff pointed out one of the windows on the left. "Over there."

Annette was surprised at how big the planes seemed even from a few miles away. It was not something she had ever thought about, least of all on her honeymoon, but it was a pretty impressive sight. The B-2 Bomber looked like no other aircraft she had ever seen. Bat-like, it was one big wing and didn't have a normal tail arrangement. It looked even more unusual attached by a boom to the larger jet above it, and as they watched, the boom retracted from the nose of the bomber, and the two planes separated. In seconds, the gray ghost slid left and away from the gigantic tanker.

"Wow, it turns slightly and just disappears into the sky," Annette commented as she watched it vanish into the horizon.

"Part of its design, I guess," Cliff said. "Between the angular surfaces, titanium skin, and radar-reflective paint, that bird is supposed to be harder to find than a seagull. At fifty thousand feet, it's probably almost impossible. I wonder where it's going?"

Annette nodded thoughtfully. "I wonder who the pilot is?"

~~

Colonel Jill Ruffe had trained for the last thirty of her thirty-seven years for this day. With over 7,000 hours since her seventeenth birthday, she was one of the United States Air Force's top aviators, male or female. Command-pilot-rated, she had flown everything from the four-bladed turbo-prop T-6A Texan II twin-engine two-seat trainers at the Air Force Academy in Colorado Springs, to the incredible supersonic stealth of the invisible F-22 Raptor. But sitting in the pilot's seat of the multi-billion-dollar big bird was what she had dreamed about for ten years.

The delta-wing Northrop Grumman B-2 Spirit bomber was clearly in a class by itself, and for many of the United States Air Force's hottest pilots; the most expensive plane ever built was also the ultimate stick. A posting to the high-profile 509th Bomb Wing in Whiteman Air Force Base in Montana, the home of the only squadron of B-2 bombers on the planet, was a promotion of success.

Whiteman AFB held special significance for Jill. Group Commander Colonel Tibbets, assigned to the wing, had led B-17 raids in North Africa during World War II and piloted the B-29 Superfortress that had dropped the world's first atomic bomb on Hiroshima in 1945. Getting transferred to the elite fleet of only twenty aircraft had been a coup in itself, but connecting history in such a manner had been more than she could have ever dreamed for.

Mission commander for the long flight to Diego Garcia, she had flown with her aircraft commander, Captain Doug Johnson, only a few times before. He had a few hundred more hours on type than she did and a background not dissimilar to hers, but Jill had been promoted to mission commander last year.

Their flight plan had fuel waiting over the Pacific, and the KC-767 tanker had pumped almost 100,000 pounds of fuel into the massive tanks of the flying wing of the Spirit of Oklahoma. Tail number 93-1085, the B-2 had been one of the last built in 1993 and, unlike many of the early models, was delivered to the Air Force as a fully configured Block 30 capable.

The upgraded variant included full defense avionics arrays, enhanced terrain-following ground radar and almost double the radar modes. Carrying a wide range of weapons systems, and virtually invisible at 50,000 feet, AV-18 was the official Air Force tag of the third last of the twenty-one planes assembled, and capable of far more destruction than a squadron of conventional long-range bombers. One of the airplanes had crashed on take-off in 2008, but loaded with sixteen intermediate AGM B61 thermonuclear bombs, each capable of delivering their 340 kiloton warheads to a separate target, any one of the remaining twenty four-engine leviathans possessed more military power than many small countries' entire arsenals.

"Traffic at nine o'clock," Doug said, pointing down and to their right. A white executive jet was a few miles off their starboard wing.

"Some rich guy on his way somewhere," Jill said, unimpressed. She had flown military versions of business jets on a few occasions, but after years in a G-suit, not much compared.

Doug set the aircraft into its autopilot mode. "Big day, Commander."

"Bigger than the two of us." Jill reached discreetly for the 9mm pistol in her leg holster.

Her co-pilot had his eyes on the color displays and he looked up just as Jill raised her hand. He was far too late to do anything. She fired twice. The first bullet hit him in the chest, and the second bullet tore through the carotid artery in his neck, blood spurted everywhere and the dead man collapsed forward into his harness.

She pushed him back into his seat, and he slumped towards the window. She smiled. Her father had been right; killing was easy. She also knew it could be very dangerous in an aircraft, so she had fired at an angle that ensured the slugs would embed in the co-pilot's seat.

She turned the transponder off before radioing the base."Whiteman Control, Big Sky 1085, belly full, commencing run. Talk to you on the other side. Over."

They would be looking for her for hours, but Camp Justice, the British base the American Air Force called home in the middle of the Indian Ocean, would never see the shipment of weapons or the aircraft.

"Roger that, Big Sky 1085, we have lost your signal, good luck, over."

Jill pushed the throttles to full power. The four huge General Electric F-118-GE-100 power plants, with over 17,000 pounds of thrust each, could push the plane over 6,000 miles without refueling, more than enough time to lose any and all followers.

She leveled off at the maximum operational ceiling of the B2 bomber of 50,000 feet. Adjusting her radio to the land-based frequency, she pressed the call button. "Algiers Base, this is the Lost One. Do you read? Over."

"Copy that, Lost One." Thousands of miles away, Tariq's voice was surprisingly loud and clear. "You are not lost anymore. Glad to have you back. Over."

"Copy that, big brother. I'm on my way home, and I've got a present for you. Over."

Made in the USA
Charleston, SC
02 July 2014